HOW
FLORA
FINDS HER
FABULOUS

Stella wrote most of How Flora Finds Her Fabulous
While visiting various places around the world.
Although the book is not autobiographical, she found
inspiration in the joy of unexpected friendship
and cultural differences. Stella travels regularly,
always with her laptop, and writes whenever she can.
When she's home, she lives in Gloucestershire.
She carries out speaking engagements about her life
as a writer and social entrepreneur.
How Flora Finds Her Fabulous is her debut novel
and the first in the Finding Fabulous series.

Also in the Finding Fabulous series:
Ready for Fabulous
Forever Fabulous

Sign up to receive special offers, bonus content,
book promotions or events and updates from the author

www.stellabookchat.com

If you'd like to connect on social media:
Instagram: StellaBookChat
Twitter: @stellabookchat
Facebook: stellabookchat

HOW
FLORA
FINDS HER
FABULOUS

STELLA STONESTREET

Speedwell

First published in 2021 by Speedwell Publishing
First produced in paperback in 2021

Paperback ISBN 978-1-8383109-0-5
Ebook ISBN 978-1-8383109-1-2

Typeset in Garamond by Jo Guillen Aguilar
Printed in Great Britain by Clays Ltd, Elcograf S.p.A.

As a commitment to a sustainable future this book
is printed on paper made from responsible sources

MIX
Paper from
responsible sources
FSC® C018072

For my family

ONE

MONDAY:
Boil egg (4½ mins)
Lay table
Toast (2 slices)
Tea
Prepare packed lunch

In a housewife's champion finish, Flora slapped fish paste onto thin white sliced, clattering and see-sawing the knife's serrated edge on the glass jar. Sounding busy was her speciality. She squashed the sandwiches into an old Stork margarine tub on top of a slice of fruit loaf and jammed the lid on. After pouring tea into a thermos and hurling a banana into John's briefcase, she grabbed a slotted spoon to hook his breakfast out of boiling water. She eyed the kitchen clock with a sense of satisfaction; it had taken years of practice to shave one minute, twelve seconds off his precious schedule.

As usual, John ate his all-too-snotty egg, drank his tea and left for work without a word. The sound of the front door closing heralded a certain calm that left Flora feeling ever-so-slightly lighter. She tuned in to *Wake Up to Wogan* just as Terry was saying 'Did you know cows moo in regional accents?' As on most weekday mornings, he was the first person to speak to her. She hummed along to Bananarama while beating her own breakfast egg, throwing in a wiggle here and there. 'It Ain't What You Do, It's the Way That You Do It'. French toast with sugar sprinkled on top.

1

It was amazing what she could make with John's prescribed breakfast ingredients.

Back in 1970, as a newlywed, she had followed his written instructions to the letter. 'So you don't need to think,' he'd said and, in case she was in any doubt, presented her with *Mrs Beeton's Book of Household Management*, with 'To my wife' inscribed inside. Mrs B was John's second-in-command, unless you counted his long-deceased mother, who still held sway over the decor and furniture.

Over the years, in order to cope with a disappointing husband, she had turned to various sources for advice that was often conflicting and therefore confusing – romantic novels and *Ladies' Circle* versus daytime telly and whatever women's glossy was in the doctor's surgery. Yes, she was her own woman, but thanks to John, Mrs B's bulky authority and old Mother Marshall's ghost, she only truly triumphed during office hours, home alone in the Coventry suburbs.

Moving on to the next of her daily tasks, she wrestled the old twin tub out from under the worktop and forced its hose nozzle onto the kitchen tap. She left the water running and raced upstairs to strip the bed and bring the fully-loaded laundry basket down before the tub was full. She'd only once flooded the kitchen, the day she had stopped to rescue a butterfly trapped in a spider's web.

Coming back down the stairs with a week's worth of washing obscuring her vision was a skill in itself. She concentrated on counting the steps. Terry Wogan was wrapping up his show with a closing pearl of wisdom. 'Don't worry,' he said, 'everybody else thinks they are better looking than they are as well.' Not everybody. She had no illusions about her looks: mousy hair, a few freckles, overweight. It didn't matter anyway. She passed the hall mirror, avoiding eye contact.

First into the machine were her all-too-familiar skirts and blouses, a tangle of American tan tights and a nightie so washed and worn the pink roses were barely discernible. After a ten-minute swish around, she transferred them to the smaller tub for a rinse and spin. The bedding and towels could be washed in one go, but they had to be divided into two separate loads to fit in the spinner. A minor inconvenience compared to the old mangle, now rusting in the back yard.

Finally, it was the turn of John's shirts, socks and pants to struggle and drown in the murky beige sea, and time for her next challenge. She arranged four Jelly Babies on the lid of the washer and watched them trembling in their sugary overcoats. Far below, with each judder, water dribbled from the undercarriage of the ancient machine and puddled across the honeycomb-patterned lino. Swish-churn, swish-churn. There were so many ways to eat Jelly Babies, other than just biting off their heads. She hovered her face a few inches above the dusty little bodies, enjoying the soft, candy-floss scent of icing sugar, then gently licked the nearest one until its tummy turned green before sucking it into her mouth.

Another hexagon of lino succumbed to the soapy flood. It was like a slow game of Blockbusters – *'Can I have a P please, Bob?'* She stuffed a rolled-up newspaper under the fridge; if the water got that far she'd leave it for John to see. Maybe then he'd agree to buying another new-second-hand 'bargain'. She reached for the next sweet without looking and tasted the colour. Red? She took it out to check, then gave the machine a nudge and watched soapy water ripple towards yesterday's crossword.

With the final rinse and spin dealt with, Flora carried John's collection of muted mixed fibres out to the back yard where the sun was yet to shine. Given the time of year, it would be close to two o'clock before the grey concrete turned a few shades brighter. While pegging out the last of the eleven socks, she planned the rest of her day. Saving up things to think about helped to pass the time, made her feel busy. Next on the agenda: choosing lunch. As per John's instructions, she was supposed to be finishing up the jar of fish paste. She pictured him tucking into his sandwich of squashed, sweaty bread with fishy-scented fruit loaf for afters. More fool him. She couldn't remember the last time she'd eaten one of those lifeless grey rectangles.

John maintained that anything more than one filling per sandwich was an unnecessary extravagance. In a satisfying act of defiance, Flora always created her own sandwich with a minimum of three. Today she'd have cheese, salad cream and grated carrot. Nice and colourful. And instead of sitting at the kitchen table, she'd have it in front of *Judge Judy*, followed by a little something from the treat tin stowed behind the ironing board. A French Fancy perhaps, with *The Flying Doctors*. Having lunch to look forward to was an incentive to get on with the rest of the morning's chores; carpets and lino, according to John's rota.

After mopping the kitchen floor, skirting around the now soggy barricade in front of the fridge, she hurried upstairs to wipe down the bathroom lino. She would leave the stairs and landing for another week and make do with a speedy hoover around the visible areas of carpet in the rest of the house. Finally, she began to line up lunchtime ingredients. Why have an ordinary sandwich when, for just an extra slice of bread, you could have a toasted *club* sandwich? A top deck of grated carrot and salad cream sprinkled with salt and pepper, toast buttered on both sides and cheese down below. She was weighing up the merits of triangles versus squares when she heard the unmistakable sound of a key in the lock. The front door opening.

John.

Quick! Switch off the radio, hide the salad cream.

'Flora, love.'

'Eh?' He never called her 'love'. She prepared for the worst.

'Something wonderful's happened.' He plonked a bottle of Lambrusco down on the kitchen table, followed by a blue-and-white striped bag from the butcher. Chops, by the look of it. 'Have a guess.'

'I can't imagine—'

He pulled her towards him, planted a quick, dry peck on her cheek. 'As of now and for the rest of my life I'm to be a gentleman of leisure. Retired.'

While she half-listened to what he was saying, a shroud of despair was already creeping over her like a cold, wet floorcloth. Everything would have to stop. Dancing to the radio, the stash of Mills & Boon, daytime telly, Gail's Cafe where the girls were so friendly. 'But you've only just turned sixty-three. Surely you'll want another job, something to keep yourself occupied?' Even the Jelly Babies were at risk.

'Don't you understand? They're *paying* me not to work! They don't want me going to the competition; insurance is very cut-throat these days. And I can't start a new career, not at my age. So, from now on, I'll have the life of Riley.'

What about Riley's wife? Presumably she fried a couple of chops and drowned her sorrows in cheap fizzy wine.

⁓ↂ⤜⤛⁓

John said he'd taken to early retirement 'like a duck to water'. He especially enjoyed digging the allotment on a weekday, while everyone else was at work worrying about the Millennium Bug and the havoc it would wreak on the new computerised system. Flora's ability to adapt was far less gainly. The age gap of seventeen years had hardly been noticeable in the early years, but now it became a yawning chasm; still waiting for her life to begin, it felt as though she were lying in a coffin with John sitting on the lid.

The only benefit of a househusband was having a second pair of hands to carry the weekly groceries home on the bus.

Soon they developed a routine: John waited in the newsagent, reading *Gardeners' World* without having to pay for it, while Flora followed the shopping list unencumbered, skimming a few pennies off the housekeeping and wrapping them in a hankie for later.

On a day much like any other, after the usual Wednesday breakfast of a fried egg on toast, they caught the number twenty-three to Coventry South Retail Park, chosen for its convenient triangle of bus stop, bargain-priced groceries and free reading matter. They stepped off the bus into a light drizzle. As Flora was about to rummage in her bag for an umbrella, a coin glinting on the pavement caught her eye.

'Ah, finders keepers,' said John, swooping down to claim it.

'I saw it too,' she said.

'But you didn't pick it up, did you?'

'Shouldn't we give it back to whoever—'

'And who's that, exactly?' He gestured at the empty pavement ahead.

'Then we should share it, buy something for both of us.' As they approached the newsagent, she pointed at a pair of giant-sized crossed fingers. 'How about one of those?'

'What, a lottery ticket? I don't think so – gambling's a mug's game.'

'It isn't actually gambling because some of the money goes to charity.'

The discussion went on for some time, but Flora knew if she kept it up, he'd eventually see his way to spending someone else's money on a chance to win even more. She clinched the deal by agreeing he could choose the numbers.

'Alright then, one pound can't hurt, can it?'

John's numbers were random, not the birthdays or anniversary dates she would have picked. No matter, they were in with a chance, and for the rest of the week she daydreamed about winning the big prize. The usually silent mealtimes became more animated. In between snorts of ridicule at her hopes for a new three-piece suite, John let slip he would like to spend the jackpot on a geography field trip, and left a copy of *National Geographic* magazine featuring the Jurassic Coast on the coffee table.

By Saturday evening they were equally keen to watch the live draw on television. No matter that John insisted on holding the ticket; she had already memorised the numbers and written them on a slip of paper that she wrapped around her lucky four-leaf clover keyring.

Spooky music and a swirl of studio fog heralded Mystic Meg's arrival in a full-length, purple cloak. Flora crossed her fingers on both hands. The fog lifted to reveal a crystal ball.

'What a load of old codswallop,' said John.

As the music stopped, Meg made meaningful eye contact with the camera. And then she began.

'I see a house,' she said in a spooky voice, 'with a blue door.'

'Get on with it, you daft woman!' John shouted.

'Lucky numbers are one and seven.'

'Hang on,' gasped Flora, 'that's us; we've got one and seven!'

'. . . a lady with long hair,' Meg gazed into her crystal ball, 'brown in colour.'

'What a load of bunkum. Complete waste of time and money.'

'Well, it's not your money,' Flora murmured as Meg disappeared behind a velvet curtain.

The drum roll for the draw made her heart beat faster.

John was supposed to cross off the numbers but he wasn't ready when number seven was the first to be drawn, and he was still putting his reading glasses on when the next number was announced.

'That's us!' shrieked Flora.

When the final number was called, she jumped up and hugged John. She'd already checked the rules – three numbers were a win.

'Calm down,' he said, 'it's only a fixed prize of ten pounds.'

First thing the next morning he went to the corner shop to claim their winnings. Flora had suggested a takeaway. Finally, she might persuade him to try something different. Chinese. Even fish and chips would be nice.

'Why waste money when you can cook a perfectly good meal at home? No, we'll reinvest our original fund,' he said, putting a pound coin on the mantelpiece and pocketing the rest of the winnings.

And so they began a weekly routine, taking it in turns to pick numbers for a single ticket and then sitting together to watch the draw. Their hopes for a big win were occasionally fuelled by another ten-pound prize. On one memorable occasion, Flora's numbers won fifty pounds, after which John poured her a glass of leftover Christmas Baileys and opened a can of John Smith's for himself. At last, they had a shared interest.

Hitting the jackpot would put an end to dreary old Grove Road; number ninety-three was the only house in the entire street without double-glazing, or a patio in place of the old outdoor privy. Flora searched the property pages until she found the ultimate dream – an executive home on Miller's Reach Estate. She would have animal print soft furnishings, a marble bathroom suite and a luxury fitted kitchen. Going to London for a makeover, like a woman in a before-and-after magazine feature, would also be a must. While she was there, she'd have tea at the Ritz with Barry Manilow – but she kept that to herself.

John said if she wanted to waste her winnings on bricks and mortar when they already had an adequate house, it would have to come out of her half. His share would be spent on a global adventure. Geography was his passion, but apart from a long weekend in 1959 when he had joined an excursion to Hadrian's Wall, he had never travelled. Everything he knew about the world had been gleaned from books and his annual subscription to *National Geographic*. His share of the winnings was destined to bring those pages of colour photographs to life. He drew up a list: the island of Molokai, the Salinas Grandes of Argentina and New Zealand's Punakaiki Rocks were just the beginning.

John seemed to enjoy the list for its own sake. Keeping it folded inside his pocket diary, he carried it with him at all times, handy for adding snippets of information. On the evidence of geographically fascinating criteria, a new destination would be added.

'I'll show you one of the most amazing sights you'll ever see when we go to Belize,' he promised. He spoke with so much familiarity and confidence, an eavesdropper would have believed they were heading off the following week. Occasionally, Flora suggested they should redouble their efforts with another ticket if they were ever to see such 'geographically fascinating' places, let alone know the comforts of a Parker Knoll in Maple Blush, but John was resolute.

'No need to go spending something we haven't got.'

'But that original pound wasn't ours and we won with that so—'

'Exactly, so we're ahead of the game.'

In the six years that followed, Flora encouraged John to embellish his list with extensive research. By arming him with a packed lunch, he'd go to Coventry's central reference library with a list of diverse questions – visa requirements, the national living wage, local delicacies – she could keep him out of the house for the best part of a day. John's fully informed world tour grew into the retirement hobby they both needed.

~◦◦◦~

'I'm off to the allotment.' John buttoned his jacket and checked for his bus pass. 'I'll sort out those spring greens and be back at six.'

Take as long as you like, thought Flora. It was always a welcome sight, him putting his coat on and leaving the house. She watched the front door close, waited to hear the gate clang shut, then filled the kettle and turned on the radio. Contact with the real world was music to her ears.

It had been years since she had referred to John's old school exercise book; she knew the housework timetable by heart and could cook the meal plan without needing to weigh or measure. Very occasionally the menu had been amended, but only when the cost of ingredients went up or there was a shortage of something. She had fond memories of the 1988 salmonella scare – with eggs off the menu she was able to come up with several 'emergency' dishes. But once the crisis was over it was back to John's boring routine. 'So we know where we are,' he'd said.

As it was Thursday, Flora quickly prepared the batter for toad-in-the-hole and fried the sausages to a pale golden brown, then emptied a tin of rice pudding into a saucepan for afters. With the basics done, she could settle down to a nice cup of tea and do the quick crossword in the free newspaper. At a quarter past five, she popped a heatproof dish in the oven with a dollop of lard. The trick with toad-in-the-hole was to pour the batter into boiling oil so that it began cooking from the get-go.

The next part of the afternoon's routine depended on where John was. Since he had gone to his allotment, she could catch up with *Home and Away*. Otherwise, if he was somewhere nearby, she would have had to stay in the kitchen and carry on with the crossword – it really wasn't worth being caught 'polluting the airways with inane chitter-chatter'. With the remote control in hand, perched on the edge of the sofa where she could keep an eye on the front gate, she tuned in to watch a heated altercation between Sally and Shauna. Other people's domestic disharmony often cheered her up. It was also reassuring to know that even in the eternal sunshine of Summer

Bay, where parakeets were as common as sparrows and barbecues were an everyday occasion, people still had problems.

She gradually relaxed into a soapy haze, enjoying the nuances of yet another petty scandal in Sally's unfortunate life. The front gate clanging shut alerted her to John's return. In a well-practised move, she zapped the remote and hurried through to the kitchen. Instantly, she knew something was wrong; the customary warm, soft smell of baking sausage and batter was missing. She opened the oven door to see what looked like albino moles peering out of gluey, lukewarm batter.

'What are you playing at, woman? It's almost six o'clock.' John was washing his hands at the sink.

'It's not me. It's the oven. It's on the blink again.'

'You'd best fetch my toolbox.'

John had repaired virtually every appliance in the house. Some of them, like the vacuum cleaner, had been practically rebuilt, which thwarted Flora's dream of ever having a Dyson. The cooker had been second-hand from Buy and Sell in the local paper several years ago. The fact it had only cost ten pounds was a source of pride to John. He loved a bargain.

Flora returned with the toolbox just as he was spreading newspaper on the kitchen floor – something he did for virtually all repairs.

'Now, get out of my way while I sort this out.'

'Shall we have fish and chips? I could get some while you—'

'And let this perfectly good dinner go to waste? Over my dead body.'

Flora knew better than to argue about the batter being unlikely to rise and crisp up, let alone the toad's chances. She would dish it up regardless and see how he liked being right all the time. She'd refuse to eat hers and then have a quick cheese sandwich later, when he wasn't looking.

She sat on the sofa, itching to put the television back on, but picked up her latest library book instead – *The Tumbleweed*, a gloriously bulky romance following the trials and tribulations of Jericho Blake, a swarthy, broken-hearted man who travelled the world selling household items door to door. Flora knew if he offered her clothes pegs or a feather duster she'd swoon on the spot.

Just as Jericho was rescuing a drowning puppy, she heard a loud clatter in the kitchen.

'You alright?' she called, with a finger marking her place on the page. She read the next paragraph while she waited for an answer.

'John?'

She reluctantly put the book down and went to investigate. John was stretched out on the floor, staring at the ceiling with a shocked expression.

'Whatever's the matter?' She dropped to her knees and shook him. No response. She leaned closer to check his breathing, then laid her head on his chest. Nothing.

She sat beside him on the lino for a while, not sure if she should dial 999. It wasn't an emergency now. The house was perfectly still. Until then she hadn't noticed how loudly the clock ticked on the mantelpiece in the front room. There was a strong smell of acrid smoke and something that looked like scorch marks around the cooker socket. The old screwdriver was still in his hand.

His glasses were askew, so she took them off and smoothed down his hair. A pointless demonstration of affection, John would have said. She took his bony hand in hers. It was still warm. Why wasn't she crying?

Later that evening, after the ambulance had left without the need for blue flashing lights, Flora remembered what John had said and put her coat on. Although she didn't fancy fish and chips anymore, she would have her own way, just for once.

~⁂~

Waking up on the sofa wasn't new to Flora; whenever John's snoring became too much, she would creep downstairs and watch a late film. Lying full-length under an old eiderdown with a cup of tea and a packet of Rich Tea was a secret time of night she cherished. In the morning, a stiff neck would be compensated for by John's almost apology when he'd blame the snoring on his excessive nasal tissue and offer to take the eiderdown back upstairs.

A stiff neck was normal, but the thudding rhythm in her head was a new experience. Still lying down, she tentatively reached for a bottle of Baileys on the coffee table and held it up to the light. She shook it from side to side, trying to see how much was left through the thick brown glass. Empty. At least the Bristol Cream was still half-full. The crumpled remains of a packet of biscuits explained the sandy crumbs squashed into the carpet.

She vaguely recalled playing Jim Reeves and Val Doonican at full volume. John's entire record collection was strewn all over the floor; some discs were out of their sleeves. The static would be attracting carpet fluff. He would be furious. She propped herself up, momentarily confused; she still had her clothes on. Something was different.

No. Everything was different.

A pile of crumpled tissues. Bouts of wailing and blubbing. If only she didn't have a headache, she was sure she would feel better for letting off steam. There were more tears to come, she knew that. Thirty-five years of being Mrs Marshall had created quite a build-up.

TWO

An old Andrew's Liver Salts tin had been custodian of the housekeeping allowance since 1970. 'No need to trouble yourself over money,' John had said, carefully counting one pound, fifteen shillings and sixpence into the tin and placing it on the top shelf in the kitchen. 'It's my job to pay the bills; you just do the shopping and look after me.' At the time, Flora had thought it romantic, so gallant of John to shield her from money worries. She soon realised three pounds ten and six a week was barely enough to cover the basics. After decimal currency he had grudgingly increased the amount, but always below the rate of inflation.

Flora shook the tin and, with a satisfying rattle, tipped the contents onto the kitchen table. But it was all noise and no substance. With the weekly shopping already done, and the fish and chip supper that she'd hardly eaten, there were only four pounds seventy-two left. Housekeeping day would have been Saturday, after John had checked the previous week's receipts and change. Balanced the books. She hastily swept the money back into the tin.

She'd never looked in his wallet before. Just rummaging in his coat pocket, even without the chance of being found out, made her heart beat faster. Three fivers and a few coppers. Twenty pounds or so wouldn't last long, not with a funeral to pay for. There would be a pound on the mantelpiece, ready for that week's lottery, but even so, she would have to go upstairs.

With curtains half-closed to keep the sun out, the spare room had a gloomy atmosphere. Stale air with a ghostly whiff of Yardley English Rose talcum powder; 'the scent of Mother', John had said, insisting on displaying the remains of a Christmas box set on the dressing table. They'd never had a guest. The double bed hadn't been slept in since old Mrs Marshall. If she hadn't died, John probably would never have married – she knew that now.

Since the sixties the bed had served as a storage area, primarily for *National Geographic*. A tributary of knowledge flowed throughout the house towards the cave-like room. The distinctive yellow rectangles swelled into a flood of back issues, stacked in year and date order all over the floor, eventually piled so high they cascaded onto the pink candlewick bedspread. For once she had agreed with John: *National Geographic* was an excellent publication, far too good to throw away.

She cleared the mattress enough to heave up a corner, shoved a hand underneath until she felt the weight of the magazines above, then, reaching a little further, pulled out a silver-sequinned boob tube. She held it against herself for a moment – had she ever been that slim or quite so deluded? She'd never even been to a disco, so how could she have been spotted by a scout for Pan's People, let alone have joined the girls on a cruise ship to dance all the way to Honolulu?

Further under the mattress her fingertips brushed soft fabric. Velvet piping around the collar with a miniature pocket for a tiny hand. Newborn size. She resisted the urge to pull it into the light and smell it. Not now. Not today. Sweeping blindly to either side, she eventually made contact with what she was searching for. A large brown envelope contained everything to ensure speed and efficiency when the time came.

Over the years, writing and rewriting a letter to John had become cathartic, a form of therapy; and in case he considered it a 'typically female outburst', the accompanying diary of misdemeanours contained actual, powerful evidence. He couldn't argue with forgotten birthdays or confidence-eroding insults – she'd read up on the subject – 'blithering idiot' and 'brainless wonder' amounted to emotional abuse.

To officially reinforce the evidence, she had '*Is Your Man a Keeper?*'. Snipped out of a magazine, he wouldn't be able to argue with his score of two out of twenty, only achieved because of '*Does he bring you breakfast in bed?*' – and even then, he'd only done it once when she was ill, just a cup of tea and a bowl of cornflakes. He hadn't thought to decorate the tray with a little vase of flowers like the man in the picture. She'd already known John was not a keeper but with the quiz agreeing with her, it was official. In her imagined confrontation, she would triumphantly show him his dismal score, read evidence from her diary and leave the letter for him to read and reread into his miserable old age.

Slamming the door on her marriage had been a recurring daydream, particularly enjoyed when biting the heads off Jelly Babies. John leaving first and so abruptly had never occurred to her. The bundle of notes in the envelope was supposed to buy her freedom, not pay for a funeral. With a few pennies saved here and there over the years, she had accumulated three hundred and twenty pounds. She had no idea if it was enough but it would keep her going while she found out what to do next.

John kept his important papers in an old shoe box in the bottom of the wardrobe: his driving licence, a few yellowing photographs, their wedding certificate. *Last Will and Testament of John Reginald Marshall* was near the bottom. She sat on the edge of the bed to open it. There was no need for ceremony – she'd read it many times before and just needed the details of the executor.

Three days later she was sitting before Mr Gregson of Hearle & Gregson Solicitors, hoping the appointment would fit into the first quarter-hour pricing increment. How much would a coffin cost? And what about the bills, the electricity and so on? Once everything was sorted out, she would get a job. At least that was something – she'd always wanted to be part of a team, to have workmates. But at fifty-two, who would employ her? John had insisted she stayed at home. Old-fashioned. She waited for Mr Gregson to look up or at least speak; she could barely breathe with nerves. What if there wasn't enough money for the funeral?

'I'm just checking the mortgage status, Mrs Marshall.'

The mortgage. What mortgage? She'd heard about repossessions; she'd have to move out. Homeless widow. Could it get any worse?

'Ah, here it is.' He checked the document. 'I am pleased to say you will have sole ownership of ninety-three Grove Road. There's no mortgage, it's yours outright. I believe we have the deeds here. We can continue holding them, if you so wish?'

'Thank you, yes,' she said quickly. What a relief. At least that was good news. What's he looking for now? She furtively glanced at the clock behind the solicitor's desk. Forty pounds an hour. Let's go, disco. Hurry up.

'Your husband also had savings, a residual pension and of course, there's the balance of his current account. The—'

'Sorry?' Flora tried to keep up. 'Did you say savings?'

Mr Gregson glanced back at the document and flipped over a page. 'Ah, yes, a high-interest savings account with the Bradford & Bingley Building Society. I have taken the liberty of obtaining the balance as it stands today. The total sum of monies being two hundred and ninety-six thousand, four hundred and thirty pounds.'

'Two thousand four hundred.' She let out a long sigh. That should be enough. 'That's such a relief. I've been so worried about the cost of the funeral and repairing the cooker, I—'

'Not two thousand, Mrs Marshall, two *hundred* and ninety-six thousand, four hundred and thirty.' He leaned over and showed her the figure written down. 'You can have a copy of this to take away.'

She looked at the printout with her hand pressed to her mouth. 'Good gracious.' Her muffled voice was barely audible. She stared at the paper, unable to focus. 'I don't know what to say. I mean, that's such a lot of money. Where did it all come from?'

'Well, as I'm sure you know, your husband was the sole beneficiary of his late mother's estate, and of course, there was the redundancy issue.'

'Redundancy?'

'Yes, from your late husband's former employer. We negotiated quite a severance payment. Constructive dismissal. I believe it was an insurance company? Quite a nice little payout, I seem to remember.'

'Payout? He said it was early retirement. I thought we – well he, John, only had his pension.'

'Of course, there will be disbursements, funeral fees and so on, but you have a healthy legacy, plus of course the value of the property, should you wish to sell.'

'We were doing the lottery, you see. I was having a Parker Knoll recliner in Maple Blush if we won. I thought—'

The solicitor gave a small smile and nodded. 'You'd be surprised, Mrs Marshall, we often have to tell a surviving spouse something they didn't know. I'm pleased that in your case, it is of a beneficial nature.' He slid some papers over to her side of the desk and handed her his fountain pen. 'Now, if I could just have your signature, here and here, I'll set the wheels in motion.'

As soon as she'd signed, he stood up to signal the end of the meeting. 'I'm sorry for your bereavement, Mrs Marshall, but I'm glad your late husband left everything in good order for you. I wish you all the best.'

Outside the solicitor's office, Flora felt shaky. Two hundred and what? She rummaged for the papers in her bag then, thinking better of it, crossed the road to the nearest coffee shop. She had better sit down. As soon as she had settled at a corner table, a waitress appeared.

'A pot of tea, please,' said Flora absently.

'For one?'

'Yes. Er, no.' She should have something special to celebrate, something with chocolate sprinkles. 'Sorry, can I change to a cappuccino?' Then remembering the broken cooker she added, 'And a toasted cheese sandwich.'

She'd left the house that morning so worried about money she'd even considered selling her wedding ring; now she was an heiress to a three-bed semi and a small fortune.

'Brown or white?' the waitress was asking.

'Oh, white please.'

Quite a big fortune, actually. And the severance payment, whatever that meant. What had John been playing at? All those times they'd gone without or bought the cheapest – everything patched up and on a shoestring. No holidays or outings, not even enough to have her hair done. Once a month she trimmed his hair with the kitchen scissors and occasionally snipped the split ends off her own. There was no style to it; she had to wear it up in a bun. Around the time it started to go grey she'd cut out a special offer from the local paper: *'Give yourself a boost with a new look'*, it said. There were photos of careworn, lank-haired women morphing into smiling babes with perky bobs and pixie cuts. She had left it on the kitchen table for John to see; she could have done with a boost. 'What a waste of money,' he'd said, 'with all that fuss and titivating, you'll still be you.'

'Cheese toastie on white?' The waitress plonked it down and was already walking away before Flora could answer. All that money, just sitting in a savings account. Why the big secret? She cut the two triangles in half to help them cool down. Things could have been so different. They wouldn't have had a wonky cooker for starters. Still, it was nice having food made for her, in that respect it had done her a favour. She took a tentative bite. Be thankful for small mercies – if it'd been the washing machine that had finally gone kaput, she'd be sitting in a launderette watching her smalls go around.

Fancy John forgetting to switch the power off before he stuck a screwdriver in the socket; he always thought he knew best when it came to repairs. When the boiler had broken down the year before, they had endured two freezing days without hot water or heating while he fiddled about. It was only after a third day of wearing gloves at breakfast that he finally called a plumber.

'Well,' he'd said, 'sometimes you have to push the boat out.' Push the boat out? He had plenty of money all along. He could have phoned an emergency plumber on day one, but he'd rather freeze.

Being mean, or careful, as he called it, had cost him his life. Poor John. But all that time, sitting on a pile of money and not poor at all. Scrooge. Spiteful, too. How different things could have been. A holiday for starters, even if it wasn't one of the lottery-winning places, a little jaunt away. A mini-break would have been something.

She stirred her cappuccino slowly, admiring the chocolatey swirl. She wouldn't bother getting the cooker repaired, it was goodness knows how old, already second-hand when they bought it. No, she could afford to have a new one now, something with an up and over and a glass hob. Easy to clean. But how would that look next to the old formica work top? And the fridge; the door handle had broken off years ago. She had grown used to prising it open with her fingers but sometimes it was a two-handed job. A new fridge would be nice, too.

By the time she had popped the last of the toasted sandwich into her mouth, she was wondering how much a whole new fitted kitchen would cost. She was still mulling over colour schemes at the bus stop. Moving on to tiles and lino, she found a seat on the intercity heading back out to the suburbs. Normally she liked to sit next to someone and strike up a conversation – public transport was one of the few places she felt she could talk to people without seeming weird – but today there was too much on her mind.

The bus growled along Beechwood Road, stopping here and there to pick up and drop off passengers. The two women sitting in front of her were talking non-stop, gossiping. John would have called it tittle-tattle. Odd words filtering between the seats caught Flora's attention.

'Dead as a dodo.'

'I know. It's not often we get a blue flashing light in Grove Road.'

'When it stopped outside number ninety-three, I said to Len, I wouldn't be surprised if she hasn't gone and murdered him, the way he was.'

'I wouldn't blame her – he gave me the absolute do-dahs. What was he like before he married?'

'Lived there with his mother. She died in the sixties, before he took up with what's-her-name. Once, our Len asked him down the Legion, just to be friendly, but he wouldn't go. I don't know if he was weird or just stuck-up. Never speaking and always in that brown suit.'

'A right old skinflint I'd say, too mean to buy anything new.' Flora felt an indignant rage mixed with a strange sense of satisfaction. It wasn't just her then; she hated those suits too. He insisted on wearing them after he'd retired because they were 'still perfectly serviceable'.

'His poor wife. When I first saw her, you know, after they married. I couldn't believe it.'

'He got the sack for that and quite right too.'

'You can't go around willy-nilly marrying your pupils, can you?'

'Not in a civilised country.'

'And she's just like him, creeping around, keeping herself to herself. Len says it saved spoiling two good 'uns, them two together.'

There was a pause. I should tap them on the shoulder, thought Flora, just to see the look on their faces.

'What a way to go though. Imagine. Fried to death.'

'I said to Len, I'm risking my life every time I cook the tea.'

They laughed at this and began gathering their bags. Flora ducked down and looked out of the window.

'We could do with a nice young family in that house, liven the place up a bit. She should move away, start again.'

'If it's not too late – I mean, have you seen the state of her?'

The women stood up as the bus stopped at the end of Grove Road. She would get off around the corner by the shops and walk back. The fresh air would do her good.

To give the neighbours time to get back behind their net curtains, Flora walked slowly, stopping to look in the occasional shop window. She played the conversation over again in her mind; they hadn't said anything she hadn't already suspected. Undoubtedly, she and John had been the odd couple in the street, the subject of gossip from the very beginning – her old high school geography teacher and the obvious age gap – Flora knew that, but they should get their facts straight. John hadn't been sacked, just asked to resign. And she had already left school by the time they got together. It didn't really matter now; even with John gone, she wouldn't invite the neighbours in to see her newly fitted kitchen. They'd never be friends.

Outside The Golden Wok, she studied the menu. With John's aversion to 'foreign muck', she could only imagine what

Chinese food tasted like. Aromatic duck, chow mien, crispy won tons, butterfly king prawns – it all sounded so exotic. Exciting. It was difficult to choose, but the special offer mini-banquet meal seemed to have a bit of everything, and they'd deliver it to her door, all for nine ninety-nine.

~≈≈≈~

Flora laid the table ready for six o'clock and put out a Christmas paper napkin – it was a sad reflection that the same pack of twenty had lasted so many years. She tuned the radio in to *Classic Hits* and poured herself a Baileys, then reapplied her lipstick so the delivery man would know it was a special occasion and the neighbours could think whatever they liked.

When the doorbell rang Flora was disappointed not to see a Chinese man or a lady in colourful silk but a spotty lad with ginger hair, wearing headphones. He handed her a large warm bag wafting a delicious aroma.

'Oh, gosh! And it's all for me.' Flora laughed and quickly handed over ten pounds so she could take the bag with both hands.

'Is that it then?' said the youth.

She could hear tinny music leaking out around his ears.

'I don't know, is it?' The bag looked pretty full. Already she was wondering how many meals she could have with what now seemed like a crazy over-indulgence.

The lad shoved the money into his jeans and turned on his heel, muttering something that sounded like 'tightwad'.

'You can keep the change,' called Flora.

She carefully unpacked the bag, savouring the moment. It was possibly a life-changing occasion, deserving of a top-up of Baileys and a respectful pause before removing the lids. For thirty-five years, John's meal plan had only allowed for seven meals with hardly a variation, besides birthdays and Christmas –

even those occasions had become predictable. Roast chicken for Christmas and a steak for birthdays. Once, Flora had decided to make carbonara for her birthday – it had only been once and that had been a mistake.

'What do you call this?' John had said, prodding the heap of steaming spaghetti.

'Try it with some parmesan on top – it's what the Italians do.' Flora passed him the pot of dried cheese and he sniffed the lid.

'Christ alive! I'm not eating that.'

'Couldn't you just try it? It's my birthday.'

'Just because you're celebrating doesn't mean I should have to suffer. No, I'll not have that,' he'd said, pushing his plate away. Flora looked at her own food, already starting to go cold.

'I'll make you a ham sandwich then, shall I?'

'I should think you'd better and don't try dishing up foreign muck again, birthday or not.'

'How will you manage when we win the lottery then, when we do the list?'

'Well, that'll be different; I'll have whatever I want, I'll be a millionaire then.'

'Actually, you'll only be half a millionaire, John. And with my share of the winnings I'll be eating anything but sodding sandwiches and shepherd's bloody pie.'

'Language, Flora.'

In the kitchen, Flora had cried small angry tears, then cheered herself up by sprinkling the ham with an excessive amount of salt and 'forgetting' to butter both pieces of bread. For the rest of their marriage, she stuck to cooking steak on their birthdays, although John sometimes complained that his was over-done or tasted a bit off.

She vowed to never again eat the seven most boring meals ever invented and took a sip of Baileys to seal the deal. The tin trays covered virtually the whole of John's side of the table. She slowly removed the lids and admired the spread. The smell was intoxicating, confusing. She tried to identify each dish by re-reading the menu and inspecting the ingredients, then used a teaspoon to taste the sauces. It was a revelation. So many contrasting flavours. Sweet and sour. Hot. Spicy. The only thing she recognised was the apple fritters rolled in sesame seeds because they couldn't have been anything else.

THREE

As the only chief mourner, Flora had the front row in the crematorium to herself. The soft music and hushed voices were strangely comforting. She sneaked a glance behind. There were far more people than she'd expected. Mr Singh from the corner shop and the nice elderly couple from two doors down. Clive and Shirley from Neighbourhood Watch. Maggie and a few others from the allotment. Thankfully, Len and his awful wife from over the road were nowhere to be seen. A youngish man with trendy hair came in and sat at the back. She didn't recognise him. Gail arrived at the last minute with two girls from the cafe and gave her a discreet wave. It was a good turnout; John would have wanted a church affair but the crematorium was on the bus route. Ease of use – it was all the rage these days.

The service opened with 'The Lord Is My Shepherd'. A couple of wavery tenors kept track while the rest joined in with enthusiasm, then tailed off when familiarity wore thin. The mood was slightly lifted by the effusive eulogy, spouted by a reverend with soft pink cheeks and a northern accent. He'd only met Flora briefly but appeared to have first-hand knowledge of John's passion for gardening and geography. Very convincing.

There was the occasional sniffle from the congregation, followed by muffled laughter when John's unusual approach to growing prize-sized dahlias was mentioned. They could all picture him playing an old Roberts radio to the rows of bobbing, frilly pompoms. His mother's pride and joy.

She had visited the allotment a few days before, hoping to make up a wreath of dahlias, but it turned out spring was too early for his 'girls' to make an appearance. Instead, she'd bought imported hot pink and zesty lemon chrysanthemums to wave goodbye as the coffin was lowered out of sight. Then the electronic curtains made a discernible whirr and the show drew to a close.

'Well, that's that, then,' murmured Flora. Picking up her bag and stuffing her unused hankie back inside, she followed the vicar into the afternoon sun. He seemed keen to move on to the funeral tea and was soon steering her through the memorial gardens, over the road towards the community hall.

The tea table was an arena of competitive baking. She knew it had little to do with John's popularity and more to do with the hierarchy of the Women's Institute. She'd been to a meeting once, thinking she'd make some friends, but John had grumbled about subscription fee and really, they weren't her kind of people. Ever-so-slightly smug with their twinsets and salon hairdos.

'Such a lovely service,' parroted the cake pushers. Even chief mourners had to run the gauntlet.

'Have a slice of my Victoria.'

'You must try the gingerbread.'

They quickly encircled the vicar, proffering plates of fruit loaf and fairy cakes. Flora could hear John, as clear as a bell – 'look at him, like a cockerel in a henhouse', and then, 'they're a proper money-spinner you know, funerals; most likely he's touting for more business.' She watched the vicar accept a slice of prize-winning Battenburg and then elegantly side-step towards a cluster of silver-haired pensioners, neighbours she hardly knew.

She was tired. It had been a long day; everything had already been said and done – maybe she should stay longer to be polite, but what difference would it make in the long run? The girls from Gail's Cafe had already hurried back to work, and she had done the rounds to thank everyone for coming.

The number seventy-two took her six stops along Great Western Road, then there was just a short walk home. As soon as she got in through the front door, she kicked off her shoes and left them lying where they landed. She could feel John's agitation but refused to put them neatly on the rack. Instead, she poured herself a large glass of Baileys. She was about to sit on the sofa, then plumped herself down in John's chair. She heard his protest as though he were there in the room.

'A few things are going to change around here,' she muttered, reaching for their wedding photograph. She stared at the black-and-white couple: Johnny M with his geography teacher's side parting and her in a white cheesecloth dress, holding a bunch of marguerites. She stroked his monochrome face with her finger.

'You silly old sod,' she said.

She had loved him then, when he was still Johnny M. She cradled the frame on her lap and sipped her Baileys. It had been on her eighteenth birthday at The Berni Inn that he had popped the question. She had just picked up her Knickerbocker Glory glass to tip the remains into her open mouth.

'Flora?'

'Eh?' Her tongue was out, ready to catch the strawberry as it gathered speed.

'I've something important to ask you.' He moved his chair closer to hers and waited.

'Mmm,' she patted her midriff.

'Flora, my love, I was wondering if—'

'That was the bees-knees.' Barely registering his agitation, she picked up her spoon to scrape a few hundred and thousands off the edge of the glass.

28

'Flora, would you do me the great honour of becoming my wife?'

'Oh!'

'You'd make me the happiest man alive.' He waited. 'We're a team, you and I. So, what do you say?'

'Yes,'

'Yes?'

'Yespialidoshus!' Her only friend and a ticket to freedom – of course she said yes.

Later that evening, her parents had been watching *Opportunity Knocks* – 'It's make-your-mind-up-time!' said a perma-tanned Hughie Green. Not wishing to compete with the clap-o-meter, she had turned the sound down and stood in front of the screen to make her announcement.

'Marry?'

'Mr Marshall? Your old geography teacher, the one with the dicky leg?'

'It's John. And for your information, he got his leg in the war.'

'For goodness sake, Flora!'

They begged her to reconsider, said she was throwing her life away and eventually refused to have any part in the proceedings. She didn't care – he was Romeo to her Juliet. Her parents' disapproval had made their love tryst all the more intoxicating.

What a silly girl she'd been.

She could still see her father's red-faced fury, shouting as she pushed past him on her wedding day. 'Listen to me, young lady! If you leave this house, you'll not come back!'

Her mother on the doorstep in her housecoat and slippers, arms folded, tight-lipped.

As a final act of defiance, Flora had picked all the marguerites from a pot in the front garden and carried them proudly past the twitching curtains to the end of the street where John was waiting. She felt empowered, excited.

She had settled into married life on the other side of Coventry, almost an hour and three buses away. Within a couple of weeks, she'd begun to wonder if she'd made a terrible mistake, but there was no going back; even a visit home would have seemed like admitting defeat.

Years passed before she tried to bridge the gap. As an only child of much older parents, a sense of duty finally prevailed, by which time it was too late. Her father died of a heart attack. Although she attended the funeral, the relationship between her and her mother remained cool. Awkward cups of tea two or three times a year were all they had. Eventually, the family house was sold to pay for a nursing home.

'She didn't know who I was,' Flora had cried after she'd finally been to visit.

Gone completely *gah-gah*, according to John.

First an orphan and now a widow. A widowed orphan at the age of fifty-two; truly alone in the world.

'A fine state of affairs.' The sound of John's voice came from nowhere and gave her quite a start.

Flora picked up the remote and flicked through to the news. That'll shut him up, she thought and went into the kitchen. The morning's washing-up was still in the sink. It didn't take long. One cup, one plate. A sad sight on the draining board. Alone. Tears built up and stung her eyes, then with one blink they were running down her face.

⁓⁂⁓

An assistant from Hearle & Gregson phoned to provide Flora with guidance on setting up a bank account. They would soon make an interim payment. However, probate meant it would be a while longer before the bulk of her inheritance could be transferred. Plans for a new cooker would have to wait. This could have been bad news, but Flora enjoyed the excuse of going to Gail's Cafe. She'd been a regular there since 1972, when she'd been so lonely she'd begun skimming a little off the housekeeping money. Since then she had dropped in for a coffee and a chat whenever possible – the staff were as close to friends as anyone.

The lack of a cooker encouraged further experimentation with meals at home. Sometimes, as a sort of celebration of independence, she'd have breakfast early, an extra snack before a late lunch, and then a tray on her lap for an evening in front of the telly. John never had a meal on a tray. He liked to do things properly and sit at the table. His most frivolous of meals was what he called high tea, reserved for Sundays, but limited to sardines on toast and a fig roll or two. High tea was begging to be reinvented. Sandwiches were brought up to date with artisan bread and an unlimited choice of exotic fillings: brie balanced on grapes, peanut butter with banana. Crumpets were introduced, with butter sliding over the crispy surface and sinking deliciously into the dimples, then slathered with jam. Somehow comforting and fun at the same time. A delightful chewy mess. And instead of fig rolls, she'd go for a chocolate eclair, or more usually a pair of eclairs, boxed side by side from the supermarket. Who needed a cooker when high tea could be slotted in between takeaway meals, pot noodles and a variety pack of cereal?

Since John's death, Flora's life was changing shape significantly, and so was her figure. There was more eating and watching daytime television and less housework or reading of improving books. And now, thanks to the interim payment from Hearle & Gregson, she could venture on a few shopping sprees. Mainly to Marks and Sparks, where she knew where she was with sizes and styles, then upstairs to the cafeteria for lasagne or tuna bake followed by a slice of cheesecake and a cappuccino. If she fancied a chat, she would also pop in to Gail's Cafe for afternoon tea on the way home.

'Nice to see you again, Flora. Is your cooker still on the blink?' asked Gail, wiping a nearby table.

'Well, I'm waiting for my inheritance to come through so I can have a fully fitted kitchen.'

'That'll be a while by the time it's done. What about a microwave for TV dinners and the like?'

'Well, I'm not sure.' John had refused to get one, saying the radiation gave people cataracts. 'Don't they cause cancer or something?'

'If they do, I'm a walking miracle. I've had one for at least twenty years.'

It was hard to ignore John's ghostly disapproval, but the thought of a TV dinner won over. Second-hand microwave ovens had their own column in the local paper with comments like 'glass plate missing' or 'knobs broken – free of charge'. If John had actually approved he would have gone for one of those; however, she chose 'Small microwave. Perfect working order. Buyer collects.' A bargain at fifteen pounds.

The final part of the purchase meant catching the seventy-two and navigating the unchartered territory of a housing estate. After taking a wrong turning, she eventually found the house, with a pile of cardboard boxes stacked outside the front door. She enjoyed the brief encounter with the young couple and two children who had only recently moved in, a rare glimpse into a normal family life. While grappling with her new second-hand bargain, carrying it from the bus stop, she wondered what had been packed in the box before they'd put the microwave in it. In any case, it'll give the curtain twitchers something to think about; the sight of her walking past wrestling a large cardboard box with 'Bedroom – JASON' written on each side in black marker pen.

The microwave's shiny chrome and glass with a digital timer and optimistic ping provoked a sense of frustration in Flora. Surrounded by half-broken appliances and dreary decor it was like a spaceship in a third-world country. Getting a new fitted kitchen wouldn't be enough; she should look at decorating the rest of the house. It was important to make sure things went together: she was getting a little ahead of herself, but one day, when she was the person she wanted to be, she hoped to have friends around and be part of a social circle.

She'd had the same aspirations as any newlywed, thinking she'd invite the neighbours for cheese and wine, coffee mornings, a fondue. She and John could learn to play bridge, join a club. Fuelled by the dream of becoming a kaftan-wearing suburban wife with a hostess trolley, she had visited Laura Ashley.

Slightly overwhelmed by the jungle of floral print, she'd been quickly put at ease by a friendly sales assistant named Belinda. With the help of their home survey form, Belinda ascertained a complete revamp was in order. Her already upbeat tone took on a sing-song confidence as she snipped matchbox-sized samples of fabric. Pixie Rosebud, Clematis Seaspray and Iona Misty Morning were coupled with Belinda's authority on wallpaper and paint, who then stapled into a personalised colour swatch.

Still on a high that evening, Flora had repeated the sales spiel to John: it would add value to the property and appeal to buyers, should they decide to sell. 'Laura Ashley is very happening, very 1970s,' she said, trying to mirror Belinda's confidence.

John's silence spoke volumes.

'It's what everyone wants—' she trailed off.

Already opening his newspaper, he said, 'This matchy-matchy business is women's nonsense. And as we'll not be moving house, give me one good reason why it serves us better than what we already have?' Belinda had said a beautiful home would be the envy of all her friends; that she'd feel super confident when she entertained. But Flora didn't have any friends and they never entertained. No one knew or cared about the horrid brown curtains or the cracked lino.

Since then, she had made do with *Changing Rooms*; she liked to imagine Lawrence Llewellyn-Bowen and the team arriving at number ninety-three and laughing at the murky interior before ripping everything out. They'd discuss her ideas for a romantic yet sophisticated overhaul and then push the boundaries with a surprising new colour scheme. She would be overwhelmed, even cry with happiness, when they painted the walls fuchsia pink and reupholstered the old beige sofa with zebra print.

Ever since the first lottery ticket, Flora had been collecting articles from magazines. While she waited for her inheritance, she would use the time to plan. She would do the whole house. Paper over the past and paint a brighter future. Flora found a decorator in the corner shop window: Bob's Brushes. FREE ESTIMATES. Friendly, clean, reliable. He sounded very nice on the phone. When he learned she'd recently been widowed, he offered to come round to price up a complete revamp the following afternoon.

Up until the moment he arrived, Flora had assumed they'd walk through each room, discussing peachy tones and coordinating carpets, with the suggestion of a dado rail here or a feature wall there. Then they'd sit down to go over the finer details. She'd offer him a nice cup of tea and a Gypsy Cream. She laid the tray and warmed the pot ready for his four o'clock arrival, then checked her hair in the hall mirror and retouched her lipstick.

The last visitor she'd had, apart from the emergency services, had been months before John's accident – a nice pair of Jehovah's Witnesses. Flora had invited them in for a chat. It made a change from watching *The Flying Doctors* and they'd given her a copy of *Watchtower*. She'd stuffed it under a cushion in the front room before John got home, then disposed of it in the bin outside the corner shop. He didn't like people coming to the house. Well I'm in charge now, Flora said to herself as she checked her watch, wondering if she'd got the time wrong. At a quarter past four, she poured herself a cup of tea and drank it standing up in the kitchen. Two Gypsy Creams later, the doorbell finally rang.

'Mrs Marshall?' *Bob's Brushes* was embroidered on his blue overalls, which, undone at the front, showcased a beer belly. 'Sorry I'm late, you know how it is.'

'Um,' said Flora. He didn't wipe his feet.

'Right!' he said, rubbing his hands together. 'Let's have a butcher's.' As he pushed past into the front room, Flora caught a whiff of cigarette smoke. 'Crikey! When was this place last looked at?'

She wouldn't offer him a biscuit.

'This stuff's pre-war.' He tapped the plaster in several places.

Or a cup of tea.

Upstairs, he only briefly looked in the bathroom. There was no point in showing him the snippets of wallpaper she'd collected or asking for his opinion on a dusky pink carpet with a plum skirting board.

On the landing, Bob stamped on the floorboards. 'You want to get a surveyor in. This place ought to be condemned. Or put in a museum.' He laughed as though he'd told a joke. He didn't bother looking in the spare room, which actually was in the best condition due to lack of use. Already halfway back downstairs he added, 'Sorry love, I'm not touching this; there's all sorts going on here. Could take months to sort out.'

Flora closed the front door, tight-lipped, more to stop herself crying than anything else. Ever since she'd moved in, nothing more than emergency repairs and patching-up had been done. Most of the decor was inherited from John's mother, who had moved there in 1940 after the family home had been bombed out. The walls were punctuated here and there by small rectangles of ghostly colour where pictures had once hung. The lino in the bathroom was so worn that the pattern in front of the sink had disappeared altogether.

It might have been described as a three-bedroomed house, but there were only two bedrooms. The third was a junk room, full of fractured furniture and retired domestic gadgets hoarded by John. Still smarting from the decorator's comments, Flora dragged everything out onto the landing: an upright vacuum cleaner, so old the canvas bag had rotted through, an eiderdown spitting feathers, a mirror clouded by age and freckled with black blotches, a wicker chair with a hole in the seat. She would have to get a man and a van. She needed one in any case to take all John's books. She was going to donate them to Autumn Leaves Nursing Home. Old books for old people.

Before the lottery, reading had been their only shared pastime. Together but apart. He with his geology, global history and the occasional biography, she with her westerns and dreamy romances. John had often scoffed at such 'frothy nonsense' and pushed her to read something more academic. 'There you are,' he'd say if she showed the slightest interest, 'we'll soon have you sitting down to *Theory of the Earth; or an Investigation of the Laws Observable in the Composition, Dissolution, and Restoration of Land upon the Globe*'. It was his idea of a joke, but she knew it was only partially in jest. He conveyed his expectations regularly by tearing strips off the local paper to mark certain pages of his books for her to read. Flora stacked the books into boxes, still with limp newspaper tails hanging out of them.

～∞∞～

The only household item of any value was the clock on the mantelpiece. John had said it was late Victorian. A clumsy, ugly thing in a dark wood. The next morning, Flora wrapped it in newspaper, like a baby in a blanket, cradled it in her arms on the bus and sold it over the counter at Bygone Days, Antiques & Collectibles. She knew it was worth more than forty pounds, but it seemed pointless to take it home again. She already planned to fill the space with a porcelain shepherdess figurine she'd seen in Samuels.

Instead of dropping in to Gail's Cafe, Flora hurried home. She was in the mood for sorting out and the bedroom was next. None of John's clothes were worth passing on but before bundling them into bin liners, she checked the pockets. Apart from the odd handkerchief and a couple of cable ties in an old pair of gardening trousers, there was nothing of interest. She dragged the bags downstairs to the coat rack and threw in his cap and scarf. He'd been wearing his coat on the day he died. Inside she found his bus pass, keys to the allotment shed, and his Collins week-to-view. Every year he bought the same pocket diary; same style, same colour. Every year he had fewer appointments. Doing the lottery had given the diary a new purpose. As well as providing ample blank spaces for ideas – to be worked upon, critiqued and occasionally deemed worthy of adding to the list – it was used to carry the list itself.

She tucked the diary into her handbag for want of a safe place. It was a sad fact that, besides her wedding ring, it was the only relic of a happy memory of John. Every Saturday for the last six years, they had enjoyed a window of companionship, watching the lottery draw. John's list had brought about conversations they would never have had, even if that meant discussing the rock formation at Punakaiki rather than her dream of an executive home on a new estate.

Knowing now that he already had the money, and they could, in fact, have gone away any time, didn't detract from her feelings on the matter. The list had been his way of communicating, a desire to share experiences. He'd developed the list for them. For her.

With all John's belongings bundled up and boxed in the hall, Flora's thoughts turned to the allotment. He had taken it over from his mother and continued to grow the exact same vegetables and two rows of dahlias, just as she had. Flora had no interest in growing flowers or sprouts; she would hand it back to the council, but first, she'd have a last visit and check the shed was tidy.

She caught the bus to the outskirts of town. What would it look like? It was already three months since John was last there – overgrown with weeds most likely. Momentarily, she felt guilty. John's pride and joy. She could just hear his annoyance. 'About time too. You've let everything go to pot.' I'm sorry, John, there've been other things on my mind. 'More important than my dahlias?' Yes.

She opened the gate and looked past the assorted sheds and water butts to see John's plot on the far side. A few early dahlias, adding a splash of colour to the green surroundings. She'd never met the late Mrs Marshall. They wouldn't have got on. The fact John grew flowers in her memory told her everything she needed to know. She sensed a tummy swirl, something close to jealousy. Mummy's boy. If she hadn't died, John would have been just as happy spending the rest of his life with her.

She stepped over a few fallen bamboo canes on a well-trodden path around plots of patch-worked vegetables, vaguely interested to see what was growing while trying not to get mud on her shoes. She'd never been one for the countryside. Apart from a hurried, fruitless visit to pick dahlias for John's funeral, it was a couple of years since she'd been there. It looked surprisingly well-kept, all things considered. She unlocked the small shed and peered inside. Nothing of value, just a few seed packets, a stack of empty pots, and half a bag of compost. The fork and spade were in good condition, but she didn't want to take them on the bus; they would be useful for the next owner. She closed the door and put the key back in her pocket.

'Hey. Hi? Over here!' A voice, seemingly from nowhere.

Flora looked around. 'Hello?'

'Over here.' A well-dressed man emerged from a forest of runner beans on the far side of the garden and waved. As he trotted towards her, he pulled off his gardening gloves and flicked his hair back. About thirty-five, she guessed.

'Hi, I'm Marty. I saw you at the funeral.' He held out his hand.

'Yes, I remember you.' There'd only been one person with hair like that.

'I'm the sweet peas and salads over there,' he said with a nod towards a riot of colour beyond the runner beans. 'I'm so sorry about your dad – he was a lovely old chap.'

'He was my husband, actually.' She was used to people's assumptions; it had happened a lot when she was younger.

'Husband? Oh wow.' He seemed genuinely surprised. 'It's just that you look, well, a lot younger than him. Sorry. I feel terrible. He never mentioned a wife.'

'We were married for thirty-five years.' Flora folded her arms – she was there to do right by John and his blessed allotment, only to discover she didn't even exist in his gardening world. And who was this man in any case?

Marty broke the awkward silence. 'Have you seen Mary's Jomanda?'

'Mary's what?'

He stepped towards the row of dahlias. 'Jomanda. She's new. Shame John didn't live to see the first flowering. I don't think we can expect a proper show until the end of summer. Unlike this little lady.' He gently cupped a solitary bloom in his hand. 'You can't beat her for pinkness. John taught me all their names. Also, in the pinks we have First Kiss, and next to her there's Gay Princess, which he said he planted for me.' Marty laughed, but Flora was still trying to get past Mary's Jomanda. How come this man was on first name terms with John's dahlias?

'I've been keeping the girls "topped up", as John used to say. And I've done a bit of tidying, I hope you don't mind, but nature was trying to take over. He had planted out a few seedlings before he, well, passed away. Carrots, beetroot, potatoes of course.' Marty flicked his fringe awkwardly. 'Sorry, I'm talking too much. I just wanted to say hello. I didn't mean anything by what I said – I shouldn't have jumped to conclusions.' He paused. 'I really don't know why John didn't mention you in any of our chats.'

She began to feel sorry for him. 'Give him a spade, and he'll dig himself a grave' is what John would have said. 'It's alright. I only came up here to see if there's anything to sort out before I hand it back to the council. I'm not much of a gardener.' She looked around. There was nothing she needed to do, this Marty had done everything for her. 'Thanks for tidying up.'

'You're welcome. By the way, I don't know if you have anyone to help, but if you want a hand with anything, I'm here pretty much every day.'

'Every day? Don't you have a job?'

'Well, I sort of do, but it's part-time, afternoons and evenings mostly – I sell tickets at the theatre. The Guild on Elizabeth Street? I'm in the box office.'

'That must be nice – to see all the shows.'

'Yes, it's great sometimes, except we've been on *An Inspector Calls* for almost a month now. Not my scene. But we're putting on *The Mikado* next. I can't wait.'

'I've never been to the theatre, I've often wondered—'

'Oh, it's wonderful. The make-up, the costumes. I'd love to work in Wardrobe but, hey, at least I'm there. I tried to persuade John to come, but he never did.'

The idea of John going to the theatre was almost as unimaginable as him having a friend like Marty, who was nothing like the dungaree-wearing ladies and tweed-capped pensioners she'd met on previous visits. Why had John never mentioned him? Yet another of his secrets.

'No, he wasn't very keen on public entertainment.' Another thing she'd missed out on. 'Which was a shame.'

'Why don't you call by? I'm sure I could get you a comp.'

'A comp?'

'Yes, a free ticket. We usually have a few floating around. Call in and ask for Marty. Everyone knows me.'

'Thank you, maybe I will.' An invitation to the theatre. She felt herself smiling as she turned to go. 'And thanks for keeping an eye on everything.'

'I didn't catch your name,' he called after her.

'I'm Flora.'

'That's beautiful,' said Marty, 'and very fitting,' he added, nodding to the row of dahlias.

FOUR

Since Marty had suggested calling in to The Guild, Flora had thought about little else. Not because she wanted a 'comp', although a trip to the theatre would be nice; no, she wanted to talk to Marty, find out a bit more about him. Maybe they could be friends.

Four days seemed a reasonable amount of time to wait. He said he worked in the afternoons, so she caught the two o'clock into the city centre. Elizabeth Street was bustling with shoppers. School holidays. Mums with prams and runaway toddlers, young girls in uniform pink and purple. A group of teenagers rushed past, laughing. 'Up to no good', John would have said. The Guild Theatre was easy to find. She'd never been inside, but it was just after the arcade where she liked to window shop. Samuels had a lovely display of figurines, but she walked straight past. Today she had a purpose.

The entrance lobby looked like Christmas, all red and gold. Glamorous. Red embossed wallpaper and ornate golden frames to show off autographed photographs. Posters of forthcoming shows. Cherubs played musical instruments on a painted ceiling.

'Hello, young lady, how can I help you?' Marty grinned at her from behind the counter.

'Oh, I just thought I'd pop in.' Flora felt a bit silly now she was there. He'd probably only said 'call in' to be nice.

'It's so great to see you. How have you been?'

'Oh, you know, sorting things out. This and that. It's lovely to see you too, Marty,' she said shyly.

42

'Listen, I've got a break coming up, do you fancy a cuppa? I'm gagging for a coffee.'

Keep calm, thought Flora, it's happening. I'm actually going for coffee with a friend. 'Oh, yes, that would be nice,' she said, as nonchalantly as she could manage.

'Okay, give me five mins, and then I'm done for half an hour. We can pop over the road if you like? I'll see you in there.' Marty was obviously used to it.

'Yes. Okay. Oh, can I order you something?' Keep calm, try to sound casual.

'That would be amazing. Tell them it's for me – they know what Marty wants,' he laughed knowingly. Was that a double entendre? Luckily, his smile was cut short by the phone ringing. He held his hand up to keep Flora's attention while he answered it. 'Good afternoon, The Guild Theatre. Could you hold the line one moment, please?' He then covered the mouthpiece and said in a loud stage whisper, 'I can't wait to have a proper catch-up. See you in five, darling.' And then, 'Hello, sorry to keep you waiting, how can I help?'

Flora loved the idea of someone else being put on hold so she and Marty could finish their conversation. She was more used to being cut off in mid-sentence or completely ignored. And he'd called her darling – that was a first.

A warm coffee aroma embraced Flora as she squeezed past a crowded table near the door. She scanned the room hoping she didn't stand out or look odd. No free seats. Her heart pumped a little faster until she was rescued by the handsome young man behind the counter. When she said she was ordering for Marty, he quickly cleared a table in the window and made a show of taking her coat and getting her settled. Then Marty ran across the road and greeted the waiter with an exuberant hug.

'It's so lovely to see you, Flora,' said Marty, sliding into his chair in one easy move. 'You must tell me all. Oh, I like your nails.' Without waiting, he took her hand for a close-up inspection. 'You should let me have a go at them: I could sort out those cuticles. Sorry, am I too much? It's just, you know, show me a tiny glimpse of a star in the making and I'm on it.'

'Oh.' Flora found herself in a girlish giggle, not knowing what to say. The arrival of the coffee helped to break the ice further.

The half hour was filled with Marty's chatter about life in the theatre and his thwarted attempts to work in the wardrobe department. 'It's where I belong; backstage amongst the sequins and satin. All the buzz of opening night. I just love it. And I'm an absolute whiz with the eyeliner. You should let me show you. Let's have a look at you.' Marty leaned over the table and cupped her face in his hands. 'Beautiful.'

'Oh,' she said, turning pink. 'Don't be silly; he's just being kind.

'Trust me, you have a fabulous structure. Just look at those brows. With the right make-up, we could turn heads. I'm not kidding.'

'I doubt it, Marty. I've always been plain, I know that.'

'Listen to me, gorgeous girl, no one's plain, everyone has something. It's the skill of the artist to find the inner diva and bring her out. Let me have a go, I'll prove it to you.'

'Well, I don't think—'

'Can you meet me tomorrow? It's my day off.'

Before she had time to change her mind, she agreed to meet at the stage door. 'They won't mind – I'm always tinkering around in there,' he assured her as he got up to leave. He kissed her on both cheeks and then wove his way out between the tables. 'See you at ten, babes,' he called over his shoulder before running back over the road to finish his shift.

꧁

That evening Flora went through her wardrobe, pairing up tops and bottoms, trying to accessorise with her only decent scarf and two necklaces. Everything seemed dowdy. Even the tops she'd recently bought in M&S looked old-fashioned. Not surprising; they were just newer versions of what she'd always worn. Marty had promised a complete transformation and she could see she needed it.

It's strange how he had appeared just at the right time, when she felt in need of a helping hand. She wanted to spend some of her inheritance on a makeover and had tried to do a few things to get up to date with other women her age, but somehow she lacked confidence. When was the last time she'd had a compliment? John hadn't seemed to notice or care what she looked like; if anything, he'd mock her whenever she made an effort.

'What you women get up to is pointless primping, just looking for more ways to waste money,' he'd said.

Another time, when Flora was watching her favourite programme, *Make Me Beautiful*, he'd said, 'When will you learn? You can't turn a sow's ear into a silk purse.' She had added that to the list of insults stowed under the mattress in the spare room, picturing the day when she would finally leave. Then he'd be sorry.

With John no longer there to mock her, there were still obstacles. A lack of confidence was at the top of the list, followed closely by her shape and size. Flora stripped down to her new Marks and Sparks underwear and looked at the full horror in the wardrobe mirror. A human-sized Jelly Baby squeezed into floral sateen smalls. At least they were matching, with lace trim and ribbon detailing. She pulled the pants up to cover a bit more tummy and turned to the side. Whatever Marty did would be an improvement. Hopefully, he could make her look slimmer too. She would forgo her customary nightcap of a Baileys poured over ice cream; it was time to take control of the situation.

Before the alarm went off, Flora was already up and dressed. She had a black tea and a single slice of toast for breakfast. Then just before leaving the house she went back to the fridge and ate four serving spoons of strawberry yogurt straight out of the family-sized pot. By the time she arrived at the stage door her tummy was rumbling, so she furtively broke off a chunk of chocolate in her bag and quickly ate it.

By ten past ten, there was still no sign of Marty; perhaps she'd misunderstood or had the wrong day. She thought about going back to the little cafe from the day before – she'd noticed they offered a brunch special. Poached eggs on toast would be nice and still quite slimming.

'Flora! So sorry I'm late.' Marty almost collided with her. He was looking a little less lively than the last time she'd seen him. 'Got a banging head. Clubbing last night. Sorry, babes.'

'That's fine, I only just got here,' said Flora, hoping there wasn't any chocolate between her teeth. There was something about his groomed hair and neatly ironed shirt that made her feel slightly dishevelled, even though she'd made an effort. And he had such an easy way of speaking; so open and friendly.

'Don't worry,' he was saying, 'I've had an espresso and a couple of paracetamols. I'll be right as a rainbow any minute now.' His smile was convincing. Lovely, like an advert for toothpaste. She grinned back while keeping her lips pressed together. Teeth whitening might not be such an extravagance after all. 'Right then,' he said, unlocking the door and ushering her in. 'Come through heaven's door and prepare to be amazed.'

Marty walked around, snapping on lights and then cleared a chair in front of a mirror. 'Sit here, babes,' he said and flicked a switch under the countertop. 'Don't you just love the lights? It's proper showbiz here.' The bulbs all around the mirror illuminated a plain, middle-aged woman with wrinkles and mousy hair. Going grey.

Marty leaned over her shoulder and peered at his own reflection. 'Where did you go to my lovely?' he murmured and then dusted his face with a bronzing brush. 'I look a mess. Typical of Adam, he disappeared with some piece of trade last night. I couldn't wait around so I went on to Rockerfella's and that was that, if you know what I mean.'

'That sounds fun,' she said.

'Trust me, it wasn't worth it, not with a hangover from hell and nothing to show for it.'

'If you'd rather do it another day I—'

'No, no, absolutely no! That's not what I meant, I'll be fine in two ticks. I wouldn't usually get up so early on my day off, but I absolutely live for this. I literally can't wait to get started.' He slipped a hairband over her head and then spoke to her reflection. 'I only ask one thing.'

'Yes?'

'You have to give me a free rein; trust me until we're done.'

'Okay.' She had nothing to lose.

'And you need to relax. I'll put some music on – how about a bit of Aretha Franklin? She knows how to work it, eh?'

The intro to 'Respect' immediately lightened the mood. Marty danced around, occasionally bursting into song, using a brush for a microphone as he got to work. Being a makeover subject was far more fun than she'd imagined. Virtually everything Marty did was a revelation – primers and plumpers, contouring and shadowing. Her efforts with Tangerine Dream and a swipe of blue eyeshadow suddenly seemed very child-like.

'Now for your crowning glory.' Marty swivelled her chair away from the mirror. 'You can't look till I say.'

'Is a wig really necessary?' asked Flora.

'Trust me, it absolutely is. Especially with the amount of relaxed blondes you've got going on.'

'You mean grey?'

'I couldn't possibly comment, darling! There. Now you're done.' He turned her chair back to the mirror. 'See how it's lifted you?'

'Wow!' Flora turned her head this way and that. Stuck for words, just smiling. Something else was different – not just how she looked. She was happy without trying. That was a feeling she hadn't experienced for a very, very long time. 'I look like someone else. I feel new!'

'I told you, didn't I? Now, beautiful girl, we're ready for the fun bit. Come with me to Narnia.' Marty went through a door with 'Wardrobe' written on it in thick black letters. The room was full of hanging rails crammed with costumes, each labelled with forthcoming plays or past productions. A dazzling array of colours and textures.

'Isn't this the best place in the world?' Marty's voice came from the other side of Cinderella. 'What do you think?' He was holding up a pink satin ballgown. 'Pink's not really my colour, but I just love the fabric.' He pulled out another. 'This emerald's fabulous, don't you think?'

'Beautiful,' agreed Flora. There was so much detail. Beads, fancy stitching, just for a play.

'Anyway, never mind about my ballgown fixation, let's go over to Modern and Contemporary. Where are we on the sizes?' Marty appraised her. 'I'd say a curvy twelve?'

'Um, somewhere closer to sixteen actually.' Her new M&S top was only loose-fitting because she'd gone for an eighteen.

'Really?' said Marty, not looking at all surprised. 'With some strategic foundation garments, I could easily get you into a twelve, but just for today we'll be a little more generous.' He walked along the rail, pulling out several outfits for day and evening. Flora watched with amazement as he loaded her up with an array of styles and colours. Things other women wore.

'Let's pop you over here to change.' Marty propelled her behind a screen. 'Give me a shout if you need a hand. I'm going to Accessories. I know just the thing to go with that gorgeous yellow chiffon. Put that one on first – I'm going moist at the thought of it!'

Flora caught his last comment but wasn't quite sure how to reply. Besides, she had to agree – the floaty lemon jumpsuit was dreamy. When she stepped out from behind the curtain, she knew something wonderful had happened.

'Oh. My. Goddess.' Marty had stopped in his tracks. 'Amazing! I told you, didn't I?' He steered her towards a full-length mirror. 'What do you think, princess, you like?' Flora nodded vigorously, too overwhelmed to speak. He added a simple belt, a silver necklace, and a pair of nude heels. 'Hang on, one more thing. I know what's missing.' A pair of designer sunglasses topped off the look.

'I could be in Saint-Tropez,' Flora marvelled as she did a little practice walk with a sideways glance in the mirror.

'Yes, you'd fit right in. You look a million dollars.'

'Marty, do you think you could come shopping with me? I think I've been doing it all wrong.'

~ago~

The day her inheritance finally came through, Flora hurried back to the theatre and arranged the first of many shopping trips with Marty. What better way to start a new life than to buy a whole new wardrobe? She would delay ordering the fitted kitchen until she had developed a style and knew who she was. Flowery designs in pink and mauve had been her absolute favourite, but she was learning so much from Marty.

With more than enough money to spend, Flora developed a collection of designer clothes, not because she preferred them or knew the labels, but because Marty steered her in that direction. He had a good eye – with his guidance, she looked younger, healthier and for the first time in her life she felt attractive. Glamorous. Even when she wasn't looking her best, he'd find something genuine and heartfelt to say. Noticing when she'd changed her nail colour or done her hair slightly differently.

In between fashion tips and confidence-building comments from Marty, he chatted continually, filling the void where she should be sharing stories of friends and aspects of life that didn't yet exist. He told her about his thwarted attempts to find a boyfriend and the goings-on at The Guild. The theatre was a whole new world. She enjoyed the gossip about the backstage staff, especially Marty's nemesis, Colette, who had stolen his dream job in Wardrobe.

With a healthy bank account and enough money to negate the need to get a job, Flora passed the time between catching up with Marty by reading romantic fiction; without John's disdainful comments, she could lounge on the sofa with a swashbuckling hero and a dish of Jelly Babies to hand. After each blissfully optimistic ending she'd watch an hour or two of daytime television and then perhaps do a little light housework – no need to go mad, there were no visitors to tidy up for. Besides the odd foray to Gail's Cafe, meeting up with Marty was her only social life.

On a wet and windy Thursday, after a fruitless search for a mustard tote and a pair of daffodil sling-backs, Marty suggested Little Italy for lunch. The delicious aroma of warm garlic bread wafted towards them as they sat down, and roast tomato with rosemary undertones made Flora's tummy rumble.

'Oh, I love Italian food.' She'd only ever cooked pasta once, years before but more recently there had been M&S lasagne and microwaved spaghetti bolognese.

'Me too. Don't you wish we could press a button and our table would land in a fabulous little trattoria on the Amalfi

Coast? Maybe we should go one day. Rome for the sights, Capri for the sun and Milan for the fashion. And all of it for the amazing food and wine, topped off with a limoncello or even a fragoncello, you know, the strawberry one?'

'Oh, yes. Lovely.' Even the names sounded delicious.

'Mind you, my dream holiday is Rio de Janeiro. How about you?'

'I don't know.' Flora paused. Best to own up before this went too far. 'Actually, I've never been abroad.'

'What? But surely you—'

'John wasn't a great believer in holidays. We didn't even have a honeymoon.'

'Crikey, that's a very different John to the one I knew. He was always telling me about these amazing destinations around the world. I can't remember all the names – mostly they were places I'd never heard of. I suppose he went there before you two met, you know, given the age gap?' Marty was expertly twiddling spaghetti onto his fork while Flora had to cut hers up or risk dropping it down her front.

'No, he didn't have a passport either. He was interested in other countries, but never actually been anywhere.'

'Really? I thought he was well travelled. I s'pose being a retired geography teacher makes sense.'

'He didn't really retire from teaching. He had to give it up when we first got married.'

She could still remember how, as a new wife, she had made John's breakfast, packed his lunch, and waved him off for the first day of the autumn term at St Margaret's. After clearing away breakfast and washing up, she had consulted his housework rota and decided she'd do it all later, maybe after lunch. First of all, she wanted to enjoy being a housewife in her own home, alone.

She picked up her latest romance, *The Navaho Queen*, but a stack of LPs piled neatly next to the record player caught her eye. She carefully lowered the stylus onto Nat King Cole, and with the words *When I Fall in Love* she grabbed a cushion and waltzed it around the sitting room, humming along to the tune.

With her eyes half-closed, it was a while before she first saw his shoes, then his mackintosh. He was still holding his briefcase.

'Oh, John! You startled me.'

'What in heaven's name are you playing at?' He strode over and stopped the music.

'I, I was just—' Flora tried to gather her thoughts.

'Well, it's all very fine, you prancing around like a fool while I've just been given the heave-ho.'

'What do you mean, the heave-ho?'

'I've been sacked. Asked to resign is the way they put it.'

'What? From school?'

'Yes, Flora! Your intellect sometimes astounds me. I have been asked to resign my position as geography master on account of marrying an ex-pupil of the school.'

'Me?'

'Of course you, you imbecile.' John sank down into his chair and took his glasses off. 'I'm sorry, I'm a bit overwrought. They said it had been brought to their attention that a teacher from St Margaret's has shown a grave misjudgment, and if they are to retain their reputation as custodians of young ladies, they would have to make an example of him. Me.'

'Oh, no.' She sat on the arm of the chair and slid her arm around his shoulders.

'Don't do that, Flora; it's your fault we're in this position.'

'It wasn't just me!' she said, jumping up. 'It takes two to tango.'

'That's a typically inane assertion. It might take two, but you led me on. I was alright on my own. I should have stayed a bachelor. Teaching was the love of my life.'

'I thought I was the love of your life, that's what you said. You said I'd make you the happiest man alive by marrying you.' When he didn't say anything, she added. 'Do you want me to leave, so you can go back to what you love?'

He took out a handkerchief and blew his nose. 'Put the kettle on, I could do with a cup.'

In the kitchen, Flora realised John hadn't actually answered her question, and that worried her. She couldn't go back home after all the trouble with her parents, whereas John could quite easily do without her.

Marty had been listening to Flora's story with a forkful of spaghetti frozen in mid-air. He put it back down and took her hand. 'Oh, babes. I'm sorry. You mean all this time you've felt it was your fault? That you'd ruined his career?'

'Yes. He said some cruel things and never apologised. He made out he had to give up teaching for the sake of our marriage. He never recognised my sacrifice, of falling out with my parents; they hardly spoke to me after I married John. Whenever there was an argument, he'd always remind me how I'd wrecked his beloved teaching job.'

'But that's ridiculous. For a start, he was much older than you. He should have known the school wouldn't approve.'

'I don't suppose he thought of that. Besides, I had already left school. I was working in Fine Fare when we got together.' She paused. 'I was silly back then; I thought I was in love.'

'So, what happened after that? Did he leave teaching altogether?'

Flora told Marty how she had dutifully followed the housework rota, cooked the scheduled meals, and tried to keep out of John's way while he searched for work. He spent a lot of time at the library. In the evenings they sat together nursing their respective books, barely breaking the tension with anything other than necessary conversation.

When he was finally offered a job at an insurance firm, he became more talkative. But Flora knew he would always hold a grudge – because of her, geography was now history and so was the chance of a happy marriage.

'Well, from what you've told me, I think you were wasted on John.'

'He wasn't all bad, but he used to put me down all the time, make fun of things I said, especially if I got something wrong.' She barely remembered the fun-loving man who had shown an interest in the Top Forty and used words like 'groovy' and 'far out', just to make her laugh. As soon as they were married, he seemed to deride everything relating to her age group, including Flora herself. 'I was a very plain girl; boys barely looked at me. I wasn't popular or good at anything. I was actually grateful John had chosen me. I didn't expect more than that.'

Marty drained his glass. 'Well, I hope you know that's not true. And speaking of more, let's have some more prosecco.'

'I'll be getting tiddly,' said Flora.

'Come on, live a little. You've got some catching up to do. Prosecco is just the start.'

'I haven't been on holiday, that's true, but what else is there apart from decorating my house? I mean, I'm middle-aged and a widow. I've never had a proper job. I don't even know how to drive a car. There's not much I can do about it now.' The waiter cleared their plates.

'To be honest, babes, I wouldn't rush for the job; working's overrated if you ask me. Unless of course it's also your passion.'

'I'll take your word for it,' said Flora, eyeing the dessert menu. She had a sudden need for something chocolatey.

'The thing is, if John hadn't actually travelled to all those places, how come he knew so much detail, the food, the transport, all of that? The way he described the local customs, the cooking techniques and all – I genuinely believed he'd been there.'

'Well, we used to do the lottery. Just a pound. John wrote a list of all the places he'd read about in *National Geographic* and so on. Then, if we actually won, we'd be able to pack our bags and start travelling straight away.' Flora took a sip of her drink. 'I often wonder how different our marriage would have been if we'd actually gone somewhere.' She paused. 'But knowing what I know now, I probably would've divorced him and taken my share of the winnings. We were very different people you know. The only reason I stayed with him was because I had nowhere else to go and no money of my own.'

'I'm sorry about that,' said Marty.

'Anyway, it wasn't to be. John's gone and all that's left is his list.'

'So, are you going to carry on doing the lottery?'

'No, I don't think so.'

'But you might win, then you could—'

'I don't want to live for Saturday-night lottery numbers, Marty. I want reality. Maybe I'll get a little job, try and meet some new people?'

'Good idea, babes, you need to get out of yourself, as my grandmother used to say. To be honest I could do with getting out of myself too. I know tons of people but I don't have many proper friends, and none to go on holiday with.'

∾∾⟩⟩⟩∾

The conversation about John and the list had somehow unsettled Flora. She couldn't just buy clothes and shoes for the rest of her life; besides, she had no idea where she'd wear half the things now filling up the wardrobe. Shopping for another thirty years sounded almost as dull as being married to John.

Married life had been boring, but in later years, the lottery list had made the future seem almost exciting, hopeful. Unlike everything else, John had no budget when it came to his imagination.

Slowly it dawned on her – John had never expected to actually win the lottery and if he had won, he wouldn't have spent the money on a trip around the world. He actually enjoyed being mean, scrimping and scraping pennies together each week, making out he was doing his best for the two of them. It was all just a perfect fantasy. It gave him complete control over her and it saved him from actually doing something real. And by alluding to the fact he was a global traveller to Marty, well, that made him interesting to talk to. Which in every other respect he wasn't. No, the list wasn't for someone like John. It never had been.

While her dreams of winning the lottery had centred around an obsession with an executive home and all the trimmings, John's faraway lands, exotic food and all the sights had also caught her imagination. It had been so built up, so real – winning the lottery had been a matter of *when*, rather than *if*. Thinking about it now, in a way she *had* won the lottery with John's secret savings. Surely there was enough for an adventure, and besides, what else was she going to do with her life?

FIVE

In the seven months since John's death, significant changes had taken place in Flora's life, the absence of a husband being the least remarkable. In just a short time, she had morphed from a frumpy housewife into a blonde babe with the confident air of an heiress. And thanks to the discovery of body-shaping undies, she was the curvy wearer of a designer wardrobe, empowered by an arsenal of shoes, handbags and accessories. John's influence was in the past – apart from two things he had never planned to activate: his secret savings account and his lottery list. Both of which were about to unite into a life-changing reality.

Marty was easily persuaded to join her. All it took was a cup of coffee and the promise of a two-week detour to Rio.

'So, let me get this straight, babes.' Marty hadn't touched his cappuccino. 'You want to spend John's life savings on visiting his list of geographically fascinating places around the world *and* you'll include a two-week stay in Rio with tickets to the carnival?'

'Yes. And I'll pay for it if you organise everything and look after me.'

'Of course. I'd do that anyway, but are you sure? It's going to cost a bomb. What about the future? I mean, I can take a break from work; they'd have me back in a heartbeat, but spending your lifesavings? I'm not sure, babes.'

After he'd made her promise to set a budget and keep enough money in reserve to last until her retirement age, he was happy to take over planning the trip and organise an online bank account, tickets, visas and a passport for Flora. With regular meetings for coffee, Marty soon drew up an action-packed itinerary, based on John's suggested route but with what he called a Marty twist.

When Flora's passport arrived in mid-September and the shops began to fill up with Christmas stock, she didn't feel the usual regret, that everyone apart from her would be having a lovely family get-together. Instead she felt sorry for them. While they were passing around a tin of Quality Street, watching Eastenders on the telly, she'd be in an exotic location, sipping champagne on a beautiful white sand beach.

With a fortnight to go and a checklist supplied by Marty, Flora cleared the bed in the spare room and began packing. After experimenting with folding and rolling, she managed to squeeze the last few items in and promised herself she wouldn't repack for a fourth time, or add anything else 'just in case'. Then all she had left to do was a farewell lunch at Gail's Cafe and a trip to have her hair and nails done.

Dressed in a non-crease outfit advised by Marty, with a roomy waistline chosen by her in anticipation of the inflight hospitality, the day finally came. With a courtesy limousine from the airport waiting outside, Marty ushered Flora and her nest of pink metallic suitcases out of number ninety-three, and the geography field trip of a lifetime began.

~*~

It was a day of firsts for Flora. A chauffeur-driven car to the airport, flying business class, and now wearing her first set of silk underwear – not the Midnight Panache she'd contemplated after reading *Undercover Story – Over Fifty and Fabulous*, but long johns and a high-necked, long-sleeved vest. The guidebook had been quite clear: to enjoy the full delights of Greenland, warm clothing was a must. Underneath her goose-down salopettes, the silk undies were keeping her toasty warm. Not that she had time to think about underwear as she hurtled through a snow-sculpted wonderland towards the Kulusuk mountains. Dog sledging wasn't on John's list. He hadn't liked animals, but she wanted to experience everything, and thanks to Marty, everything was possible.

'I'm here, and I'm actually doing it!' Her words were drowned by the dogs' joyful barking as they raced beneath a bright blue sky with boundless energy. Fresh, flinty air with an earthy scent of pine and moss. Skimming through magical scenery was a perfect moment she wished she could freeze-frame forever. Rising bubbles of euphoria tickled her into laughing out loud, something she'd never experienced before. This is life. This is what it's all about.

Kulusuk and the rest of Greenland's archipelago had been at the top of John's list. He had written a few notes and underlined most of it in red: *Explore one of the wildest, most beautiful and near-deserted ice-scapes on earth.* He sounded almost poetic if you ignored the bit about instantly freezing rain and the crystalline rocks of the Precambrian Shield.

As agreed, Marty had booked everything according to the list, adding a little twist here and there. They would see the aurora borealis while cruising the ice fjords, with the added promise of whale-watching and polar bears. However, the dog sledging had been Flora's idea; she'd always wanted to experience the thrill of it, ever since reading *The Ice Maiden's Prince*, a tempestuous romance thwarted by a snowy wasteland.

When the dogs were finally called to a halt, a snowmobile taxi was waiting to take her back to Marty. The Inuit sledging master, Nuniq, said something indistinguishable and gave her a bear hug she could barely appreciate through his sealskin coat. It had been a wonderful, breath-taking afternoon; with the language barrier, she made do with smiling and nodding, accompanied by the gesture of namaste, which she felt was suitably international.

By the time another silent, sealskin-wearing local had driven her back to the private snow lodge, it was almost dark. Through the large picture window she could see Marty sitting by the log fire reading a guide book. The sound of her stamping snow off her boots had him leaping up to open the door.

'Quick, come in,' he said, dramatically wrapping a woolly blanket around her shoulders. 'You must be freezing, sitting on that sledge for hours.' He brushed her cheek. 'Colder than a penguin's chuff.'

'No, I'm fine,' said Flora, 'I was toasty in my Maxiheat Skinnies. You should've come, it was fantastic.'

'I'm sure it was, and I want to hear all about it, but first you could do with a nice hot soak. You could catch your death out there.' He disappeared into the bathroom and spoke over the sound of running water. 'I've already ordered room service. We're having the Inuit dog sledger's menu of choice.'

'Not seal blubber, I hope.' With Marty's taste for theatre it could be anything.

'No. Arctic mushroom soup and a couple of shots of Siku.' He paused. 'It's sixty-thousand-year-old ice from the Qaleraliit Sermia glacier, made into vodka.'

'Is that on the list?'

'The glacier? No, but at sixty thousand years it should be; that's a shed-load of time. You have to have it neat of course, none of your coke or orange concoctions.'

'You're starting to sound like John.'

'Maybe I am, but when you really think about it, a sixty-thousand-year-old anything is mind-blowing. It deserves to be revered.'

'I know. It's amazing,' Flora said in mock sincerity. She had had enough of facts and figures. Marty had spent most of the flight from Manchester to Nuuk telling her all the things John had missed off the list, putting it down to the fact he had only gleaned his information from books rather than using the internet.

The musky bath oil filled her nostrils. Marty had sprinkled dried polar poppies on the water, lit floating candles and dimmed the overhead light. How romantic. Her only candlelit bath until then had been during the great storm of 1987 when a power cut had caught her by surprise. She had thought about making it a regular thing after that, but it never came about.

'Don't be daft,' John had said, 'you could set your hair on fire.'

Flora sighed as she relaxed into the warm water, half-listening to Marty in the next room. She caught the end of something about an ice massage and hot springs, things he'd organised for the following day. John would have been beside himself. She could hear him saying 'What about the expense? What'll you do for money when this lot runs out?' Just the thought of his pinched, mean expression made her giggle.

By the time she'd pulled on a large fluffy robe and a pair of fur-lined slippers, a Ski-Doo and room service trailer had pulled up outside. A waiter in a regulation white puffer and knitted beany was expertly unpacking their order. He poured their vodka from an ice-encrusted bottle, then carefully ladled Arctic soup into striking black bowls, stopping just beneath the hotel's gold polar bear motif near the rim so that the bear appeared to be walking on the steaming liquid. The tasting menu was beautifully arranged in an ice sculpture, with a bottle of champagne on a bed of arctic moss as the centrepiece. John could say what he liked, but you couldn't beat room service and a little bit of luxury.

'Okay, babes, come and sit by the fire. Bubbles?' Marty was already easing the cork out in a well-practised move, the kind that gave a satisfying pop without fizzing all over the place.

'Mmm, yes please.'

'And then you must tell me all about your day.'

'You're taking your role very seriously, Marty. You don't have to wait on me hand and foot.'

'I do, and I like to – I'm a natural people-pleaser.' He passed her a glass. 'Besides, our deal makes me happier than a high-kicking chorus girl. The Rio Carnival. I still can't believe it.'

'Well, you'll have earned it if you carry on like this.'

'Of course I will. It's what we agreed. Organise everything. Choose the menus.'

'And look after my—'

'Outfits and do your hair. That's the best bit.'

'That works well for both of us then.' Flora raised her glass and Marty reached over to chink it with his.

'Here's to our wonderful adventure,' he added.

Flora was developing a taste for champagne, not so much for the actual flavour but because every bottle took her further away from the past. The closest John had come to pushing the boat out had been the day of his so-called 'early retirement', when he'd come home with two lamb chops and a bottle of Lambrusco. On reflection, he had been in an unusually good mood for someone who'd just lost their job, but now she knew about the redundancy payout, it was obvious. And to think he'd kept it secret all that time. There was no doubt, she was much better off without him. In fact, she giggled; she was well off without him. Who cared how much this holiday cost? It was payback time.

'Okay babes, I just want to check you're happy with tomorrow's fun and games. Is it okay if I come along? The Fire and Ice Experience is for two in any case.'

'Of course you can; you can pretend to be my toyboy.' She was getting the giggles again. 'Imagine John doing the fire and ice thingy. He was only interested in the geology and whatnot.'

'A shame, because the list is so much more. Take the next stop for example, Canada's Bay of Fundy.' Marty consulted his notebook. 'This was going to be a real highlight for John because it has the greatest fluctuating tidal system on earth, the rarest whales in the world, and a whole heap of semi-precious minerals and dinosaur fossils. So, of course, you'll see all of that, but I've booked you on a gorgeous little cruise with just a handful of other people so you can experience the tidal shift and see the whales while enjoying the services of a private chef and a five-star cabin.'

'Sounds lovely,' said Flora.

'And while you're cruising, I'm going to arrange a few little surprises for our two nights in Fundy National Park. I'm going to make old bones and fossils both exciting and glamorous.'

'Really?'

'Trust me, a night with your personal palaeontologist will be the experience of a lifetime. Following that, there's a quick scoot down to Niagara Falls – it's going to be fantastic. Then we're on the trans-Canadian train to the Rockies.'

'And that's Canada ticked off the list. All done with a Marty twist.' She sipped her champagne.

'I don't know about you but I'm having a ball, and the best part of doing all of this is seeing you so happy. You came back from that dog sledging today a changed woman. Look at you. You're glowing!'

'It was wonderful. I've never been so excited. The scenery, the speed of the dogs, even the air smelt different. Fantastic.'

'Here's to John's list.' Marty raised his glass.

'And here's to happiness,' she replied.

⌒⁓⁓⌒

Flora gazed into the fire in a post-dinner haze. She was having the time of her life. When was the last time she'd felt so full of joy? Probably aged eighteen when a heady cocktail of dreams and hormones collided with John's marriage proposal.

Strangely, her parent's disapproval had been deliciously empowering. Freedom.

Finally, she'd get to do 'it'. She read *Nova* magazine's '*Sex and the Expectations of a Patriarchal Society*' and made an appointment at the Family Planning clinic. This was 1970 – no need to invent a reason or answer awkward questions; as a bride-to-be she qualified for a bare-bottomed turn in the stirrups, fair and square.

The appointment temporarily deflated her ego: knees prised apart, with a spotlight on the star of the show. And the whole process in silence, performed by someone with cold hands and an even colder metal speculum. Then in the waiting room, a brown paper bag was thrust through the service hatch.

She had hurried home, pushed past her mother who still wasn't speaking to her, and locked herself in the bathroom. Inside the bag was a leaflet entitled '*On Your Wedding Night*', a tube of spermicidal jelly, and a blue flying-saucer-shaped box containing a Dutch cap with a disquieting diagram of a woman sawn in half.

A new beginning. She even looked different. She held her gaze in the bathroom mirror, untied her hair and shook it out. Pouting Brigitte Bardot style, she unbuttoned her blouse and pushed her breasts into a plausible cleavage; yes, she thought, now I'm ready.

What a silly girl, believing in happily ever after.

Cloud nine had lasted for almost four weeks, during which time she bought her wedding dress, planned dinner party menus, practised inserting her Dutch cap and experimented with a few new signatures; she couldn't wait to leave dreary old Flora Jones behind and become Mrs John Reginald Marshall.

She would stand on the doorstep in a pink silk dressing gown to wave John off to work. Bake cakes, attend coffee mornings or paint her nails. In the evening, after a three-course candlelit dinner, they'd wash the dishes together and chat about their respective days. Later, while he watched the news, she'd sit on a quilted velvet stool in front of her new kidney-shaped dressing table and brush her hair with a hundred strokes for extra shine. Each night, before finally falling asleep in John's arms, they'd make tender love.

Thirty-five years of disappointment, and finally, another new beginning.

She looked around her at the luxurious decoration, the picture window of a floodlit snowscape, the firelight and the sumptuous sleigh bed she would soon fall asleep in. She had money, a bunch of plane tickets, and a great friend in Marty. She was in fine health, and yes, she was happy beyond all imagining. Long may it last.

SIX

Flora gave Marty a credit card and access to her new bank account; so far as she was concerned, he was in charge of finances and she left it to him to book and pay for everything. Now and again, she checked the account against the receipts, much in the way she'd seen John do with the housekeeping, but more to show support than look for mistakes. The system worked well. Besides organising the travel and accommodation, Marty had managed to make the geological marvels of Greenland and Canada unforgettable and fun, adding an interesting or luxury twist to John's least exciting ideas.

After the trans-Canada train journey, timed perfectly to catch the fiery beauty of autumn colour, they had two nights in a boutique hotel on Vancouver Island before flying over the border to Salt Lake City. According to John's list, America was all about the national parks and unusual weather phenomena; New York and Vegas would have to wait. Marty had arranged a tour of The Great Lake, followed by an 'American Beauty' tour to see the best of the national parks from Utah to Arizona.

On arrival at the Grand Canyon, they quickly settled into a suite at one of the best hotels, where a few days of relaxation and local sightseeing would allow Marty time to organise the next leg of the journey.

'Hey, listen to this,' said Marty. '*See art come to life when you enter the broad region of rocky badlands and head into a painting encompassing more than ninety-three thousand acres.*'

66

'The Painted Desert?' Flora had heard this description many times. It was one of John's favourites.

'Yes. It says, from deep lavenders and rich greys to reds, oranges and pinks. Sounds amazing, eh? We're doing the Grand Canyon by helicopter and then landing at a helipad in the desert. From there, we'll hire a jeep to drive through Monument Valley. That's the one you see in all the Westerns. Belongs to the Navajo people.'

'Actual native Americans?'

'Yup. Apparently, it takes five years of building trust before they allow a whitie to make eye contact. I read that when I was a kid. I used to be fascinated by the whole American settler thing.'

'Me too. I love reading Westerns, especially if there's a lonely, handsome cowboy in it.'

'You and your romances. Mind you, I'm pretty partial to a handsome cowboy myself.'

'Rusty, the lone rodeo-rider,' Flora said, clutching her heart, 'looking for love amongst the saloon girls and never finding it until—'

'Yeh, yeh, but that's just fiction. We're on a real-life adventure now. Who knows, you might find your real live cowboy.'

'Do they still exist?'

'Of course. They probably drive pick-up trucks and drink beer these days. We could try and find some in Texas if you like? On the way to Dallas, we'll travel through the Chihuahuan Desert,' Marty consulted his notebook, 'which according to John is *the most biologically diverse desert in the world and home to the Bristlecone pine tree and some of the world's most unusual cloud formations.* Anyway, we could stop somewhere along the way.'

'Oh yes, we need to find a cowboy or two.'

'Definitely two. One each.' Marty grinned at Flora. 'Anyway, before we find romance in a Texan saloon, we're going to the Petrified Forest. John has underlined this and written, *must-see – the phenomenon of America is Racetrack Playa in Death Valley National Park.*'

'Oh, I remember him telling me about those – the huge rocks that move?'

'That's it, but my hunch is they don't zoom around like bumper cars. I'm going to have my work cut out to make those geographical gems into a bundle of fun, so if you'll excuse me, babes, I need to get organising while you cool off in that amazing ozone pool.'

'Oh, okay, I think I can manage that.'

'Then cocktails on the terrace? See you at sundown, *pardner.*'

'Are you trying to sound like a cowboy?'

'Just practising,' said Marty, with a grin.

～ঞ্জৣ৶～

The hotel pool room was positioned high above the Canyon, affording a sweeping bird's eye view of the area and a glass platform for those wanting to see to the very bottom, where the Colorado River cuts through on its way to the Gulf of California. Despite the chilly temperature outside, there was a glass-domed roof to keep in the artificially warm air. The pool was one of the key features of the hotel, with tropical plants and flowers, it was designed to look as though it was carved out of the rock itself. With most of the guests still out on day tours, Flora had the place to herself. Before taking off her robe, she edged near the glass for a view of the sheer drop into the canyon.

The water was deliciously warm. A faint scent of marzipan and jasmine came from the mass of exotic flowers; soft jazz music was playing from the undergrowth. She pushed herself off from the steps and floated on her back, watching the clouds overhead through half-closed eyes. It felt natural to just float and relax.

She drifted into a dreamy state, imagining a handsome cowboy on a white stallion. He would pull her up in front of him and with his arms around her, they'd gallop into the sunset. Just as her thoughts turned to the little log cabin where they would spend the night, there was a loud splash behind her. Flora panicked, thrashing her arms and legs, trying to stand up as quickly as possible.

'Sorry, I didn't know anyone else was here.'

Flora swivelled to see the voice.

'I sorta ran and dove in,' said a large moustache.

Flora bobbed down in the water, it was the best she could do to cover herself.

'I was here yesterday and did the same thing, only it was empty then. I'm sorry, it was too late to stop when I saw you.'

Flora wondered if she should get out. He'd spoiled the moment. 'It's okay,' she said.

'Here.' He waded over to her and held out his hand. 'My name's Cal. I'm a complete idiot. Please forgive me?'

'It's fine. Really. I was just daydreaming.'

'Are you English? Your accent tells me, yes, but I get most things wrong most of the time.'

'Yes, I'm from Coventry in Warwickshire. How about you?' She tried to see who was behind the moustache. Brown eyes, quite good-looking, late forties, maybe fifty. American.

'I'm a Haligonian. Nova Scotia.'

'Um . . .'

'In Canada,' he added.

'Really? I've just come from Canada. Are you on holiday?'

'Nope. I'm working up in the Canyon. Specialist electrician. All the dangerous stuff. I'm the idiot guy hanging out there in a harness.'

'Oh, right.'

'But it feels like I'm on holiday, I'm supposed to be in the

Canyon View Motel instead of here but there was a mix-up. Lucky me, eh? I'm sorry, I didn't catch your name.'

'It's Flora.'

'Great to meet you, Flora. Let me say sorry properly, and I'd love to hear all about your trip. Can I buy you dinner?'

'Oh no, there's no need, really. I have to get going. I was about to get out when you arrived.' Flora moved towards the steps, trying to think of a way she could exit without displaying her bottom. 'It's an amazing view, isn't it?' she said indicating towards the Canyon. Quick, get out.

'Yes, it is!' he said, staring after her.

She grabbed her towelling robe and hurried towards the door. How humiliating. She heard him call after her and pressed the lift button several times in quick succession. Finally, the doors opened at an agonisingly relaxed pace. Her heart was still beating double time when she got back to the room.

'That was quick; I'm still in Death Valley.' Marty was sitting on the floor with a map and brochures spread out in front of him. 'But that's because I'm trying to fit in a trip to Tombstone while we're—'

'Marty I—'

'You know, the Wild West town, where actual cowboys had a real gunfight at the O.K. Corral, they're buried at Boothill and—'

'Marty! If a man with a moustache tries to speak to you, you must ignore him, he's just seen my bottom.'

'What, your actual bottom or your Fendi one-piece, covering your bottom?'

'Well, that really, but all the same you mustn't speak to him.' Ugh, an expanse of white dimply cellulite.

'Why not babes, it's not a crime to look is it?'

'He's just asked me to dinner!'

'Wow! A date?' Marty was grinning. 'So, when are you going? I can easily cancel—.'

'No.'

'Why not?'

'I just don't think I'm ready for that kind of thing.'

'But you may as well get in some practice. We'll be in Texas soon, darling. And then you're going to be swamped by cowboys.'

'You've got cowboys on the brain.'

'Maybe I have, especially if they're just wearing leather chaps and a ten-gallon hat.'

They both laughed at the image.

'Well, cowboys are completely different to a dinner date,' said Flora.

'I don't see how. A hot-blooded male who likes the look of your bottom is a prince among men. Trust me, it's not easy on the dating scene, so unless he was downright repulsive, why not give the moustache a bit of a test drive.'

'I don't feel—'

'Come on, you might enjoy it. And you must be getting bored of little old Marty at every mealtime. A change of scene would do you good.'

'Well, I suppose it's only dinner.' After dinner, they might go for a walk under the stars, maybe hand in hand. The Electrician and the Widow would make a good romance.

'That's my girl. What's his name?'

'Cal. He's Canadian. And he's working here as a specialist electrician.'

'Leave it with me,' said Marty, already halfway to the door.

'But only if you think he's not a weirdo or an axe murderer.'

'Don't worry, I'll suss him out and even if he passes my inspection, I'll still be stalking the pair of you the entire time.'

'Maybe you should come too?'

'No way, I'm not going to be a gooseberry.' Before she could change her mind, he left the room.

Flora paced up and down in her towelling robe. A date. The first since she was a teenager, and even then she already knew John, so it wasn't the same. Cal was quite good-looking and easy to talk to. Completely different from John. She giggled and then thought of his broad, hairy chest. She was just trying to recall what kind of swimming trunks he had on when Marty returned.

'Well, I'm impressed with your choice.' He arched his eyebrow knowingly.

'Did you see him?'

'Of course I saw him, all six-foot-four of his manly Canadian physique.'

'And?'

'He's going to meet us on the terrace for drinks.'

'So what did you say to him?'

'I just explained that my lovely friend is new to dating and was a bit flustered.'

'Do you think he's a weirdo?'

'No more than you are, babes. He said he just wanted to take you to dinner. Nothing crazy, and he seems a nice, down-to-earth person.'

'So, we're all meeting for drinks first?' Flora was smiling now.

'And then you two lovebirds are going to the hotel restaurant while I hide behind a large potted palm and keep an eye on you.'

'Oh my god,' shrieked Flora, 'I'm going on a date. An actual date with a man.'

'Yes, you are, and I'd say he's all man through and through!'

'Oh, stop it!'

'First things first, what to wear?' Marty already had the wardrobe door open and was flicking through hangers. 'I'm thinking smart casual, you need to feel comfortable. Relaxed. Slightly understated but with a bit of Flora personality.'

'Heels or flats?'

'I'd say heels for sure. He's a giant of a man.'

'It was hard to tell in the pool, but you reckon he's six foot?'

'And the rest. He was just getting out when I went down there. I got an eye full, shame he's straight. I'd quite like him for myself.'

'Well,' she laughed, 'you can keep your hands off. He's mine.'

~⁂~

With trembling fingers, Flora frantically tried to unlock the door. The key card was the wrong way round. Finally inside, she kicked her remaining shoe off. The other had fallen off outside the lift.

'Marty! Are you awake?'

'Hey, what time is it?' He sat up in bed and pushed his sleeping mask up. 'Are you okay?'

'Not really,' said Flora. She had tried not to cry but now she let go.

'Hey, come here, babes. What happened? Is it the Canadian, did he hurt you, because if he—'

'No.' Flora slumped down beside him.

'Hey, come on, why are you crying?' Marty reached for a tissue on the bedside table. 'Here. What happened, babes?'

'I can't believe it. We were having such a lovely time. We talked for hours.'

'I know you did.'

'That's why I told you to go to bed, I felt really comfortable in his company. I told him everything. Really opened up.' She suddenly felt ashamed of the way she'd exaggerated John and his penny-pinching ways, just to get a laugh.

'Here.' Marty passed her another tissue.

'He was such a good li-listener,' she hiccuped, 'really lovely. And he sh-shared my snickerdoodle. Two spoons, one doodle. We were having fun.'

'Blow your nose, hon, there's a bit of a snot fest going on.' Marty held out the tissue box.

'Sorry.' Flora blew her nose.

'But why are you crying? When I left, he was holding your hand.'

'We went back to the bar for drinks afterwards. He was all over me.' His hand on her thigh, inching towards unchartered territories had been deliciously exciting. 'He said nice things about my hair and kissed my neck.' That moustache! 'He wanted me to go to his room.' How different the evening could have been.

'You didn't, did you?'

'I was quite tipsy, I was thinking I might.' She definitely would have.

'But you didn't?' insisted Marty.

'There was a phone call, the receptionist came over, said his wife had been trying to contact him.'

'Whoa! His *wife*?' Flora held the tissue to her mouth and nodded. She wanted to howl. Marty flung his arm around her. 'What a love-cheating scumbag.'

'Yes, he's a love-cheat,' she wailed. 'He didn't even take the call, Marty. Said he'd ring back, then carried on as though nothing had happened.'

'Wow. That's not very classy.'

'He said, "it's only sex, we don't need to see each other again", as though he did it all the time.'

Marty rubbed her back and passed her another tissue. 'Well, he's right about one thing, you don't have to see him again. I'm so sorry, babes. It's my fault – I pushed you into it.'

'No, you didn't. I really liked him.' Flora sniffed. 'I'm such an idiot. I thought he was going to be my first proper boyfriend.'

'Hey, look at me,' Marty grabbed her hand. 'You are a wonderful, kind and trusting person. He doesn't deserve to even speak to you. Let alone anything else.'

'No, but—' Perhaps he was trapped in an unhappy marriage.

'Listen, he's a sleazy nobody and you're a beautiful somebody. You looked absolutely gorgeous last night.' Marty dabbed at the mascara on her cheeks.

'Bet I don't now,' she said with a weak smile.

'No darling, you look more like Alice Cooper at the moment, but we'll soon have beautiful Flora back on show.'

'Thanks, Marty, you're a true friend.'

'So, how shall we play this? Are you okay to carry on using the pool? I can make a complaint to the management, maybe they can move that cheating scumbag to the motel, where he should have been in the first place.'

'No, I don't want a fuss and I won't be able to relax. Let's move.'

'Okay, darling, but I'm going to tell them why. I don't want you paying for the time we're not here. And I'll get them to help find a really nice place to move to.'

Later, after a room service breakfast, Marty went to speak with the manager. Within the hour they were collected in a white limo and driven to the sister hotel just a short distance away. It was a surprise to Flora when they were shown to the penthouse suite.

'Wow, I can't believe it. Is this all for us?'

'Yes, we've got it for two nights.'

'I love it.' She stopped in front of a floor-to-ceiling glass tank, up-lit from a bed of live coral and full of tropical fish. Mesmerising.

'Come and look at this,' called Marty.

'Where are you?'

'Up those little stairs next to the cocktail bar.'

Flora found him reclining on a huge beanbag, looking up through a glass ceiling. She slumped down next to him. 'This'll be an amazing place to stargaze, almost as good as the swimming pool in the other place.'

'No, it's better. Look over there.'

'The spaceship thingy?'

'It's a flotation chamber. You can either have the lid up and float around looking at the stars or you can close the lid and be in complete darkness, play music or have a light show.'

'I love this place! Thank goodness for Cal, the cheating Canadian, otherwise we'd never have found it.'

'No, apparently it's not advertised. It's usually reserved for people in the movie business. They come out from L.A. for a break.'

'So, how did you—'

'Let's just say, my frustrated inner actor collided with my law degree.'

'Law degree?'

'Okay, so I didn't complete it, but I studied law at uni.'

'You went to university?'

'Mainly to please my dad. He and I, well, ever since I came out, things changed. He's always been homophobic, and the idea I was never going to have a pint down the pub or give him grandkids, well, whatever. He's a lawyer, so I thought if I could be a barrister, I'd prove something.'

'I don't think it works like that.'

'No, I found that out. In fact, I think he'd have been even more put out if his gay son had become more successful than him. Parents, eh, who needs them?'

'Well, they should be very proud of you.' It was rare to see Marty look so down. She tried speaking in an American accent. 'And you got us this place, my oh my, you're smarter than a hooty owl.'

He smiled. 'You been reading up on Texan phrases?'

'I sure have.'

'Well, we have the lap of luxury to enjoy before we get to cattle country, so don't get too far ahead. How about we make a couple of cheeky cocktails?'

'Might as well,' twanged Flora, 'can't dance, never could sing, and it's too wet to plough.'

SEVEN

The fiddle and the banjo players finished tuning their instruments and the caller stepped towards the microphone, tipping up his black Stetson to reveal a strong jawline covered in light stubble. Flora elbowed Marty in the ribs. He looked just like Tom Selleck.

'He can rustle my cattle anytime he likes,' she murmured, but before she could catch Marty's reply, she was swept along in a tide of bandanas and waistcoats as the whole room followed the caller's instructions in a stampede of collective energy.

'Yeee-haa!' Marty propelled her into the middle of the square with the other cowgirls.

'Ladies do and the gents you know, it's right by right by wrong you go.' The caller's sing-song voice was strong and commanding. 'You can't go to heaven while you carry on so.' The fiddler stepped up to play a fancy solo.

'What's that about heaven? It doesn't make sense,' shouted Flora over the sound of clapping and stomping.

'And it's home little gal and do-si-do.' The caller seemed to be looking straight at her, speaking to her directly. Was her clumsy footwork attracting his attention? Flora tried to ignore him. 'And oh by gosh and oh by Joe,' he sang, tapping his snakeskin boot to the beat.

By the time the third dance was coming to an end, Flora had worked out the moves and was beginning to relax. She ended with a flourish; the caller nodded appreciatively, showing his straight white teeth and a pair of dimples. It was only a moment, but she felt a connection and quickly smiled back as Marty grabbed her hand and led her towards the bar.

'That was so much fun,' he said.

'How come you know all the steps?' Flora glanced back at the stage but the caller was talking to the band.

'I've been researching. Yesterday, while you were on the Space Center tour.'

'You're such a cheat!'

'You soon got the hang of it. Anyway, are you enjoying it?'

'It's great. And I love our outfits. I thought they'd be over the top but we blend right in.'

Marty stroked his stick-on moustache. They had spent a small fortune on kitting themselves out. Marty had been in his element; he'd insisted, to truly get into the role, they should have alter egos.

'Well, you know Mary-Lou,' drawled Marty, 'I took to the life of a cowboy like a horse takes to eatin' oats.'

'Why, Randy Applewhite, you sure did,' said Flora as she twiddled her nylon plaits and giggled.

'Miller High Life?'

'Eh?'

'It's what all hoedowners drink after a few a do-si-dos.'

'Oh, okay, why not. I'm just popping to powder my nose.'

'Sure thing, sister,' said Marty, turning to the bar.

Flora wove through the crowd towards the wooden weatherbeaten Cow Belles signpost. She was on such a high. Why hadn't she been dancing before? John. In the seventies she'd suggested they go to a New Year's Eve disco, just a bit of fun. 'What, with my leg? Don't be absurd,' he'd said. He hadn't talked about his childhood injury, except that when the family home was bombed during the war, only he and his mother survived. Dancing was something she'd only ever done at home. Always on her own, and usually in the kitchen to the radio. It had been years since she'd even done that. Not anymore, though.

Back at the bar, Marty was in full flow, chatting to a couple of unlikely-looking cowboys from Asia.

'Ah, here she is. Flora, this is Wu and Chun, they're on their way to Vegas. I was telling them we're going to be spending a lot of time in China next year.'

'Oh yes, I can't wait. I love everything Chinese.' Crispy won tons and bang bang chicken from The Golden Wok, at least. 'We're going to see those giant animals and plants. The limestone place?'

'Ah yes, Shilin, the Stone Forest,' said Chun, nodding appreciatively. 'Very beautiful. Full of wonder.'

'We're also going to the Torch Festival there.' She looked to Marty for confirmation. 'In June? We've a lot of travelling to do before then.'

'And a whole heap of dancin' too,' said a voice behind them. 'Howdy. Y'all from outta town?' The caller flashed another of his gleaming smiles and held out his hand. 'I'm Smokey Brooks,' he said, looking straight at her.

'Oh, hello, er, Smokey, I'm Flora,' she heard herself giggle. Stop it. 'Pleased to meet you.' Up close she could see he had blue eyes and thick black eyelashes. He was exactly like every cowboy she'd ever imagined. Rugged and charming. Sexy. She stifled another giggle. 'Oh, this is Marty and our new friends Wu and Chun, from China.'

'Pleased to meet y'all.' He tipped his hat to the others and kissed Flora's hand. 'How's about I show you a few more steps, Miss Flora? I'm done for the night, now we got ol' Whiskey George up there.' They followed his gaze to an elderly caller on the stage: with his long, grizzled hair and bushy side-whiskers, he looked like he'd just ridden into town from Tombstone.

'Can I get you a drink, Smokey?' asked Marty.

'That's mighty kind, but I've a hunch the lady wants to dance.' Without waiting for a reply, he took Flora's hand and led her towards the dance floor.

Smokey Brooks was as good a dancer as he was good-looking. Every inch of him a cowboy, he guided her through each set with surprising tenderness. He would be very different out on the open plains, roping cattle and galloping on his horse in the hot sun. The perfect man: strong and silent with a soft centre. Better still, he appeared to only have eyes for her. Occasionally, he took her back to Marty who was still deep in conversation with Wu and Chun.

'Do you want to dance, Marty?' Flora felt she should offer.

'No thanks, babes. Wu and Chun have seen every single musical I can think of, what're the chances of that?' Marty was in his element and Smokey seemed only too pleased to take her back for the next dance.

Flora was planning ahead, trying to think of some way she and Smokey could continue the night somewhere a little more private, or perhaps meet up again the next day. But as the last dance came to an end and the band took their leave, she was disappointed when he took her back to Marty and abruptly wished her a good evening.

'It's been a privilege, Miss Flora; you're a mighty fine dancer.'

'Oh, but I thought—'

'I wish I could stay a-whiles but I gotta pony up back to the ranch.' He kissed her hand one more time and nodded at Marty. 'You take care o' Miss Flora.' He nodded towards the exit. 'It's rainin' yonder, like a tall cow pissin' on a flat rock.'

'I sure will,' Marty called after him.

Flora watched him disappear into the crowd. 'Well, that was—'

'Was what?'

'Amazing. So wonderful to be treated like a lady by a real live cowboy. He said my skin was softer than peaches in the morning sun. Who'd have thought it? Me and a rancher called Smokey Brooks. It's a romance and a Western all in one.'

'That's the perfect story, eh?' Marty smiled at her fondly. 'Come on, babes, I'm starving, let's go and find a late-night diner. We need to talk about Guatemala.'

'Guatemala?'

'Yes, it's Mexico next and then Guatemala. I have to book the itinerary tomorrow and I need to check you're happy with everything.'

'I thought we were going to Belize?'

'We are, but I found this fabulous little place in Belize for Christmas, right on the beach, so I've swapped them around. Is that okay?'

'Yes, whatever. First, can we talk about Smokey? I think I'm in love.'

Sure enough, it was raining heavily when they stepped outside, but a diner right next to the dance hall was buzzing with life. With Hank Williams on the jukebox and ham 'n' eggs with a side of grits on special, it was the perfect choice. The neighbouring tables were crowded with bandana-wearing ranchers and cowgirls in gingham shirts.

'Look, there's even a Western saddle over there, do you think it's real?' There were old Wild West posters and paraphernalia all over the walls. 'Smokey would fit in here, eh, Marty?'

'He sure would,' Marty smiled, opening a double-fronted menu designed to look like saloon doors. 'Tombstone crackerjacks. Chuckwagon steak bites. What shall we have?'

'You choose. I'm still dreaming about my dreamy cowboy. I can't believe he picked me out of all the other cowgirls there. Little old me!'

'He picked you because you're gorgeous. You were the cowbelle of the hoedown,' said Marty, catching the eye of a waitress.

'Hi, guys. I'm Tammy.'

'Well, hello, Tammy, can we have the buckaroo buffalo sharing platter and two six-shooter skinks, please?'

'Sure thing, cowboy,' she said with a smile and hurried away.

'Don't you love the accent? Sure *thang*, cowboy,' mimicked Flora.

'I sure do, Mary-Lou. And I sure do have a thirst on me,' he said as he spotted Tammy returning with their drinks. 'Wow, that was quick.'

She gave Marty another winning smile as she put the drinks down then placed a sheet of paper on the table. 'Maybe you'd like to enter our competition, seeing as you folks are dressed up an' all?'

Flora picked it up. It looked like an old poster with '*Wanted*' in Western writing at the top and a cowboy pointing at the reader.

'Best-dressed diners win Texan wings and rodeo ribs for two,' said Tammy.

'It's okay, thanks, we're leaving tomo—' Flora was just about to hand it back when she noticed the photograph. The pointing cowboy looked familiar. 'Actually, can I keep this? He looks just like a cowboy I met this evening.'

'You met Kieran, over at the hoedown?'

'Oh, no, his name was Smokey Brooks, but they look very similar, don't they, Marty?' Flora held the poster up. Marty nodded without really looking at it.

'He's an amazing caller. Not bad for an Irishman,' laughed Tammy.

'Smokey's a caller too. He did the first half of the hoedown, but he's not Irish, he's a Texan rancher.' Flora could talk about him all night. 'And a great dancer, too.'

'I'm just popping to the gents.' Marty slid out of the booth and touched Tammy's arm. 'I wonder if you could tell me what whiskey you have over there, on the shelf behind the bar?'

'I'm sorry, sir, they're not for sale, they're just part of the decor,' she said, turning back to Flora. 'I wonder who this

Smokey is? I thought I knew everyone over at the hoedown, especially the callers. So far as I knew there was just Kieran and Whiskey George on tonight.'

'Well, Kieran and Smokey are doubles, they even have the same outfits and the same blue eyes.'

'Kieran's from The Old Town Theatre Company, so maybe they both borrowed outfits from there? He's an actor in the Wild West show when he's not calling at the hoedown. Though I happen to know he tends to buck the trend when it comes to footwear; he likes to wear his own snakeskin boots. Anyway, listen to me prattling on, I better get back to waiting tables. Enjoy your drinks.'

Flora was still staring at the poster when Marty came back.

'How can there be two callers who look exactly the same, right down to the same snakeskin boots?'

'I don't know, babes,' Marty said quietly.

'Why would he say his name was Smokey?'

Marty was silent.

'I don't think he was a real cowboy after all. But why pretend?' wailed Flora.

Marty reached for her hand. 'Listen, babes, why not remember it the way it was. It was fun and romantic. He picked you out of all the other cowbelles and was a true gentleman.'

'I think we should go round to that theatre place tomorrow and find out. I want to ask him myself.'

'That's not going to achieve anything, and besides, this time tomorrow we'll be in Mexico, the birthplace of the dahlia and John's absolute favourite on the list. I can't wait to see the flowering valley. The day after that there's a fiesta. You've been looking forward to that for ages, remember?'

'I don't feel very fiesta-ish anymore. What's wrong with men, why are they all such liars?'

'Hey, now come on, Flora. There are plenty of really good guys out there and even Smokey didn't tell a big lie if you come to think about it. Just that he was a rancher. And don't forget, he was lovely to you and made your night really special.'

'Yes, but—'

'We're leaving tomorrow in any case, so cherish the memory. It was never going to come to anything.'

'I know that, but—'

'It was so much fun. Don't spoil it, babes, take it for what it was.'

'I just liked the idea of him in a pair of chaps, wielding his lasso like a real cowboy.'

'I know,' he grinned, 'I liked that idea too, Mary-Lou.'

Flora wavered. He was right; it was just for fun. Silly to think otherwise.

'Well, Randy Applewhite, I'm keeping the poster as a souvenir. A reminder for when I get old that I once danced the Whiffletree Reel with Smokey Brooks.'

EIGHT

Apart from the white sands of Alamogordo, Mexico had been a kaleidoscope of colour. At the spectacular dahlia specimen gardens the likes of Hot Tamale, Spartacus and Neon Splendor competed with the newest hybrids from around the world. Seeing the national flower of Mexico in such a profusion of colour would have been a highlight for John, but almost as soon as they had ticked it off the list and returned to the hotel, the experience paled into insignificance for Flora. All she could think about was attending her very first fiesta to see ladies in swirling skirts, dancing to 'La Cucaracha'.

After a light supper of black bean tostadas with avocado salsa and tres leches cake for afters, Marty suggested they had an early night. If they were going to see the fiesta through to the end, they would need to get some rest.

In the early morning, while the majority of the townsfolk were already dressed in their finery and attending church, Marty and Flora had wandered out to find a little cafe for a leisurely breakfast. The town was almost deserted, but when the bells finally rang out and broke the sombre atmosphere, musicians appeared from side streets to compete with the cacophony of chimes across the city. It was time to join the celebrations.

With an almost overwhelming combination of music, dancing, deliciously spicy food and assorted tequila-based cocktails, it was far more than just a party. Neither Flora nor Marty had been prepared for the locals' insistence that they join in; sweeping Flora's inhibitions aside, she was dragged into the tide of dizzying dancers and swept along, buoyed by the joy of those around her.

It had been the most fun she'd ever had; partying, eating and drinking with friendly strangers throughout the day and long into the night. It was almost dawn when she found herself walking back up the steps to the hotel. Marty had mumbled something about feeling sick as he staggered past her, while she trailed behind. With her shoes in one hand and a slightly battered pink straw sombrero in the other, it was all she could do to keep her balance, then finally, back in the bedroom she crumpled onto the bed and fell asleep.

Waking to find she had the mother of all hangovers coincided with Marty's discovery that his credit card and a substantial amount of cash were missing from his money belt. After searching frantically and questioning the hotel staff, they had no alternative than try to retrace their steps of the previous evening by taking a taxi back to the late-night taco bar they had gone to with a group of their new fiesta friends.

It was a struggle to remember the address, but they both recalled the place had been decorated with so many sombreros it had seemed over the top, even for Mexico. Walls and ceilings, covered in hats of all colours and sizes and even giant sombreros were used as sunshades for the outside tables. With much explaining to the taxi driver they finally turned down the correct side street, where a row of sun-bleached sombreros nailed around the sign 'Amigos' came into view. The shutters, painted with bright green cacti, were closed. It looked very different in the daylight but it was enough to jog Flora's memory. They had gone there at the end of the evening, almost immediately, Marty had fallen into a tequila-infused sleep while Flora and their newfound friends had carried on partying. She'd taken the card out of his money belt to pay for a round of drinks, and later when they had both been helped into a taxi, she'd also eased out a wedge of cash to pay the driver.

After hurrying back to the hotel, she searched her clothes from the previous evening and found the missing credit card in a pocket. What a relief. Marty's mood switched from worried to angry – she'd never seen him so cross.

'Why didn't you just put it back? Or better still, why don't you carry your own card?'

'But you said I should put my purse in the hotel safe with the jewellery and passports.' For the first time since John's death, she felt small again. Worthless.

'How much was the taxi? Virtually half our cash is gone.'

'I don't know. I was confused about pesos and dollars, so I just told him to keep the change.'

'Why didn't you wake me? I'm in charge of the money. If you want to take over, get your own money belt!' Marty had shouted.

It had been a quiet journey to the airport, followed by a short silent flight to Guatemala. As soon as they had arrived, they opted for a room service dinner and an early night. When Flora awoke, she was relieved to see that Marty was all smiles. The Mexican stand-off was forgotten.

After a lazy morning by the pool, they would be ticking Tikal National Park off John's list. Compared to the frantic pace of the previous week, Guatemala seemed like another universe. Calm. A leisurely afternoon excursion up into the mountains sounded perfect.

~~~

The coach was gear-grindingly slow. Initially, it had been soothing and rhythmic, but for the past hour Flora had been silently perched on the edge of her seat with her buttocks clenched. She tried not to look out of the window, but the sheer drop was mesmerising. She couldn't even see the side of the road; the first solid surface in view was some distance below, where boulders provided small relief from the otherwise vertical drop. Marty had stopped speaking soon after they'd reached the first plateau. He said he wasn't himself and had assumed the crash position, gripping the seat in front of him, his eyes squeezed shut.

She imagined one bump too many in the road – everyone beginning to panic; whimpers and prayers first, then screams and shouts as the coach hissed and groaned. The driver struggles to keep it on the road as it lurches to one side, unable to right itself. Then a moment of suspended hope before it topples over the edge like a clumsy beast. The roof shears off and the windows smash, passengers flung out of their seats to freely bounce down the rocky shale, occasionally turning Olympian cartwheels. By the time they reach the bottom, they're all silent. From the road above, they would look like sleeping babies.

Babies. She'd been thinking about them a lot recently.

If hers had lived, there would have been a wonderful twenty-first birthday party: vol-au-vents, Asti Spumante and cards with a key in silver foil on the front. They could have gone on this trip together. The Marshall family holiday. John in khaki shorts, socks pulled up to the knee. Mother and daughter in matching sundresses, sharing an ice cream and posing for photographs.

She always imagined a girl. A boy might have looked like John, who had more than a passing resemblance to Norman Tebbit. Not a good start in life. People don't cuddle an ugly child in the same way.

She had loved carrying her secret baby. She had planned to share the news with John when she was absolutely sure; at four months, she could feel the slightest bump. She had hugged and loved that little bud of life. She had plans. Things were going to change; John would change. She spent her days looking at baby clothes, blissfully dreaming of a new life to come. She found the sweetest baby-grow, white, with a rabbit on the front. Newborn size. She bought it with the housekeeping money and was planning to drape it over the arm of John's chair so he'd see it on Friday after work.

'What's this?' he would ask.

'Guess.'

She'd even practised a mysterious smile.

At first, there was just a dull ache. She lay down, hoping it would go away, while all the time it crept through her belly and curled around her back. Perhaps it was normal. When the dull throbbing turned into a sharp, ripping pain, she began to cry. She wasn't prepared for the shocking amount of blood as her precious little secret slipped away.

The space where joy had been, instantly filled up with sadness, staying with her, growing dull and foggy with the passage of time, but always there. It was even with her in the coach, clinging to the mountainside, looking into the abyss. The idea of plunging to her death wasn't so terrible; she'd thought about dying many times in those difficult early years. But not now that life was finally becoming interesting.

A barely audible groan came from Marty. He still had his eyes shut. A sheen of sweat glistened on his ashen face. The tour guide stood at the front, swaying with the bumps in the road like a very slow dancer as he tapped the microphone and blew into it. When the coach lurched suddenly, he did an involuntary two-step down the aisle.

'Okay, *amigos*! I hope you enjoyed the amazing view, provided free of charge by Turismo Tours. Soon we arrive at Tikal. We must stay together, nice and cosy, eh? Tikal National Park is home to an ancient Mayan city. It covers two hundred square miles, so if you get lost, it's *hasta la vista, baby*.' A few nervous laughs came from the queasy-looking passengers. 'But don't worry, there are royal palaces, temples and of course the ceremonial areas to keep you entertained during your bewilderment.'

'Interesting approach,' murmured Marty.

'What's he saying?' asked Flora.

'Don't get lost, but if you do, you won't be bored.'

'I don't know about you, Marty, but I'm getting tired of all this excitement.'

'I know what you mean. Mexico was so full-on. I'm tired too.'

'And Guatemala seems to be all about Mayan ruins and human sacrifice. It's giving me the creeps. Those poor sacrificed babies. I just can't stop thinking about it.'

The guide was reeling off his spiel with a slightly bored undertone. 'And if you're lucky you might catch a glimpse of a bear, coyote, jaguar, or puma.'

Flora leaned back in her seat. The coach journey was taking much longer than the advertised *'Two hours of spectacular scenery, best viewed from your coach window'*.

'Our national bird is the highland quetzal, also our symbol of liberty.' The driver shifted down a gear, and the coach slowed to a crawl. 'It is a protected species and the penalty for capturing the quetzal is prison.'

The coach pulled in to a passing bay to let yet another tour bus go by. There was no doubt about it, thought Flora, Marty had carried out his side of the bargain to a very high standard. He had made sure every destination on John's list was action-packed and fully informative.

'I can't wait to get to Belize and just lie on a beach for two whole weeks,' Flora murmured.

'I can't wait to stand on solid ground.' Marty was sitting up now, mopping his face with a paper tissue. 'Don't forget, Belize is where you're going to learn to scuba dive. You're going to have to get your PADI certificate before you can properly see the Great Blue Hole.'

'Oh, I didn't realise I'd actually have to go in the water. What is it we're going to see again?'

Marty pulled out his notebook and flicked through the pages. 'Hang on, here we are. *The Great Blue Hole is a natural underwater sinkhole. Formed in the Ice Age by the opening of a dry cave and the melting of huge ice blocks.* John's notes are all about white carbonate sand – apparently, that's what makes the water appear so amazingly blue. I can't wait to see it.'

'And to do that, we have to scuba dive?'

'No, but you're going to want to scuba dive because it is an amazing place to see tropical fish, corals and all kinds of wonderful things you'll never see anywhere else. Trust me, you have to dive to make the most of it.'

'I'm not a very good swimmer. Apart from the pool at the Grand Canyon, I haven't swum since I was at school.'

'Don't worry; swimming's like riding a bike and besides, scuba diving is more about gently floating about admiring the view. It's going to be amazing. White, white sand, translucent blue water, and all those gorgeous tropical fish.'

Flora sighed and closed her eyes. There would be plenty of time for scuba diving. First, she was planning to relax.

The coach crawled into the parking area and stopped with a resounding hiss of the brakes. The tour guide tapped his microphone again.

'Okay everyone, please check you have all your personal belongings. We can't take responsibility if something goes missing.'

Theft of personal belongings had been a continual warning from the guide. Poverty and crime seemed to go hand in hand. Each time it was mentioned, Flora felt guilty, with her designer clothes and the extravagance of John's list; all of this was only supposed to happen after they'd won the lottery. Instead, she'd decided to do it almost on a whim, not because she wanted to visit the world's most geographically fascinating places, but because she had no other plans for the rest of her life.

The more countries they ticked off the list, the closer she came to having to make a decision about the future. Seeing all the married couples sitting side by side on the coach magnified the life awaiting her back in Coventry. Alone. She was old enough to be a grandmother and yet she had no one.

Everyone began to file off the bus. Marty had recovered his composure and was chatting to a couple in matching orange tee-shirts. He always made friends, while she didn't even know the names of her next-door neighbours back home. People didn't gravitate to her; she wasn't a natural mixer. Maybe she should get a pet. She pictured herself shuffling around in a velour tracksuit with a horde of cats winding around her ankles. Stop it, Flora. She stepped onto the gravel and moved to one side, waiting for Marty to appear.

'Okay. My friends, please come together.' The guide stood on the coach's steps to address the small crowd. 'We're going to start our tour here and end with the most important surviving pyramids in Tikal.' He raised his yellow umbrella. 'Please keep together and follow me to the ticket office.' Marty and Flora dutifully merged with the group.

'Sorry about this, babes.' Marty rolled his eyes. 'It's the only way I could get Tikal National Park ticked off the list, although, now we're here, I could scout around and find someone to take us separately.'

'It's fine. In a way it's fun to be a proper tourist: it's only for today, isn't it?'

'Yes. Tomorrow we start on a quest which I believe is close to your heart? The one that takes us over the border to the Ixcacao Chocolate Factory in Belize.'

'Oh yummy, I've been looking forward to the choccy part. So clever of you to find it.'

'It all started in Guatemala, so although the Maya sacrificed babies, they also gave the world chocolate. Yin and yang.'

A pair of orange tee-shirts walked purposefully towards them.

'Oh, hi again,' said the husband in a strong American accent. 'Just in case we lose you later, could we grab your contact details? We're so excited about the Cotswolds. You're definitely on the list when we do Europe.'

'Oh right, great. Yes, of course.' Marty took out his notebook and tore off a page.

'Coventry's not really in the Cotswolds,' said Flora.

'They're pretty much one and the same,' said Marty, handing the couple a hastily scribbled email address, not looking at her.

'Gee, thanks. We just loved hearing about your adorable cottage garden full of dahlias. So awesome.' The group was forced into a single line as they were funnelled through the turnstile.

'Enjoy the park,' Marty called after them and let a few people step in front of him. As soon as they were out of earshot, Flora grabbed his arm.

'What are you doing with John's dahlias?'

'Oh, it's nothing, just having a chat. They're touring South America to trace the origins of the dahlia. Apparently it's also the official flower of San Francisco, so they —'

'And what's that about a cottage in the Cotswolds?'

'Oh, you know, to give them the perfect picture, something lovely to think about. An allotment in Coventry isn't the same.'

'No, but it's the truth.' What was he playing at? 'Do you do that often?'

'What?'

'Make things up?' How come she'd only just noticed?

'No, of course not, but why not sew a sequin on here and there, sprinkle some magic? There's nothing wrong with embellishing.'

'Eh? Have you been doing that with me?'

'I just, well, not really—'

'Not really? That's a yes then!' The tour was moving into a clump of trees, almost out of sight. She walked quickly towards them.

'Flora, wait. Listen, I don't mean anything by it. I just want to make people happy. You especially.'

No one had ever paid her compliments like Marty. He always managed to find something nice to say, made her feel good about herself, attractive. Was any of it genuine?

'All this time I've absolutely trusted you and I suddenly discover you just make stuff up.'

'Yes, but not all—'

'What's wrong with you? I thought I knew you quite well, but now—'

'Come on, babes, you're being overly dramatic. I only want you to be happy and you know what? Sometimes it has cost me dear.'

'Like when?'

'Remember when you came to the theatre for a makeover and I said I had permission? Well, that wasn't one hundred percent true, but I wanted to show you how beautiful you were, give you a chance to shine.'

Flora faltered. Beautiful wasn't a word she'd related to before meeting Marty. Even if it was just flattery, it was a nice thing to say. 'So another lie—'

'It was worth the risk to see you so glammed up and gorgeous, but I didn't think you'd come if I didn't say I had permission.'

'No, I wouldn't have, but no harm done.' It had been life-changing, the best thing ever.

'Well, actually, I was caught putting the key back and they gave me a second written warning. I was already in trouble for taking Carmen Miranda home for Christmas – it's such a lonely time of year, I was feeling miserable and that tutti-frutti headdress just—'

'So, what else have you lied about, where I'm concerned?'

'Well, if I'm honest—'

'Yes, honesty would be nice.' Flora carried on walking ahead of him. She didn't want to look at him when he told her she wasn't a curvy size twelve with great skin and film-star eyes.

'Well, in the Grand Canyon, remember I got us that amazing hotel room?'

'Because you pretended to be a lawyer, yes, I know.'

'Well, I did study law, but I also told them you were Goldie Looks.'

'Eh, Goldie who?'

'Looks. She's a travel blogger mainly followed by retired wealthy Americans. You're about the same age, with similar hair, so all I had to do was tell them Flora was your real name and show them some of her articles. She's an amazing online influencer, estimated to be responsible for millions of dollars of the American vacation market. I love her blog, it's full of—'

'So, you said I was this Goldilocks person to get us a nicer hotel?'

'I don't see it like that. You were so upset about Cal the cheating Canadian. I wanted you to enjoy the Grand Canyon and forget all about him. You were inconsolable. I didn't know how else to cheer you up.'

True, she had been very upset, and Marty had been wonderful – whisking her away to a much nicer hotel. The amazing suite, normally reserved for film stars, and at no extra cost.

'I don't know, Marty. How am I supposed to believe anything you say?'

'I don't make things up just for the sake of it, you know.'

'Hm.'

'You've got to admit, that hotel suite was fantastic.'

'That's not the point.'

They walked in silence. Flora barely heard the tour guide's spiel. Slight nausea from the coach journey stayed with her and added to a congealing drag of doubt. Just how much of Marty's friendship with John had been true? He had simply appeared from nowhere on the day she'd visited the allotment. He could have been anyone. John had never mentioned him. True, she'd seen him at the funeral, but he didn't sit with Maggie and the others from the allotment. And what about all the nice things he'd said to her? His flattering comments were addictive, a breath of fresh air after all those years of John saying she looked like a dog's dinner whenever she'd made an effort.

Back on the coach, Flora relaxed into her allocated window seat. This time she had a closeup view of the carved-out rock face. On the other side of the coach, a group of Americans were dealing with the sheer drop by exclaiming 'Wowzers!' and 'Get a load of that!' at every turn in the road. Did they have to be so loud? So different from the nervous laughs coming from a family of Asians. She stole a glance at Marty – normally he'd say something funny but his eyes were closed. Good. She was still cross with him.

∽◦◦∾

Usually, they would have had dinner in a nice little bar or restaurant serving local food. Marty had already found a *Comedor* serving the best *tamales* in the district, but instead Flora opted for dinner at the hotel. Laying off the wine might be a good idea, too. She'd have another early night.

Only a set menu was available in the crowded restaurant. Two disinterested young men in ill-fitting suits and coloured bow ties pushed a trolley between the tables, delivering soup. She waited for Marty to ask what it was, but he didn't. Maybe minestrone? He was usually so talkative, always discussing the next thing on the list, cracking jokes. Making her laugh. Being married to John had conditioned her to what could be called a companionable silence. They had stopped trying to have conversations years ago. Pointless chit-chat, he'd called it. But Marty? The continued silence was unbearable.

'Why do you do it?' Flora finally asked.

'Hm?'

'All this making stuff up?'

'You're not still on about that are you? It's nothing, just a matter of adding colour, embroidering reality.' He sounded as annoyed as she was.

'It's called telling lies, Marty.'

'It's not proper lies.' He looked at her, but she said nothing. 'Alright. I've always found real life a bit monochrome. Boring. And I can't bear to see people I care about being sad. My imagination just skips over the bad stuff and comes up with a much better version.'

'That doesn't make it alright.' Skipping over the bad stuff? Did that mean she had actually looked like a pig fighting with a curtain in those white embossed capri pants? He had wolf-whistled and said, 'Very Jackie O.'

Seeing him upset was awful, but she had to know – was he completely fake? John had never thought twice about saying something unkind: that she was stupid or deluded. On the other hand, he'd had secrets too. His ginormous savings account, for starters. Secrets or lies, which was worse?

'What else have you "embroidered", Marty?'

'Smokey Brooks,' he said slowly.

'The Irish so-called cowboy? Another liar in my life. I must attract them.'

'No, listen, I was trying to make your cowboy dreams come true. I hired him to—'

'You *hired* him?'

'With my own money.'

'Blimey, Marty, that's not the point. You paid him like a gigolo?'

'No, not like that. After Cal the cheating Canadian, I thought you could do with a little boost. I never intended to upset you. I'm sorry.'

Deep down, she'd known all along he'd been too good to be true. 'What else?'

'Does it matter? I would never say or do anything to upset you, I only—'

'You have upset me. What else?'

'I can't think of—'

'What about my bum?' She wanted to know, but only in a roundabout way. Too late, it was out now.

'Your bum?'

'Yes. Bum. And everything else. You always say such nice things, but what's the truth? Those capri pants – what does my bum look like in those?' She braced herself.

'Honestly? Those capris are really well made, the embossed fabric is gorgeous and you look fabulous in them.'

'And my—'

'And from behind, you look like a forty-year-old woman. Confident and classy.'

'Oh.' More than ten years younger. Better stop now.

They ate the main course in silence, then Marty said, 'Shall we skip the dessert? I bought a Mayan chocolate selection box in the gift shop, we could have it in our room and watch a film?'

'One of your musicals?'

'*My Fair Lady.* Let's go before those bored trolley boys get here.'

On the way to the lift, Flora felt him put his arm around her and kiss the top of her head. The evaporating negativity was such a relief. So what if he exaggerated sometimes? Everyone had their failings. How could she manage without him? He was her best friend and family all in one.

NINE

'This place is amazing,' Flora said dreamily, gazing out of the window at hummingbirds sipping from flaming orange and yellow hibiscus. The garden in front of their villa was paradise in motion: scarlet macaws in the cashew nut trees, a kaleidoscope of butterflies dancing over exotic plants around the saltwater plunge pool, and creamy-pink conch shells all along a neat little path, leading to an impossibly white sandy beach.

And then there was the sea. The previous day's snorkelling trip had opened a magical turquoise window into a swimmingly beautiful underworld of psychedelic art. Shoals of humbug-striped angelfish and zesty yellow tangs mingled with purple-finned, lilac-pink triggerfish, green and blue bar jacks, and Flora's favourite, princess parrotfish. Belize was far more beautiful than the guide book had promised.

'Belize. Even the name sounds relaxing,' Marty said, still trying to tie a complicated yet casual-looking knot in Flora's sarong. 'The flowers are absolutely gorgeous. I'd love to take some cuttings, but I can't see them enjoying a Coventry allotment.' He stepped back to admire his handiwork 'There. What do you think?'

She'd never imagined herself in a gold lamé swimsuit before. The delicate cream and gold sarong softened the glitz, but still, it was outrageous. 'It's a lovely gift, Marty, but it's not my usual style. I think it would look better on someone thinner and younger.'

'Oh, pish! I know it's a bit over the top, but if you can't have a bit of bling at this time of year, when can you?' Marty appraised her. 'You look a million dollars, darling.'

'I look like an over-wrapped Christmas present.'

'That's because it *is* Christmas – you look wonderfully festive.'

'Well, I suppose everyone here is a bit over the top.'

'So work it, girlfriend. You never know, you might attract a nicely minted husband who'll look after you for the rest of your days.'

'Actually, I've been thinking about that a lot recently. Marriage. I think I'm ready to move on. Not a fling,' she said quickly. She'd had enough of Marty's matchmaking. 'But properly move on and settle down again. I know I should still be sad about John, but I can hardly remember what he looked like. It seems a lifetime ago. Is that normal?'

'Not after thirty-five years, but I don't think you two had a normal marriage. Not by any stretch.'

'How would you know?' Flora was surprised at how defensive she felt.

'I'm not being judgey; I mean, from my point of view, the John I knew at the allotment was a very different person, but from what you say, he was so controlling. You never made any decisions.'

'Maybe I liked it that way.'

'Babes, I don't think it was healthy, and you said yourself you felt depressed virtually the whole time.' Marty paused. 'Look at you now, how far you've come. Do you remember that frumpy grey tweed coat you used to wear and those brown, flat lace-up shoes? It was all a bit old lady-ish.'

'I wasn't old.' Tears prickled her eyes.

'No, but you dressed old and you acted old.' Marty took her hand. 'I'm sorry, darling, but John did that to you. Think about how you were then and look at you now.' He steered her towards the mirror.

Flora studied herself, turning this way and that. Marty was right, she looked festive, in the way normal people did at Christmas – just as she had for her first Christmas with John when she'd squeezed into the same outfit she'd worn the previous year with her parents: a red, long-sleeved mini and white go-go boots. Very Christmassy. She applied mascara, frosted blue eyeshadow and a generous application of her wedding lipstick. Tangerine Dream.

She half-closed her eyes and pouted, Brigitte Bardot style. 'Happy Christmas, darling,' she would say, picturing John's delight when he realised what a Christmas cracker he had for a wife. He'd give her a little box wrapped in gold paper, tied with a red ribbon. The necklace she'd been dropping hints about. He'd kiss her neck as he stood behind her to fasten it. 'You're so beautiful,' he'd murmur. She had tiptoed downstairs and waited outside the door to savour the moment. John had never had a proper Christmas. He was about to find out what he'd been missing.

He was standing over the stereo, about to give Jim Reeves a turn on the player. He stared at her, the record frozen in midair.

'Whatever have you done to yourself?' he laughed.

'I thought—'

'Little dabs of powder, little pots of paint, makes a girl's complexion, something that it ain't.' He spoke to the album cover as though only Jim would appreciate his little rhyme and Jim, who seemed equally pleased with his *Twelve Songs of Christmas*, smiled back.

She had wept quietly in the bathroom, then wiped her make-up off and splashed her face with cold water to subdue the pinkness. Not wanting any more upset, she pulled off her go-go boots; according to John only slippers should be worn in the house, to save the carpet. She took a deep breath and forced a smile in the mirror until her reflection was convincing.

Back downstairs, John was humming along to 'Blue Christmas'.

'Here you are, Flora love, Happy Christmas!' he said, handing her a small, neatly wrapped parcel in the shape of a book. It wasn't the love token she'd been hoping for and a few more tears trickled the remains of mascara down her face.

'Come on now,' said John, taking her by the shoulders. 'There was no need to titivate yourself. You know I prefer you just the way you are.'

'Yes,' she said.

After that first Christmas, Flora secretly put her Tangerine Dream lipstick on when she needed to cheer herself up. Sometimes she'd add blusher and mascara, just to go to the shops. She made sure to wipe it all off by five-thirty, before she heard John's key in the door.

Thanks to Marty, she looked years younger; with her new hair colour and make-up, she finally felt attractive. Apart from the swimsuit, he had great taste in clothes and seemed to know exactly what would flatter her shape and colouring.

Marty was standing behind her, so she spoke to his reflection, 'I might look different, but I don't know how I feel. I look glamorous and confident, but without you, I wouldn't be able to pull it off.'

'That's not true. What I mean is you had it all along, but John crushed you. Believe in yourself, Flora Marshall.'

'I hate being a Marshall, I have done for years. I was Jones before.'

'Okay, so believe in Flora Jones.' Marty wagged a finger at her reflection.

'I don't think Flora Jones was up to much either. She left school with two O-levels and became a shelf-stacker. She didn't even get to work the tills.'

'Hey, come on.' Marty kissed the top of her head. 'It's Christmas Day; let's sprinkle a little magic on it. How about a new name – who would you like to be?'

'Well, still Flora, but not Marshall or Jones. I'd like to sound glamorous and feminine. Something with a bit of mystery.'

'You can be whoever you want, babes. You'll have to keep your passport name for now, but as soon as we get back to the UK you can change it officially, by deed poll.'

'And then I can have a new passport?'

'Yes, then the new Flora can blossom in all her golden glory.'

'That's it!'

'What?'

'What you just said.'

'Glory? Flora Glory sounds a bit iffy.'

'No, blossom, or something like that. Bloom?'

'Flora Bloom. I love it! That's exactly who you are.' Marty hugged her. 'A gorgeous Flora coming into bloom, bold and bright, just like a dahlia.'

'Thanks, Marty.' Flora laughed. Already she felt different.

'Right Ms Bloom, I'm thinking those cute mother-of-pearl sandals and the Gucci shades? Let's start Christmas on the beach with a lovely bottle of pink bubbles.'

~※~

While Marty was on a long-distance call, wishing his parents a Happy Christmas, Flora lounged on the beach, enjoying the soft warm sand beneath her toes. Who'd have thought it, she giggled to herself, sunbathing on a tropical island and sipping champers on Christmas Day.

In the Marshall household it had been an improving book and Bristol Cream in front of the Queen's speech. She'd tried to force some festive cheer into the occasion, but gradually she'd resigned herself to something so lacking in joy, it scarcely served to break the monotony of the rest of the year. The exchange of a gift – always a book from John – was carried out with little enthusiasm on either side. Flora's only pleasure was derived from rearranging her books each Boxing

Day in order of boring to almost interesting. *Exciting Geology for Beginners*, *The History of Domestic Appliances* and *One Hundred Moneysaving Tips* jockeyed for pole position.

Lunch would be a Tesco chicken with Paxo stuffing, roast potatoes, sprouts and carrots. Each year Flora folded red paper napkins into triangles the same way they did in restaurants. By the time the first box of twelve crackers was used up, she had been married for six years and knew another box would be deemed a waste of money. 'Bits of pointless plastic and a daft paper hat,' according to John. In thirty-five years, only one Christmas stood out.

'Sit down, Flora love.' John had pulled out a chair at the kitchen table.

'Why, what's happened?'

'Nothing's happened, I just want you to sit down. I'm going to surprise and delight you,' said John, flipping his tie over his shoulder.

'Oh.' She couldn't begin to imagine what he had in mind. There were so many things that would have surprised and delighted her. John, nipping upstairs to change into a silly Christmas jumper; that would have surprised her. A different gift, something pretty, would have been delightful. Or the suggestion they go out for Christmas lunch, treat themselves to the five-course extravaganza advertised at The Bell Hotel: prawn cocktail to start, soup, roast turkey with all the trimmings followed by a selection from the sweet trolley, continental cheese selection and minty chocolates with coffee – that would have delighted her more than anything. She had been dropping hints for weeks, saying it would be nice to be among other people on Christmas Day, feel more festive and enjoy a proper celebration. Of course, she knew John wouldn't want to spend the extra money, but she'd worked out the difference in cost and said she'd go without a present if they could book a place at The Bell, just once.

'Now, I know you think I haven't been listening to all your little hints about doing something different for Christmas.'

'Are we going—'

'And I realise it must be rather boring for you to have the same old routine. It's not as though you go out to work, whereas I have quite enough stimulation during my working day.'

'So, are we—'

John held his finger up, something he was prone to do when interrupted.

'I've not been fair on you, Flora, I realise a woman like you needs a little spoiling now and then, so I've decided, Christmas is as good a time as any.' He picked up the kettle and began to fill it up. During mid-flow, he turned to smile and nod at Flora, who was still hopeful; Christmas lunch at The Bell would be such a treat.

While the kettle boiled, John put a saucepan of water on the stove and then took off his watch and laid it on the kitchen table.

'What are you doing, what's the surprise, John?'

'Just you wait.'

'The suspense is killing me.' Just as she said this, the kettle began to boil. John made a pot of tea and set it on the table. Flora got up to get the cups.

'No, no, you just sit there and enjoy yourself. One egg or two?'

'Boiled?'

'Yes, boiled.'

'That depends on if we're going out for Christmas lunch,' said Flora.

'Out for Christmas lunch? Why on earth would we go out for Christmas lunch?'

'But I thought the surprise would be—' Her voice tailed off. There was no point in saying more; of course they wouldn't be going out for lunch. The chicken was already in the fridge. Although Flora had imagined they could have it for Boxing Day, she suddenly realised the whole idea was in her head.

'This is the surprise. Me, making you breakfast. I don't suppose you expected that, eh?'

A shadow loomed over her sun lounger.

'Hey, babes?' Marty was speaking.

'Yes? Sorry. I was miles away.'

'I was saying, how about the lobster for lunch? Today everything is my treat. You've done so much for me; this trip is the best thing that's ever happened in my entire life. I want Christmas to be my way of saying thank you.'

'You don't have to thank me, Marty. You were right about what you said before; I'd still be the old Flora if it weren't for you. It's me who should be saying thanks.'

'Blimey, listen to us. Let's just agree that Christmas is a day to be grateful for loved ones past and present. And loved ones in the future.'

'Definitely ones in the future, and not just for me. Isn't it about time you found yourself a lovely man, Marty? I mean, you've never said much about it, but I'm presuming you want to settle down sometime?'

'Yes, I suppose I do, but there's never been anyone special. Then again, I've not exactly had the opportunities. The gay scene in Coventry isn't much to write home about and before that, I was trying my best to be the son my parents wanted, which was a much straighter version of the Marty you see now.' He wiggled in his tight pink swimming trunks until the little gold anchor on a chain tinkled and made them laugh.

'Hopefully, Rio will be full of gorgeous guys and you'll be spoilt for choice,' said Flora.

'Well, if they're not there, I don't know where they are.'

'Hmm, imagine. All those lovely Latinos.'

'I am,' said Marty, leaning back in his lounger with a smile.

TEN

'Anyone sitting here?' A woman with grey hair braided into cornrows and wearing tie-dyed harem pants was hugging a rucksack with suntanned, sinewy arms.

'No, not at all.' Flora pulled her handbag a little closer as the woman sank down with a resounding sigh.

'Oh man, I thought I'd never make it,' she said half to herself as she took out her water bottle. 'Sad to be leaving. Isn't it beautiful here?'

Flora was waiting for Marty to sort out their luggage – he had been in the queue for half an hour already.

'Yes, it's wonderful.'

'Still, I've got Peru next.' She opened a bag of plantain chips and held it out.

'Thank you.' Flora took one to be polite and nibbled the edge. 'Peru sounds exciting. Are you travelling alone?'

'Yes. I've been working my way around the world for almost a year now. Tour guide in Mexico, bar job in Belize. Now I've put enough cash together for a month of exploring. How about you?'

'Oh, I'm travelling around too. My friend's over there, in the excess baggage queue, the pink polo shirt. We're going to Bolivia.'

'Great choice! I hope to make my way there sometime soon.'

The woman was a global traveller. They were fellow free spirits. Soon Flora was telling her all about John's list and how Marty came to be her travelling companion. She usually enjoyed people's reactions; they'd ask questions, say how much they admired her for taking up the challenge.

'So, what about you?' asked the woman. 'All that time your hubby was putting his list together, didn't you have a hankering of your own?'

'Well, yes.' Suddenly a Parker Knoll upholstered in Maple Blush seemed ridiculous; even an executive home sounded lame. 'Actually, I've always wanted to go to Honolulu.'

'Another great choice.' She pointed to a small turtle tattoo on her ankle. 'I get inked every place I go. Honolulu is okay, but Hanauma Bay is the bomb, far from the tourist traps. I worked on a turtle breeding program there after my divorce.'

'You're divorced?'

'Yup. Seven years ago. I'm fifty now.' Flora listened to her potted life story, hoping she'd get to the end before Marty reached the front of the queue. This woman was all the things she could have been. 'Life began at forty-three and I'm getting younger every year! So, what do you do back in England?'

Flora's heart sank. What could she say to someone who was a qualified physiotherapist, did horse whispering as a sideline and had been to over thirty countries? She wasn't even between one thing and another. Past or future, there was nothing. She was relieved to see Marty approaching and stood up.

'I'd love to stay and chat but I'd better go.'

'Yeh, see you around. And be true to yourself, okay?'

'Lovely to meet you. Cheerio.' Flora gave a small wave, hoping to look like one of the sisterhood, and hurried over to Marty.

'We'll have to get rid of some of our clothes, excess baggage is a fortune. Imagine how much it'll be by the time we get to Asia.' He tucked the credit card back into his wallet. 'I know it's your money, babes, but I think we should economise where it doesn't affect the trip and besides, it's a pain, lugging everything with us. We've already had to buy an extra suitcase.'

'I know, it's crazy,' said Flora, 'but the things we've bought are souvenirs. I love my cowgirl outfit and that genuine Inuit coat was a one-off.'

'When are you going to wear them again?'

'I don't know. Never probably. Maybe we can give a few things away.'

'Let's see what Bolivia has in store, you never know, you might decide to wear your seal skin while playing the nose pipe.'

Flora laughed. 'Are we actually going to play the nose pipe? I don't trust you after the scuba diving.'

'Not that again. It's not every day you get to see something underwater that dates back to the stone age.'

'The sharks, Marty. No one said anything about sharks. I can't get them out of my head.'

'I knew you wouldn't go if I told you. Anyway, you have to admit, the other fish were stunning, even the sharks were pretty special in my opinion.'

'They were horrible.'

'Well, we're not going anywhere near another beach until we get to Rio, so you can relax.'

'Bolivia, Argentina, then Rio?'

'Patagonia is before Rio as well.'

'And after Rio? I don't suppose you can think past your two weeks of partying.'

'I can, but I prefer not to.'

'Well, it's your well-earned reward for all your hard work. I wonder what I'll do while you're at all those gay bars, hanging out with gorgeous new friends.'

'Don't worry, we have the most amazing hotel, and I'm going to book a personal guide for you. Also, we have some great seats for the carnival and then there are the after-parties. We're going to dress up in some crazy costumes and party all night.'

'I'll definitely need a rest after that. If Mexico was anything to go by I don't think I can do more than one all-night party before I'm pooped.'

'So you won't miss me,' said Marty.

'Of course I will, but most likely from the relaxed position of a sun lounger.'

'By the way, I've been thinking, it might be a good idea to learn a bit of the language, just in case you get lost or something.'

'Don't be silly, I'll be with my guide or in the hotel and besides, I'm rubbish at languages.'

'Okay. All I'm saying is, it can help to break down barriers with the locals. I've got a few choice sentences tucked up my sleeve.'

'I bet you have,' said Flora, 'and another one in your jeans I expect.'

'Flora!' said Marty, in mock horror, 'whatever became of that shy and retiring lady I first met at John's allotment?'

~ ∘ ~

According to the guide book, Casa de Huespedes Isabella was the only accommodation available in such a small Bolivian mountain town. The driver had refused to take them all the way to Coroico; the tropical downpour had made driving conditions almost impossible. He stopped the car momentarily while Marty read from the guide book.

'It says *"Homely and unique. Authentic Bolivia"*, what do you think?' He almost shouted as the rain hammered on the roof of the car and lashed at the wipers.

'The name sounds so romantic.' Flora was trying to focus on the small photograph in the half-dark. This was proper travelling. Exciting. And a nice change from marble foyers and porters in uniform.

Once inside the tiny guesthouse, rain clattered relentlessly on the tin roof and in places, ran down inside the walls and drained away through cracks in the floorboards. It was definitely unique. The ancient landlord ushered them further in to sit at a table in the single downstairs room. Under a battered hat still dripping with rainwater, the man's face was creased by age and sun; a broad grin displayed a single gold tooth among discoloured stumps. He instructed someone to carry their bags upstairs and then, after further shouts to a room beyond the small make-shift bar, a young woman hurried in to lay the table.

Flora and Marty appeared to be the local attraction. Several villagers crowded into the bar to watch them eat dinner – only two or three bought themselves a drink, the rest were content to stare at the tourists enjoy cornbread and goat meat, washed down with bottles of Saya Dorada beer.

Soon after they'd finished a tall man with shoulder-length hair and a moustache pushed through the crowd. His shirt might have been red at one time, but it was faded to a dusky pink and soaked through from the rain, clinging to his torso so tightly that they could see the outline of something at his waist.

'I think he's got a gun,' whispered Flora.

'Or maybe a knife. Let me do the talking.'

'My name is Ramiro Gonzalo Salvadore de Lozada, how about you?'

'Um, I'm Marty, pleased to meet you?' Marty tentatively extended a hand. There was a murmur from the onlookers as someone translated.

'Not shake hands unless we plan wedding or death. What is your wife name? Very lovely with the blue eyes and the yellow hair. She is *churra*.'

'Her name is Flora, but she's not my—'

'Ah, Flora, yes, we have this also. On the mountain, in the market, everywhere is flora, very beautiful. So now we play poker.' Without waiting for a reply, he pulled up a stool and the barman brought over a well-worn pack of cards.

'Well, actually we've had a long journey getting here, we're really very tired, so I don't think I—'

'You are pussy cat.' A small time-lapse while this was translated ended in a roar of laughter. 'Your wife can sleep, but you are the man. You have US dollar?'

'Well, I—' Marty paused. 'I don't have much, maybe twenty dollars? We usually use a credit card, it's only because I couldn't use it here in the bar that I asked about spending dollars. We didn't realise it was going to be quite so remote. We're on our way to Coroico you see, but the rain was so heavy and—' Flora kicked him under the table.

'You're gabbling,' she murmured, then said loudly, 'he would love to have a game, wouldn't you, Marty?'

'Yes, just a quick game would be great, thanks,' Marty added.

'Your wife, she has your balls in her hand.' Ramiro demonstrated the squeezing of Marty's testicles for the benefit of the audience.

'She's not my— oh, never mind. What are we playing, um, Ramiro, can I call you Ramiro?'

'Yes, call me Ramiro, it makes no difference to me what you say, they call me many things, is just a name.' Ramiro took out a slim cigar and one of the villagers hurried forward and struck a match for him. 'We play Bolivian poker.' He clicked his fingers and the barman brought over two bottles of Saya Dorada. '*Chupar.*' He raised his bottle. 'Drink, *amigo.*'

Flora didn't mind that she hadn't been included in the round; it was as though her well-thumbed copy of *The Faithful Brigand* had come to life. It was disrespectful to buy another man's wife a drink. Wife. Given the age gap and Marty's good looks, it was flattering. At least he didn't presume she was his mother, as some people had.

Ramiro shuffled the cards and the game got underway. Flora watched for a while – it appeared to be the same game they had played in Texas when Marty had come out winning. After a few rounds, a pile of Ramiro's grubby, well-worn single dollar notes had been added to his original stake.

'You play well, my friend,' said Ramiro as he pushed two more crumpled dollar notes into the centre of the table.

'Thank you. Can I get you another beer?' Marty seemed to be enjoying himself. 'How about you Flora, beer?'

'Actually, I think I'll go to bed. That drive up the mountain has played havoc with my back. I need to lie down.'

He leaned over and in a stage whisper said, 'I won't be too long, just need to get to the bottom of Ramiro's stash.'

'Really? You don't have to take all his money, Marty, what if it's all he has?' She whispered back, concerned there was perhaps a Mrs Ramiro and a clutch of malnourished children; on their way into the village, they'd seen several run-down huts with a seemingly endless number of children spilling out of each.

'Don't worry, Missus Flora.' It was the first time Ramiro had spoken to her directly. 'I only use dollar tips from the tourist, is just for fun, no?' When he smiled, a dimple puckered his stubbly cheek. He could definitely have been the hero in *The Faithful Brigand.*

'Don't worry, babes, I won't be long, just a couple more rounds.' Marty was picking up his latest win and grinned at her. 'Trust me, it's fine.' She patted his shoulder and said goodnight.

In her room the thundering rain on the tin roof overhead was strangely soothing, and soon she was asleep.

～☙～

A percussion of exotic of birdsong, accompanied by a pair of roosters competing outside Flora's bedroom window, told her it was morning. The rain had stopped and sunshine was leaking into the room around faded curtains. She had slept soundly and her back felt much better. Where was she again? Travelling for almost three months meant she often woke up and struggled to remember which country she was in. A distant clamour of children's voices jogged her memory. Such a happy sound. Despite the care-worn room, the basic bathroom down the hall and the chewy tasteless dinner, she liked the simplicity. She flung open the curtains, opened the window and inhaled the clear mountain air; after all the glamour and glitz of Belize, it was perfect.

She quickly washed and dressed. Marty would probably have a hangover. She made her way down the rough-hewn wooden stairs. There were large gaps between the steps and the distance between each one varied. It required concentration. The staircase led straight into the empty bar; apart from the kitchen, it was the only downstairs room other than a sort of rustic outhouse tacked onto the back. She sat at the same table as the previous night and waited. There was no rush.

'*Buenos días*, Madam,' said an elderly lady. Perhaps the landlord's wife? She was dressed in a combination of a traditional skirt, oversized wellingtons that had been rolled down, and a bright pink sweatshirt with '*Beach Babe*' printed on the front. She was carrying a large tray laden with fresh fruit, small pastries and a pot of coffee.

'Good morning. Thank you, this looks delicious.' Flora was pleasantly surprised by the breakfast. The pastries were something Marty had told her about, a Bolivian delicacy. 'Are these those traditional pastries?' she asked.

The old lady just nodded, pointed to the coffee and gave a thumbs-up sign.

'Oh, yes coffee is perfect, thank you, and what about these?' Flora pointed to the neatly formed pastries.

'*Salteñas, me gustan mucho*,' said the old lady, nodding vigorously and patting her tummy.

'Ah, yes, that's it, *sultanas*. Marty was telling me about them. I know they can have different kinds of filling, so what are these made of?' Flora picked one up and turned to the old lady, but she was already leaving the room in a shuffle that suggested she was trying to keep her boots from sliding off. That's a shame, thought Flora, I was enjoying our chat. She took a bite and tried to work out the filling for herself. A mild chilli heat and a sweetness; she inspected the contents and could work out raisins and olives, among other things. Delicious. Seeing as there was only one cup for the coffee, she presumed the breakfast was just for her and selected a second pastry; they could order more when Marty finally made an appearance.

Bolivia was turning out to be her favourite place – even the coffee was great. She would talk to Marty about sharing his poker winnings among the families in the run-down huts they'd seen on the way in. They could go for a wander around after breakfast and give the dollars out before they headed on to Coroico, or maybe now they'd go straight to La Paz. She'd let him decide.

Half an hour later, Flora knocked on his door. No response. She waited another ten minutes, then tried to open it, but it was locked. Back in the bar, she called 'hello!' several times, but the place was deserted. She went through to the kitchen; just a small room with a table and storage jars and an old, blackened wood-fired stove. A tray of pastries was set on one side with a cloth over them, but besides that, there was no evidence of recent activity. Where was the old lady?

'Hello? Um, *oh-la*. Anyone there?' She was starting to worry.

Back outside Marty's room, she banged on the door so hard it hurt her hand.

'Marty! Are you in there? Open up!' Still nothing. Flora went to her room and scribbled a note saying she was out in the village and would be back in half an hour, then pushed it under his door.

The sunlight was dazzling after the night's rain. It had been so dark and gloomy in the guesthouse, she hadn't thought to bring her sunglasses. She shaded her eyes and looked around. Previously she'd heard children playing, the clatter and murmur of women going about their daily chores, but now there was no one to be seen. She walked past several houses. Doors and shutters were closed. Even the cockerels had stopped crowing. Strange. The only sound was the buzzing of insects and the occasional squawk from invisible birds in nearby trees

'Hello?' Flora said loudly, not wishing to shout. '*Oh-la!*'

The dirt road was still wet and slippery from the rainfall. Mud stuck to her sandals as she picked her way over large stones or ruts in the road. A mangey-looking dog lay in a patch of shade and studied her as she walked past. She was glad it didn't get up – she had had a rabies injection but she was still nervous of foreign dogs. A neat vegetable garden with old tins on sticks for bird scarers distracted her for a moment. John would like that. Then a few more small houses. It was hard to believe so many people lived under one roof. Families of maybe twelve squeezed into what looked like a single room. That en-suite bathroom in Texas was bigger than any of them. It was an eye-opener.

As she turned a corner, a murmur of voices coming from a small stone building attracted her attention. It was a single-storey with faded blue double doors and a small tower. The relief made her laugh. Of course, it was Sunday. Church.

She would wait. When everyone came out she could ask Ramiro how the poker game went. Meanwhile, it was lovely to sit in the sun and hear the background of the service. What a view. The canopy of trees falling down the mountainside speckled with flashes of colourful birds.

Bolivia was such a delight, by far the most diverse and interesting country she'd been to so far. Where would it rank by the time they had finished the whole list? There was so much more to come.

Finally, the doors opened and the congregation poured out into the sunshine, looking very different from the dishevelled group she's seen the night before: women in layered skirts of sweetie shop colour and shawls woven with rainbows of thread, men in clean white shirts and waistcoats. Flora searched for a familiar figure. Ramiro had been distinctively tall. He wasn't there. In fact, the congregation was mainly women and children with a few older men – searching for a familiar face. Now dressed in her Sunday best, it took Flora a moment to recognise the old lady who had served her breakfast.

'Hi, I'm from the, um—' Flora indicated back towards the guesthouse.

'*Si.*' The old lady nodded with a gummy smile. A small crowd of similarly elderly ladies gathered around and began talking. One of them reached out and touched Flora's hair and said something that provoked a resounding cackle. The women continued with an animated conversation. Flora waited for a slight break and spoke quickly.

'Excuse me, ladies. I'm just wondering if you've seen Marty this morning?'

Her voice was drowned by their running commentary. They obviously didn't understand her and seemed to have moved on from her hair to the size of her breasts, comparing their child-weary bosoms to her chest with exaggerated hand gestures and gales of laughter.

Trying to join in, she pointed to herself and said, '*Me no bambino.*' This seemed to satisfy their curiosity and gradually they moved away to gather their grandchildren or go back to work. After walking back to the guesthouse with the old lady, who chatted amiably unperturbed by the language barrier, Flora hurried to Marty's room. His door was still locked and the shadow of her note could be seen on the floor just inside.

Downstairs the old lady had started sweeping the bar with a bundle of twigs bound to a stick, humming an indiscernible tune.

'Excuse me, do you think I could have the key to my friend's room?' Smiling and nodding seemed to be the only common language, so Flora took out her own key and showed it to her, then beckoned for her to follow her up the narrow staircase where she gestured to Marty's door and performed an exaggerated display of trying to unlock it. Flora was relieved to see she had communicated clearly and the old lady quickly reappeared a few minutes later with a key.

The bed hadn't been slept in. It looked as though he'd just dropped his suitcase off when they arrived, gone down to dinner and not come back. Flora gave the old lady an exaggerated shrug, hoping it was international. In case it hadn't filtered through she pointed to the bed and then shrugged again adding the word '*que*?', something she'd gleaned from Manuel of *Fawlty Towers*, and then, '*que pasa*?' – a regular phrase in her old Western novels and hopefully something close to whatever they said in Bolivia. The old lady began reeling off a plethora of exclamations, adding a shrug in here and there, indicating that she too was puzzled. Eventually, she gestured for Flora to follow her, relocked the door and went back to the bar. She pointed Flora in the direction of a chair and seemed to suggest she might wait there.

'What is problem, *Señora*?' The landlord appeared in the doorway, followed by the old lady, who was still speaking excitedly and gesticulating through a rapid line of questioning. For good measure, she shrugged in Flora's direction and said '*que pasa*?' to keep her in the loop.

'Your friend, he is Coroico.'

'He's gone to Coroico without me? But why would he do that?' Surely Marty would never leave her without saying something. 'And Ramiro? Where's Ramiro, did he go with him?'

'*Si Señora*, he is Coroico.'

'Can you telephone? Can I speak to him?'

'No telephone, *Señora*.'

'When are they coming back? Why are they there, should I go to Coroico as well? It's our next stop anyway.'

'*Señora*, relax.'

'Relax? How can I relax when Marty might be kidnapped or in danger?' Flora had read about drug trafficking. Ramiro's wet shirt had revealed the outline of something that looked a lot like a gun. Who was he? He could be using Marty as a drug mule right now. Or maybe Marty had carried on winning and there'd been a fight. How did the landlord know they were in Coroico? Maybe he was covering up something more sinister. Why hadn't Marty left her a note? There were so many questions and no one to answer them.

'Relax, *Señora*,' was all the landlord said, and he left the room. Flora was alone. What if something terrible had happened to Marty? Losing him would be unbearable, on top of which she had no idea how to organise anything. She had handed all responsibility over; he'd booked and paid for everything using her credit card. She didn't even know how to exchange money, let alone what the currency of Bolivia was.

She went up to her room to assess the situation. In her handbag, she had forty American dollars and a gold credit card. She already knew that was useless in remote areas. She didn't have any Bolivian money. Perhaps she could get someone to drive her to Coroico. But what would she do if she didn't find him? Forty dollars wouldn't last long.

There was no point searching Marty's room; she already knew he would have their tickets, passports and money in his money belt and strapped under his shirt. What if Ramiro had spotted it? Why had the landlord told her to relax, were they all in on it?

Each scenario Flora imagined was worse than the last until all she could think of was Marty being murdered by Ramiro and his gang. She needed a plan. If she left and Marty returned, they'd never find each other. But waiting at the guesthouse could be wasting time. He could be in life-threatening danger, but where was he? And if everything had happened the previous night, Ramiro would be far away by now. Having no one to talk to was frustrating; why hadn't she learned a bit of the language?

It was almost lunchtime when Flora went back down to the bar. She would try and get more information out of the landlord, even if it took a long time. She found him filling a stack of crates with empty beer bottles and carrying them outside. He was surprisingly strong for such a small man. He gripped a cigar between his worn-down teeth and smiled broadly as she approached.

'What time, Ramiro come back?' Flora spoke slowly and clearly while pointing at her invisible watch. Nothing. She repeated the action speaking slightly louder. '*Que pasa* Ramiro and Marty *returno* here?' She couldn't remember the name of the village but then went out to read the sign for the guesthouse. It was so faded she could only just make out the words *Casa de Huespedes Isabella*. She copied them down onto a piece of paper.

Slowly she said, '*Que pasa* Ramiro and Marty *returno Casa dee Hewspeedie Isabella*?' She was virtually speaking the language but still nothing. Maybe an exaggerated mime of Ramiro with his straight, shoulder-length hair and moustache walking back into the bar with Marty would work. She styled Marty on

John Inman's character in *Are You Being Served?* When she did this the landlord called out to the old lady who in turn called the neighbours, and soon Flora had an audience. Momentarily forgetting the severity of the situation, she hammed up the characters, to the obvious entertainment of the villagers. The more she exaggerated the two missing men's return, the more the small crowd seemed to like it. Laughter ensued, but at the end of each performance they took the lead from the old lady, who was now sitting down in the front row of spectators. She shook her head and shrugged.

'Okay, one more try and I'm sure someone will get it.'

'*Si, una más por favor, Señora!*' The landlord was wiping tears from his eyes but still managed to convey a certain gravitas.

Flora threw all her effort into the mime. Just as she portraying Marty mincing back into the bar, she noticed everyone had stopped looking at her and was staring past her.

'So, you have fun also, Floritta?' Flora spun round to see Ramiro and, behind him, Marty. Flora could only guess how long they'd been standing there.

'Oh, thank God! I've been so worried. Marty, where have you been, are you okay?'

'I think Marty need lie down in dark,' said Ramiro 'How do you say? The avenging angel is in his head.'

'Marty, you look terrible, what happened? You left without telling me.' Flora grabbed his arm as he walked past.

'Sorry, babes, not now. I need to sleep.'

'Yes, Floritta, babes,' said Ramiro. 'Marty, he left a boy, he comes back a man!' Ramiro quickly translated for the benefit of the crowded bar and there was a cheer, although Flora noted it seemed to come more from the menfolk.

'What have you done to him, Ramiro?'

'Don't worry, Floritta, *Señor* Marty with Ramiro, nothing bad can happen. Now, excuse me I must see my grandmother.'

'Grandmother?'

'Yes, I am hungry. She makes the best *salteñas* in Bolivia.' Ramiro smiled at the old lady who had served breakfast. 'Lita, *estoy hambriento.*'

Ramiro stooped down to hug his grandmother. She shot Flora a toothless smile and retreated to the kitchen.

While Marty was in his room, Flora gleaned little from Ramiro except that Marty had been a very willing participant in the trip to Coroico. There had been too much rain to make the journey back and they'd spent the night in a bar, playing cards and drinking. Ramiro seemed to have a high regard for Marty's card skills – they had won a lot of money.

By the time Marty came back downstairs, still looking pale and exhausted, Flora had tried to rationalise the situation. He was entitled to do whatever he wanted, she didn't own him, they were just friends with a travelling arrangement.

'Marty! What were you thinking? I've been worried sick, I didn't know what—'

'I asked the landlord to tell you where I was. Didn't he say anything?'

'Well, yes, but that didn't mean you were okay. I didn't know what to do. How could you just leave me here? Not even a note.' She was beginning to sound hysterical. Tears stung the corner of her eyes.

'Hey babes, it was just high spirits.' Marty reached for her hand. 'We went to Coroico because they ran out of Saya Dorada and there was only some kind of moonshine left to drink. I won every single dollar off Ramiro; he's not a very good player by the way.'

'I don't care about the poker, Marty, you left me here and I didn't know where you were. I was terrified. For you and for me.'

'I'm sorry if you were upset, but I can look after myself and besides, they're lovely people. We just went to Coroico to get some more beer. That was the idea anyway. But when we got there Ramiro bumped into two of his mates and challenged them to a game of Bolivian poker. It's different because they play with the forty-card Spanish deck. To be honest, he hustled them. He made out I was a dumb tourist with loads of money.'

'I knew it. He set you up.'

'No, he set them up. We won over a thousand dollars, babes.'

'A thousand dollars! That's a lot.'

'Yes, it is. The thing is, by the time we'd finished playing it was daylight and our driver had gone to start his day job, so we couldn't get back before you woke up, which was the plan. Or at least to be back in time for breakfast.'

'You should have left me a note, I was frantic with worry.'

'I'm sorry, babes, but we were stuck. There were no phones, otherwise of course I would have called. I presumed because Ramiro's grandparents own the guesthouse, they would tell you not to worry.'

Flora remembered the old lady, chatting with her friends outside the church and then the landlord telling her to relax. No one had been worried apart from her.

'What are you going to do with the money? Split it with Ramiro?'

'Well, he's such a nice guy and the people here are so friendly I thought we should give something to the community,' said Marty.

'Good idea,' said Flora.

'And we brought a whole load of beer back for the bar. Maybe we could have a bit of a party for everyone and stay one more night? We can go straight to La Paz tomorrow, then on to Salar De Uyuni. Believe me, there's not much to see in Coroico.'

'Okay.'

'So, do you forgive me, babes?'

'I suppose so.'

'That's good, because I forgive you for making me out to be such a mincer.'

ELEVEN

'If anyone says, when you've seen one salt flat, you've seen them all, I'll ask them if they've been to Salar De Uyuni,' said Marty, clicking through the stills on his camera.

'I know,' Flora said, leaning over his shoulder. 'Amazing. Like a ginormous mirror. And look at those flamingos. Just beautiful.'

'Your John was onto something with his lottery list. When you first mentioned it, I thought going halfway around the world to see a high tide and a few multi-coloured rocks would be boring, but we're having the most amazing adventure.'

Flora smiled. 'Well, maybe he got something right after all.'

'He wasn't all bad, surely?'

'No, not all bad, but he never made me feel good about myself. At least Cal the cheating Canadian said nice things, made me feel special and, well, how I imagine other women feel.'

'But he wasn't right for you,' Marty said quickly.

'I know. But I want more of whatever made me feel different about myself.'

'More flirting or more of something else?'

'Um, more of something else.'

'Ooh la la! You mean sex?'

'Well, I suppose I wouldn't mind. I'm curious. If Cal hadn't been a love cheat, I would probably have gone to his room.'

'I hear you, sister. You've been solo for almost a year and you have needs.'

Flora hesitated, then blurted out, 'I haven't had sex for over twenty-five years!'

'What?' Marty was staring at her. 'Twenty-five years? You mean you were married to John all that time without a banana in your fruit salad?'

Flora nodded slowly. Should she tell him about the baby? Maybe later. 'At school, all the girls had a thing for John. Compared to the other teachers, he was the only choice. We used to call him Johnny M behind his back. The girls talked about his prowess in the bedroom, even though we were all virgins. I probably married him so I could have something the other girls only talked about. I thought it would be so romantic. You know, with a lot of sighing and heavy breathing. But it turned out to be two minutes of nothing much.'

'Oh no, poor you. So, after a while you gave up on it?'

'I suppose I did,' Flora said quickly. Tell him about the baby now? No.

'That's a long time out in the cold. Weren't you tempted to have a dalliance, a little extra on the side?'

'Well, no. I mean, I thought about it, but no, not really.' Micky's flower stall. That could have been something. He said she had a lovely smile, and once he'd held out a single rose and said, 'C'mon, give us a kiss. It's Valentine's Day.' A quick peck on the cheek. She'd pressed the rose between Mrs Beeton's jams and pickles. Once a week, she undid her ponytail just to walk past the stall on her way to Gail's Cafe. If she timed it right they'd have a quick chat in between customers, but that was it.

And there'd been Raj, the milkman. Friday afternoons. The climax to a week of exchanging bottles and an occasional note. One pound twenty, a friendly chat and a glimpse of exotic flesh in the V of his nylon overalls. The tetra pack ruined everything.

'It's thirty percent cheaper in the supermarket,' John had insisted. Oh, Raj! She listened out for him whirring past in the early hours and hovered around the front gate on Friday afternoons, but a polite nod was the most she got out of him after that.

'So, Cal—'

'When he kissed my neck, I just sort of melted. I've never felt like that before.' She paused, reliving the moment. 'I want more melting moments.'

'Hmm, Uncle Marty needs to fix this situation.'

'I'm not asking you to do it!'

'Phew, that's a relief, I could never be a vagitarian.' They both laughed. 'Anyway, it's not men who hold the key, it's you.'

'Me?' Flora was amazed.

'Yes, it's in your power to attract a mate. Just switch it on and dial it up,' he said, doing a little showbiz wiggle. 'You just need a few lessons in hunter-flirting. That's flirting with a purpose, rather than just flirting for fun.'

'Okay, I'll give it a go.'

'Fabulous. So, imagine I'm this gorgeous guy sitting in a bar. I've got Cal's moustache. You'd like to feel those whiskers on the back of your neck.'

'Or a bit lower down?'

'Hang on, you hussy! First, without actually using words, how would you let me know how much you'd like my fanny duster tickling you in a way that makes you giggle, fizzle and pop?'

'Oh, I see, well, if you're across the bar, I'd smile and maybe give you a wink?'

'Hmm, that's a bit Widow Twankey. Let's say you can only convey your feelings by looking at me.'

Flora concentrated hard.

'Yes, much better! I felt the connection, I'm interested. Maybe I'll come over and offer to buy you a drink.'

'Did you really feel something, Marty?'

'No, babes, that was role play. I'm so gay I can't even think straight. But let's put it to the test tonight.' He jumped up. 'Oh, my. I've just had a fabulous idea. Of course! We're in Argentina – you simply must learn to tango.'

'The dance?'

'Yes, but it's much more than dancing. Hot, sizzling passion as you gaze intensely into each other's eyes. It's sexy and sensual. The perfect pick-me-up for your sleeping beauty.'

'My sleeping—'

'Your fou-fou, darling,' he said, pointing to Flora's crotch. 'In fact, your whole lady garden and surrounding provinces. Tango is catnip to the libido. Before you know it, you'll be doing a horizontal tango with some tight-trousered Latino.'

'Crikey!' Flora giggled. Touch another man's naked body? With only a distant memory of John's spindly torso, always in his pyjama jacket, she could only imagine.

Marty was pulling his shoes on. 'I'll probably be a while, I want to find you the perfect dance teacher. Why not have a nap? It's going to be a long night.'

As soon as Marty closed the door, Flora let out a sigh. Exciting. She stretched out on her bed and went over the conversation. It was a relief to share her secret: twenty-five years was a long time to go without someone's arms around you, even John's, but the reason behind it was still too painful to talk about.

John had found her upstairs. She'd been sitting on the bathroom floor most of the afternoon, crying.

'What do you mean, you've had a miscarriage?' Initially, his tone was sympathetic, then as the story unfolded, it was less so. 'Since when did I agree to cease using a contraceptive device?'

'I wanted to surprise you, I thought—'

'I'll not be a father, Flora.'

'But we can try again, I'll be more—'

'A child is a ridiculous notion at my age.'

'But I've always wanted children.' She had presumed it would be a natural progression after getting married.

'Well, you should have thought of that before you tricked me into marrying you.' John still blamed her for losing his job as a teacher.

'I didn't trick you. If anything, you tricked me into thinking we'd have a normal marriage, with kids, just like everyone else.'

'I think you'll find I did no such thing. It was never discussed.'

'Neither was your stupid bloody job.'

'We don't need language like that, thank you very much.'

Flora had thought of leaving him. She wrote to her parents, still aware of how she had marched out to get married. She hinted at coming back home. Their brief reply reminded her that marriage was for better, for worse. They hadn't approved of her making her wedding vows but would not support her in breaking them either. John didn't seem to care if she stayed or went.

His final remark, 'Use contraception or we'll simply cease sexual relations altogether,' had told her how little he desired her. Already, sex had dwindled to once a month. She had presumed all men had sex on the brain, but not John.

Occasionally it crossed her mind he might have been gay. On the way to Machu Picchu, she had asked Marty if he thought that might be possible, but he'd laughed at the idea.

It had been a relief not to have ferrety sex with John, but there ended the hope of having a baby. All she had left was a small velveteen secret under the mattress in the spare room. Sometimes she'd take it out, hold it close and have a good cry.

~~~

'Flora, Flora, wake up. You'll never guess what! I have found you a gorgeous, and I mean GORGEOUS tango teacher. He was recommended by the concierge, so rise up Madame Butterfly, make ready.'

Flora pushed up her sleeping mask. She had shed a few tears before falling asleep; her eyes were puffy and pink round the edges.

'Oh my god, you look like one of those albino rabbits. Come on, darling, we have work to do.'

Marty ran a bath while rummaging through his emergency supplies. 'Here, let's try this cooling aloe eye gel.' He applied it to a couple of cotton pads. 'I can't wait for you to meet Fernando.'

'Did you say Fernando?' Flora was now fully awake.

'Yes, I know, it's his actual name, AND he's a tango dancer. It can't get much better than that, can it?' Marty swished some powdered kelp and sea salt into the water. 'But first, we're meeting him for something else Argentina has bequeathed to the world. The *asado*. I hope you're hungry?'

'Yes I am, but what is it?'

'Think beef, think fire, think macho men with,' he paused for dramatic effect, 'extra-large skewers.'

'Something like a barbecue?' asked Flora

'No, this is so much more. It's all about the theatre and testosterone. The perfect start to you getting your mojo on.' Marty was now looking through Flora's shoes. 'Now, which ones would you be most comfortable in? We have a long night ahead, possibly including breakfast. The red or the black?'

'For dancing? The black I think,' said Flora.

'Great, I was hoping you'd say that. I've bought this adorable dress, it's perfect for tonight. Come on, babes, I need you up and at it, so we have time to do your hair and make-up.'

'I think you're enjoying this more than me,' smiled Flora as she pushed the bathroom door closed.

'I think I am,' called Marty from the other side. 'It's so much fun. And that Fernando's going to blow your socks off. Put those pads on your eyes, we need you at your best, darling.'

~~~~~

Flora's cheeks were pink. 'It's the barbecue,' she said, fanning herself, knowing full well it was Fernando, who seemed to be standing just a little too close. She detected a spicy cologne. Earthy.

'What did I tell you?' Marty whispered. 'Sex on a stick.'

She muffled a giggle. He *was* gorgeous – in his tight satin black trousers and open-fronted shirt, there was little left to the imagination. Fernando's thick curly hair brushed her cheek as he leaned in and spoke softly, as though sharing a private thought.

'So, Flora, tell me, how do you like it?' His breath tickled her ear deliciously.

'Um,' she said, still feeling a bit giggly, 'the food?'

'Yes, the meat.' Did he just slightly thrust his slim hips at her or was it her imagination?

'It's lovely, thank you.'

'No, not lovely. It is sensational!' Fernando smacked his lips. 'It is the taste of Argentina. No place in the world will you taste like this.' He took Flora's hand and led her towards the fire. 'You see, all is meat, not just the beef steak but *morcillas*, *chinchulines*, *mollejas*. Everything from the *criollo*, we cook it here.'

She suppressed the desire to put her hand over her mouth; the small, crispy things had been tasty, but if she'd known they were intestines, she wouldn't have eaten them.

'So you see, beautiful Flora, you already have Argentina inside before we make love with the tango.' His white teeth gleamed in the firelight.

'Now I must prepare for our evening together.' He stooped and kissed her hand. 'Please take time to digest this fantastic *asado* and enjoy a night tour of beautiful Buenos Aires.' He kissed her hand once more. 'And then, we will meet again.'

Flora watched him walk away, admiring his taut buttocks. What would he look like naked?

'I know,' said Marty as he appeared at her side.

'I'm—'

'Speechless?'

'Isn't he wonderful? So tall and handsome. Muscular. I think I'm going to love dancing the tango,' Flora said dreamily.

Marty chuckled. 'Come on, babes, the limo's outside. First stop is Plaza de Mayo, you know, where Eva Perón wowed the workers.'

They drove slowly around the plaza, past Casa Rosada's famous balcony, and as a mark of respect, broke into a rendition of '*Don't Cry for Me Argentina*'. Marty insisted on stopping to pose for a photograph – *Evita* was one of his favourite musicals. They went on to El Obelisco and the magnificent Teatro Colon. Then at the ornate gates of Recoleta Cemetery, the driver told them the story of how Evita's burial had taken over twenty-four years to complete.

'My lovely Evita, we must come back and walk around the cemetery tomorrow. I won't forgive myself if I don't,' said Marty as he wound his window back up. 'Right, now we are going to our first *milonga*.'

'Is that a tango dancing place?' Flora was trying her best with the language and the culture, but there was so much of everything in South America, it was hard to keep up.

'That's right, just a small show first to get the feel for it and a couple of drinks for courage. We'll have to pace ourselves: some places don't get warmed up till well after midnight.'

'When are we meeting Fernando?' His arms around her. Yum!

'We'll see him in a couple of hours. First, we're going to watch a few shows and have a lesson.'

'But I thought Fernando—'

'Don't worry, he's the main event, but I thought a sneaky lesson would be better than going in cold.'

'Good idea, I want to get up to speed as quickly as possible.'

'Of course you do, darling,' he said.

༺ ༻

As the red velvet curtain closed, the crowd stamped their feet and cheered for an encore. Blimey, tango was so much more than dancing. It had been a whirl of colour, full of smoulderingly sexy women and men who were almost as handsome as Fernando. The steps were complicated and so intimate it was hardly decent. All that squashing together. And soon I'll be doing it with Fernando, she mused.

'Don't you just love it, the drama, the sheer theatre of it all?' Marty was in his element.

'It looks so, well, intense. Are they always like that?' How could she ever look as elegant and sultry as the women she'd just seen?

'Pretty much. Isn't it wonderful? Hey, I found out there's a gay tango club in town. I might slip off there once you're in Fernando's care, would you mind?'

'Not at all. It's amazing how you find these places.' With Marty in another club, she'd be alone with the most handsome man she'd ever seen. 'I don't want to make a fool of myself, Marty. I really like Fernando.'

'Don't worry, babes, it's mostly attitude,' Marty said authoritatively.

'How can I learn attitude in an hour?'

'Well, we can start right now. Hit me with your best sultry look. Imagine being one of those proud Latina *señoras*, then pout.'

'Like this?' Flora puckered up.

'No, that's Bonnie Tyler sucking a lemon. It's more of a super-hot, bitch-babe thing. Have another go.'

Flora closed her eyes for a moment. The best bitch-babes had been in *Dynasty*. She could be Crystal or Alexis, without the shoulder pads.

'Hey, yes, that's it, now straighten up, but look a little bit softer at the same time,' he held her chin. 'Okay, now, head back a little, and – sultry pouting, one and two and three and, hold it! Smoke in the eyes, chin up, back straight, yes, that's it! Now all you need to do is learn the footwork.'

'I'm glad I wore these shoes,' murmured Flora, trying out a saucy strut on the way out.

~ ⚏⚏⚏ ~

When their taxi arrived at the final *milonga*, Fernando was already there, leaning against the doorframe. He stepped forwards, opened the car door and with a smile, offered Flora his hand.

'*Hola de nuevo*, Flora! How was your evening?' He took her hand, looked over to Marty and nodded. 'Don't worry my friend, she is safe with me.'

'Okay, I'll just pop on over to Villa Cabre then, Flora. Look after her, Fernando, she's a very special lady.'

'I know this already,' said Fernando, 'I see fire behind her eyes, passion in her heart.' He was walking tall and proud as they entered the club, his jaw angled, showing off his wonderful profile. She stretched her torso and raised her chin. Immediately she felt more powerful. Right, she said to herself, I'm a woman in control.

'Come, Flora, sit. We can discover each other before we start with the dancing.' Fernando pulled out a chair at a table marked '*reservado*'.

The place was filling up. Couples were on the dance floor practising, stumbling and laughing at their mistakes. The atmosphere was lighthearted on the surface, but underneath it all there was a tangible buzz of pent-up emotion, a charge of something wonderfully exciting.

'So, lovely Flora, tell me, what makes fire in your belly?' Fernando leaned over and placed a perfectly manicured brown hand on her tummy. Luckily, her proud Latina posture temporarily reduced her muffin top to a lower-fat version.

'Oh, um, fire in my belly?' she gulped. The heat of his hand. Electric!

'Yes, what makes passion swirl around inside, what gives you energy, zest for life?' Fernando beckoned to a passing waiter who came over with two glasses of wine. She was trying to think.

'I don't know really.' She felt slightly embarrassed. Where was her passion? 'I'm probably still trying to find it.' Fernando nodded encouragingly. 'I like reading, does that count?'

'It depends. What do you read?'

'Well, I know it's silly,' she gave him a weak smile, 'but I like romances. Historical romance.'

'*Perfecto*! The romance. The history. This is tango!' Fernando hugged her shoulders. 'I knew it! You have the fire inside, you understand desire. You want love, no?'

She felt naked, as though he'd switched a spotlight on her; seen and heard for the very first time. If Marty had been there she probably would have cried. Slightly bewildered, she furtively let the bubbles of emotion seep out as she exhaled and tried to smile at the same time.

'And for the drink of love, we have Malbec, the best red wine in South America.' He raised his glass. 'To your passion, beautiful Flora.' Flora chinked glasses and sipped her drink, glad of the chance to gather herself.

Fernando raised his glass again. 'And tonight your passion will come out and show me everything. You will expose yourself. Your fire, your love, even your anger – all is passion.'

'My goodness, Fernando.' Flora imagined herself stark naked next to his firm thirty-something body and felt quite giddy.

'Do not worry, I will show you my secrets also. We shall expose together, share everything.' Fernando took her hand. 'Come, let us start.'

Under his expert guidance, she soon had the confidence to fully immerse herself and follow his whispered commands.

'*Abrazo*,' Fernando's breath was hot in her ear. '*Entrada*,' he said, sliding his leg between hers. His eyes were closed, seemingly lost in the moment. His long lashes cast a shadow on his cheek. He'd look like that if he were asleep in her hotel room after a dreamy session of horizontal tango.

'Please be careful, Flora, your mind is on holiday.' His voice prompted her back to the crowded dance floor. Concentrate.

The evening was a whirl of music and colour. When they finally sat down for a break, she was out of breath, gently perspiring.

'I can feel you, Flora, your heart, your passion. We are sharing everything, if someone ask me to change partner, I will say no. You are perfect for me. Tonight, we are one.'

'Oh, gosh. I'm not sure I've fully mastered it, but it's really enjoyable,' said Flora, still trying to catch her breath.

'Enjoyable?' Fernando looked at her intently. 'No. You must feel something more. Tango is life! Sad, sexy, sensual, passion, even aggression, it is everything. You must give more Flora. Let go and show everything. You can tell your life story in tango.'

'Yes, I understand. It's just that British people don't let go very easily. I'll try my best.'

'That's good. See how brave you are. I know you have a story still to tell me. Come, we will dance to 'Adios Muchachos', a song from a dying man who must say goodbye. I will be the man, and we will say goodbye.' Fernando led her to the dance floor without waiting for a reply.

It was a slower dance, which gave Fernando the chance to translate some of the words.

'I must say farewell,' he whispered, 'no one can stop destiny.'

Flora hadn't thought of John recently, but knowing the song was about a man at the end of his life, she suddenly found a lump in her throat. Perhaps it was the drink, but the soulful music and the fact Fernando held her close made her realise just how little love there had been in her life. John hadn't said anything nice to her for years; his last words had been 'get out of my way'.

Years of pent-up emotions, her desire for just a little romance, and the ensuing disappointment overwhelmed her with sadness. It wasn't about John as he was, but what he could have been. By the end of the dance, tears were trickling down her face.

'Yes, yes! This is fantastic, Flora. Now you feel everything. You are free.' Fernando steered her back to their table.

'I'm sorry, I don't know what came over me.' Flora dabbed her face with a napkin.

'You must not hide the truth. Truth is passion, and passion is tango.' Fernando called a waiter and placed a final order.

'It is enough for tonight. Soon will be daylight, so we drink one more time together and I will escort you to your hotel.' Suddenly Fernando looked tired and Flora realised he probably had a day job, maybe a wife and family.

When the waiter reappeared, Flora was glad to see there was no alcohol. Fernando set a tall glass down in front of her.

'For you I have *submarino*. Warm milk with the piece of chocolate in the bottom, it tells you the story of our night together. First it is nothing, then the chocolate melts when you must disturb it – just like your heart when you discover your passion. Stir everything together and it becomes complete and delicious. That is life and life is tango.'

'Thank you for a wonderful evening, Fernando, I will remember it,' she fought the urge to cry again, 'and you, for a very long time.'

It was sad she would never know him better, but something important, more intimate than sex had happened that night.

She was exhausted, both mentally and physically. She looked around for her handbag and shawl. It was time for bed. It was only as reality began to seep into her consciousness that she became aware of her aching feet.

TWELVE

Patagonia. Granite spires towering over picture-book landscapes of wild flowers, rocky outcrops and lush green pastures, waterfalls thundering into icy-blue rivers of glacier water. The vast, wind-whipped steppe gradually crumbling into the sea, creating a mass of uninhabited islands. The snow-capped Andes painted a dramatic contrast between a beautifully blue sky and impossibly turquoise water, just as the guide book said.

'Oh, my goddess! Isn't it amazing?' Marty called from the prow of the boat. 'I mean fantastic in the true sense of the word.' Flora remained huddled into her coat. 'Babes? This is awesomely wonderful. Come up and have a proper look, I can see the marble caves in the distance.'

'I've seen enough,' said Flora in a monotone.

'Hey, what do you mean?' Marty sat down next to her. 'You've been off with me since Buenos Aires. Is it because I went to see Evita's grave without you?'

'No, I was too tired to go. It's not that. It's not you, either.'

'Well, something's sucked the sunshine out of you. What's going on?'

'Dunno. I just feel differently about what I'm doing. All this travelling around stuff. What's the point?'

'What's the point? Only the most brilliant experience anyone's ever had. We're doing what virtually everyone on the planet would love to do.'

'But why are we doing it?'

'Well, I think you decided to follow John's list for a few reasons, but the most important one is you owed it to yourself. All that time, just talking about something and never doing it. Years and years of dreaming, and you never went further than Coventry's city centre.'

'I know, but—'

'And maybe it's a lot of money, but what else were you planning to spend it on?'

'It's not about the money. It's about what I'm doing, or not doing.'

'With what?'

'My life. I mean we're on this trip and who knows how long it'll take, but it's not reality. It's an escape. All the time I was married, life was passing me by and now I'm out here in a boat in the middle of this blue lake in a faraway place and life is still passing me by.'

'No, it's not, this *is* life, Flora. And you're living it to the full. Look at all the wonderful places you've seen, the things you've done and the people you've met. That's more than most do in a lifetime and we're not even halfway through yet.'

'But it's not a real, everyday existence with a proper home and a family, is it?' She was feeling tearful again.

'Come here, babes.' Marty put his arm around her. 'No, it's not everyday, but some of us will never have that kind of life and you know what? A lot of people who do have it would swap with you in a heartbeat.'

'I've got nothing,' wailed Flora. 'No children, no proper home, no friends, no job even.'

'Hey, you've got me.' Marty pulled her closer.

'I don't mean you. I mean friends who are girls and my age group. I've never had that, even at school. I thought being married would make me feel better about it, but it just closed everything off. Now look at me.'

'I am looking at you, and I see a brave, kind, beautiful woman who I'm proud to call my best friend, and anyone you care to make friends with would feel the same about you as I do.'

'You're just saying—'

'No, I'm not just saying anything. You've got to give it a chance. When we get back home, you're going to be so different from the person you left behind. Remember her? The Flora who didn't even have a passport and had spent all those years polishing the lino? She's already gone.'

'I suppose so,' sniffed Flora.

'Now get your tango-toned arse upfront and admire the view. You can't help but feel uplifted by the whole glorious magnificence. The eight hours to get here is definitely worth it.'

Flora knew that wasn't the end of it; dancing the tango had been life-changing, just as Fernando had said. Maybe there was still more work to do, to dig deep and find her true passion, something to define who she was. If not a fifty-three-year-old widow, then who was she?

'Come on, Flora,' Marty called, 'life's out here.'

⁓༄⁓

The boat took them through deep fjords and past groaning glaciers to the Cape Horn archipelago, where the world's southernmost forested ecosystem could be crossed off John's list. So they could have their passports stamped with 'the end of the world', Marty had organised a scenic detour to El Fin del Mundo, en route to the airport.

'I've just been to check, and the flights are delayed,' said Marty. He set a tray down on the table. 'But fear not, for I have hot chocolate for my lady, with the best seat in the house. The view is the finest I've ever seen from an airport lounge. Just look at those snowy mountains.'

'I know. Patagonia and especially Ushuaia have been stunning.' Flora sipped her hot chocolate.

'It's going to be a culture shock going from here to Rio, eh?'

'Well, I'm looking forward to being warmer, but I'll miss the wilds of Patagonia, and the people were lovely. Who would have thought they speak Welsh?'

'That tickled you, eh? Especially with your name. I bet there are more Joneses here than in Coventry.'

'That's probably true.'

'But there's only one Flora,' said Marty, giving her a meaningful look.

'Are you saying I'm unique?'

'Yes you are, and don't you forget it.' He squeezed her hand.

Flora knew he was referring to the incident on the boat, and said, 'you know, there's something about feeling very small compared to the huge mountains and glaciers, it puts a lot of things into perspective.'

'It sure does. I felt tiny, like a speck on the planet,' said Marty.

'The thing I realised is the past doesn't matter, life goes on regardless. It's what happens next that counts.'

'Well, look who's being profound today. I'm glad you see it that way, babes. It's made me do a lot of thinking too.'

'What about?' Flora was glad to turn the spotlight on Marty for a change. It wasn't often he talked about himself.

'Well, I've never had a serious relationship. I wasted so much time trying to be someone else, just to please other people.'

'You mean by not being gay?'

'Well, I was always gay, but I knew coming out would break my father's heart. I had to make a choice, you know, between keeping him happy or by being me. In a way, you and me are the same, babes.'

'We are?'

'I mean that we've both made choices that have hurt our parents and we've suffered for it. Neither of us had a proper family relationship once the decision was made.'

'That's true; I never thought of it like that. Once I married John that was it, I couldn't go back. The same for you I expect. You can't get back in the closet once you're out, can you?'

'Not when it took all those years to actually open the door, no.' Marty sighed. 'Maybe I'll meet my true love one day, but it's been tough at times. Being gay in the theatre is fine, it's so full of luvvies I feel at home, but I should've gone to London, tried my luck in the West End – had a proper go at life. At the very least, instead of growing sweet peas at the allotment, I should have joined an evening class or something. Tried to meet a partner. Out here in the wilderness it's easy to see what a mess I'm making by doing nothing much at all.'

'Oh,' said Flora, with a twinge of guilt. She always expected Marty to cheer her up without thinking about what was going on in his life.

'What I'm trying to say is, we all have something that makes us feel the odd one out, and just because I'm all cheerful and make jokes about everything doesn't mean I'm any more sorted than you are, or anyone else for that matter. The only things not screwed up are those mountains out there.'

'I'm sorry I seem to make everything about me. I presumed you were happy with life, but I can see now it's just as hard for you.' Flora paused. 'Hey, I really, really hope you meet someone lovely in Rio. I know he wouldn't be for keeps, but it would be nice to have someone else besides me to enjoy your time there.'

'Yes, I'm pinning my hopes on there being a gay scene. It's hard to know in a Catholic country. But besides that, I can't wait to see the carnival. It's been my dream from the moment I heard about it as a teenager. You're going to love it too. And not just for all the party pizazz. I've booked us a fabulous suite for the two weeks. Top floor, jacuzzi on the balcony, views over the beach.'

'I can't wait either.' Flora picked up the empty cups. 'Shall I get us two more?'

~·♦♦♦·~

Marty made the most of his freedom in Rio – he was either out enjoying the various clubs and bars, or sleeping off the excesses. Flora soon settled in, although having time to herself felt strange at first; virtually every moment of the last few months she'd either been with Marty or on a tour.

The hotel suite was a magnificent statement of extravagance. Apart from their bedrooms, and accompanying luxury en-suite bathrooms, one on either side of the living area, the whole place was open-plan and designed to make the most of the view. A neat, white marble-topped kitchen was set back from a wide dining platform with a glass dining table and velvet button-backed chairs. Three wide steps led down to a lounge area with cream leather sofas positioned to showcase the sweeping views over Copacabana Beach. The entire outer wall was made of sliding glass doors opening onto an *al fresco* dining area. Also on the balcony were a crescent-shaped cocktail bar with four high stools, a spa-plunge pool and sun loungers.

Flora would have been happy to spend the entire two weeks just lounging at the hotel. But she made the most of her personal guide and went on a couple of shopping trips and a few excursions; by the end of the first week she had holidaying alone down to a fine art. After an afternoon in the

145

hotel spa enjoying a hot stone massage, followed by a chilli hot chocolate and a pedicure, she took the lift back up to the suite feeling thoroughly pampered. Later, she would watch a film on the widescreen television and order room service.

As she kicked off her shoes in the lobby, she thought she could hear someone inside. Maybe housekeeping. 'Hello,' called Flora, 'anyone there?' She could hear voices. One sounded like Marty. His unmistakable laugh.

Whatever ran through her mind as she entered the room, she wasn't expecting to see a nut brown, well-toned bottom wiggling backwards and forwards.

'*Um dois,* you see? Now like this, *três quatro,*' said a voice.

A naked Marty was sitting on the sofa facing Flora. He grabbed a cushion and stuffed it into his lap, still laughing.

'Enrique!' he spluttered.

'*Yes? Um dois, três quatro—*'

'Er, hello, I'm sorry to inter—' Flora stopped mid-sentence as Enrique turned around.

'Enrique! This is Flora.' Marty stood up and handed him a cushion. 'You might want to cover up, babes.'

Even with only John's pale and puny body as a point of reference, she knew she was looking at the most perfect naked man she was ever likely to chance upon. And he was beautiful – deep brown eyes and long thick lashes with a sensuous mouth and a toothpaste advertiser's smile. She forced herself not to look down for a full appraisal. But then as he stepped towards her, she furtively skimmed the rest of his physique. Lovely! Well-toned with smooth velvety looking skin.

'Flora, I am Enrique.' He held out his hand, still without covering himself.

'Hello, Enrique, pleased to meet you. You must be Marty's new friend?'

'Sorry, babes, I thought you were at the salon for at least another hour,' said Marty with a sheepish grin. 'I was just having a samba lesson. Um, Enrique, how about you put some clothes on?'

While Enrique walked to the bedroom, Marty's smile broadened. 'So, what do you think? Isn't he gorgeous?'

'He looks like a model, Marty. Where did you find him?'

'It's more the other way round. He found me. Can you believe it? Little old Marty pulls a Latino hottie!'

'Well, why not, and he's lucky to have you as well.' Flora paused. 'What does he do?'

He smiled mischievously and raised an eyebrow.

'For a job, I mean,' she quickly added as Enrique reappeared in tight jeans and a plain white shirt.

'I am, how do you say, the jack-of-all-trades?' he said. 'But most of all I love to dance. Will you come dancing with us, Flora?'

'Oh, no, I don't like to intrude. You two need to get to know each other.'

'We're already quite well acquainted,' said Marty, laughing. 'We met on my first night out, actually in the first club I visited, isn't that lucky? Why not come tonight? He's performing there for a couple of hours, so you can keep me company.'

'Well, I was going to watch a film and—'

Enrique walked over and took her hand. Brazilians were so tactile. 'You can watch movies when you are old, Flora,' he said. His big brown eyes seemed to envelop her. 'Now you are young and beautiful, you must enjoy. Come. Marty is right, I have to work, so you must look after him for me.'

'I suppose I could, just for a while—'

Marty began walking backwards towards his room with the cushion still firmly in place. 'How about the yellow chiffon and those gorgeous tassel earrings?'

'Oh, I like the sound of that. May I see your clothes, Flora?' Enrique was already heading to her room, pulling her with him.

'Of course,' said Flora, feeling a bit giddy.

～⁂～

The club was busy, but there was already a table reserved at the front for Marty. Enrique had gone to get ready.

'I can't believe it, babes. I think I'm in love.' Marty was pouring Flora a glass of champagne. 'He's totally gorgeous, a fantastic lover and to top it off, he's in showbiz! I have to keep pinching myself.'

'He's your prince, Marty. Did you meet him in here?'

'Yes, I was sitting near the back, just watching the show. I spotted him on stage. He had these little sequinned silver shorts on. I couldn't take my eyes off him. I never thought he'd end up with me. I just sort of daydreamed about buying him a drink after the show, but I didn't know if he was going to come out front.'

'Oh, how romantic,' said Flora.

'Anyway, after the show, a few of the dancers started to filter out, so I hung around and waited. Just when I thought he must have left by the stage door, he came through and walked straight over to me.'

'Wow! Just like that? Amazing.'

'I know. I couldn't believe it. I still can't. I'm completely smitten.'

'I'm so pleased for you, Marty. It just goes to show how love conquers all.'

As the lights went down and the show began, Flora was lost in thought; she had feelings she couldn't quite work out. Enrique appeared to be perfect in every way and Marty was the happiest she'd ever seen him. It seemed so easy for him; to just go to a club, meet the man of his dreams and fall in love. As a middle-aged woman, the chances of that happening to her were close to zero.

After the show, Enrique joined them at the bar and suggested going on to a nightclub. Looking around at the mixture of tourists and locals, all seemingly in couples, Flora felt out of place now they were a group of three. And going to a club where Marty and Enrique would obviously want to dance together made up her mind. Despite their protests, she insisted on going back to the hotel.

'Well, only if you're sure,' said Marty. 'Promise you're not going because of Enrique and me?'

'Absolutely,' she fibbed, 'I've had a lovely time, but I'm really tired. You go and dance the night away.'

Enrique gallantly hailed a taxi and spoke to the driver in Portuguese.

He opened the back door. 'Here, for you, lovely Flora. He is friend – no need for paying anything. He will take you to your hotel and see you are safe inside.'

'Are you sure you don't want to come?' Marty put his arm around her. 'It'll be so much fun. The clubs here are crazy.'

'It's okay, I'm looking forward to a quiet night. You two lovebirds go and enjoy yourselves.'

'Okay, babes. I hope you don't mind if Enrique comes back with me?'

'Of course. Just don't wake me up if you're going to have another samba lesson.'

They both laughed at this. Had she accidentally insinuated something else?

Enrique hugged her for a few seconds longer than she expected, which was rather nice. Then, still holding her shoulders as he spoke he said, 'I am so happy to meet the beautiful lady Marty is always talking about. You know, sometimes I feel quite jealous.' He laughed and then kissed her on both cheeks. 'Tomorrow, I hope I can know you better. Bye for now. *Tchau*!'

'*Tchau*, Enrique,' said Flora, rather pleased with her pronunciation. 'Bye, Marty, have fun. Don't do anything I wouldn't do.' She laughed waved and smiled from the taxi while wishing it were her standing on the pavement with a lovely man of her own.

THIRTEEN

Flora awoke to the sound of someone singing. It wasn't Marty – despite being keen on musicals, he wasn't very tuneful. Neither was she; 'caterwauling' is how John had described her attempts. It must be Enrique. She pulled on her Chinese silk robe. Even if he didn't mind being naked, she preferred to cover up.

'*Bom dia*, beautiful lady.'

'Good morning.' She was slightly disappointed to see him fully dressed in Marty's white sailing shorts and black silk shirt. How nice though, sharing clothes.

'I am making breakfast on the terrace, please to join me? Marty is sleeping. He put all his energy into dancing last night. Now he is like a baby.'

'Oh, he's probably exhausted. I expect he told you, he's been looking after me all this time. It's his turn to relax, so I'm glad he's still asleep.'

'I have *pão de queijo* from the market. Our special cheese bread. And you must try this smoothie with *acai* and *guaraná*.'

'It looks delicious, thank you, Enrique. How was your night?'

'Last night I was so happy to dance. Not here, I am sorry for that.'

'Don't be sorry,' she said hastily, trying not to picture his pert, wiggling bottom.

'I mean to perform at the club with you and Marty watching; it made my heart sing. I was so happy to show you.'

'You were great. Superb. How was the nightclub?'

'It was okay but is not so great. More better, I talk with you. So now I make breakfast, we can sit together.'

'That's nice,' said Flora. 'Do you think Marty wants some?'

'Let him sleep. We can go for lunch together. I know the perfect place, – is belonging to my uncle. He makes the best *moqueca* in Brazil. It is like a fish stew we serve with the rice, *farofa* dumplings and *pirão*. Please come and honour my family.'

'I would love to.' Flora was delighted to be invited; she was conscious of invading their space, but if Enrique was okay with it, she was sure Marty would be.

'So now it is just you and me together, we can talk. I want to hear everything about you.' Enrique poured her coffee and passed the basket of cheese rolls. 'Please try. They go together like, how do you say, love and marriage.'

Flora enjoyed talking to Enrique, he was so interested in everything she had to say and had a way of making her feel relaxed. She didn't mind his lack of personal boundaries, the probing questions he asked, and the way he seemed to touch her all the time.

'So, we must find you a good man. Marty says you are widow. I am sorry to know this, it breaks my heart to see a beautiful lady by herself.'

To be called beautiful by someone who was possibly the most beautiful person in the world was thrilling, even if it wasn't true. 'Well, I must confess, I do feel a bit lonely at times. I wonder what the future holds, you know, when we get back to Coventry.'

'Maybe you never return there. Perhaps I can find you a nice Brazilian man, who will love you and take care of you? Would you like that?'

'Well, I—'

'If you don't mind, maybe I can introduce you? There are a lot of bad men here, in Rio, you must be careful, but also some of the best men in the world. You are the delicate flower. You are *florzinha*, little flower – you need sunshine to grow, no?'

'I don't know about that, but I do dream of meeting my Prince Charming one day. I'm a great believer in romance and living happily ever after. I had hoped I'd do that with John, my husband, but right from the start he was wrong for me.'

'Yes, Marty tell me. Very wrong. I am sorry to say, but he did not see your true heart.'

'Hey, why didn't you wake me?' Marty stepped onto the balcony. He kissed Enrique on the cheek and did the same to Flora. 'I just came to say good morning, but I need to hop in the shower.'

'Good morning, handsome man,' said Enrique, jumping up. 'Shall I get you some coffee? I think you need it.'

'Yes please, babes. *Dois minutos*, first I need to *tomar um banho*,' Marty called after him, then to Flora he said, 'You see how fluent I am? It's amazing how much easier it is to learn the lingo when there's a gorgeous guy on the receiving end.'

'Well, on that subject, Enrique says he might introduce me to some nice friends of his. What do you think, have you met any of them?'

'No, I haven't but if they're anything like him, you're in for a long-overdue treat.' Marty patted her shoulder affectionately and went back to his room. Flora felt a warm fuzzy buzz of excitement. Rio was turning out well, after all.

When Enrique returned with fresh coffee, she asked him if he might keep in touch with Marty after they leave – perhaps he could join them for some later part of the tour?

'Oh, Flora, already my heart has been heavy about this. I have been praying to Christ the Redeemer on Corcovado Mountain to just have a little longer with Marty. If only it won't be over so soon.' A tear was trickling down his face.

She passed him a napkin. Marty was undoubtedly smitten with him too, but everything was already booked. 'Our next stop is New Zealand. You're very welcome to join us there, or maybe China?'

'Is not possible. I have to work. If only you could stay longer?'

'I wish we could too, but two weeks is all we have, and Rio isn't meant to be a big part of the trip; it was just for Marty.'

'You don't love Rio?'

'Yes, of course I do, and I've really enjoyed meeting you too, but our tickets are booked, I don't think we can change them.'

'My sister works in a tourist office, maybe I can ask her if it's possible?'

'Well, I suppose there's no harm in asking, but I—'

'And we keep it a surprise for Marty, yes?' He kissed her on both cheeks, as though to seal the deal, then sat down quickly as Marty reappeared. Flora caught his furtive wink and under the table, he squeezed her hand.

'What's going on? I heard my name being mentioned.' Marty looked at Enrique and then Flora. 'You two are up to something, I can tell.'

'Flora was just telling me what a great friend you are, and I agree with her, that's all,' said Enrique as he poured the coffee.

⁓◦◦⁓

Around midday, they caught a cab and drove away from Copacabana towards the foothills of Rio. On the way, Enrique talked excitedly about his uncle's restaurant, saying how no one cooked better, not even his mother. When they pulled up outside a simple single story building, Uncle Gabino was already waiting and hurried over to greet them with open arms. Talking all the while, he ushered them to a table overlooking the city, with views of the sea beyond.

'Ah, you have come for my famous *moqueca*. I will cook especially for you the whole meal myself. Please sit. Jago will take good care of you. I will go to the kitchen and prepare a feast for you.'

Flora looked around at the other diners and said, 'Enrique, your uncle doesn't need to cook especially for us, we'll have what everyone else has.'

'If you do that you will insult him, he is a proud man. Any friends of mine are family. Please, enjoy.' Enrique turned to speak to Jago the waiter in rapid Portuguese.

Flora discreetly elbowed Marty. 'Look at him. Brazilian men are so yummy.'

'Enrique? Yes, I know, he's a living god.'

'No, not him, well, yes him, but I meant our waiter,' said Flora.

'Hm, yes, he's pretty handsome for an older man. Enrique will look a bit like him in ten or twenty years' time.'

'What's his name again?'

'I think it's Jago,' said Marty.

'Do you think he's single?'

'Hey, babes, do I detect the twang of cupid's bow? Let me find out.'

'But don't say I asked.'

When Enrique turned back to the table, she stood up. 'I'm just nipping to the *Señora*s to powder my nose,' she said, giving Marty a nod as she left the table.

In the sanctuary of the ladies' loo she scrutinised her face in the mirror. Not bad for the wrong side of fifty. Thanks to Marty, she could easily pass for ten years younger. How old was Jago, the waiter? Marty was right – life was for living. If he was at all interested, she was going to go for it. And if 'it' included having a dalliance in the boudoir, then why not? She'd soon be back in gloomy old Coventry, stuck on her own. Best make the most of it.

Back at the table, the first course was already waiting.

'Wow, this all looks amazing. What is it?'

'Well, it's a mixture of things to try before the main event,' said Marty. 'These palm hearts wrapped in bacon are delicious, you dip them in the sauce. I've already had one, sorry, I couldn't wait.' He guided her through the other small tasting dishes. Rio had the best food and such good-looking men. Boom bang a bang!

Plates were cleared, more dishes arrived. Flora furtively stalked her heart's desire, noting his agile ease, carrying trays high above his head while twisting and weaving between tables. Now and again Uncle Gabino emerged from the kitchen to explain a dish in detail, how the sauce was unique to the village where he grew up or how his own secret ingredient made all the difference. When he switched languages to talk to Enrique, Flora seized the moment.

'Marty,' she whispered, 'have you asked Enrique about Jago?'

'I'm sorry, babes, he said he didn't know but he will find out. He was going to ask his Uncle there and then, but I told him to be discreet.'

'Oh right, well, discreet is good, but I hope he gets on with it, you know while we're still here. He's yummilicious.'

They were nearing the end of the meal. Several times Jago had smiled at her and she smiled back. There was a connection. Smokey Brooks and Cal the Canadian had been ages ago – she'd learned a lot about herself since then, and was much more confident.

'*Bolo de rolo*,' said Jago, setting down a dish in front of her.

'Roly-poly?' said Flora. It looked similar.

'I'm sorry, you want roly-poly?' Oh, hello! Was this sexy banter?

Oblivious to her smirk, he explained the thin layers of cake and guava paste, rolled together. 'Soaked in *porto, bolo de rolo* is our most famous dessert.' Even their roly-poly was better. Exotic.

Jago said something to Enrique, then reverted to English. 'Please enjoy the rest of your meal, I have to leave now.' With a warm smile in Flora's direction and a nod to Marty, he said goodbye.

'That's a shame,' said Flora, 'he was lovely.' Beautiful hands.

'Yes, I'm sorry he had to leave before the end,' said Enrique. 'It's not usual to do this but he must help with the carnival preparation.'

'He's a dancer?' Flora asked a little too quickly.

'No, he is working on the construction.'

'I hadn't thought of that,' said Flora. 'Building all the displays, I mean. How do you put them all together?'

'Oh, we have a warehouse. It takes a lot of organisation, almost a year. But Rio has the best carnival in the world, we must work until everything is perfect.'

'I'd love to see behind the scenes,' said Marty. 'I can't wait for the actual carnival, but to be backstage where all the buzz is going on must be amazing.'

'It is not for tourists. I'm sorry, I mean it's just for us to prepare without distraction. Like Jago, we all have normal jobs, then build the set and rehearse in our free time.' He glanced at Marty who was making puppy-dog eyes at him. 'Hey, stop it!'

'Pleeaase!'

Enrique tried to ignore him. 'Also each display is a secret. It is a competition, so it is not possible to show outsiders.'

'But we're insiders. Marty's with you, and so am I.' Flora held back from adding Jago's name.

'Please, please, please make my day, darling, lovely boy. My whole year.' Marty flung an arm around him, his face more doleful than ever.

Finally Enrique laughed. 'Okay. I can't promise, but let me speak to someone.'

～∞))∞～

'So all the samba schools are taking part?' Flora almost shouted over the cacophony of drums and whistles accompanying the dance rehearsal.

'Yes, even after we leave the school, we are still a community. We are family.'

Enrique and Marty were walking towards a large, solid-looking sliding door, Flora quickly scanned the room for Jago before following them. On the other side, the surdo and snare drums provided a muffled, frantic back-beat to the heavy rhythm of sawing and hammering, shouting set-builders. They passed an intense conversation between two women wrestling with an oversized pineapple, through another sliding door, and they were in the relative calm of the costume department.

'Our theme is The Creation. We have the best *carnavalesca* in Rio. These are all the drawings,' said Enrique, pointing to the walls, covered with detailed sketches, bordered by swatches of fabric, ribbon, sequins and feathers. Marty had his hand at his mouth. Speechless. 'Here is Adam and this is Eve. The serpent is almost twelve metres.' Thousands of gold and white sequins sewn together for a realistic interpretation of snakeskin. Red illuminated eyes, and a forked tongue connected to a complicated-looking hydraulic mechanism. The creature would be set on a moving base for added theatre.

'Oh my goddess.' Marty studied each illustration with the intensity of an art lover.

'And over here is the result.' Enrique drew back polythene curtains as he spoke. 'Each costume is months of work and costs many thousands.'

'Oh, Flora, look.' Marty grabbed her sleeve. 'The detail. And feel this. I can't quite believe it.' He was gently stroking the first garment, inspecting the stitching.

He had tears in his eyes. 'The Garden of Eden,' he whispered.

What did it feel like to be so passionate about something, she wondered. He had swapped a job in the theatre to share her quest and complete John's geography field trip, but only on the condition it included two weeks in Rio. Now she could see how much it meant to him, she understood why he had insisted on adding it to the list.

Enrique was explaining how many thousand sequins were in Eve's headdress, the consideration of weight and the skill needed to dance on a moving platform. Judging by the overloaded racks of costumes, they were going to be there for ages. When would they get to Jago? She wandered around, half-listening to Enrique while the dazzling array of bling and feathers saturated her senses.

'Wow, making the float must be like building a house,' she interjected.

'Bigger than many houses, you can see for yourself.' He opened a side door, ushered her through, then looked around for Marty. 'I will go and get him, I think he's gone back to the headdresses.'

Flora stepped into a jungle of scaled-up foliage; every giant leaf and petal was full of detail. The sheer scale and imagination were impressive.

'Hello?' A voice from behind a clump of lilies. 'Lovely lady from the restaurant, yes?'

'Do you mean me?' said Flora. There was no one else there.

'Yes, please wait there. I am coming.' Jago? Who else could it be?

A hand on her shoulder made her spin around. 'Hello again. Can I show you everything?'

'Oh. Yes.' Her heart was beating double time. Daisies spun around her tummy. Hold it together, girl. 'Yes, please, it's beautiful.'

'Just like you, if you don't mind me to say so.' He held out his hand 'I am sorry I forget my manners. I am Jago.'

'I'm Flora.' She wrestled a nervy laugh into a smile. Lovely firm handshake. Manly.

'Flora. It means a beautiful flower, no? You belong here, in our garden.'

'It's lovely to meet you properly, Jago. I mean not at the restaurant but here at this amazing place, I'm completely in awe of what you're doing. Did you make the lilies?' Stop gabbling. Nerves. Hopefully, it would pass as a cultural difference.

'No, I am not artist, I am in charge of, how you say, *mecânica*. Mechanic? Can I show you how I make the flower open and move?'

'Oh, yes please.' Perhaps you could open my flower too. Stop it!

Jago held out his hand. 'Come with me. Please take care, everything is made of paper.' He pulled Flora up onto the platform, into the middle of the garden.

'You see the dot on the grass? The dancer must stand here. Enrique will be higher up, near the front. He's one of the best.'

'Oh yes, he's very good, I've seen him dancing.' How could she forget his naked bottom? What about Jago's? He was older but more muscular with such lovely smooth caramel skin. His tee-shirt was ripped at the shoulder. Strangely sexy. When he bent down, she caught a glimpse of a hairy chest. Yum.

'Here.' He grasped the huge petals of a lily and pulled. 'The person underneath can control, to open like this.' Jago gently opened the flower. 'If you don't mind to come underneath, I can show you how I do it.' Jago was already at the edge of the platform. He helped her climb back down, parted the grass curtain and ducked underneath the structure. It was almost dark inside. She was close to other people – she could hear them talking, hammering the odd nail, shouting orders – yet also alone in the semi-darkness with Jago. When he took her hand and guided it towards an overhead lever, her knees almost gave way.

'Hold the handle and gently pull down.' He smelt of work – sweat, paint and sawdust.

'Like this?' The warmth of Jago's body behind her. His breath on her neck.

'Let me help you.' He spoke softly. 'Now gently pull so the flower will open.' He exhaled slowly into her ear. His chest pressed gently on her back. All she had to do was turn around.

And so she did.

Jago's arms closed around her. His mouth brushed hers.

'You must tell me to stop,' he whispered.

Her body was trembling. No words. She stood on tiptoes to make it easier for him.

Was this French kissing? It seemed natural to let her tongue join in. Tickling, teasing, wonderfulness. Don't stop, please don't stop. She pulled him closer. She wanted his taste, his smell. Everything.

How long did it last, minutes? At least two minutes of blissful, floaty heaven.

'Can I call for you tomorrow evening? I am sorry, but now I must work. We must complete everything today.'

'Yes. Please,' said Flora, still dazed by what had happened.

~•~

The next day seemed to pass at an agonisingly slow pace. All Flora could think about was Jago.

'I keep having flashbacks. I can't tell you how dreamy it was.' Flora was perching on a kitchen stool while Marty made a pot of tea. 'He's the best kisser in the world.'

'I think he's into you, babes. Did you see the way he looked when we were leaving?'

'And now I'm going on an actual date. He's just so gorgeous, I can't stop thinking about him. You know what? I know it's a bit soon, but if he asked me to sleep with him I'd seriously think about it.' Definitely would.

'Ooh la la! That's up to you, you're a grown woman. You've plenty of making up to do.'

'I know it's early days, but I think I'm in love. I can't even breathe properly and my heart's all of a flutter. Oh Marty, he's a dream come true.' And, if the kiss was anything to go by, an amazing lover.

Marty carried the tea tray out to the balcony. 'I can see you're smitten, but try not to fall in love properly. I'm already in too deep with Enrique, and we're leaving in a few days.'

'Perhaps not.'

'What?'

'Oh, nothing, it's just, well, we could always come back. After the trip. There's no need to spend the rest of your days in Coventry.'

'Well, I definitely won't be doing that. Maybe I could get a job here. Something to do with costume would be amazing.'

The conversation drifted back and forth; the costumes, the carnival, Jago, Uncle Gabino's lovely lunch, then back to Jago. Another cup of tea and a dip in the jacuzzi helped to fill the agonising wait for Enrique's return from his afternoon shift.

When the conversation ran dry, Marty picked up a magazine and Flora said, 'I think I'll have a little lie-down.'

'Good idea, babes. I'll wake you up in plenty of time to get ready. We need you looking your best,' Marty grinned.

'We certainly do, if I'm ever to do the horizontal tango. Or the samba.'

'It's all the same when you're lying down,' Marty called after her.

Flora lay on her back. She was too excited to sleep. Jago. Perhaps he'd try to seduce her. She could resist a little at first, play the game, enjoy the attention. And then? She had nothing to compare him with. Not John. His seduction technique had been simply to marry her. At eighteen and still a virgin, she'd wanted to experience Lady Chatterley's muted 'strange thrills': at the time, sex was about all she could think of.

She'd thought John would woo her first. How naive. After the registry office wedding and a pub meal, they'd walked home from the bus stop. She'd made him carry her over the threshold of number ninety-three, then all giggles and nerves, she had dashed upstairs to gather her thoughts.

The bathroom whiffed of mildew and cold tar soap. She stood on tiptoes to fully see her married face in the mirror – that cabinet never did get moved down: John said it was the perfect height for inspecting his nose hair. The whole place needed a freshen up, a feminine touch, but on her wedding day, nothing mattered more than easing her new rubbery diaphragm into place and reapplying her lipstick. Perhaps he'd ravish her on the sofa.

Back downstairs John had said, 'How about a nice glass of sherry? It's Bristol Cream.'

'Oh, *rah-ther.*' She said, hoping to sound like Madeleine Carroll in *The Prisoner of Zenda*; if only I smoked, she thought, I could light a pink cocktail cigarette and lounge in a sophisticated pose. John passed her drink and poured himself a Double Diamond.

'Here's to us! Mr and Mrs Marshall,' John said, raising his glass.

'To us.' Flora quickly sipped her sherry. It tasted like the smell, only stronger.

John drank his beer and drummed a silent tune on the antimacassar. They had chatted all the way home on the bus, but now it was awkward.

She burst into half-singing the advert, '*Double Diamond works wonders, works wonders!*' She wished she hadn't. He didn't laugh. Nerves. His naked body next to her. His penis. Erect? She'd only seen diagrams. Recent bouts of heavy petting, albeit still fully clothed and in the standing-up position, suggested he was an experienced lover, which was both thrilling and terror-inducing in equal measures.

The clock ticked on the mantelpiece.

Somewhere an ice-cream van chimed the first tinny notes of 'Greensleeves'.

Flora fiddled with her glass and then moved a hand onto John's knee and cleared her throat.

'It's been a smashing day, hasn't it?' she said.

John nodded and said, 'That photograph'd better come out alright – ten shillings is a scandal.'

'Yes, but we'll have two copies. One for us and one for Mum and Dad.' She hoped for a reconciliation, perhaps when a grandchild was on the way; then she'd give them the picture. 'I'll get a nice frame from Woolies,' she added, half to herself.

John did a pretend yawn. Flora laughed nervously and topped his glass up a bit too fast so there was a head of froth.

When he took a drink, it left him with a thin white moustache. She imagined licking it off.

Eventually, he said, 'You'd best go and get ready then.'

She hurried upstairs. Oh my giddy aunt, here we go! She opened a new bar of lavender soap to wash her underarms – no-one wants a sweaty bride – then brushed her teeth for the full two minutes and put on her new satinette midi nightdress. She shuffled over to the middle of the bed and arranged herself in an alluring pose, ready for the seduction to begin.

She heard John rinsing their glasses at the kitchen sink, then locking the front door and slowly climbing the stairs. As he pushed open the bedroom door, Flora tried to pout and look out under her lashes at the same time. He switched off the light before he could appreciate the combined effect or the way she'd spread her hair on the pillow.

He undressed in the dark, then pulled back the blankets and climbed straight on top of her. He covered her face with clumsy wet kisses, simultaneously smearing her with perspiration from his upper lip.

'Now, let's get on with it shall we, Mrs Marshall?' he slurred. With a clammy hand, he fumbled for the hem of her nightie and pulled it up to her waist.

The sharp pain of penetration dulled into a numb throb as he relentlessly jabbed into her. With hot, beery breath and gargled grunts, he sounded more like a frenzied animal fighting with itself than the thoughtful lover she had hoped for.

And then, with one final thrust, it was over.

He collapsed on top of her and soon began to snore. Flora struggled to breathe as she lay in a patch of cooling semen, still waiting for the exquisite moment to begin. That night formed the stencil for any future lovemaking. Despite being married for thirty-five years, she had never been naked next to a man, let alone experienced Lady Chatterley's 'strange thrills'.

~ஐஜ஠~

Flora awoke from her afternoon nap to hear Marty attempting to sing 'Bohemian Rhapsody' in the shower. She found Enrique on the balcony.

'Hello, lovely Flora.' He kissed her cheek and whispered, 'I have good news.'

'About the tickets?' she whispered back, enjoying the charade.

'Yes, is possible for you to change. My sister, she says it is easy for you to do – just with the internet and it is simple. My sister says you must take care with your credit card. There are many bad people try to steal your money. Make sure you have all correct information and double-checking the flight. Be careful with your credit card number. You must print everything for safety also.'

At the word internet, she more or less stopped listening. The idea of using a computer was about as possible as flying the plane herself. Marty did all that.

'Oh no, I don't feel confident using a computer. Could you help? There's one downstairs in the hotel. We could sneak down there while Marty's asleep.'

'I am dancer, Flora. I love to dance, but I am a dancer because I do not go enough times to school. I am sorry, I cannot help.' He paused and swallowed, his voice cracking slightly when he continued. 'Every time I think of you and Marty leaving, it breaks my heart. But you must fly to New Zealand in five, no, four days. It is fate.'

Twenty-four hours ago, before The Kiss, she would have agreed. 'No, it isn't! I'm sure there's another way. What about your sister? Can she help us?'

'Maybe she can, I will ask.' Enrique cut the conversation short with a staged, 'Shhh!' as Marty appeared in the doorway.

'What are you two whispering about? You can't have secrets unless you include me.' He slipped into the middle seat and flung an arm around each of them.

The suggestion of a double date had been a relief. She liked Jago too much for anything to go wrong. With Marty there, the conversation would flow, and later if all went well, he and Enrique had promised to disappear. Nerves tangled with excitement until she felt slightly queasy. This was it: her very own Brazilian prince had invited her on a date – not someone hired by Marty and not a Canadian love cheat. This time it was for real.

Could he be her happy ever after? Flora and Jago had a nice ring to it. She and Marty could move out to Rio. No, it was silly to think so far ahead. She'd settle for just another kiss, maybe more. Definitely more.

What about condoms? Should she be a modern lover and get some? Kissing seemed to be under control, but what about the other stuff, would all her bits be in good working order? After all, twenty-five or so years was a long time. Houses go derelict in that time. Dry rot sets in. And what 'extras' would he expect her to do? The things people got up to these days. She'd only ever read about them.

There had been a time when she tried to rekindle her dwindling sex life with John. Glossy magazines, liberated from the doctor's waiting room, virtually shouted at her to do it. '*Sex After Marriage*'. '*Claim Your Orgasm*'. '*Dare to Be Desired*'. She had admired the photograph of a bare-bottomed wife in her husband's black silk pyjama top, hair piled up in a messy yet sexy up-do. It was worth a try. She wouldn't bother with the stilettos, they might rip the sheets and she'd never wear them outside the house. A pair of black stockings would do and instead of John's blue and white, flannelette pyjama top she found a black nylon baby-doll nightie in a charity shop. Slightly see-through. Alluring, not sluttish. She waited for the end of the *News at Ten* to make her entrance. Standing in the doorway, she struck a *Cabaret*-style pose. He still had the remote control in his hand.

'Let's make love,' she said, puckering her Tangerine Dream lips.

'What on earth are you playing at?'

She had expected that. The article said, *Take control, surprise him*. She sashayed towards his armchair in her imaginary patent leather stilettos. 'Come with me,' she said, pulling him up by his tie.

'Have you taken leave of your senses?'

'You know you want to.' She tried a saucy wink. It seemed to work wonders in the photo. Be cheeky, they said.

'For goodness sake, Flora.' He batted her hand away with the remote.

'Who's a naughty boy?' Her voice was spot on. Husky. 'You need to be punished.'

'I most certainly do not. Stop this nonsense at once.'

She wavered. Discover his desires, cajole, tantalise. Tease. It had sounded so easy.

'And what's this ridiculous get-up?' He prodded her baby doll. 'You look like a trollop.'

It had taken years to realise she had the right technique, but the wrong man. John had always been more interested in propagating his dahlias than exploring his sexual boundaries.

~~~

When Flora and Marty arrived at the club, Enrique was already backstage and Jago was waiting at a table near the front with a bottle of Cava on ice and three glasses. Jeans and a crisp white shirt had transformed him from a worker to a romancer. Even more handsome. He stood up as they approached, kissed Flora's hand and pulled out the chair next to him. The glitter ball lighting made his eyes shine, and a thick gold chain around his neck twinkled. She caught a waft of rich, spicy cologne. Like Christmas, but better.

The club had squeezed extra tables and chairs indecently close together in order to maximise the harvest of carnival tourists. Being shoulder to shoulder with unknown neighbours provided Jago with every good reason to put his arm around Flora. With Marty on her other side, she was firmly wedged.

'Hey, I'm in a manwich.' She'd never understood the word until then and seeing Jago's puzzled expression, quickly explained the joke.

'So, can I eat you?' Jago whispered into her ear.

The warmth of his body, pressing against her capri pants, sent delicious tingles up her thigh. Did he feel it too? Bubbles of excitement whizzed around her body, forcing out an involuntary giggle at almost everything he said. In between stilted conversation he filled the silence by twirling her hair, or occasionally squeezing her shoulder. Now and then during the show, he leaned in and nuzzled her neck. He was so at ease, they could already have been together for ever. When the curtain closed on Enrique's finale, he led Flora towards the exit. Holding her hand like a proper boyfriend, they waited outside the stage door.

When Enrique appeared, he shook Jago's hand and kissed Flora on both cheeks. 'So exciting, now we are all together. I'm starving, shall we go to Siqueira? I know the owners, they do the best *picanha*.'

Jago was already scanning the rows of motorbikes. 'Flora, will you ride with me?'

'On your motorbike? I, er, I don't know.' She looked at Marty.

'It's okay, babes. It'll be fine.'

'I've never been on a motorbike before—'

'Tonight we will do many things for the first time.' Jago smiled as he took a helmet from Enrique, eased it onto her head and fastened the chin strap. 'Now, you must hold me. I will be careful.'

'We'll see you there,' shouted Marty as they roared into the traffic.

At first, all she could think about was clutching her handbag while keeping a grip on Jago. As they zoomed past the neon-lit bars and clubs along Copacabana Beach, she relaxed enough to look around and enjoy the thrill of hugging a handsome man while overtaking gridlocked taxis. The revving engine, wind on her face and somewhat pleasurable sensation of Jago almost sitting on her lap were a strangely liberating combination.

Siqueira was heaving with locals, high on the pre-carnival vibe; they greeted Jago and Enrique like long-lost brothers with animated exchanges and slaps on the back. Flora followed them, feeling slightly overwhelmed. No one was speaking English. Already seated in the middle of a long trestle table, she tried to catch Marty's attention, but he had struck up a conversation in faltering Portuguese with an elderly woman. Both were laughing at something he'd said. Jago was talking to a group of men nearby. Enrique was at the bar.

Waiters in black tee-shirts began circling the tables with walking-stick sized skewers sizzling with hunks of meat. What was it with men and barbecues? Her idea of a dream date would have been a candlelit table for two at a little place down by the harbour. Somewhere they could chat. Flirt. There hadn't been much of an opportunity to talk so far and now Jago was sitting opposite her, still chatting to men on a neighbouring table. At least when the tip of a giant skewer was thrust into a metal groove at their table Jago stopped talking and smiled at her while the waiter carved the sizzling meat.

As Flora helped herself to a sausage, Jago said, 'You must have the *picanha*,' while loading his plate with several slices. 'Brazilian men like meat.'

'And what else do they like?' He had virtually ignored her since arriving.

'Most important is beautiful ladies. They come before the meat and the samba dancing.' He was already eating. Using his knife to point, he added, 'This is why I bring you here. I have everything I love all together.'

He said love! He didn't mean it properly, of course, but maybe he felt something. Never mind that he hadn't talked to her very much, he'd been working hard – she shouldn't begrudge him time to chat with his friends. Anyway, now the food had arrived everyone seemed to have calmed down. The skewers came round twice more before Enrique and Jago held up their hands in defeat. Marty had tried a bit of everything but Flora only had a taste of the famous beef to keep Jago happy.

'Now we will dance.' He held out his hand.

'I'm not very good.' She'd learned the basics from Enrique – hopefully it was enough.

'Don't worry, is just for pleasure. I want to see your body move.'

Luckily she'd paired the capris with a floaty silk shirt to hide the Jelly Baby belly she'd never managed to shift. Jago guided her through the basic steps. He wasn't the teacher Fernando had been, but he manoeuvred her this way and that until she was able to add a cheeky bottom wiggle to her quick-quick-slow, quick-quick-slow. If only she'd worn comfortable shoes. She'd chosen the strappy heels simply to add inches to her kissing height.

'Let's sit down for a moment.' How much had she drunk? Who cares, she was a dancing diva. 'Hey, Marty, did you see me?'

'Yes, you're finding your groove,' Marty laughed.

'How about you and Enrique? Why aren't you up there?'

'It's not the right place, babes, not for us, but we're thinking of going on to a club. You two fancy a bit more dancing, a few cocktails?'

'Or maybe somewhere more quiet. To talk?' Jago winked.

'Oh, yes, talking. No more dancing. My feet are killing me.' She linked her arm through Jago's. 'Perhaps you could motorbike us back to the hotel?'

~∞∞∞~

As the lights streamed past and the engine thrummed, her mind turned to what might happen next. Was tonight the night? She'd suggest a drink in the suite, then pop into the bedroom and 'slip into something more comfortable' – just like they did in films.

The Chinese silk dressing gown with not much underneath should do the trick.

At the hotel Jago walked towards the lift without waiting for Flora's invitation. Once inside the penthouse, she was still wondering how to suggest 'slipping into something more comfortable' when a warm hand steered her towards the sofa.

'Lie down, take off your shoes,' he said, turning to delve in the minibar. Then, he handed her a large brandy and, as she took a sip, he began massaging her dance-weary toes.

'Oh, stop, it tickles,' she laughed, not knowing what else to say. Should she resist his advances? Play hard to get, or was it too late for games?

'Shh, please relax. Close your eyes.' He leaned over, kissed her ear and whispered, 'Now I will love you.

FOURTEEN

Soft, floating, sleepy bliss and the slow, reassuring inhale and exhale of her lover. So this was spooning. John had always kept to his side of the bed, even in the early days. Flora hadn't known how much she craved physical contact until she'd awoken to find Jago's strong, hairy arm casually thrown around her. His warm, naked body pressing into hers, radiating a sense of belonging, security, maybe even love.

He shifted position slightly, then he was licking her ear, sucking it. Oh, lovely! Pretend to be asleep. She enjoyed a few moments of delightful ravishment until an involuntary moan gave her away.

'I am sorry to go, my Flora, but I must hurry. The carnival—'

'Oh. But first can we—'

'I wish also. You have done something to make me want you more and more. Last night you were sensational.'

'I was?' She sat up a little.

'Oh yes, you give me the *sensação especial* – I don't know how to say such a good sexy time. I wish to see you again, but is not possible.' Jago was already pulling on his jeans. Flora gazed longingly at his disappearing thighs.

'Not possible tonight?'

'I want more than anything in my life, but the carnival is big crazy time. I must help my team, then work in restaurant. We stay open all night for celebration.'

'Oh. How about tomorrow?' A whole day to wait.

He perched on the bedside, pulling on his socks. 'Tomorrow is same, also the day after until fiesta is over.' Then he was buttoning away the last glimpse of his torso. She quickly slipped her hand in. Warm, hairy. Compared to John's bony chest, Jago was so macho – almost animal. A wonderful, hot-blooded man who made her want more, more, more.

'Please,' he said, gently removing her hand. 'You drive me crazy, you sexy girl.'

Sexy girl? That was a first. They were mad about each other.

He leaned down and kissed her on the cheek. '*Tchau*, beautiful Flora. Can you wait for me?'

'Yes, I'll wait, my love.' Just like a scene from *Casablanca*, 'Then we can be together.' He was slipping his shoes on – the gold chains were a nice detail she hadn't noticed the night before. 'You can come and stay here.'

'Stay here?' He took a comb from his back pocket and carefully swept his hair back. Those lovely hands. The things he'd done with them.

'Yes, stay here with me. Don't tell Marty, but I'm extending our stay in Rio.' Everything was falling into place. Enrique had talked about taking Marty on a sailing trip after the carnival. Flora had planned to spend time by the pool and catch up on her novel, but now Jago could stay with her and enjoy the hotel.

'You are a kind woman to think of this.' Cupping her face, he kissed her quickly and stepped back. 'I drink the vision of your face, until we meet again.'

'I'll be waiting for you, my love.' She watched him leave the room, then there was a soft click of the lobby door. She fancied she could hear him fire up his motorbike and drive off into the dawn light. She rolled over to his side of the bed, still warm with a whiff of musky cinnamon. Jago. The perfect man.

Tall, handsome and a Romeo in the bedroom. She giggled; I have a Latin lover who has made actual love to me. Twice in one night!

She hadn't understood a word of whatever he whispered in her ear while his fingers stroked up and down her spine, but the combined effect had been intoxicating. A delicious soft fizzing sensation had started at her toes and worked its way up – swirling, warm caresses, layer upon layer, he tantalised her senses into unbearably exquisite heights of pleasure. Held her there, dancing on the edge of something magically thrilling, deliciously tingling to the point of near agony. Then imploding, blissful release into one ecstatic, mind-glowingly wonderful finale.

Finally she was on par with Lady Chatterley, whose 'strange thrills rippling inside her' now seemed somewhat understated. Clearly Jago was an exceptional lover, more so than Lady C's passionate gamekeeper.

~∞∞∞~

She dressed quickly. The sooner she could get Enrique to sort out the tickets, the sooner she could start planning the next two weeks. Picnics, romantic dinners, and plenty of bedroom time. It was going to be so much fun. She began laying a tray for breakfast, making sure to rattle the cups and saucers. Come on Enrique, I need you out here. As soon as Marty's bedroom door opened, she pounced.

'Good morning!'

'*Bom dia*, lovely Flora. How was your night?' he asked with a smile. 'You look happy. You and Jago had a good time, yes?'

'It was wonderful. A very special night.' He was right: she was as happy as she could ever remember.

'I will make coffee then you can tell me all about it.' Enrique headed towards the kitchen.

'No! I mean yes, but first I was wondering about your sister. The tickets? There's no way I can leave Jago now.'

'Yes, of course, she is coming to help my family for the carnival so she is in Rio. I hope she is not too busy.'

'Okay, what do you need?'

'My sister says I must take the tickets you already have and your passports, also the cost of changing the ticket, my sister will do this, no charge, but the airline will make a fee.'

'Can you go now?'

'I must call her first.' He was already lifting the receiver.

Flora went to the safe and retrieved the documents bag. Marty's organisational skills had paid off so many times and now, with everything neatly filed, it was easy to extract what she needed. 'How much is the fee, Enrique? Is it in pounds, dollars or Brazilian?'

'I'm not sure. My sister says we must use your credit card, the same one you make original booking, I think that will work best.' He was pulling his shoes on.

'Oh, okay,' Flora hesitated slightly before handing over the card.

'Do you want to come with me? I can borrow a motorbike helmet from—' he was interrupted by the phone ringing. Flora grabbed the receiver. Mustn't wake Marty up.

'Jago!' Flora put her hand over the mouthpiece. 'It's okay, you go on your own. It's Jago.' He was ringing her, even though he was busy. So thoughtful.

'I want to hear your beautiful voice,' he said. 'I hope you have good sleep this morning? To leave you is sad for me, but the carnival—'

'I was sad too, Jago. We had such a wonderful night together, didn't we? I can't wait to see you again. Just as soon as the carnival is over, we can be together.'

'That's true, *meu amor*. I am sorry, I must go. I will say goodbye for now.'

'Goodbye, my darling.' She waited for him to ring off and cradled the phone in both hands. This was it; she had finally found love.

To her surprise, Enrique was back before she'd even had time to lay the table for breakfast. 'My sister is expert on computer; it was easy for her to do.' He held out her credit card. 'The passports will come back with the new tickets. This afternoon I hope, but maybe tomorrow because of the festivities. My sister will bring them to hotel and leave them at reception.'

'Thank you, Enrique. I'm so excited! Are you still taking Marty on that sailing trip?'

'Yes, my cousin works on a charter yacht, they have already reserved our place, I was just waiting to know if Marty can come. We will leave immediately after the carnival. He's going to be so excited, we will go scuba diving.'

'He'll love that,' said Flora with a passing grimace, remembering the reef sharks in Belize. 'Oh, I must let the hotel know we'll be keeping the penthouse for another two weeks, I already told them it was a possibility, they booked it provisionally. Now it's actually happening.'

'Do it later,' said Enrique. 'First, we have the carnival to enjoy.'

The sounds of Marty moving around the bedroom caught their attention and Enrique quickly busied himself in the kitchen while Flora stepped out onto the balcony. The sun was sparkling on the sea. Diamonds dancing on silk. She was just about to give her best friend the surprise of a lifetime, then enjoy two weeks of sheer bliss with her gorgeous new boyfriend. Life was perfect in every way.

FIFTEEN

Flora and Marty arrived in good time at the carnival stadium. With their five-star tickets, they were funnelled past the heaving crowds to the relative calm of the club enclosure. Marty had wanted to be in the crowd for the atmosphere, but Flora had been worried about the vast numbers, so they compromised on a private balcony for the first day and a seat in the stalls the next.

'Wow! Look at this place. Who'd have thought it – the box office boy from Coventry is at the greatest show on earth.' said Marty. 'All this and then sailing the blue seas with my boy, Enrique.' He hugged Flora. 'All thanks to you. I still can't get my head around the whole extension thing, how you changed the flights all on your own. You're the most wonderful friend anyone could ever have.'

'It was worth it just to see your face this morning. What a picture.'

His initial silence had been a worry. At first, she thought he was angry, trying to choose his words, then she realised he was crying. Eventually, when he was able to speak, he said it was the single most thoughtful thing anyone had ever done for him. He hadn't stopped talking all morning. It could have been annoying if she hadn't also been excited for her own reasons.

'Look, Marty! On my seat, it's a flower just like the ones Jago made for the carnival float.' Flora picked up the lily and read the attached note. 'For my love. Until we meet again.' She read it again and for a moment the chaos of the carnival, the trumpets and the thumping music faded away while she pictured Jago in an open-necked shirt and leather trousers, coming to claim her, carrying her in his arms through the parting crowd as everyone cheered and threw their hats in the air. He would set her down on the sands of Copacabana Beach and from there they'd find an old fishing boat and sail away into the sunset.

Marty was speaking, 'I just love it! Look at the colour, the glamour, the costumes. And this is just the warm-up! It hasn't even started yet . . . Flora?'

'Hm?'

'Oh, don't tell me, Jago has you by the heartstrings?'

'He's wonderful, isn't he? And the flower, it's just so thoughtful. It's a mini version of what's on the float – he must have made it himself, just for me.'

'It's beautiful.'

'And in his note he says "my love". It's a sign Marty, I think he's the one for me.' She couldn't stop smiling even if she wanted to.

'I'm excited for you, babes. You deserve to find love. And now, thanks to you extending the ticket, we can look forward to two more weeks of fun and games – who knows where we'll end up?'

A waiter appeared with a tray of savoury pastries and two tall glasses adorned with exotic fruit and a straw in the shape of a pink flamingo, all topped off by a fizzing mini sparkler.

'Please,' he said, 'Rio Samba Smile for you.'

Whooshing fireworks in crackling bursts of silver, blue, emerald and gold sparked together and a huge Brazilian flag magically floated above the stadium. The crowds roared as a band burst into an ear-drumming rendition of *A Voz do Morro*, the voice of the favela – a hundred and thirty beats per minute of polyrhythmic dance music competing with the cacophony of pyrotechnics and a deliriously happy crowd.

Marty, already cheering with complete abandon, was on his feet ready to catch the first glimpses of the greatest show on earth.

～॰జుॐॐ～

Drunk on the electrifying performances, the charged atmosphere of the crowds and a steady flow of Rio Samba Smiles, Flora and Marty made their way to the after-parade party.

'Did you see the way that waiter was looking at me?' slurred Flora.

'And he patted your bottom when we were leaving.' Marty linked his arm through hers. 'He was like a bee around a honeypot.'

'Well, as of last night, my honeypot is well and truly spoken for!' she giggled.

'Ooh la la! Jago's definitely the man for you.'

'He is.' Flora brought the hand-made lily up to her nose, 'I can even smell him in this – that's how close we are.'

Enrique was already at the after-show party and joyfully greeted them at the door by grabbing Marty into a bear hug. 'I have exciting news,' he shouted over the noise. 'One of the walkers has a motorbike accident today. His place on The Creation, Marty, you can have it!'

'What? As a walker, walking alongside The Creation? Me?'

'Yes, you will be in our parade.' He turned to Flora, 'I hope you don't mind? It's, how do you say, one lifetime opportunity?'

'I don't mind at all. Marty, you're going to be in the carnival! Will he get a costume?'

'Of course. He will be palm tree.'

'With a headdress?' Marty clapped his hands, 'The olive and gold? Oh my goddess! It has ostrich feathers, Flora. Actual showbiz.'

After a few drinks and a quick bite to eat, they went back to the hotel. Marty needed to collect a few things so he could stay the night at Enrique's place. He needed to rehearse his part in the parade and help with the finishing touches to the float first thing in the morning.

'I'll be completely fine,' Flora had forced herself to sound upbeat. 'Go and enjoy your moment. I'll try not to have too much fun without you.' Even as she said it, the idea of sitting in a huge crowd on her own seemed daunting.

Marty had wanted tickets in the stalls, to 'soak up the atmosphere'. Flora had found even the private box today a bit overwhelming with the heat and the noise. Having to weave her way through hordes of drunken revellers on her own tomorrow filled her with trepidation.

'I'll be in the crowd, cheering you on.' What else could she say?

'And you're sure you'll be okay getting to your seat?'

'Yes, yes, the seat number is on the ticket and the ticket is in the room safe. I'll get a taxi from the hotel in the morning. I'll be fine.'

'And you'll take a photo as we go past? I don't know if you'll be able to spot me, I might be on the other side, but take loads of pics, babes. This is my moment!'

'Yes, of course. I'll have my camera at the ready.'

They would meet at the club after the parade. Jago wouldn't be there, but as soon as the third and final day of the carnival was over they would have their time together. Enrique kissed her on both cheeks. Marty hugged her, then climbed on the back of Enrique's motorbike and they zoomed off into the tangle of traffic. She wore a smile to wave them off, then wearily walked up the steps to the hotel. Just two more days, then she'd have Jago all to herself.

Before going to bed she checked the ticket. She would get there nice and early, before the crowds. Getting out of there afterwards, squashed in among a heaving mass of party-goers, would be a challenge – she'd seen the crowds today from the luxury of a private box and that was bad enough. If it weren't for Marty wanting a photograph, she would happily stay in her room tomorrow and watch the fiesta on television.

Waking up the next day, and sitting on the balcony without Enrique's exuberance or Marty's late but cheerful appearance, felt a bit strange. She checked her watch – still early. She made a cup of tea and drank it perched on a stool in the kitchen. It wasn't worth laying the table just for her. She looked in the cupboard. No *pão de queijo*. Enrique usually nipped out early and bought them fresh from the market. In any case, nerves had overcome her appetite. She forced herself to eat a banana and an almond biscuit, then phoned the hotel reception to order a taxi. At least she wouldn't have to use public transport – without Marty, that really would be a nightmare.

'Yes, madam. A taxi is possible, shall I book for you?'

'Yes please, and one for return as well.'

'Oh, no, return not possible, too difficult. Too much people. You find one when you come out of the stadium, is better that way.'

Flora's heart sank. She'd just have to manage.

'Oh, one other thing. I am now able to confirm we'd like to keep the suite for another two weeks.'

'Certainly, madam. You were checking out tomorrow? We have limousine booked for the airport in the evening, shall I cancel as well?'

'Oh, yes, please, we're not going anywhere just yet.' She toyed with the idea of keeping the limo to take Jago on a surprise drive up into the mountains, but she'd wait. He'd come to the hotel as soon as his shift was over the following evening, and that was where she wanted him. In her penthouse suite, preferably in her bed, doing something deliciously naughty.

The receptionist was speaking. 'So, I can confirm, you are now booked for two more weeks. If you please settle your original booking with payment tomorrow, I can re-open the same account for you.'

'Great, I will pop down after breakfast.' The tickets and passports would have been dropped off by then as well. She'd organised everything without needing Marty.

Feeling more empowered, she opened her wardrobe and selected a bright pink sundress with a matching straw hat and a pair of comfortable sandals. Perfect for staying cool and keeping the sun off in the stalls. No need to look glammed up – there was no one to impress. May as well be comfy. As soon as Jago, Enrique and Marty had passed by on The Creation, she'd dodge the crowds and come back to watch the rest on television. She could have a little nap, get changed and then get another taxi to the after-show party.

~❦~

'Excuse me, I think you are in my seat.' Flora waved her ticket at a large bearded gentleman in a baseball cap and a black string vest. A pair of tattooed snakes twisted around his forearms.

'*Nein, es ist mein Platz,*' he said, giving her a hard stare.

Flora pointedly checked the tickets again. He was in Marty's place; she had planned to put her handbag there so she could keep an eye on it.

'Never mind, I'll just sit here,' she said and plumped down, glad to be off her feet at last. It had taken almost two hours to get from the taxi rank to finally find her seat. Shuffling slowly in with the crowd she'd gone up the wrong aisle. Weaving back down against the flow of hyped-up party animals in lurid wigs and face paint, she'd had her toes trodden on twice. A group of teenagers were shaking beer cans and chanting the chorus to 'Copacabana'. The spraying foam splatted Flora sideways-on – she could feel it running down her arm.

If she'd been in a private box she would have been shown to her seat by an usher who would've offered her a cold flannel and a bottle of water on arrival. She scanned the surrounding area for refreshments: she could only see a couple of bikini-clad girls selling cigarettes and tequila shots from a holster. Luckily, she still had half a bottle of water and another banana zipped up in her handbag and wedged it between her feet, so she could feel if someone tried to steal it.

She didn't like the look of the German. On her other side, a young girl in a cropped top and minuscule silver shorts was daintily texting with pink, sequin-studded fingernails. She wasn't wearing a bra. Next to her, a girl in a cowboy hat was chewing gum, an arm slung casually around her texting friend. She caught Flora's gaze, removed her gum and, maintaining eye contact, licked her friend on the mouth and kissed her passionately. Flora quickly looked away. Not wishing to attract attention either side, she looked straight ahead, arms folded so as not to accidentally touch anyone.

The parade began with a magnificent display of acrobats who somehow managed to combine cartwheels and backflips with samba dancing. The music amped up several decibels and the crowd went wild as the first float came into view. A few rows behind Flora, someone began blowing a whistle; the shrill pitch competed with others in the crowd. Cameras clicked and flashed as the first display passed in front of them. Booming speakers announced the procession of floats in several languages. The Mercy of God; Power of the People; Save the Planet.

Flora was glad she'd brought a sunhat – the brim shielded her face nicely – but already her shoulders were glowing almost as pink as her Boho-Chic sundress. Her water hadn't lasted long and she'd eaten the slightly squashed banana. Where was the loo? Better wait until The Creation had been and gone, she'd never forgive herself if she missed it. It was a shame the people around her were so unfriendly; she'd love to tell them all about her friends and The Creation. All her favourite men in one place. Enrique would be dancing on top, Marty waving a palm leaf from the side. Then lovely, muscular Jago out of sight, one of the men chosen to guide the float. He was going to be exhausted; two more days at the carnival, followed by his evening shifts at the restaurant. When they were finally together she'd make sure he had plenty of tender loving care. Maybe run him a nice relaxing bath, some ylang-ylang bath foam and a glass of wine. She could wash his back. Room service dinner. Steak.

Flora drifted into a pleasurable daydream involving Jago and a champagne bucket full of ice. She had just got to the bit where she seductively popped an ice cube into her mouth and Jago was groaning in ecstatic anticipation when she heard The Creation announced on the loudspeaker. There was a roar from the crowd. She jumped to her feet, echoing the crowd's cheers while frantically rummaging in her handbag for her camera.

The sky seemed to cloud over. Waves of nausea pulsed through her body, cold and hot at the same time. Then everything swerved and faded as her legs gave way; half-crumpled onto her seat and half in the hot denim lap of the hairy German, she was helpless.

'Heiliger Strohsack!' he growled.

She heard him speak but felt a strong desire to stay just where she was. It was easier to keep her eyes closed. He heaved her upper body back into her chair.

'Okay?' she heard him ask, then a large hairy hand held a bottle of water in front of her. *'Wasser ist gut,'* he said and nudged her.

'Thanks,' said Flora weakly. She sipped a little water and handed it back, trying not to think of all the germs she was ingesting.

She leaned forwards, remembering an occasion when she and John had been queuing for a half-price kettle at an End of Summer Sale. Standing in freakishly hot sun for over an hour, snaking slowly towards the doors of BHS, she had felt faint, but John had refused to lose his place in the queue and told her to find somewhere to sit down and put her head between her knees. Good idea.

By the time Flora felt normal enough to sit up, The Creation had passed out of sight. Still feeling shaky, she squeezed past the row of spectators and made her way down to the ground behind the stadium. In the relative peace, standing in the shade of the striped awning, she assessed the situation. She'd missed the moment. Marty would be upset but there was nothing she could do about it now. Spying an ice-cream stand, she went over and held up a finger and said, 'Um, *uno*, one, *por favor*, please,' hoping she'd covered the language barrier. Feeling restored enough to find a taxi, she made her way back to the hotel.

Back in the safety of her penthouse suite, she turned the air-conditioning to the coldest setting and had a long lukewarm shower, then wrapped herself in a soft, fluffy dressing gown and settled down to watch the rest of the carnival from the sofa. Perhaps The Creation would be shown again; maybe they would even win.

~ↄ☙ℬℬↄↄ~

Darkness. The phone was ringing. Still half asleep, Flora stumbled towards the small red flashing light. As soon as she raised the receiver, she knew it was Marty; the booming music in the background told her he was in a night club.

'BABES!' he shouted. 'Where are you? We've been looking for you.' She clicked on a nearby lamp and checked the time. She was missing the after-show party. She stifled a yawn and hoped he wasn't going to insist on her going out to meet them.

'Did you see us? We came second! The Creation won a prize, Flora! I was actually on a prize-winning float at Rio Carnival. Enrique made it happen for me, babes. He's the best human being in the universe! And you are, Flora! I love you, you know that, don't you?'

Flora giggled. 'And I love you too, Marty.' He was her family and best friend, she loved him more than anyone. It was good to say, 'I love you.' She could imagine whispering it to Jago sometime soon as well.

Marty was saying something about sailing into the sunset with his lover and how he'd see her soon. Of course. Enrique's charter yacht. Wasn't that a day early? Yes, they were setting sail at first light.

'So, see you in five days, babes. Have fun with Jago.' Marty hung up.

Flora smiled. He was having a great time and so would she. Love is in the air: she absently hummed the tune, then, channelling Barry Manilow, she switched to 'Copacabana' while swishing and gliding around the room in a happy haze.

'*Her name was Lola . . . da-dah-da showgirl . . . The Copa, Copacabanahhh, di dah-da, di dah do di-da dah.*'

She didn't know all the words but it sounded like a love story. Lola with her chap and Flora with hers. With a final twirl she arrived next to the phone and called room service for a club sandwich, then poured herself a glass of chilled orange juice. So, Marty and Enrique were going sailing earlier than expected. In a way she was glad, she'd had enough of the carnival. She'd have the following day to herself. She would plan everything around Jago's arrival in the evening. She glanced at her nails. A manicure and pedicure were a must. Pale pink or red? Red nails for a seductress. Not that Jago would need much encouragement. Maybe she should have a massage as well, loosen herself up, get in the mood. And while she was at it, she may as well have her hair done.

She totted up the time allocated for each treatment – she only had to have a late breakfast, a leisurely lunch and perhaps a swim in the hotel pool and the whole day would be taken care of. Then she'd have a candlelit soak in fragrant bath oils, slip into something alluring and wait for Jago to end his shift at the restaurant. He would be exhausted after the last day of the carnival – it was her job to make sure they had everything they needed. She'd order some champagne and a few nibbles in case he was hungry, and then the following morning they could have a room service breakfast.

Deciding what to wear required thought. She flicked through a magazine and read *Be Precious to Someone*. It said, strike just the right balance between sexy and vulnerable. Temptress and peasant girl. Thinking back to the stadium, the girl hadn't been wearing a bra, maybe she should go freestyle as well? No, she would wrap herself up like a precious gift. In between passionate kisses, Jago could unwrap her, while gently guiding her in the bedroom direction. After laying out a few options ready to decide upon in the morning, she went to bed hoping to dream of Jago. Too excited to sleep, she got up again and watched *Camila*, a love story set in Buenos Aires, which was almost in Brazil.

SIXTEEN

'I am sorry, madam, this card is declined.' The receptionist's red-lipsticked smile conveyed just the right amount of professional warmth in case it was a genuine mistake.

'Beg pardon?' Flora had only stopped off to pay the hotel account on her way to the beauty salon; she didn't want to be late for her appointment.

'Can I suggest we try a different card? Sometimes this happens.' A perfectly manicured hand returned Flora's gold credit card.

'Oh, right. I have another one here.' Flora hadn't used her bank card since leaving Coventry, and even at home she'd hardly touched it. She preferred to go to the counter and fill in a withdrawal slip, like John used to. While the receptionist inserted the card, she feverishly tried to remember the pin number.

When the machine declined the second card, she still didn't panic. Marty would be back in a few days – he'd sort it out. Clearly, there was a misunderstanding. She looked at the confusing array of numbers. However much it was in Brazilian money, John's life savings was more than enough for any hotel bill, no matter what.

'How much is that in pounds?' she asked. The receptionist's fingernails click-clacked as she quickly worked out the exchange rate and held up the calculator.

'Gosh, that *is* a lot.' Just over eleven thousand pounds. 'I'll sort it out in a day or so. There's some sort of mistake. I'm here for another two weeks now, so there's plenty of time.' Flora smiled while tucking the second card back in her purse. 'Now, if you'll excuse me, I mustn't be late for the salon.'

'I am sorry, madam, but without payment of your bill we cannot extend your booking.'

'What do you mean?'

'We require you to settle your account today.' The lipstick was no longer smiling.

'But I don't know what I can do. Can you try the cards again? There's been a mistake.'

The girl shrugged. 'Your bill must be paid,. Meanwhile, we would like to hold your passport.'

'But you already have a copy of it. Isn't that enough?' When there was no answer, Flora continued, 'I'm afraid I don't have a passport, you see I gave it to Enrique, but it's not a problem. His sister will bring it back today.'

'I'm sorry, Mrs Marshall, please wait here. I must call security.'

~ஸ்ஸ்~

Two over-sized security guards watched Flora pack. She'd tried speaking to them, but they didn't understand. If only Jago were there, he'd explain everything, but he wouldn't arrive until much later. And what about their romantic night together? She'd had it all planned. How disappointing. In an attempt to salvage something of her date she'd even suggested moving to a cheaper room, but they insisted she settle the bill first. Where would she go? Perhaps she could stay at Jago's place. He probably had a bachelor pad somewhere. She could cook him a special meal, maybe something British.

All of Marty's clothes were neatly folded and ironed ready for use, so it was just a matter of sweeping everything into a suitcase. In her room, still under the scrutiny of the security guards, she felt pressured to be equally as quick. She wasn't naturally tidy, everything had become quite disorganised since

Marty's break from looking after her. She quickly bundled things together and threw them into the remaining suitcases, then squashed the lids down. How did she manage to fill three suitcases to the brim and still not fit everything in? Marty always managed. One of the security men called housekeeping and a maid brought a couple of refuse sacks to take the overflow of shoes and handbags.

With all her belongings piled up in reception, Flora had another go at calling her credit card's international helpline. The first time had been confusing as she couldn't remember the passwords. Eventually, they had asked her an assortment of security questions and then said the card was over the limit and the direct debit from her bank account had failed to be forthcoming. It wasn't possible she argued, but the voice, which had started out sounding reassuringly British, began to lose patience, saying interest on the balance of the card was accruing at a rate of twenty-nine percent, and she was advised to pay it off immediately.

Without the correct passwords to hand, the call to her bank was equally confusing. After several questions and the need to wait for her bank manager to return from his late lunch, Flora was informed that the account had been closed when all funds were transferred to Dominguez Corporation. 'Domini who? I've never heard of them.' Silence. 'That wasn't me!' shrieked Flora. What had Marty been up to? A patient voice said if she didn't recall making the transaction, perhaps she could come into the branch to discuss the matter. They assured her that accusations of malpractice were taken very seriously and they would file an investigation just as soon as they could see some form of identity and proof of her address. Two utility bills would suffice.

The hotel manager had been hovering nearby.

Marty! What had he done?

'If your bank is not helping, please find another way. Call your family to pay.'

'There's no one. Look, how about I give you my jewellery?' Her Longines watch, the Chanel earrings and maybe the sapphire necklace should be more than enough.

'We run a five-star hotel, madam. Not a jewellery shop.'

'But what am I to do?' What was the name of the restaurant where Jago worked? Even if he was currently at the carnival, surely the owner, Enrique's uncle, would be there? But all she could remember about the place was Jago, carrying a tray above his head while weaving in and out of tables – she had no idea of the address. Not even the food stood out in her memory.

'What about your companion?'

'Marty? He's away for five days, but I have a good friend arriving this evening. His name's Jago. He's local – he will help.' He wouldn't have the money, but he would know what to do, maybe how to contact Enrique and Marty. It wasn't going to be the evening she'd planned, but the idea of him coming to her rescue was still romantic.

'Maybe he will help if he is a rich man. You must wait here until your passports arrive. Then it is up to you, but you must pay the bill, one way or another.'

The manager ordered her a sandwich and a cup of coffee at lunchtime. As the afternoon wore on he asked more questions about her trip, about Marty.

'Ah yes, I believe the gay man is a fun-time friend for the ladies, no?' He didn't seem perturbed.

'Yes, he's great fun and very caring. He seems to know just what I need, whenever – which is more than I could say for my husband.'

'Oh, you are married?' He looked quizzically at her ring finger.

'Widowed. He died. Electrocuted.' She tried to convey a suitably sad face.

'Electrocution?' The manager leaned forward now, as though studying Flora anew. 'So he was a bad man, how do you say, on death row?'

192

'Oh, no, just with a screwdriver.' She paused, noticing his confusion. 'An accident, he forgot to switch off the power when he tried to fix the cooker. Silly mistake.'

'Fatal mistake,' the manager nodded. 'So, you are a single lady.'

The phone interrupted their conversation. After a brief discussion the manager said, 'Something has just been delivered, maybe for you, Mrs Marshall. Please excuse me. I will check.' He returned a few minutes later waving two British passports and airline tickets, presumably to New Zealand. 'This is good news for you, I will keep them here. You are now free to go. I look forward to receiving full payment of your bill before you leave Brazil,' he glanced at the tickets, 'in two weeks' time.'

'But where should I go? I only have a few Brazilian reais and some American dollars. Could you recommend somewhere?'

'I am sorry, I think our sister hotel is too expensive. Maybe stay with your friend, did you say his name is Jago?'

'Couldn't I stay here, until Marty gets back?'

'I am already taking a risk. Really I should have called the tourist police, but they are too busy with the carnival. I take care of you today to wait for the passports. I am sorry, but you had our best suite for two weeks, you charge everything to the room, then you don't pay. I cannot do more.' He paused, but Flora had nothing to say – the whole situation seemed ridiculous. The penthouse suite, the beautiful clothes, partying every night and the private box. They had spent more money in Rio than in their combined tour of South America.

'Can I at least wait here? My friend is working in a restaurant. He is coming to see me after his shift this evening.'

'You can leave your luggage here and come back later, but I advise you to find somewhere to stay. The whole of Rio is full of carnival party.'

The club was crowded with tourists, even at four in the afternoon. It had taken a couple of wrong turns to find the place and she could have done with a sit down, but without wanting to spend any money Flora waited by the bar. As the show came to an end and people were getting up to leave, she worked her way around the room to speak to the waiters.

'Have you heard from Enrique? The dancer?' Her questions were met with a shake of the head or a shrug. No one knew where he was. As soon as the young lad who had taken Enrique's place in the show came through the stage door, Flora hurried over to speak to him.

The boy shook his head. 'Enrique? He quit. I am Carlos.'

'Isn't that just temporary, while he's on a sailing trip?' Enrique loved dancing. Why would he give up his job?

'I don't know. He is gone. I have his contract for the season.'

'Do you know where he lives? His uncle has a restaurant. Do you know it?'

'No, sorry.'

As a group of dancers pushed past a girl called to him, '*Vamos, despache-te!*'

'I must go,' he said quickly and followed his friends towards the exit.

Flora walked back to the hotel. A taxi now seemed like a luxury. Charcoal smoke and charred beef wafted from a row of street vendors, followed by the exotic scent of roasted chillies. Flora paused in front of each stall. Little meat pasties fried in sizzling oil, spicy barbecued meat skewers. *Coxinha* – a pastry case shaped like a chicken drumstick, stuffed with shredded chicken and rolled in breadcrumbs. She was sure they'd be delicious but she stuck with familiar territory and purchased a bag of *pão de queijo*, the little cheese rolls Enrique usually bought from the market.

Checking her watch, she still had hours until Jago would come. The hotel foyer was virtually empty. A couple were sitting together drinking coffee, and at a corner table a teenager was playing a computer game with headphones on. The receptionist was on the phone. She went to the Ladies to retouch her make-up. The wall-to-wall mirror reflected a less-than-perfect-looking Flora, who appeared to have a lot on her mind. She must try and relax; it was all just a big misunderstanding. Jago wouldn't find frown lines attractive. It was bad enough her nail polish was chipped. She was supposed to have had a day of pampering.

Back in reception, she asked if there had been any messages, but of course, Marty and Enrique were on a yacht somewhere, completely ignorant of the situation. The only other possible person was Jago and he was going to be there in person in a few hours. She settled down to wait in a seat facing the door.

〜◦))))◦〜

'Excuse me, madam?' A hand on Flora's shoulder was gently shaking her. For a fleeting moment, before she opened her eyes, she thought it was Jago. Instead, the night watchman, Alberto, was looking down at her with a concerned expression.

'Is almost morning. Where is your friend, Mr Marty? I do not see him.'

'He's away for a few days. I was waiting for someone else but—' Flora couldn't bring herself to finish the sentence.

'Please don't cry.' Alberto offered her his handkerchief. It was crumpled and warm from his pocket and smelled faintly of peppermint. The gesture made her cry even more.

'Alberto will find you some coffee,' he said gently. 'Everything is better with Brazilian coffee.'

He left her for a few minutes, enough time for Flora to have a bit more of a cry, smudging mascara and traces of lipstick onto the handkerchief in the process. She hurried to the Ladies and wiped her face on a damp hand towel and returned to the foyer just as Alberto was coming out of the concierge's office with a mug of coffee.

'I'm sorry, Alberto, you're very kind, and now I'm afraid I've messed up your hanky.'

'Please, for you to keep. My wife, she makes them for the market.'

'Your wife made this? How lovely. I can't sew.' John, standing over her and tutting at her attempt to sew a button on his overcoat. 'I can't do anything like that. I'm useless.' John had been right; she had no special skills.

'Everyone has something, madam Flora. You must find out what it is,' said Alberto. He eyed the row of world clocks above the reception desk. 'I have to go now. I hope you find your friend.'

Friend? Jago wasn't a friend; a night of foolish hope had told her that. At first she'd envisioned a terrible accident or the restaurant staying open longer than usual. Then, when the traffic was quietest and the hotel lobby was deserted, she was forced to accept the facts. She'd been taken for a fool. He was probably married. Of course he was.

She sipped the coffee and ate the last *pão de queijo*; they were much nicer straight from the market, still warm. She must work out a plan. Find a place to stay until Marty returned. She'd like to find Jago as well. Hadn't he left her a lily and a note? She deserved an explanation. If only she could remember the name of the restaurant, or even where it was, but all the streets behind the main strip looked the same. Without Marty everything had gone wrong.

How could the bank have transferred all her money to the Dominguez Corporation without her permission? Maybe Marty had requested it but if so, why? Perhaps it was a special investment, she had no idea about money. No, he would have discussed it with her. Perhaps the hotel manager would let her make another international call? But even if she did, the bank seemed impossible to sort out without a face-to-face conversation. There must be another way. Maybe sell all her jewellery and surplus clothes? It was all designer wear – even second-hand they must be worth way more than eleven thousand pounds. Don't be hasty, wait for Marty. He'd know what to do.

She assessed her financial situation more thoroughly. She had forty-three Brazilian reais left. What was that in British money – about ten pounds, maybe less? She doubted it would be enough for accommodation, let alone food; she would definitely have to try and sell something.

When the concierge finally came on duty in the morning, Flora explained she would like to sell her gold Chanel earrings. He seemed surprised, but ordered her a taxi and explained to the driver what she wanted. Confident she would make more than enough for a comfortable four-day stay in a nice hotel, she asked the driver to wait while she went into the second-hand jewellery shop.

She was still trying to work out how much one hundred and seven Brazilian reais was in sterling when she got back into the taxi. It wasn't enough – but how could she have negotiated a better price without Marty's language skills? At least she'd raised some funds on her own initiative. Feeling a little more empowered, she felt brave enough to look for accommodation. She asked the driver to take her to a cheap hotel.

'How do you mean, cheap?' asked the driver.

'Not costing too much money, maybe ten reais a night.' She could always sell the sapphire necklace.

'Ten reais is not much expensive. Rio hotel is expensive. Is minimum one hundred reais a night.'

'Oh dear. How about just a simple room? Four nights. Ten reais a night. It's all I can afford.' The driver glanced pointedly at her expensive watch. 'No,' she said, covering the Longines with her other hand.

'Okay, *barato demais*. I know.' Shaking his head and muttering to himself, he drove away from the wide pavements and neat shop fronts, into the depths of the sprawling suburbs. 'We go more outside the city,' he said.

As the streets narrowed and potholes forced the driver to slow down, Flora watched a group of grubby children playing with sticks and an old tyre. They passed old stone houses with rusting tin roofs and cardboard patching up broken windows. Tables and clusters of mismatched chairs set up on the side of the road, serving beer under faded umbrellas. A pair of dogs copulated lazily in the shade of a small dusty tree. The taxi pulled up outside what appeared to be a little pub. It looked smarter than the other houses in the street. It was freshly whitewashed, with shutters at the windows and *Vila Eloa* painted on the door.

A middle-aged woman in a flowery apron opened the door. How homely. Flora caught her eye and performed her international namaste gesture with a smile from the back seat of the taxi. After a rapid interchange with the driver, the lady, who had inexplicably laughed several times, finally agreed there was a room available for the price of six reais a night.

A quick calculation; four nights would be twenty-four reais. That left around a hundred and twenty reais for food, maybe even a drink or two in the bar and a chance to get to know the locals. She could probably afford something better, but it was only for four nights. Then Marty would sort everything out and they could have their suite back.

On the way back to the hotel, the driver explained the room was currently occupied; she could move in after six o'clock. He couldn't guarantee to be available to take her but he wrote the address down and charged her forty reais for the round trip. Forty reais. That was a big chunk out of her survival fund. He suggested she use the underground instead of paying for a taxi later but that was out of the question. Firstly, she'd never used it before and didn't know how to, but secondly, she had two bin bags full of shoes and three suitcases – four if she also took Marty's.

SEVENTEEN

As early evening approached, Flora took a taxi to her lodgings – already half the value of the Chanel earrings had gone on fares. When she didn't tip the driver, he drove away without offering to help carry her suitcases. Flora quickly heaved her belongings inside while keeping an eye out for possible bag snatchers. There was no reception area, just a small entrance hall and a bar decorated with posters of pouting Latin beauties in various stages of undress.

'Hello?' She knocked on the door marked *Não Entre*. 'Anyone there?' She would ask the landlady for a cup of tea; perhaps they could share a pot and get to know each other. Tea crossed all language barriers, just like music and smiling. The door was opened by a petite girl wearing just a small pink towel and silver platform heels.

'Oh, hello, I was here earlier,' said Flora.

'Yes.' The girl flicked her long black hair.

'Um, is the proprietor here, could I speak to her?'

'Theresa? No. Come.' She was already clonking towards the stairs.

'Could you just give me a hand? I don't know how I've managed to accumulate so—' The girl didn't seem to hear, so Flora grabbed a suitcase and double-handedly heaved it up the stairs. Why hadn't she just picked out enough for four nights and left the rest behind with Marty's stuff? Too late now. A couple of bannisters were missing. The whole structure seemed to creak with every step. She kept close to the wall. As she neared the top, panting and slightly sweaty, the landing came into view. Not as nice she'd supposed: bare wooden boards served for both the floor and walls, no decoration to speak of. Four doors. She peered through the only one already open, and there was Little-Miss-Clunky-Shoes sitting on an unmade bed.

'Gosh. It's very cosy, isn't it?' Flora said with a laugh, shuffling herself and the bag in sideways. A single bed, covered in soft toys and a scattering of clothes. No window, just a lightbulb hanging from a cable tied to the roof rafters. Screwed to the wall was a small plastic fan, buzzing a slight breeze.

'Is this your room?'

'Yes. You also together,' said the girl.

'Share? But I'm paying—' Flora was still slightly out of breath.

'You pay only six reais – is half price. You can have from six until six. Night-time.'

'Night-time?'

'Yes, I am working, you sleeping. In the morning, I sleep also.'

'Well, it's not what I was expecting, I—' She needed to think. It was already early evening, the chances of finding another taxi to take her somewhere better were slim. She'd better make the most of it. What would Marty do?

'I'm sorry, I'm forgetting my manners. I'm Flora, pleased to meet you.' She held out her hand, feeling slightly ridiculous when it was left there in mid-air.

'Is just a few days, no? No need to get related.'

'Well, no, but what is your name?'

'Bonita.' She stood up and undid her towel. Starkers underneath. Crikey. Flora watched her select a silver bikini from the bed. 'Don't you have boobies of your own?'

'Oh, er, sorry, I didn't mean to, er— I'll just go and get the rest of my stuff.'

By the time she had lugged the other two suitcases and bin liners upstairs and stacked them in a corner of the room, the girl had added a pair of purple-sequinned botty shorts to her silver bikini top and was applying a set of false eyelashes.

'Ah, you're a dancer?' Maybe she'd know Enrique.

'Not really,' said Bonita, and without further explanation she hurried out of the room, clattering down the stairs in her five-inch heels.

Flora looked around for hanging space. She wouldn't be able to unpack very much, but she could reorganise her bags so the essential things were to hand. She'd packed in such a hurry, she hadn't thought about what she'd need in the short term. Not her Nicole Farhi cocktail dress or the Gucci clutch, for sure.

There were three nails in the back of the door. Flora redistributed Bonita's tangled collection of bags, Mini Mouse umbrella and denim jacket and hung up a couple of Prada sundresses and a boho blouse, then hooked her silk dressing gown over the top. If the bathroom was downstairs, she'd need to keep it handy – it was alright for a beautiful young girl like Bonita to walk around half-naked but she intended to stay covered up.

She laid her nightie on the pillow and gathered up Bonita's residual clothing, mainly bikini tops, and folded them up as neatly as she could. A cardboard box half under the bed was an overflowing mass of clothes. Without wanting to presume, she placed everything in a neat pile on the floor, next to which she lined up the soft toys in a sitting-up position, hoping it conveyed mutual respect for each other's belongings.

Now she felt a little more at home, she took out her compact and reapplied her lipstick. Time to socialise. Who knew how the evening would go? She could hear lively conversation through the floorboards. Her room must be directly above the bar. Female voices, so far as she could make out; she would order a drink, perhaps make a friend or two, find out more about the local area.

'Hello, everyone.'

The chatter instantly stopped.

'I've just moved in upstairs.'

A dozen teenaged girls were staring at her. Smile. Marty would smile and carry on talking. Why were they all wearing bikini tops? Theresa, the landlady, was nowhere to be seen. Sit at the bar. Keep smiling. Even in her embossed capri pants, the ones Marty had said made her look ten years younger, she felt like an ancient lumbering old lady as she walked across the room. A drink would calm her nerves.

The bar was really just a high table with a chiller fridge behind it. She looked for a bell or some way of attracting service. Nothing. Feeling all the more awkward, she sat down and smiled weakly at the staring girls.

'Why are you here?' one of them asked.

Good question. Why was she there? 'Oh, it's a long story. It doesn't matter,' she said, conscious she was holding back tears.

A couple of girls were whispering, then one said, 'We no want you here. We are *ocupada*.'

'I see,' said Flora. Embarrassed and at a loss to know what else to say or do, she walked back out of the room. As she closed the door behind her, the talking started up again as though nothing had happened.

She had hoped to order food in the bar. Clearly, that wasn't an option. She would have to go out and perhaps find a cheap restaurant or maybe another bar. It was almost dark. Better go now. She stepped out into the street, narrowly missing a motorbike that swerved around her and beeped. She looked for a landmark. Her sense of direction had never been great and she couldn't read a map – John had been right when he's called her 'geographically illiterate'. She had the address in her bag and now it was evening, a neon light flickered above the door; she was sure to spot Vila Eloa on her return.

The street had no pavement, just earth and rubble that ran beside a strip of rough tarmac, pockmarked with potholes. She picked her way through litter and skirted around slimy trickles of water coming from leaking pipes. Occasionally, she was forced to cross the road when an old wreck of a car blocked her path. A dog ran out barking, then circled her with a low growl. Marty would have said, 'Keep walking. He's just doing his job, guarding his territory'. She passed between a row of blacked-out houses. The absence of outside lights meant the stretch of road was in almost complete darkness. A man smoking a cigarette in a doorway made kissing noises. Flora fought the urge to run, and kept an eye on the better-lit area just a little further ahead. She would eat at the first place she came to. She wasn't very hungry now in any case. All she wanted to do was go to bed and sleep until Marty came to get her.

She had pictured herself blending in with the locals, chatting to neighbours over a cold beer, making new friends. How silly. The only good moment was spotting a stall selling *pão de queijo*. She bought a dozen and a can of fizzy orange and walked as quickly as she could back to Vila Eloa. Once inside, she hurried to use the bathroom then crept upstairs. As she passed the bar she was glad to notice there was less chat coming from inside; she dreaded the thought of bumping into any of the sulky girls.

She sat on the single bed listening to the odd car passing. Occasionally someone came in or went out of the room below. Flora ate a cheese roll and opened the can of orange. Tomorrow she would have to leave the room at six a.m. and stay out for twelve hours without spending her savings. A few days with no money and nothing to do wasn't all that different to being married to John. She'd only become used to the high life thanks to Marty – but being stranded in a foreign country without speaking the language presented new challenges.

And so did being heartbroken, humiliated and completely alone.

She went back through all the possible scenarios: had the bank made a mistake? Maybe she was a victim of identity theft. Whatever it was, Marty would sort it out. But he couldn't help where Jago was concerned. She had been used for a night of sleazy passion, then thrown aside – a discarded conquest. But the flower on her seat at the carnival – why would he have gone to so much trouble? The note said, 'For my love'. Was it some sort of elaborate game? Just when she thought she might have found her prince, everything had fallen apart. With that thought, the last reserves of bravado dissolved and Flora buried her face in Bonita's Little Mermaid pillow and allowed herself a good cry.

~~~

'Hey! Old woman in my bed. Get out.'

Flora awoke from an exhausted, dreamless sleep. The stress of the previous two days and a night of sitting in the hotel reception meant she could have slept anywhere. Surely it wasn't six in the morning already?

Without a window there was no way of knowing if it was daylight, but voices on the street carried through the weatherboard walls. Animated conversations, traffic, children: different sounds to the night.

A few more hours would have been nice, but she levered herself out of bed. Best stick to the agreement. Six till six. Bonita had already changed into an oversized Care Bears tee-shirt and was sitting on the plastic seat, taking her make-up off with cotton wool and a bargain-sized bottle of baby oil.

'Good morning, Bonita, how are you? Did you have a nice time at work?'

Bonita examined her teeth in the mirror.

Try again.

'You have lovely white teeth, not like mine.' Still nothing. 'Well, I'll see you tonight. Can I bring you anything back? I'm going into the city. A magazine, perhaps?'

'Maybe a new life.' Bonita was already in bed, facing the wall.

'Oh, well, yes I'm sure we'd all like that.' Flora gave a little laugh. Silence. Then she heard Bonita say '*chok old*' in a small, tired voice. Did she say chocolate?

~ ❧ ~

There was no way around it; without enough money for a taxi she'd have to brave the underground. It couldn't be that difficult. No more than the bus system in Coventry. Theresa walked part of the way with her and pointed to the street leading to the station. Metro Rio's blue 'M' in a circle would be easy to spot. She would go back to the tourist area near Copacabana Beach. Better to stick to familiar territory. She wrote down the name of the station in her notebook and double-checked the spelling; the place names had a habit of all looking the same, although once she read them out phonetically, they were quite different. She walked down a short flight of stairs towards the ticket booth and studied the map next to the turnstile.

'Madam, where are you going?' A young man in a uniform was speaking.

'To Copacabana?'

'Of course.' He tapped the board. 'You can get off here at Siqueira Campos. Line One. Walk down Rodolfo Dantas Road, past all the shops and there is the Copacabana.'

Easy. She'd spend the day window shopping, people watching, maybe take off her shoes and walk on the beach. Have a paddle.

~ ❧ ~

Like an inland beachcomber, Flora patrolled the streets behind the sandy Copacabana strip, hopeful of discovering some sort of delight. Local colour, culture. Instead, she found a tapestry of tourist traps: souvenir shops, ticket touts, over-priced cafes. A single designer boutique was seemingly out of place, wedged between Sexy Time Lingerie with its party of shameless dummies in the window, and Original Rio Art, selling xeroxed copies of Christ the Redeemer in technicoloured glory.

After paying in advance for four nights' lodgings and putting aside a little for emergencies, there was the equivalent of about a pound a day to spend. She would only buy food from the market or street vendors. No treats. As an investment in Bonita, she splashed out on a box of *Serenata de Amor* from a stall aptly named *Amigo Chocola*. It took up a third of her daily allowance, but a chocolate friend was better than no friend at all.

Another bag of *pão de queijo* would do for lunch. She was beginning to tire of them but at least she knew what they were made of, and they were cheap and filling. A cup of tea would have been lovely, but tourist prices forced her to take out her hankie and carefully wipe the spout of the beach-side water-fountain. By five o'clock she was hot and weary, looking forward to claiming her time-share of the bed for an early night. Only three more sleeps until Marty returned.

At the underground exit Flora was engulfed in a swathe of rush-hour workers, conscious among all the glossy black hair and olive skin that she stood out as a prime target for robbers and beggars. Now that the streets were becoming familiar, she walked with a little more confidence than she had that morning, getting used to the staring locals and the small grubby children who sometimes ran up to her with their hands out. She knew from experience that giving the slightest thing to one would open the floodgates. In Mexico she had thought a few small coins wouldn't hurt, only to be besieged by trails of children, often pushed forward by parents, who then became demanding, if not a little menacing. With a slightly more worldly confidence, a simple 'no', in what she hoped was a clear but friendly tone, seemed to work. In the same vein, she'd learned to split her money up and distribute it in several different pockets, to dress plainly and not wear any jewellery.

She turned the corner into the final street and scanned the row of dusty shacks for Vila Eloa. About halfway up on the left-hand side she spotted a woman washing the front step with a mop. None of the other homes looked quite so well cared for, and even though the place was cramped and sparsely furnished, it was spotlessly clean. At least she had that to be grateful for.

Flora walked carefully, stepping over a used nappy and a pile of broken roof tiles. A car seemed to swerve towards her until she realised it was just negotiating a large pothole. Clouds of dust billowed behind it as it passed; the woman outside Vila Eloa cursed quietly and began to mop the step anew. Flora admired her dress; pink was such a cheerful colour. She had something almost identical, only hers had been bought in Belize at an exclusive beachside boutique.

'*Olá*' said Flora, enjoying the ability to communicate. Soon she'd be fluent.

'*Olá, Senhora,*' was the woman's reply, accompanied by a broad smile.

After exaggeratedly avoiding the mopped step, Flora entered the building and spotted Theresa in the bar. The flowing yellow jumpsuit seemed quite a drastic change from the flowery apron she'd been wearing that morning; it was just a little too big, but the colour suited her.

She looked up from buffing a tray of glasses and said '*Olá, Senhora*'.

'*Olá*, Theresa. Please, call me Flora.'

'Flora,' she said slowly, nodding and smiling. Then, gesturing to her outfit she said, '*Eu gosto desta cor amarela.*'

Flora had no idea what she was saying but nodded enthusiastically. 'Beautiful. *Bellissimo*, er, it looks lovely on you,' she said a little louder, hoping the depth of compliment would translate with volume. It looked like chiffon but was probably nylon. She could see herself in something similar. She knew Marty would pair it with her tasselled earrings and a pair of nude heels.

She wanted to catch Bonita before she left for work, so gave a small wave and went up to her room. Bonita was wearing a gold bikini top and a striking blue mini skirt, with her hair tied in a high ponytail – she looked younger than ever. A pair of leopard-head earrings completed her look.

'Here, Bonita. I've bought you some chocolate.' She held out the box, waiting for some scornful reply.

'Thank you, Flora, you are kind,' said Bonita with a double-dimpled smile. She burrowed to the bottom of her clothes box and hid the chocolates, then kicked the box back under the bed. Sweet, thought Flora, she treasures them so much she wants to hide them from the others.

'I like your earrings,' Flora ventured.

'I like your earrings also,' said Bonita, with a small laugh.

Flora wasn't wearing any earrings, so it took her a moment to work it out. 'My earrings?'

'Yes, tiger is a good animal, no? Strong.' Bonita carried on with her make-up, applying frosted blue lipstick.

'Tiger?' asked Flora. Now she was completely lost. She didn't have any tiger earrings, but Bonita was wearing leopards – she had a similar pair. No, wait. She had some exactly the same. Suddenly the pink dress, the yellow chiffon made sense. The Fabergé leopard earrings. The ones she'd bought in Texas.

A suitcase was lying on the floor, not where she'd left it neatly stacked in the corner with the others. Almost empty. She rummaged through a knot of bras and knickers. Her jewellery box was gone.

'Bonita! Where's all my stuff? What do you think you're doing, taking my things? Give me those earrings!'

Bonita was already on her feet, pushing past. She ran downstairs with a familiar-looking Swarovski clutch bag under her arm. Flora hurried after her, but by the time she reached the street, Bonita was already on the back of a motorbike; the driver took off down the road while she put her helmet on.

Back in her room, Flora surveyed the remains of her belongings. The idea of Bonita going to work in a pair of earrings worth three thousand pounds and Theresa polishing glasses in a designer chiffon jumpsuit was both funny and galling at the same time. Besides the underwear, there were a couple of Inca bangles from Guatemala and a small gold ankle chain Marty had given her at Christmas, plus a pair of sensible shoes and a safari suit. Luckily the things she'd hung on the back of the door were still there. The other two suitcases and the bin liners of shoes and handbags were missing altogether.

Her first thought was to go to the police. She had seen plenty of *policía turística* at the carnival, strutting around in their berets and bulletproof vests. Intimidating. Why did they have pistols and other paraphernalia strapped around their waists? Enrique had explained they were the friendly face of the normal military police. 'I can say from experience – I love my country, but the police, they kill people. No questions.' Would they want to see her passport? How could she explain it was being held by the hotel because she owed them over eleven thousand pounds? Would the tourist police pass her on to the less friendly men, the ones in camouflage and jackboots, toting machine guns? Best stay out of their way.

Even asking Theresa for her things seemed pointless. She'd brought three suitcases and two bin bags of clothes, handbags and shoes to a house full of women who were just as poor as all the other people she passed on the streets. Ever since Mexico, she'd been hiding her jewellery and keeping her valuables in a money belt. What did she expect? She should have just brought what she needed and left the rest at the hotel with Marty's stuff, but she'd packed in such a hurry, unable to think straight.

~ஐஐ~

The next morning, on her way down to have a wash, she heard a tentative '*bom dia*' as someone vacated the bathroom, swishing past in Flora's silk zebra-print beach robe. She'd only worn it once, in Belize, and felt it was just a bit too 'jet-set'. Now, wrapped around a willowy teenager, it looked oddly in keeping against the peeling paint and chipped tiles – like a fashion shoot in a glossy magazine.

As more girls appeared, sleepy from their late nights, Flora spotted familiar items of clothing here and there or occasionally a full designer outfit, far too big but worn with a sense of pride and style. She was greeted with smiles and greetings, offers to share breakfast. Much more pleasant than the glowers and flounces she'd encountered previously. For the first time in the last three days she felt relaxed – included, even. Staying at Vila Eloa would now be much more pleasant, but at what cost? How could she get all her things back? Bonita spoke the best English; she was the only girl who could translate properly. She went back upstairs to find her already in bed and apparently sound asleep, still wearing her Fabergé earrings.

'Bonita, I need to talk to you.' Flora shook her by the shoulder, gently at first and then, remembering the rude awakening she'd had the previous day, she added a degree of force.

'Bonita! I know you're awake.' Nothing. With jolty movements in time to the words she added, 'I'm. Not. Going. To. Stop. Until. You. Talk. To. Me.'

Bonita groaned and half sat up. 'What you want?' Her eyelids were drooping with obvious exhaustion.

'What about my things? I need you to get them back for me.'

'You have too many stuffs. Better to share, no?'

Flora felt a twinge of guilt. She did have too much. Only a few months ago she would have been happy with a new Marks and Sparks cardi and a pair of slippers at Christmas. What had become of her? She would have gladly given a few things away; she'd been planning to.

She tried a different tack. 'You can't wear those earrings to work, Bonita – what if you lost one?'

'Is okay, I buy new pair.'

'But they're, you know, a bit too good for every day. Designer.'

'Is good fake, no? The real fake.'

'Not fake, they're actually real,' Flora insisted, but without being able to get them back, what did it matter.

'You must quiet now. Sleep.' Bonita turned to the wall and pulled the covers over her head.

~~~~~

Flora left Vila Eloa for another day of window shopping. She would come back early, before Bonita got ready for work, whatever that might be. She would get her to explain to everyone how valuable everything was. On the other hand, any single item would be worth a fortune to them and if they realised that, they'd probably sell it. Perhaps they should. Hadn't Marty said they needed to reduce their excess baggage? She'd go on a fun shopping trip as soon as he'd sorted out the bank account. They'd need some warmer clothes for New Zealand in any case.

Later, Theresa invited Flora to join her and the girls for dinner. It was a simple meal, but served with banter and high spirits. A couple of the girls asked her questions in broken English and then translated her answers for the others to hear.

They already seemed to know a fair amount about her. The taxi driver must have passed on a few snippets when they'd first arrived, but they weren't curious about her outstanding hotel bill; they were more interested in John.

'Your husband was good man or lazy man?'

'Did he give you the money or spend it on drinking and gambling?'

'Did he have a lover?'

Flora's answers were met with nods of approval. John had worked hard, never took holidays, wasn't interested in sex and liked to save money. They all agreed: he was the perfect husband who had the decency to die before needing to be taken care of in his old age.

As the conversation moved on to men in general, it became apparent none of them had a boyfriend or a husband.

'But the Brazilian men are so handsome,' Flora chirruped.

'I had a husband,' one girl said. 'The day we married, he took me away from my family and home in the mountains. He raped me every night. After a few weeks he was bored. He stole everything and ran away.'

A quiet girl with solemn eyes said she had been forced into prostitution by her father who was an alcoholic. Another had a boyfriend who used her as a drug mule until he was shot by a rival gang.

Flora was tempted to mention Jago. He had used her for a sleazy night of passion. He wasn't any different, but someone else summed up the situation for her.

'Brazilian men are cheats and liars. Dirty pigs who just want sex and drinking!' This brought a chorus of agreement.

'They make us do things and don't pay extra.'

Flora was confused. 'Pay extra?' The room was suddenly quiet and then someone started giggling.

'For the boom-boom time. Fucking,' said a sweet girl in Flora's Dolce & Gabbana sunglasses and a Minnie Mouse tee-shirt.

'Prostitution?'

'Yes, *prostituta. Puta.*'

'What, here? A bordello?'

～·w)))·～

Later, when the girls had dispersed and Flora was getting ready for bed, she thought about the stories she'd heard and the girls' belief that John had been a good husband. Until then she had considered her marriage a disappointment, beginning with a lacklustre wedding night. Unlike the girls at Vila Eloa, who would have woken up on their first day of marriage to a handsome but violent husband, she'd opened her eyes to find John sitting up in bed, pyjamas buttoned up to the neck, reading a copy of *National Geographic*.

And instead of giving her a slap or heaving himself on top of her to take his dues, John had simply said, 'How about a nice cup of tea?'

She'd never had a cup of tea in bed before. 'Oh, yes please, that would be lovely.'

'Off you pop then,' John nodded towards the door. 'We may as well start off in the way we mean to go on.'

And while the girls were being put to work as drug mules or prostitutes, John had handed her a copy of Mrs Beeton's *Household Management*, saying, 'If Mrs Beeton was good enough for Mother, I'm sure she's plenty good enough for you.' When he added, 'And I've something else', she had looked up from *Managing Your Household Staff*, hoping to see something frivolous: a love token perhaps. But John was waggling an exercise book at her.

'It's all written down in here, so you don't have to think. Shopping, meals, a rota for your housework, even telephone numbers. Everything you'll need, to save you asking.'

'Save me asking?'

'Here you are. See, today is Wednesday. Breakfast: fried egg, two slices of toast. But,' he held up a finger, 'at the same time you'll need to prepare my packed lunch. Sandwiches and an apple. Cheese. And don't go fussing with the crusts, I like them left on. Dinner is at six and if you follow the chart, you'll see we're having shepherd's pie tonight, with tinned peaches and Carnation Milk for afters.'

True he wasn't violent, but he was controlling, and he'd undermined her confidence. Was that also a form of abuse?

EIGHTEEN

In case Marty had left a message, Flora went to check at the hotel. The manager spotted her and came over with a questioning expression on his face.

'Ah, so you will settle your bill, *Senhora*?' He seemed less friendly than last time.

'Well, no, I was just—'

'I have many, many problem with your bill. My boss, he is very angry.'

'I'm sorry about that. I'm trying my best, but I really have to wait for Marty. He's the only one who can sort it out.'

'Marty, Marty. Where is he now? Maybe he left you and ran off with his lady-boyfriend.'

'Don't be ridiculous, he's just gone for a few days' sailing. He'll be here tomorrow, or the next day at the latest. As soon as he arrives we'll sort everything out. You have my word.'

'Forgive me, *Senhora*, your word is nothing without money.'

'I offered you my jewellery; you should've taken it.' While I still had it, thought Flora.

'If he is not here tomorrow, I have to talk with my boss again. He knows where you are living. Good day, *Senhora*.'

Flora was stunned. How did he know where she was living? She could do with speaking to Alberto, but he only worked nights. Perhaps she could come back later and ask him about a bit about the boss; he sounded very intimidating.

Maybe she should get the tourist police involved after all? The only other person she could ask without too much of a language barrier was Bonita.

'No! Tourist pigs! Have you seen them? They are same as all police and when they know you stay in favela, in a house of *puta*, what you think they say, eh?'

'But what if the hotel boss becomes violent, what should I do?'

'Rio is full of bad men. Do you think this is something new?'

'Oh, Bonita, it's such a pickle, I just hope Marty arrives nice and early.'

After Bonita had left for work, Flora lay on the narrow bed and went over the events since they'd arrived in Rio. Everything had gone so well and then so wrong – in such a short space of time. She thought about Jago, the things he'd said, his gentle touch. The things he'd done; she hadn't known such pleasure was possible. And then he disappeared. Maybe he was injured, in hospital, with a nasty bang on the head giving him temporary amnesia. Perhaps he was looking for her right now. No.

The hotel manager had her wondering about Marty. Maybe he *had* run off with Enrique. After all, Enrique had left his job but hadn't told her; maybe they'd been planning an elopement? But why would Marty do that to her? His last phone call had been enough to tell her he really did care about her. There was no way he wouldn't come back when he said he would. Ever since she'd known him, he'd always put her first. She'd go back to the hotel tomorrow morning and await his return, then as soon as he'd sorted everything out they could find somewhere nice to stay, away from Copacabana; they could make the most of their extended ticket by exploring another part of the city.

⁓✿⁓

Flora read and reread the email; it just didn't make sense. Clutching a tissue in one hand and the sheet of paper in the other, she could see the words, but they were a blur; partly from the tears pricking her eyes and partly because her hand holding the printout was shaking so much.

'So, Mrs Marshall, what are you going to do?' The man in a cream linen suit and open-necked shirt had introduced himself as Mr Marcola Lopez, owner of four hospitality centres and the two best luxury hotels on Copacabana Beach. He spoke quietly and steadily with a hint of an American accent. The hotel manager was standing a few paces to the side, giving his boss the appropriate space and respect. Flora looked beseechingly in his direction, but he averted his gaze, clearly indicating she must deal with Mr Lopez from now on.

'I—' Flora's mind was a blank.

'We have already given you five days. You said your friend is coming.'

'But—'

'You had the good life at my expense, no? You live like a film star in the Presidential Suite. So now you must pay. You gave your word, Mrs Marshall.'

'I don't know what I can do.'

'Perhaps we will take a look at your jewellery after all. Maybe with everything together we can make it enough.' He looked out of the window as he spoke, as though already bored.

'I, um. I don't have it any more.' Flora could barely breathe. 'It was all stolen,' came out in a hoarse whisper.

Silence.

'And my clothes as well,' she managed to add. Perhaps he'd be sympathetic.

'Then you must find another way,' he said, reaching into his inside pocket for his phone.

'But—'

'We have your passport. Do not try to run away. We know where you stay. We will watch you. We have people everywhere. Please understand what I am saying, Mrs Marshall.' He gave her a look that spoke volumes. 'One way or another, you will pay what you owe me.'

Flora looked at him properly for the first time. For a moment she thought he looked like Enrique's uncle from the restaurant, but of course, he couldn't be. 'But without—'

'Use your imagination, Mrs Marshall. No matter what your English manners tell you about me, I am a fair man. I give you this opportunity to pay first, before you experience something regrettable.'

'W—what do you mean?' Flora tried to control her voice.

'Let's hope you never find out, Mrs Marshall. Pay your debt.' Already dialling a number on his phone, he turned away. When Flora remained seated, unable to think of what she should do next, he simply added, 'That is all.'

The hotel manager escorted her back to the foyer in silence. She wanted to ask his advice; how long did she have before 'something regrettable' happened? What would that be? Prison perhaps, or would Mr Lopez let his security guards take over — she'd seen them around the hotel, an assortment of stocky, hairy men erupting out of shiny suits. How could she possibly find enough money on her own? How would she live in the meantime? She turned to speak to him but he avoided eye contact and propelled her past reception, through the revolving glass doors to the top of the marble steps. She tried a different approach.

'I can't understand how Marty could—'

'Good afternoon, Mrs Marshall,' the manager said, still not looking at her. 'Keep in touch.'

She grabbed the handrail to navigate the steps. It was a small relief to be back on the pavement amongst the chaos of tourists and street hawkers. She felt faint. With a racing heartbeat and sense of her limbs giving way, she staggered, arms outstretched to grab the nearest wall. Panicky short breaths stuck in her throat. Sweaty tingling numbed her hands. She slid to the ground.

No one stopped to help. Think. She tried to focus but blind terror was taking over. Slumped on the pavement for several minutes, her breathing gradually returned to normal. With her eyes closed, she inhaled slowly and deeply, then exhaled. Blindly grappling in her bag for a bottle of water, she took a few sips. When she felt strong enough, she pulled herself up to stand.

Marty, how could you do this to me?

~∙∙∙∙∙∙~

She had finished her water ages ago, and her stomach reminded her she hadn't eaten since breakfast time. She had to keep going. Several wrong turns had led her back towards the city. She would use the underground, but money was even more precious now.

Finally, her aching feet trudged along the last row of the neat houses, past the city dump and municipal buildings to the outskirts of the favela. Exhausted, Flora willed herself on, wearily navigating around piles of rubbish, an occasional burnt-out car. When she saw a collapsed building with a makeshift tent on top of the rubble, she knew she was almost there and walked a little faster. Begging children in filthy clothes ran towards her; she barely gave them a glance. '*Oi Senhora, oi!*' they called after her.

By the time she arrived at Vila Eloa it was beginning to get dark. She would have to speak to Theresa. She was supposed to move out; her few belongings were already packed in anticipation of Marty's arrival. Hopefully Bonita would still be willing to share.

She had started the day so full of hope, cheerful even, knowing Marty would be back to sort out the hotel bill and find somewhere nice for them to stay. Thinking they would maybe squeeze in with Enrique, wherever he lived – it would be fun. She even had the idea they might all go out for dinner and had planned a passable outfit from her few remaining clothes and accessories.

How ridiculous.

The girls were chatting in the kitchen over the clatter of plates. Theresa said something, and they all laughed. Sitting with them, sharing their evening meal had become a cherished time of newfound acceptance, almost friendship. She wasn't in the mood for company now. Talking to Theresa would have to wait. She pulled herself up the stairs, each step sending a sharp, complaining spasm through her body. She had never walked so many miles in her life.

Her solitary suitcase was where she'd left it, by the door. Bonita had left for work. As usual, the bed was unmade. She swept aside the jumble of sparkly bikini tops, jelly cats and minuscule botty shorts and sat down. Her hands were still shaking. She took the printed email out of her bag, addressed to her, care of the hotel:

Dear Flora
I am not coming back to Rio.
Enrique and I will start a new life together.
Goodbye my friend,
Marty

Reading it again and again, the words shouted the unthinkable. Marty wasn't coming back. As simple as that, with just an email sent to the hotel. How could it be true? Perhaps it was a dream. A nightmare. Had she done something to make him turn away? Maybe when she'd overslept and didn't meet him at the after-party? Surely that wasn't such a terrible thing? He'd been with Enrique. 'I love you,' he'd shouted down the phone. Drunk and happy.

I am not coming back to Rio. There was no mention of the problem with the bank. He didn't know about the outstanding hotel bill. Of course he didn't.

Again, she scanned the message for clues. *Goodbye my friend.* It didn't even sound like Marty. The warmth and humour, the high spirits were gone. What had happened in five days to make him change so drastically? Was this how someone behaved when they were in love? Even so, it wasn't the agreement; she'd paid all his expenses, in exchange he was supposed to do John's list with her, not leave her at the first sniff of love.

He must have thought she was having a great time with Jago – perhaps he thought *she'd* abandoned *him*! But surely he would have tried to contact Jago, or called Enrique's uncle at the restaurant. But if that was the case, he'd know they weren't together. Her and Jago. Just the thought made her heart shrink into a sharp stabbing pain. How had everything gone so horribly wrong?

Flora kicked off her shoes and lay down. The little fan whirred lukewarm breath towards her, dusty grime clung to the ventilation mesh in waving tentacles. The single lightbulb flickered overhead. She was sweating and wondered whether the heat from the bulb made the room so hot or if it was the lack of a window. Probably both.

A spider made its way lazily across the ceiling. A fly buzzed frantically in its grip. The spider seemed in no hurry. There would always be another victim. Downstairs the girls were gathering in the bar. She could hear them clonking about on their ridiculously high plastic platforms, squabbling and laughing simultaneously the way young girls do. Soon, men would arrive on the pretext of having a beer and choose one of them to undress, to lie their dolly-shaped bodies down, for little more than the price of a burrito. Old enough to be their fathers. Grandfathers, even.

What was the world coming to?

~ఴ౨౨ఴ~

Flora switched the light off and lay down in the dark. Her thoughts were exhausted, overtaken by a strange sense of numbness, close to calm. From the rooms below came the odd argument, shouting, sometimes laughter. A girl was singing. Late into the night, she heard the rumble of men's voices, the exchange of money for services, Theresa ringing the bell when time was exceeded. More money, more voices. Less laughter. No singing.

Eventually, the activities of Vila Eloa petered out and the noise from the narrow streets subsided to little more than the occasional motorbike or barking dog. She switched the light back on, ready to face the facts.

Her purse contained fifty-seven Brazilian reais. She did a rough calculation; about ten pounds. Add to that a few inexpensive pieces of jewellery. Perhaps she could persuade Bonita to give back the gold and sapphire leopard earrings; maybe Theresa could ask the girls to return a few other pieces. Then there were the plane tickets, not just the ones to New Zealand, but the business class ones for Asia as well. Whatever they were worth, if she could find out how to get a refund, maybe Mr Marcola Lopez would accept the combined value. It might just be enough to get her passport back.

Then she'd just have to find a way of getting home. Alone.

Coventry seemed such a long way away. In that different world it would already be morning. Grove Road's pebble-dashed semis in gloomy dawn, each house displaying a window or two of light. Kettles on, toast in; neighbours leaving for work, going about their business. Only number ninety-three would be dark and waiting.

She'd been in such a hurry to leave. Life had been so easy. A bit of housework, an endless supply of library romances, sitting in the front room with a nice cup of tea and a biscuit, *Corrie* or *Eastenders* on the telly. She'd even settle for making John's evening meal. Friday – fish pie with jam roly-poly and custard for afters. She had hated that rota, yet now she missed the certainty, the comfort of never not knowing. With all his faults, John had been a loyal husband. He'd provided food and a roof over her head; even if it was patched-up and dingy, it had been home. A palace compared to Vila Eloa.

She remembered Marty saying, 'Hey, babes, guess what a favela is?' It sounded nice. 'Something delicious. A dessert?' she'd said. How she'd laughed at his parody of ordering a favela and getting a compote of gang warfare, served on a bed of class A drugs, sprinkled with violent crime and a prostitution sauce. Not funny anymore.

Perhaps she should try and move somewhere cheaper than Vila Eloa, but she felt safe there. Theresa and the girls stealing all her stuff had levelled the playing field and paved her way to becoming more accepted. She needed something to cling to; even if it meant hot-bedding with Bonita, it was all she had left.

She had to get Mr Lopez off her back. Hopefully the plane tickets would sort that out. Then, when she had her passport, she'd plan how to get home. She needed more money. But where from? She'd only ever had one job as a school leaver, and look where that had got her.

Fine Fare supermarket was where she'd met John. Or Johnny M as he was then. Who would have thought stacking the deal of the week into a bargain-sized pyramid would change her life forever.

'Excuse me, Miss.' John's hand had almost touched hers when he stretched for the upper reaches of Lipton flo-thru teabags.

'Mr Marshall! Fancy seeing you in Fine Fare.' Johnny M. Next to the other male teachers – Baldy Newbald and The

Dribbler – he had been the only remotely attractive member of staff at St Margaret's, even with his NHS glasses and a slight limp. His geography classes had been the highlight of her final year.

'I was just passing,' he said, 'I spotted the special offer in the window.'

'Everyone likes a bargain, Mr Marshall,' she had replied.

She knew she was almost pretty when she smiled.

'Please, call me John.'

A few 'bargains of the week' later, John said his kitchen cupboard, once akin to the Kalahari Desert, was now under threat of a Strombolian-like eruption and suggested they meet for a walk after work instead.

She wasn't funny or clever; she had no special talents. Until John came along she'd lived in the half-dark, and from what she could gather, so had he; they were two odd socks making up a pair – better together than apart. Despite that, they didn't have much in common; she had her romantic novels and soap operas, he had geography and gardening.

It was because of the allotment and his beloved dahlias that she'd met Marty.

Marty. How could she have got him so wrong? His email was bewildering – how could he abandon her? They had an agreement. They were friends – her only friend. She couldn't dig into her feelings without a surge of panic threatening to tip her into complete turmoil. She had to stay focused. Yes, she would have to find a job. Without language skills, she doubted she could work in a shop, but anything would do. She'd scrub floors if it meant finding her way home; then, back at Grove Road, she'd let herself think properly about Marty and the whole sorry mess her life had become.

NINETEEN

Bonita didn't seem surprised to hear Flora would be staying on. She simply shrugged and said, 'I told you, men are selfish pigs. Your friend, he only think of himself, no?'

Flora didn't want to talk about Marty. She had to stay on plan. 'I was wondering if you could let me have those earrings back, the gold and blue leopards?'

'The earrings? No.' There was a pause. 'I sold them already.'

'Sold them?'

'Yes, good price. Then I buy whole new outfit, including shoes.' Bonita seemed pleased with herself.

'They were worth a lot more than one of your outfits.' Flora tried not to shout. 'Was there any money left over?'

'Yes. I had a chocolate milkshake.'

'What? Bonita! Do you have any idea—' What was the point? She'd sold the earrings and that was that.

'Look, real leather, nice and soft.' Bonita held up a pair of strappy green and gold sandals with transparent four-inch platforms. Floating inside each heel were tiny sparkly Brazilian football shirts.

'Oh, so you enjoy sports?'

'They are not for enjoying, just for working.'

Flora still wasn't sure where Bonita went each evening, dressed like the girls downstairs but with more sequins and a slightly more coordinated look. She would have to ask her, show an interest, but just then she wanted to get back on track.

'Well, without those earrings, I'll need a job. Do you have any ideas?'

'What kind of job?'

'I don't know. I don't have any skills.'

During the carnival the city had been full to bursting with extra workers. Now it was over, there was a surge of unemployment as the tide of tourists drifted away again. She'd take whatever was on offer.

'What do you think I could do to earn as much money as possible, as quickly as possible?'

'You want to talk to Theresa about giving the boom-boom?' Bonita smirked.

Flora pictured herself wearing a pair of sparkly botty shorts and lining up with the girls downstairs. It was too funny not to laugh.

'No, but seriously, Bonita, I have to get a job. I urgently need money.'

'I don't know. The most money is from drugs. Then you must deal with chief of favela.'

'No, I'm in enough trouble already. I'd better look closer to the city centre. Maybe I could do cleaning. I was good at that.'

'What is change from yesterday,' Bonita asked, 'so now you need work?'

Flora briefly explained the situation with the bank account and touched on Marty's email.

'This money just goes from the bank then your friend, he vamoose?'

Flora nodded.

'You have Lopez after you?' Bonita paced the room. 'So now your friend, he lives like a king? Why trust him so much?' she wasn't exactly shouting, but had the excitable tone Flora heard whenever there was an altercation between the girls. 'Are you *idiota*?' Bonita was pointing at her head, her face just a few inches away. Without warning, fat tears rolled down Flora's cheeks. It was such a relief to share her problem, heartwarming that instead of the usual shrug or smart remark, Bonita was angry on her behalf.

Bonita clattered downstairs and began speaking rapidly to the girls. Flora quickly wiped her face and followed. Until then, it hadn't occurred to her that Marty might have taken the money, but to Bonita it was obvious. And what about the few occasions when Marty's behaviour had taken her by surprise, the way he embellished the truth almost without thinking? Then, on one occasion he'd left a restaurant without paying. At the time, it had looked like an accident, but now she wondered. She hadn't known Marty all that well before they'd set off. They had met for coffee and gone shopping together, but she'd never been to his flat. What was he truly like as a person?

None of the girls owned up to having any of her belongings except the youngest, who was still wearing a pair of Chanel sunglasses despite the gloom of the badly lit room. Thinking about it, even Theresa had stopped wearing the chiffon jumpsuit. Flora suspected they had followed Bonita's example and sold them.

The sunglasses were solemnly handed over, but Flora felt sorry for the girl. She'd worn them continually day and night, mostly indoors. Clearly, they were her most treasured possession. 'It doesn't matter,' she said and gave them back.

~~~

Looking for work was the priority. Flora chose the tourist areas where there wouldn't be so much of a language barrier. Her enquiries were met with a mixture of responses: why was an Englishwoman asking for work, what did she really want, was she joking? By five o'clock she was exhausted and nowhere closer to finding employment. But Copacabana wasn't the only area. She would try further along the beach in the morning.

Walking wearily back towards Siqueira Campos Station, she realised she hadn't sat down all day. A nice cup of tea would be a well-deserved reward, never mind the expense. She spotted a neon sign just ahead: Cyber Cafe. Inside, Flora looked around for the service area.

'You alright, love?' Almost hidden from view was a young man with lank blonde hair, apparently playing a computer game.

'Oh, er, yes, I'd like a cup of tea, please.'

'That's so funny, nice one!' He looked up. 'You sound just like my nan. I miss her. Where are you from?'

'I'm from Coventry,' said Flora, a little bewildered to hear his accent.

'Nan's in Leamington Spa. Not that far from you, then. I'm Dave by the way.'

'Hello, Dave, I'm Flora. I was wondering—' she looked around. She could only see people using computers; no one was drinking tea. 'I don't suppose you know where I could get a cup of tea?'

'Oh, sorry, I thought you were joking about that. Um, no, sorry, tea is fairly low on the agenda of gamers. They're more into Red Bull.'

'Gamers? Playing electronic games on computers, you mean?'

'Yes. This is an internet cafe, which means kids can pay me to skive off whatever they're supposed to be doing. It's a win-win. I make money; they have fun.'

'I don't suppose I could use one of the internets to arrange a refund on some airline tickets, could I? I'm not much into gaming.' She was pleased with her use of the vernacular.

'Yes, of course. It's split into half-hour slots, and you can print stuff off for a bit extra. Shall I set you up over there?'

'Well, actually, I was wondering if you could help me. The inter-web is so—'

'Go on then, let's see what you've got.'

Dave checked the refund policies. 'So, you're going from New Zealand to China, then Mongolia, Cambodia, Indonesia – wow, that's a cool trip. You sure you want to cancel?' Flora didn't reply; she was trying hard not to cry. Everything had been so much fun, planning the trip with Marty, even before, when she and John were trying to win the jackpot. How they'd discuss the geographical wonders of the Far East. In many ways, Asia was the part of the trip Flora had most looked forward to. Especially after sampling numerous dishes from the Golden Wok – she had a feeling China would have been her favourite place of all.

'Nice!' exclaimed Dave. 'There's a lot I could do with nine grand. Oh, plus the airport taxes.'

'Nine thousand?' A surge of relief. Nine thousand pounds plus the tickets from Rio to New Zealand. That should do it. She could hardly concentrate on what Dave was saying.

'Mastercard or visa? We just need your card, the one you paid with originally.' Flora fished the credit card out of her purse. 'You need to fill in the numbers. I don't want to be accused of hacking your bank account,' Dave joked as he covered his eyes with exaggeration.

Navigating with some difficulty, Flora managed to complete the details and then pushed the mouse back towards Dave.

'So, it says here, the refund will be processed in seven days. Do you want me to print this off, so you can check your account next week?'

Flora thanked Dave and said she would be back the following day, then went straight to the hotel. Happily, she waved the print-out at the manager and asked for her tickets to New Zealand, explaining she hoped to have enough of a refund to pay the bill in full.

'This is good news, Mrs Marshall. I will give you a photocopy of the tickets. Which day will you return with the money?'

'A week tomorrow.'

The manager nodded. 'Very well, I will inform Mr Lopez on your behalf. We will expect to see you again soon.'

～ﾐﾉﾉﾉﾚﾞ～

Two business-class tickets to New Zealand bumped the refund up considerably. With airport taxes on top, there would be more than twelve thousand pounds. Enough to settle the hotel bill and hopefully buy an economy flight home.

'Just another week in this tropical paradise and you'll be back in good old Blighty,' Dave said over the whirring printer. He handed her the confirmation. 'There you go.'

'What a relief.' She glanced at the balance, just to be sure. 'Thanks for your help. I must say, I don't know what I would've done without you.'

'No sweat. Just promise you'll pop in and see Nan next time you're in Leamington Spa. She'll be chuffed to bits, knowing you've met her favourite grandson.'

'I expect you miss your family?'

'Not really. Apart from Nan, everyone was always arguing. I don't miss the weather either.'

'Well, yes, I understand that.' Outside was another gloriously sunny day. 'February in Britain isn't the best, is it?'

'It's either fog or raining sideways. Not so bad when it snows, but then there's all that grey slush. And those miserable dark mornings! Not for me,' he said with a smile.

'Yes, but you can't get a proper cup of tea here, can you?' Flora couldn't remember the last time she'd enjoyed a decent brew. Perhaps it was the water? One thing she already knew, if she ever went on holiday again, she'd take her own teabags.

'Same with the beer. I seriously miss my local – what I wouldn't do for a pint of Old Peculier.'

A group of rowdy teenagers coming in cut the conversation short and Flora said a hasty goodbye. All that talk about tea had put her in the mood for a cup of something, though she would steer clear of the local *chá preto* – it wasn't a patch on PG Tips. She drifted towards a small cafe she'd previously visited with Enrique and Marty; they served the most delicious little *brigadeiros*, complimentary with a cup of coffee. She deserved a treat after all the stress and worry of the past week. Now she had everything under control, she could afford to relax.

Until last week, going home had only been an abstract thought, happening sometime in the distant future. Travelling away from Coventry had also taken her away from the past; with each country and new experience the old version of frumpy Flora grew smaller and smaller. But now she was about to boomerang back to Grove Road before that sad little figure had completely disappeared. All the promise and excitement gone, and nothing to look forward to except a nice cup of tea.

John's list was meant to have kick-started a new beginning, to have provided a period of readjustment. By the time the mineral-rich thermal waters of Pamukkale had been ticked off the list, she imagined, she would have blossomed into her full potential, the person she'd always wanted to be. A happy, confident Flora who could stand her ground in the allotment of life.

Now she was stuck. Even if she still had the money, she couldn't do John's list on her own. In so many ways Marty had been her saviour, but now, every time he came to mind her stomach churned. She still couldn't believe he had been so conniving. Enrique must have put him up to it. Then again, he could have planned the whole thing; he was a very convincing liar. She'd seen him in action many times – so-called 'sprinkling magic and adding colour'. More fool her. Emptying her bank account and disappearing into thin air had been the work of a con man, not a magician.

For all his faults though, life without Marty back in Coventry would be lonely. She stirred her coffee absently. As lonely as being married to John, but without having to wash his smalls or put up with his snoring. Instead, she'd watch more daytime telly, do less housework and sugarcoat the expanse of time with a packet of Jelly Babies or a trip to Gail's Cafe whenever she wanted. Still, what a life.

Perhaps she'd mistaken boredom for loneliness?

She nibbled her *brigadeiro*, momentarily relishing the creamy caramel, then wet her finger and dabbed at the chocolate sprinkles left behind. She would find a way to make friends, move to a new area maybe, where no one knew her. She ran her teaspoon around the inside of her coffee cup and finished off the foam. She just needed to be more outgoing, like Marty; talk to strangers, look for the fun in life. Even now, with no money and another week at Vila Eloa, she needed to think more like him. What would he do in her shoes? Probably give all the girls a makeover. Well, that wasn't her forte, but she could try and get more involved. Help Theresa in the kitchen, perhaps even cook the girls a meal? Treat them to some British cuisine.

~※~

'Frogs in the hole?' Bonita frowned over the dish and prodded it with a fork. 'But is no frog. Is sausage from the pig, no?'

Flora had done her best to explain the dish; toad or frog, it made no difference. Bonita's translation of 'frog in the hole' was met with equal confusion until Theresa interceded. Then there was nodding and a round of raucous laughter as the girls suggested a few alternative names. It was lovely to see one of Bonita's rare smiles.

'They say it is old man's *piroca* in a lady's *chocho*,' she said.

Flora laughed and sliced into the crisp batter as the warm steam enveloped her in a misty hug. It had come out well, considering the improvised ingredients. She'd cooked toad-in-the-hole every week for well over thirty years and it had never occurred to her to give it another name, let alone experiment with the ingredients. Theresa had insisted they use Brazilian *linguiça* sausages, made from smoked pork, seasoned with garlic and spices; for the batter they had adapted the recipe for *pão de queijo* – the little cheese balls she was so fond of. The reinvention was delicious.

'Tomorrow, I show you *coxinha*,' said Theresa, which started the girls off again – pronouncing it slowly made it sound like 'cock's in her'.

Each morning after that, Flora accompanied Teresa to the market and watched her haggle for the day's groceries, then write each expense down in a well-used notebook. By spending time with her, Flora saw a woman who really cared about her girls, concocting a herbal medicine for one and mending shoes for another. Occasionally she'd buy one or two small gifts, flowers or a soft toy. The language barrier was frustrating – Flora had so many questions.

A few days later, while preparing her new version of cottage pie, she spoke to Bonita. 'Theresa's very kind, isn't she?'

'Why do you think everyone want to stay here? She is mamãe for us.'

'When I first arrived, I thought the, er, *'prostituta'* was terrible'.

'No. She never wanted to do this way. But she has no kids. Her husband is killed by gangsters. No family. She was lonely. One day a girl ask for food and a place to sleep. When the girl was beaten by a bad customer on the street, Theresa made a working room in the house for her to make safe.'

'And then I suppose she found more girls needing protection?'

'Yes, including me. She take good care of us, and we share the money. Is a good way to live. We are a family. Together, we are strong.'

In return for Brazilian cooking lessons, Flora shared the seven meals immortalised by John's weekly rota. He would never have eaten anything remotely spicy, but with added local ingredients they were so much more tasty and interesting. For her cottage pie she would cover the shredded beef in a rich spicy tomato sauce with crushed new potatoes, sautéed in garlic. She had bought a pretty little notebook from the market and asked Bonita to translate and write down the newly adapted recipes for Theresa. It would make a nice leaving present.

'In a week's time she'll have to cook them without me.' She said while applying her newfound knife skills to a clove of smoked garlic. Then began to slowly dictate the ingredients for bread and butter pudding.

After Bonita had left for work and the girls were preparing for the evening ahead, Flora sat at the kitchen table, enjoying the relative calm. Less than a fortnight ago, she'd arrived in what she now knew was one of Rio's poorest favelas, scared of everything, the place, the poverty, and especially the people. Now she was almost part of the Vila Eloa family. In some ways she'd be sad to leave.

Bonita's words, 'together we are strong', and the story of how Theresa overcame loneliness, ran through her mind: how could she apply the same philosophy to life in Coventry? Perhaps she could be the person who started something, gathered people together? And like Theresa, perhaps she could even make it into a business of some kind? In the back of her mind there was a small spark of something hopeful, exciting even. Making decisions would be part of the new Flora.

When had she ever been in charge of her own life? Even for her holiday of a lifetime, she had handed the decision-making over to Marty. Was it laziness on her part? John used to shout, 'Grow a backbone!' at the telly whenever someone dithered over something. Maybe that was it.

~◦⟩⟩⟩◦~

On the final morning, with the airline tickets about to be refunded, Flora was feeling much more optimistic about returning home alone. She drank a breakfast coffee with Theresa in the kitchen and wondered if it was for the last time. As soon as she'd paid off the hotel, she'd ask Dave to help her find the cheapest flight home. She was going to miss life at Vila Eloa. She'd keep in touch, send a Christmas card and a parcel. A Christmas cake or tin of Family Circle, perhaps.

The underground at rush hour could have been unpleasant, but today was a turning point – no amount of hot, sweaty bodies would spoil it. She walked quickly to the hotel. It would be the last time of having to push through the ornate brass and glass doors. She took a moment to look around the foyer. Until then she hadn't taken much notice of the decor; it teetered between gaudy and opulent. Very Rio.

She handed over her credit card to the manager – no need to speak, he knew why she was there. While she waited, she scanned the uniformed staff, hoping to see Alberto, although he usually worked nights. She wanted to return the handkerchief he'd given her and thank him for his kindness – as soon as her payment was processed, she'd be on her way.

'Excuse me.' The manager was speaking to her. 'Your card is declined.' This time there was no veil of politeness.

'Declined? That's not possible! There's a refund of over twelve thousand pounds.' Perhaps the time difference meant she was a bit too early. But Britain was hours ahead, already afternoon.

A brief conversation with her credit card company on the international freephone number confirmed the worst.

'Your account is still in arrears. The refund has been received and is credited to your outstanding balance. But, because you breached your credit agreement previously, we would require the remainder of the balance to be repaid before we can extend further credit.'

'But that wasn't me,' Flora said weakly.

'If it wasn't you, please contact our fraud helpline. Can I give you the number?'

Flora was still clutching the receiver tightly long after the call had ended, not wishing to let go of her last hope. Then feeling lightheaded and faint, she staggered to a chair and sat down, trying to unravel what she'd just heard. No money. No ticket home. And how would she explain to the fraud helpline that with her permission, Marty had been using her credit card for months already or that she'd given it to Enrique, who'd passed it on to his sister, someone she'd never met, in the giddy expectation of two weeks of passion with Jago? And now they'd all disappeared.

The hotel manager was waiting. Mr Lopez would like her to join him in his office.

'Mrs Marshall, I have been patient, no?'

'I thought – I don't know what to say, except I—' Flora clutched Alberto's handkerchief, she could cry at any moment. 'I'll look for a job and— '

'A job? Ah, yes.' Marcola and the hotel manager discussed something in rapid Portuguese. The mood seemed to lighten. They were smiling.

'Perhaps I could work in your hotel?' she said quickly. Were they discussing her punishment, whatever veiled threat he had insinuated last time they'd met? 'I could join the housekeeping team, I'm very—'

'You are not Brazilian. The Brazilian woman is strong and full of energy – she understands the high standards we demand. Rio is my town. How would it look to have an old English woman mixed in with my girls?' Marcola chuckled and shook his head, then removed his cigar so he could have a proper laugh unencumbered.

Marcola said Flora would be better placed working as a *cafetina* at a *terma*. He owned four of the best establishments in Rio. He appraised her appearance and said she looked okay but could do with more make-up and proper women's shoes. Flora disagreed – she'd be better off in her sandals if she was going to be working in a cafe. She imagined she'd be on her feet all day, serving coffee (perhaps with a little *brigadeiro* on the side); comfortable shoes would be a must.

With no alternative, she accepted the job readily and left the meeting, still trying to catch up with emotions that had looped from excited to devastated and desperate, back to accepting and almost optimistic once more. Starting from tomorrow, she'd be in full-time employment. She'd stay on with Theresa and the girls – better than being lonely in Coventry. And at least the fear of Marcola Lopez's threats was under control. She would be his employee; she'd have rights and gain work experience. It would be nice to chat with customers; it might even be fun.

She'd been so relieved when Marcola had seen her potential as a *cafetina*, she'd simply agreed to everything he said – the unsociable hours, the overdone make-up, even the shoes. Only later, when lying in bed back at Vila Eloa, did she realise she hadn't discussed her wages, nor how long she'd have to work to pay off her debt.

～♩♩♩～

Flora eyed the building and double-checked the address: 'Carnival' was such a pretty name for a cafe. It suggested fun, colour – pinwheel pastries and fruit flans decorating the window. Instead, the exterior was black and gold with sweeping marble steps either side of a large fountain. She had one of Theresa's flowery pinnies in her bag, thinking she could pop it on to help make sandwiches in between waitressing – she wanted to learn the business inside out. Looking at the polished black marble and inlaid gold lettering, she realised they probably supplied full-length black aprons, something more upmarket.

A man in a Hawaiian shirt and chinos sauntered out and stood on the top step, blinking into the sun.

'Good morning,' said Flora, aiming to sound both friendly and professional. 'I hope you enjoyed the delights of Carnival?'

'Um, sure,' he mumbled, looking at her askance as he started down the steps.

'Wish me luck. It's my first day,' she called after him. He didn't reply. She would have to accept that some people would be coming in for a quiet cup of coffee and wouldn't want small talk or 'nonsensical chitter-chatter' as John would have called it. She made a mental note to try and read each customer's mood before engaging them in a conversation. With a deep breath, she pushed through the revolving front door.

The inside looked more like a hotel reception than a coffee shop. Behind the counter was a beautifully coiffed woman in a shimmering peacock blue dress.

'You are Flora?'

'Yes, I'm starting work today.'

'I am Alanza. Please use the backdoor in future. You cannot mix with the customers.'

'Why ever not?' What a silly rule, surely everyone liked a cheery hello?

'They must have their privacy. And if you see them outside on the street you must not recognise them. I heard you speaking a moment ago. This is strictly forbidden.'

'Oh, er, right.' Throughout her marriage, Gail's Cafe had been a complete lifesaver. Without a cheery 'hello and how are you?' type chat with either Gail or one of the fresh-faced waitresses, she would have been the loneliest housewife of all time. John never asked her how she was or how her day was going. Without the cafe girls, no one would have cared.

'Go downstairs. Chana will get you ready, then come back up and you can start with observational training; then you can try on your own. Any mistakes and Lopez will be angry. Business has been hit by De Flamenca opening a month ago. Whatever happens, no one who comes in can leave without purchasing a gold pass. Understand?'

'Okey-dokey.' Whatever a gold pass was; but she was sure to find out and meanwhile, she could try and make herself useful. 'I could easily wash up or clear tables without any training.'

'What are you talking about? Just go downstairs, crazy English.' Alanza turned back to her computer and conveyed her contempt by click-clacking furiously on the keyboard with her manicured fingertips.

In the dimly-lit basement, Chana's lustrous skin still shone the colour of burnished copper. Her hair was teased out into a huge mass of tiny black corkscrews to provide a glorious canopy for chunky gold earrings and a very skimpy gold lamé dress. Flora tried not to notice her breasts; their sheer size and spilling-outness was quite bewildering at close quarters. Everything about Chana was extraordinary.

'So, you're Lopez's new pet?' she said with a slow smile, her husky Caribbean voice honey-coated and sexy. 'Come over here. Let's see what we can do with you.' Flora sat in front of a mirror. Just months before, she'd sat in front of something similar, while Marty performed his transformation. Flora tried to picture herself as she was then. Frumpy. At least thanks to him, she'd never be that again. Chana set about her with a pot of foundation. 'So, how do you feel about the job. Have you any experience?'

'Well, no, but it can't be that difficult. I imagine I'll just be serving tea and coffee and whatnot.'

Chana had been about to apply false eyelashes; the tweezers halted midair. 'Tea and coffee, eh?' she chuckled. 'What in sweet lovin' Jesus's name are you on about?'

'Well, I just presumed— ' Flora trailed off. Since arriving, she'd seen no evidence of hot or cold beverages, let alone any sweet treats. And now all this make-up. A bit over the top. 'Um, what does a *cafetina* actually do?'

'How about I show you around?' Chana applied the second row of spidery lashes and chucked the tweezers back into her make-up bag. 'Follow me.'

A short while later, Flora said, 'so, let me get this straight, Carnival is a brothel, disguised as a spa?' She felt a certain sense of déjà vu, except unlike Vila Eloa, Carnival's clientele had the option to pursue certain tastes. 'And the customers can pay to have their bottoms smacked or, um, other things.' She was eyeing a rack of elaborately decorated riding crops, hanging in order of size by their tasselled handles. Men paid money to feel pain. Extraordinary.

'Yes, but not always. They can just have a massage if they want, with a happy ending of course.' Chana giggled at Flora's confused expression. 'You know what a happy ending is, right? I mean, there has been a Mr Flora at some time, hasn't there?'

Flora nodded, although the idea of giving John a massage, let alone a thingamabob, was too silly for words. So, as a *cafetina*, she was she supposed to massage the customers and smack their bottoms? She'd been looking forward to working in a cafe. What was it with Rio? First Vila Eloa and now here. Disappointing. And what on earth made Marcola Lopez think she'd ever consider doing such a thing?

Chana was in full swing now. 'The ones we like best are the old guys off the cruise ships. They just want a bit of fun before they die. They're the easiest to manage, and they're good tippers.'

'I couldn't possibly, I—'

'Couldn't possibly what?' Chana looked amused.

'You know, become a—' she searched for an inoffensive word. Some of her more racy romantic novels had courtesans or scarlet women, but spanking and whatnot had never come into it. 'A happy hooker,' she finally blurted.

Chana's cool demeanour melted into raucous laughter. Flora spotted a gold tooth while she waited for her to finish. What was so funny? She had a mountain of debt – if she refused to comply, how else could she pay it off?

'No, I don't think there's much call for senior ladies scoring tricks, at least not here.'

'So, I'm not going to have to, you know?' She nodded at the whips.

'Hell no, girl. Your job is to send the old guys off the cruise ships to us, before they spill their magic beans somewhere else.'

It took a moment longer to sink in. 'As a sort of *pimp*?'

'No, a *cafetina*. There's a difference. You look just the part – younger than them, English. Approachable but respectable. The old boys will gravitate to you. All you have to do is point them in the right direction. Makes sense, doesn't it?'

'I can't do that! What about the poor girls who work here and have to, er, you know.'

'Our girls are lucky to be here. They make good money and Lopez takes care of them. They're under his protection. If they didn't have him, they'd be working for one of the favela gangs. Beat up or on hard drugs in no time.'

'I'm sorry, but prostitution, it's just—' Flora knew she sounded old-fashioned, and she was already living at Vila Eloa, but that was different. 'Well, it's just not very savoury. I can't be a part of it.'

'So running up a huge debt and committing fraud is okay, is it?' Did everyone in Rio know about her money troubles? Chana grabbed a whip off the rack and hit the table. Thwack! 'How're you planning to repay Mr Lopez?' Thwack! 'Cos I'm telling you girl, you ain't going nowhere till that little holiday of yours is settled up.'

~~~

Flora soon discovered the habits of a cruising oldie were as reliable as the high and low tide. They flowed ashore in the morning after a late breakfast, then trickled back on board two or three hours later for the inevitable '*Marco Polo* buffet lunch', followed by a short nap. After which, they returned to dry land until cocktail hour lured them back to the ship for the rest of the night. The hours fitted perfectly with Carnival's quieter times when, without the older clientele, the girls would have been sitting around with nothing to do but gossip and paint their nails. Instead, they could make easy money for minimal effort.

Disembarking passengers were signposted directly to Cafe Rio, where there was a free-admission elevated photo and viewing platform of Christ the Redeemer, who tirelessly forgave the sins about to be committed beneath his outstretched arms. It was the first of Marcola Lopez's enterprising string of strategically placed 'hospitality' venues, where the extraction of a cruising pensioner's spending money was as assured as shooting fish in a barrel of *cachaça*.

The cafe was the first hook-up for onshore tours, charter boats, game fishing, personal guides, trinkets and handicrafts. The more hedonistic services were also discreetly offered to obvious targets: drugs, gambling, and with Flora in-situ, a guaranteed happy ending. There was something for everyone in Rio, City of Saints and Sinners.

Marcola Lopez's enterprise was well organised, based on years of information gleaned from a close study of the cruising tourist. Cruise ships provided a special breed of customer, different from the hotel guest and many, many cocktails away from the backpacker or the family vacation. With each luxury liner came a whole gamut of opportunities to help fund the Lopez family mansion and fleet of armour-plated Mercedes-Benz limousines. At a time when many locals derided the increase in cruise ships, brought to gawk at Rio and litter the streets, Marcola had been quick to recognise the magical potential of these floating cities with thousands of wallets and fully-loaded Amex cards. The cruise operators had the monopoly at sea, but for a few hours, morning and afternoon, Lopez Enterprises netted the onshore catch.

Chana was right; Flora was a natural fit. Planted in full sight, apparently enjoying a quiet cup of coffee, she was well placed to strike up conversations. A knowledgeable expat and a welcome friendly face among the ticket touts and local hustlers. But what could she say to get the ball rolling? Chana's advice had been to smile and be natural. That was easier said than done. Should she use her own name or go for something a bit more exotic? There was already enough to think about. Flora would have to do.

Each morning as she walked from the Carnival dressing room towards Cafe Rio, she pictured herself as a lovely flower, admired by everyone. Big, confident and beautiful, like a dahlia. In the overly obvious make-up applied by Chana and the ridiculously high heels she carried in her bag, she felt different. Disguised. The full transformation took place when she slipped the stilettos on and took her position at a table in the window. A cup of complimentary coffee was a perk to the job, then it was down to her ability to spot potential punters and smile, smile, smile. Recalling a conversation she'd had with Marty on the subject of flirting, or as he had aptly named it, hunter-flirting had also helped.

To her surprise, she quickly learned to involve herself in conversations, offering advice on local tourist attractions, a brief history of the city and a few snippets of culture. An oasis of calm and trust, with her blonde hair neatly coiffed and in a smart designer dress, she exuded comparative glamour and assuredness. Sure enough, the widowers and wayward husbands soon gravitated towards her.

By the end of the third morning, she could be heard reeling off her patter to a cluster of geriatrics as though she was born to the job. 'So, besides the botanical gardens and the spice market, the more testosterone-charged amongst you could seek out a little spice of your own. I'm told the Carnival is the best place. Guaranteed safe and clean.' If there was the slightest awkwardness, she followed with, 'It's perfectly acceptable here. Brazilians are very in touch with their natural urges.'

Flora's ageing lotharios soon became a welcome sight on Carnival's security camera. On a split-screen monitor in the locker room, the girls would watch them arrive. Distinguishable by their diminishing tufts of silver hair, regulation cruise wear and Hush Puppy deck shoes (insoles padded for added comfort), they were a walking target, soon to be slain by Alanza's hypnotic smile. Before they could fully register the eye-popping pre-payment, their credit cards and other valuables were posted into a gold-fronted safety deposit box and Chana was leading them to the luxury spa: the respectable front for Carnival's more lucrative 'relaxation lounge' and 'activity chambers' downstairs. Chana's charm soon had patrons bathing in the salty flotation pool or enjoying champagne in one of several private jacuzzis, which saved the slightly awkward moment of asking them to take a shower later on. It also allowed them time to make friends with the bathing beauties on duty.

Compared to the regular punter – Rio's big shots and money men; mafia friends of Marcola Lorenzo, the cruising grandfather, or *gringo velho* as they became known, were courteous and grateful. They always left a tip and sometimes went to the trouble of buying the girls their favourite sweets, *bananinha cremosa* and *coloreti*. Quick to recognise this new business opportunity, Lopez Enterprises set up a nearby candy stall, thus keeping the perks 'in the family'. The girls enjoyed the gifts until they began to worry about getting too fat, so a fifty percent refund policy was agreed upon. It was a win-win, allowing the girls to make a little extra cash and diminishing the requirement to order new stock. In one week alone, the same box of *coloreti* could easily be bought and returned a dozen times.

Realising sweet treats had limited value, the stall holder introduced a few pricier gifts, each with the same refund policy: dainty silk hankies, ornate compact mirrors and 'gold' friendship bracelets. Then pretty glass bottles containing diluted coffee masquerading as perfume appeared, labelled with whimsical names: Little Flower, Pretty Maiden, Princess, and the much-coveted Sainted Beauty. At the end of each shift the girls tallied up their spoils and wrote their scores on a leader board. *Coloreti* was the lowest-value gift, while Sainted Beauty, being the least popular among the punters and therefore a rare gift, drew the highest score.

Everyone agreed, since Mamãe Flora's arrival, life at Carnival had become a whole lot more fun and business was booming.

~჻৺჻~

Marcola Lopez pulled out a chair for Flora. 'So, Mrs Marshall, Alanza tells me Carnival income has increased by thirty percent in the last two weeks. I'm impressed. Each new customer reduces your debt. Please, keep up your good work. Then we can shake hands.'

'What's my cut?' The words were out before she had time to think. Crikey, I'm a hustler thought Flora, taking pleasure in Lopez's raised eyebrows. The last few weeks had taught her a lot. 'I want to know how much longer I have to work for you.'

'Don't be so hasty. You are good at this job. Natural. Maybe you will want to make a more permanent arrangement. Don't you want to make some money for yourself, Mrs Marshall?' Marcola leaned forward, giving her his full attention.

'It's true – I need enough to buy a ticket home, but paying my debt is a priority. How much is outstanding?'

He picked up his desk calculator, taking his time and prefacing his answer with a sigh. 'I am afraid you still must pay the equivalent of ten thousand, eight hundred and thirty-two pounds.'

Flora didn't bother to work out the exact amount she had paid off. Could she really only have earned a few hundred pounds? 'What about all the new customers? You said yourself there has been a thirty percent increase.' She had no idea how much this was in monetary terms, but everyone said it had significantly changed the business.

'You have done very well, but first, you must pay for your training, your uniform. Of course there is also interest on your debt. This is a generous rate I give to all my employees, only twenty-five percent.'

'But—' Quickly she tried to work out twenty-five percent of eleven thousand three hundred and forty-three pounds, and concluded it would be a lot. She must be earning good money if she was paying extortionate interest and managing to reduce her debt at the same time. 'Okay, so how long before I can clear the full amount?'

'Keep working, Mrs Marshall. I am not a monster. Take your time with the loan – just keep working. That is all.' He got up and opened the door. The interview was over.

TWENTY

'Get me a job at Carnival.' Bonita was painting her toenails gold and sticking plastic diamonds on top. 'I need to change.'

'It's not a place for dancers, Bonita. I mean, they do have a few dancers, but they all, um, do other things as well.'

'I already know this. Do you think I am just dancing?' She looked at Flora with a mixture of defiance and humour. She had become much more friendly since Flora's transition from rich tourist to *cafetina* – they'd even met a couple of times in a downtown cafe so Flora could treat Bonita to her favourite chocolate milkshake and strawberry *brigadeiro*.

'I can't introduce you. I'm only there myself because I've no choice. What if something bad happened to you? It would be my fault.'

'What can go wrong with old man and his limp dick? Is easy money, more better than the pigs I have all the time, making me hurt just to feel like the big guy.'

'I don't know, Bonita, I feel responsible, I—'

'You're not my mother, not even a friend. I need the money. Girls at Carnival, we all know they get the good money and the good tip. You must help me.'

'It would be on my conscience if—'

'You know I work here for Theresa when I was fifteen? Then I need more money, so I go to the city on my own. I pay her the rent, but I need more money for another thing.'

'You had those gold leopard earrings, why didn't you—'

'My baby, Kalisto, he is five years old. I want him to go to school.' Flora did a rapid calculation. Bonita would have been thirteen, maybe twelve when she became pregnant.

'You have a child. Who looks after him?'

'My sister. She has also three older kids but they don't go to school. I want a better life for Kalisto and for me. For us to be together. If you do this, I give you my room. I will sleep with Theresa.'

She couldn't see a way out of at least asking Alanza if there was a place available. If something good could come out of the situation, why not try?

~~~

Unlike the majority of girls who catered for Rio's captains of industry, with their silicone boob-grenades stuffed into neon mesh bikinis, Bonita's breasts were natural and bouncy. At Flora's suggestion, she put a flower in her hair and exchanged her sparkly bikinis for something altogether more whimsical. To the day-tripping pensioners she stood out as an innocent young girl in a pink gingham bikini, and appealed to their nostalgic yearnings. Under her unwavering gaze, shy smile and gentle playfulness, Bonita transported octogenarians to a time when they'd been virile and handsome. Desirable.

While the other girls called them *velhos tolos*, old fools, Bonita said she liked them. As a result, the clients experienced a seamless fantasy, resulting in a steady stream of malleable oldies keen to rekindle the tingles of first love. Bonita quickly shot to the top of the leader board, scoring more bottles of Sainted Beauty than the others had managed collectively.

The girls put Bonita's success down to Flora. They saw how much things had changed since she had appeared. This brought Flora power and a fresh appreciation. In recognition, they began splitting their tips with her. Her popularity grew to the point that Mamãe Flora became their preferred point of contact, more than Chana and Alanza unless it was a business matter. They exchanged language lessons while sharing their *bananinha cremosa* and *coloreti* with her during quieter times, and on her birthday they presented her with a tee-shirt declaring '*Sisters before Misters*' in crystal lettering.

Whenever a police raid took place, the girls invited Flora to join them at a nearby bar. These raids were announced by Alanza, following a tip-off from the local *pelotão de polícia militar*. The first time Flora saw the girls running downstairs she presumed they were rushing to hide evidence of illegal activity, but in the changing room skimpy bikinis and cartoonishly high platforms were flung off with cheerful abandon. Within a few minutes, a group of seemingly ordinary girls were assembled at the back door, dressed in sundresses or shorts and flip-flops and ready to make the most of a few hours off.

Alanza and Chana stayed behind to deal with 'local business', which meant keeping the police topped up with cold beer until a pair of Lopez Enterprise security guards arrived with a briefcase full of mixed currency. This often took time, as paying off the various police departments required a complicated movement of cash through a network of money-laundering operations.

Away from the hypnotic music and neon lights of the Copacabana strip, the girls settled in a backstreet bar frequented by office-working locals. They drank cachaça, laughed at good-humoured banter and swapped stories from home, outdoing each other with the horrors of life in some of the roughest favelas where murder, extortion and forced prostitution were an everyday occurrence.

'What about your husband, Mamãe Flora, was he handsome?'

'Well, no, he was a lot older than me and not very good-looking.' The girls chatted excitedly, listing the benefits of an ugly, older husband.

But when she told them about his lottery list, of his plans to tour geographically fascinating places around the world, there was a stunned silence. The idea of winning the lottery and not immediately buying a custom-painted Puma to drive around the neighbourhood was unimaginable. Travelling the world to see a fluctuating tidal system or a salt flat seemed to be madness until Flora told them about Marty and how his magical flair for theatre and luxury made even the most turgid geological feature exciting.

'And this Marty, where is he?'

Flora explained about her empty bank account, the credit card debt and Marty's sudden departure. They all agreed he was the guilty party and resolved to chop his gay dick off and throw it to one of the mangey street dogs if he ever dared to come back. Although she still held out a glimmer of hope that Marty was not the villain, the girls' protective nature touched her. They were the closest thing to friends she'd ever had.

~~~

It had been unusually busy. Three cruise ships, unable to dock the previous day due to bad weather, had been moored overnight further out at sea, where the lights of the party city could only be seen, twinkling with promise. As the weather lifted, a multitude of veteran cruisers stampeded over the foreshore with pent-up fantasies, ready for action. Flora hardly had time to sip her complimentary coffee and by the end of the day she was exhausted. She was especially glad to kick off the ridiculously high heels Marcola Lopez insisted on, and slip on her comfy sandals. Then, a short stroll to Carnival, and in the locker room she was back in her simple cotton sundress with her belongings stuffed into a large straw bag with flamingos woven into the raffia.

She was looking forward to a pleasurable evening with *His Arms Around Her*, a particularly promising romance, formerly the property of Boston Public Library, now liberated from Cafe

Rio's lost property box. She had had to wait until that week's consignment of cruisers was safely on their way to Valparaiso before the spoils of the lost property could be divided. Flora regularly passed on designer sunglasses and umbrellas to the girls at Vila Eloa. She kept hold of a Mulberry handbag, a couple of pretty Hermès scarves, and a bottle of Lily of the Valley scent, but her most prized finds were always novels in English, preferably a sizzling romance.

Her collection of nearly two dozen bodice rippers was stacked beside her bed, high enough to form a little table on which to place a box of her favourite caramel *brigadeiros* – the perfect accompaniment to a nice glass of Malbec. The Argentine wine regularly transported her to happier times when she had danced all night with Fernando. Sipping her glass, eyes half-closed, she could almost still feel his taut body beneath his silk shirt, hear his whispered commands, even smell him. She checked the book was in her bag and set off towards the underground. In less than an hour she'd have her feet up with *His Arms Around Her* and a nice glass of wine to hand.

'Hey, wait!'

Oh no. Bonita. Usually, a detour to a cafe was a welcome delay before returning to the noise and squalor of the favela, but not today.

'Aren't you on the rota for tonight?' asked Flora.

'No, I am finished, and tomorrow I have day off. I will go to my Kalisto.'

Flora toyed with the idea of making an excuse, but what could she say? Bonita would only follow her home and see she preferred a paper romance to their growing friendship. *His arms* would have to wait.

'Oh, little Kalisto, that's good to hear. He'll be looking forward to seeing you.' Flora had a great deal of respect for Bonita. Since she'd worked at Carnival she'd kept her promise and moved out of their shared room. She'd set up a saving plan and had been working hard to get Kalisto a better life. She was the highest-earning girl at Carnival and Flora was the best *cafetina* ever according to Alanza. They were a team.

Without needing to discuss it, they turned down a side street towards The Amazon Cafe, eager to see if their favourite table was available.

'Look at him,' said Bonita, gingerly sidestepping a man huddled over a cardboard sign. 'Filthy! My Kalisto will never be like this.'

Flora glanced at the English words on the sign. '*Homeless and hungry. Please help*'. Rio was littered with travellers who'd blown all their money on drugs and lost themselves in hazy reality – that was the trouble with it being a party town. There were junkies and drop-outs everywhere. Even in her most desperate moments she hadn't resorted to begging, but then she'd managed to sort out a solution before true desperation kicked in. Luckily.

'No. I'm sure Kalisto will be a fine young man,' Flora said absently. She was already thinking about her milkshake: chocco mint or the rum baba?

'Flora! Hey, FLORA!' a man's voice shouted.

Bonita dug her in the ribs and laughed. 'It is one of your boyfriends. Maybe he can't live without you.' Being the conduit to a blissful albeit expensive detour to Carnival, proof of her undoubted understanding of a man's needs, Flora had received several declarations of love, half a dozen bottles of Sainted Beauty and, to everyone's amusement, a marriage proposal from an American peanut farmer.

'It's a possibility,' mused Flora, turning to see who was trotting towards them.

'Flora, WAIT!'

'Oh, no—'

'Flora, I can't believe it! I've found you.' The beggar had

dropped his sign and held out his grimy hands, as though he was going to hug her.

'Hey! *Homem fedido!*' Bonita stepped in front of Flora. 'What are you doing, you crazy *louco*. Don't touch her!'

Tears, trickling grime down his weather-worn cheeks, disappeared into his beard – for a tramp he had surprisingly good teeth.

'Flora, it's me.' Now openly sobbing he shuffled from side to side, trying to bypass Bonita.

Underneath the layers of dirt and whiskers there was a resemblance. It didn't look much like him, but – 'Marty?'

'This is Marty? *Bastardo!*' Bonita shoved him hard in the chest. He staggered back a couple of steps and, slipping off the pavement, lost his footing and fell over. Bonita rushed at him again. '*Vai-te foder, bastardo!*' she shouted, kicking him in the ribs. 'You thief-pig. I kill you!' It took Flora a few moments to gather herself enough to intervene.

'Stop, Bonita! That's enough.' She looked at him lying there and felt the urge to kick him herself. 'Enough for now,' she added.

~ഇ‍ഇ~

Marty sat at the kitchen table in Flora's Chinese silk dressing gown, eating corn pancakes as fast as Theresa could make them.

'So, let's go over it again. You're saying you didn't send that email?' Flora poured him a third glass of orange juice.

'No! I'd never do that to you. Anyway, how could I send an email when I was stranded?'

'Oh, and where did you say this island was?'

'I've already told you, I don't know. Enrique said we were going to Ilha do Mel. I looked it up before we left – it's a nature reserve. He said it wasn't open to tourists but I was a special guest, and we'd stay at a private cabana on the beach.' He gulped the orange juice and quickly ate another pancake. 'The crew sailed into this little cove. One of those picture-perfect places; the water was so clear I could see the bottom. Enrique dived over the side. "Race you to shore," he shouted.' Marty's voice cracked and he began crying again. Theresa fussed around him, proffering one of her homemade hankies.

'Go on,' said Flora. She needed to be convinced, even though they had spent most of the previous evening in conversation. There were still holes in the story.

'I just dived in and started swimming. I'm such an idiot.'

'You swam ashore?'

'Pretty much. When I got to the shallows, I looked round. Enrique was already back on the boat. I shouted and started to swim back but I was too slow.'

'They sailed off without you? Could it have been a misunderstanding? Maybe Enrique arranged to pick you up later or something?'

'No, Flora! I don't know why you're sticking up for that conniving bastard!'

'Well, you haven't always told the truth. Remember that thing about living in a cottage in the Cotswolds with John's dahlias?' Petty to bring it up maybe, but his so-called 'sprinkles of magic' had left quite a trail of misunderstandings.

'Look, I promise this is the truth. He took me out there and dumped me. I found out later it wasn't even Ilha do Mel. I didn't know where the hell I was. I spent three nights on my own.'

More crying.

Theresa caught Flora's eye and said, '*Pobre bebê.*'

'No, Theresa. We haven't heard the whole story yet. What about the money?' Had Marty planned the whole thing, maybe even going back to their first meeting in Coventry? Had he really known John, or was he a confidence trickster?

'I'm telling you, it was a nightmare. Snakes, scorpions. Horrific! I was bitten by bloody piranhas. Why don't you believe me? Look.' He held out his hands for inspection.

'And all this time you were just wearing your swimming trunks?'

'Yes! My Dolce & Gabbanas.'

Flora smothered an involuntary smile by pretending to cough. 'So, there you were, hacking your way through the jungle in your pink speedos. That doesn't explain why you decided to sit on street corners begging. Why didn't you just ask for me at the hotel?'

'I don't know how long it took to get back to Rio. Weeks, maybe months. I had to sleep rough, I lost all track of time. As soon as I got here, I went straight to the hotel. They told me you'd left soon after the carnival. They said you'd taken my passport.'

'But the hotel has our passports! And your suitcase with all your stuff.'

'I thought you'd deserted me. I went to the British Consulate, but I couldn't prove I was a British citizen. I think they thought I was a druggie. They kicked me out.'

The kitchen was momentarily silent.

'Why didn't you come looking for me?' he wailed. 'I could have been dead. Murdered.'

She hadn't thought of that. The empty bank account and the email saying he'd gone to start a new life with Enrique had been enough to stop her. Theresa began washing up, muttering under her breath. Flora studied Marty's face – drawn and haggard – with his beard now shaved off he looked like an elderly clown: cheeks and brow sunburnt, pocked with mosquito bites, then a pallid five o'clock shadow. He should grow some George Michael stubble until his complexion evened out, maybe use some fake tan. But first, she needed to find out where all her money had gone.

Flora asked Bonita to tell Alanza she was taking a day off. She needed to find out exactly what had happened, then make a plan. Between cups of coffee and more tears from Marty, who seemed to be almost at breaking point, it took the best part of the morning to piece the whole story together.

'You think even Jago was in on it?' She had tried not to think about him. Occasionally she had asked around, trying to find him, but in her heart she knew he'd stood her up for a reason. Thinking he'd probably been married, she'd concluded he'd just fancied a bit on the side. Now it wasn't even that. He was part of the scam. Faked the whole thing – only being nice to her until they had her money.

'Yes, Jago was the essential part, to make you want to stay in Rio longer. I can't believe you just handed over the credit card and passports like that. Didn't you think Enrique might—'

'Don't you dare blame me! I was trying to do a nice thing and surprise you.' In hindsight, she did feel a bit foolish, but she had been a different person then. Naive. 'But how did they get into my bank account? I mean they completely emptied it. Surely they can't just transfer the whole amount like that?'

'These people can do anything. Think about it they were already waiting for us to arrive in Rio. We were set up right at the start. Probably in Mexico. Remember the fiesta, how drunk we were. And that argument we had about the credit card?'

'Well, yes, but—'

'Enrique told me he had so-called 'cousins' in Mexico. According to him, virtually everyone we met were cousins or uncles.'

'And he said he had a sister too.'

'I doubt any of them were actual relations. Just a network of fraudsters.'

258

'So the sister didn't—'

'And a couple of times he seemed to know more about our trip than I remembered telling him. He seemed to know exactly where we'd been after Mexico, but not before then. Nothing about America.'

'Maybe you told—'

'Trust me, Flora, I've had a long time to work things out – I've thought of nothing else. Before you even said the bank account had been emptied, I already knew it was your money they were after.'

Flora's recollection of Mexico was eclipsed by her first experience of a fiesta, and the first proper hangover she'd ever had. There were blank spots, but with Marty's help she gradually pieced the day back together.

They had been awoken by *Cántico de Zacarías*, the call to morning prayer, and ventured outside to wander through near-deserted streets until they found an open-air cafe. They had enjoyed a delicious breakfast – hot chocolate and *pan dulce* while listening to the sombre Catholic hymns emitting from a nearby church. Eventually, Church bells rang out in joyful peals of collective celebration. People spilled onto the streets, dressed in their finery. Soon the collective strumming of guitars, the *vihuela* and *guitarrón*, filled the air, accompanied by trumpets, violins and a range of percussion instruments.

'Do you remember that Mexican guy who gave us our first margarita?' Marty stared at Flora, willing her to focus. 'He said, "*feliz día de fiesta*," and kissed you on both cheeks. A complete stranger.'

'They were all like that, friendly, all saying *feliz de* thingy and giving us free drinks. And those tasty little donuts.'

'*Buñuelos*,' said Marty.

The afternoon had been a giddy blur of colourfully-dressed dancers, music, and free-flowing drinks. Much later, their newfound friends had taken them for *carnita tacos* in a side-street restaurant. The place had the biggest collection of sombreros they'd ever seen, decorating the walls and ceiling.

'You fell asleep in that place. What was it called? *Amigos*?' She pictured Marty slumped in a tequila-infused slumber over his half-eaten taco; the male attention had stepped up a gear once her chaperone was out of the picture. One man with a particularly pleasing moustache had slid his arm around her and declared her his 'little flower'. Another had feigned a broken heart until she allowed him to give her 'one kiss on her beautiful cheek'. Flora cringed at the flashback. How she had morphed into a coquettish maiden, influenced by an overdose of romantic fiction and a day of intoxication. Giggling and slapping away each of the adoring *papi chulo* in turn, safe in the knowledge Marty was gently snoring a few feet away.

'Remember you took the credit card out of my money belt?' Marty's steady gaze was unforgiving. 'We had a row about it the next day when I couldn't find it, and you had it in your pocket?'

Oh no. She'd insisted on paying for everyone amidst cheers and declarations of '¡*Qué generosidad, que gentilidad!*'. Kind, rich and beautiful lady. Was that where it started? Frisking Marty and then triumphantly flashing the gold credit card. Loving the attention. Like a sunflower turning towards warm rays, she'd soaked it up, insisting on one more drink for everyone. 'One for the road,' she'd slurred, explaining the British custom. 'One for the road,' they roared 'and another one for *la senora tan generosa y amable*' What had she talked about, how did they know they were going to Rio? Had she told them about her inheritance and John's list?

Possibly.

Yes.

And worse, she had even drawn them a map. Hot shame crept up her spine with the memory of sketching out their tour on the paper tablecloth, helped by Pedro, one of the handsome, open-shirted musicians, who cupped his hand over hers to help draw an outline of South America. Each time she drew an 'X' to mark a destination, he made a juicy kissing noise. She kissed the air back, while looking at him with come-to-bed-eyes, thinking how deliciously naughty she was: flirting, laughing, having fun.

How utterly stupid.

TWENTY-ONE

While Marty languished at Vila Eloa, being cosseted by Theresa and giving each of the girls a makeover, Flora continued to work as normal. She needed to earn as much in tips as possible, and get Marty fit while she worked out a way to get their passports back.

Her reputation at Carnival continued to grow. Each day a cluster of girls waited at the back door, hoping to fill a vacant spot. Mamãe Flora had improved working conditions and introduced the best possible customers: generous older men who were courteous, clean and good tippers. Better still, with their ageing pipe-work a limp *piroca* often meant they were unable to enjoy full *relação sexual*. Thanks to Flora's experiment with Bonita, the *Namorada* experience had been added to the gold-framed list of 'treatments'. The *Sweetheart*, only available in hourly increments. With no sex, just playful groping, hand-holding, and perhaps the fumbled removal of a bikini top, it was an instant hit. The sales of Sainted Beauty had gone through the roof.

Despite many attempted copy-cat operations, Flora, with her blonde hair and English accent, was the once-in-a-lifetime *cafetina*. The only person who could effortlessly infiltrate the cruise ship crowd, to quickly steer vintage libido and bulging wallets in the right direction. And, for every customer she persuaded up Carnival's marble stairs into the embrace of Alanza's credit card machine, she received a tip from each of the girls lucky enough to entertain such pliable, easy meat.

She stowed the tips in her money belt, enjoying the feel of reassuring nylon webbing beneath her clothing. When the constant wear and humid conditions culminated in a nasty belt-shaped rash, she borrowed a needle and thread from Theresa, cut up an old face flannel and fashioned a soft, absorbent under-padding. When the wedge of cash grew too bulky, she changed the money into larger denominations to reduce the evidence.

'Let me look after it,' Marty said as they stood at a counter in the Central Bank of Brazil. 'It'll be less conspicuous on me.'

She was watching the cashier change the week's collection of crumpled notes into another hundred-dollar bill. Nine hundred dollars. Almost enough for two single tickets home.

'It's okay, thanks. I'm used to it now,' she said, slipping the note into hiding and discreetly adjusting her '*Sisters before Misters*' tee-shirt.

Did she trust him? Yes. But things had changed – a few months ago the money belt would have felt like a stick of dynamite strapped to her waist; now she wore it with all the assurance of a seasoned gunslinger, ready for anything ; and like any gunslinger, she'd feel naked without it.

She wound her arm through his and said, 'Come on, I'll take you for a rum baba milkshake at The Amazon Cafe. There's something I want to discuss.'

It wouldn't take long to earn the rest of the airfare home, but getting their passports back seemed impossible. She had tried, but as her successful track record grew, Marcola Lopez had become increasingly evasive. Often when she made an appointment, he wasn't there, and whenever she did manage to talk to him he was vague about her outstanding debt. In her last brief meeting he had simply said, 'Don't worry, Mrs Marshall, you are going in the right direction. Keep working and soon you'll be free to choose if you want to stay in Rio.' When he added, 'Maybe you will like it too much to leave,' she wasn't sure if there was an underlying threat, but it was clear to her, he didn't want her to go. She was a victim of her own success.

Marty carried the milkshakes over to what The Amazon Cafe's staff knew as Mamãe Flora's table; she sat there at least three evenings a week with Bonita, and now with Marty. She pushed her notebook aside to make way for the frosted glasses, each on a saucer with a complimentary chocolate *brigadeiro* on the side. She picked up her glass, already anticipating the rum baba flavour made with a tot of real rum. Delicious. If Gail's Cafe made them, it'd put them on the map. Maybe she'd suggest it.

'The thing is Marty, there's no way we can get our passports back unless we play Lopez at his own game.'

'I know, but what can we do? He's such a crook.'

'Yes, he's a crook, but not like Enrique's lot. He wants respect in Rio; he's also a businessman.'

'Can we not mention Enrique? Just the thought of him is curdling my baba. How I'll ever get over—'

'Shhh! Focus. We have to make a plan.' She opened her notebook. 'I write everything down. Look. For every punter I introduce to the girls, I get a tip, so I know exactly how many there've been and roughly how much extra income I've generated for Lopez, not counting the *necessidades especiais*.'

'Special needs? What do they—'

'Never mind. The point is they pay extra, so I've brought in at least the equivalent of thirty-four thousand pounds worth of new business.'

'Wow! That's a lot of shenanigans.'

'About three times the cost of our original hotel bill.'

Marty stared at her. 'So, now he's making a profit from you? Why didn't you tell me before?'

'I was waiting until you were fully recovered. So, now it's time—'

'I'll never recover, babes. I'm going to need counselling when we get home, I'm mentally scarred. I only have to think about all those creepy-crawlies and I come out in hives. What I went through—'

'So—' Flora paused to give him time to catch up. 'Now it's time for you to get involved. Confront Lopez and get our passports back.'

'Confront him? Okay. But what'll I say? I mean, I can hardly just march in there and ask for them. You already said the chances of getting an appointment, let alone—'

'What's happened? You used to be so resourceful.' A few months ago he would've sorted everything before she even knew there was a problem. Good job she was on the ball. 'Never mind. I'm going to introduce you to my friend Dave, who owns an internet cafe. You have a week to brush up on international law and all that stuff about civil rights.'

'A week? It's been years since I've looked at the nuances of law.'

'You seemed to manage okay at the Grand Canyon. Remember? Anyway, you already have an appointment. At least, Walt from Sunshine Forever Cruises has. Lopez is expecting to negotiate a deal next Wednesday before going on holiday with his family, so it's now or never.'

'Whoa! How do you know about the appointment?'

'Let's just say, even though he doesn't know it, a certain slimy so-and-so named Walt has been very useful.'

The way Walt had ensnared her had been almost gentlemanly. 'Hey, little lady. What have we here?' The last few passengers had just left Cafe Rio in an arthritic race towards the promise of pleasure. With an hour's break before the next ship put ashore, Flora had dropped her 'ex-pat enjoying a quiet coffee' disguise and kicked off her shoes. She was having a yawn and a stretch when he appeared as if from nowhere. His unmistakable uniform immediately set her on edge.

'Beg pardon, can I help?' Flora quickly clocked his name badge: Walt Harrington, Entertainments Manager, Sunshine Forever Cruises. Blimey. Now what?

'Are you hustling my passengers – sending them off like lambs to the slaughter, to be done over by merciless Brazilian hookers?'

'Um—'

'Well, why not?' He sat down opposite her. 'We all have to make a buck.'

'Oh, I—'

'No doubt you'd like me to keep this quiet? Maybe I should go along myself, check up on the old boys. After all, I am the Entertainments Manager.'

'Er, I don't know—'

'Of course, if I were satisfied the establishment was up to standard, I might be persuaded to turn a blind eye.' He winked, slowly. 'I would need to make a regular assessment of the, er, services rendered. Say, once a fortnight?'

'Oh. Right. I see. I'd have to check.' Flora froze in her seat. She hadn't given a second thought to the possibility of being caught. Would he call the police? If they weren't on Lopez's payroll, she'd be on her own. What a nightmare.

'Tick-tock. You'd best get a shimmy on, little lady. We don't want any cardiac arrests at the house of fun, do we?'

From then on, Walt came ashore every two weeks, waited until his passengers were on their way, then sat down with Flora for a coffee and a chat before wandering along to enjoy his 'perk'. After a few visits he began asking questions about Lopez Enterprises. Besides owning Cafe Rio and Carnival, were there any other establishments? A casino, perhaps? For a small fee, he could warm up the passengers before they even reached the shore.

Marty was open-mouthed and staring at Flora. 'So this slime ball, Walt, made an appointment to see Lopez? How are we going to—'

'No. Walt hasn't the foggiest. I just used his idea and asked Dave to call Lopez in an American accent and pretend to be Walt Harrington from Sunshine Forever Cruises, interested in discussing a mutually beneficial arrangement. We had to use Walt's name in case he checked.' She relayed the rest of her plan.

'So Lopez is expecting to do a deal with Walt? And instead of him, he gets me? Does that mean I'm going to have to dress up as an officer from an American cruise ship?' Briefly, the old Marty was back. A glint in his eye reminded her of their shopping sprees, the hair and make-up sessions they used to enjoy.

'I was going to say casual clothes would be less conspicuous, but yes, you could use Walt's uniform. You're about the same size, and come to think of it the name badge would get you past the hotel reception more easily. You could wear sunglasses, just in case they remember you. Once you're in his office, you can come clean. Confront Lopez and get our passports back.'

'Wowzer, babes, you've really thought this through.'

'Before you go to Dave's, I want you to meet Horado. He's Brazilian. One of Bonita's special friends.' She tore a page out of her notebook and scribbled down an address. 'I can't be seen with him in case someone reports me. Lopez has spies all over Rio.'

'This is all very 007,' said Marty.

'Horado has a serious track record as a human rights lawyer. Bonita has been talking to him for me. He says I'm a victim of bonded slavery.' Until then, she had only read about such things in *The Slave Princess*, a disappointing tale with a cowardly lover, too scared of retribution to free the heroine.

'Bonded slavery? Well, yes, and I'm a victim of kidnapping. I'm mentally scarred, I should sue for—'

'This isn't about you, Marty. Let's focus on the matter at hand. We just want to get our passports back.'

'But—'

'Horado will help you with Lopez, coach you on how to approach him and what to say. You need to read up on international law so you can stand your ground, no matter what.'

'So this Horado chap, will we have to pay him? Legal fees are—'

'Don't worry, he's a starry-eyed widower, drunk with happiness, all thanks to Bonita and a few out-of-hours dinner dates. He's more than happy to help and Bonita wants to help too. She still feels bad about the leopard earrings.'

'The gold and sapphire Fabergés?'

'Yes, I'll tell you about them later. First, you need to concentrate on getting our passports back.'

⟨≈⟩

By the morning of the meeting with Marcola Lopez, Marty had a watertight script, memorised and rehearsed with Dave, who tried to throw him off by acting out a number of rogue scenarios – Lopez is in a hurry, he tries to leave; there are other people in the room. Nothing was left to chance. Now all they needed was for someone to steal Walt's name badge; better still, his entire uniform.

Flora went to Cafe Rio as usual and after the normal rush of cruisers, she waited for Walt to saunter over. As usual, he ordered a coffee and sat down at Flora's table for ten minutes of small talk before the coast was clear and he was able to head to Carnival for his free sample. As soon as he left, she dashed to Carnival via a series of back streets, aiming to get there before him. She found Bonita below stairs, sitting on a stool in front of the CCTV monitor. Copacabana looked quite different on the black-and-white screen. It took a moment to work out what was what.

'There he is.' Flora pointed to a monochrome man in a shipmate's uniform, sauntering towards the camera.

Still on the pavement, Walt hesitated.

'Come in, nice mister *bastardo*,' murmured Bonita.

He took a furtive look over his shoulder, then sprinted up the marble stairs two at a time. The camera in reception filmed him being greeted by Alanza in her confident, businesslike manner and placing his valuables into one of the fake-gold mini safes. Without needing to hand over a credit card, he was led by Chana into the lounge – Bonita's cue to dip the lights on and off, on and off. Whoever was assigned the bald *Americano* must ensure he was out of his uniform and frolicking in a jacuzzi, *rapidamente*!

Disguised as one of the cleaning maids in a plain black overall, Bonita swept a broom into the boudoir, bundled his clothes into a laundry basket and scuttled back to the locker room where Flora was waiting with her large straw beach bag. With the bag slung over her shoulder, she set off towards Dave's, trying to look casual while hurrying. The streets were crowded with tourists exploring Rio's over-priced and least authentic souvenir shops. Pensioners she had just seen disembarking from Walt's ship, wearing 'Sunshine Forever' baseball caps, wandered two or three abreast.

As she approached Cyber Cafe, she saw a man pacing back and forth outside. The bushy moustache and dark glasses obscured most of his face, but the faded Hawaiian shirt was a giveaway. 'Marty?'

'Yes, ma'am!' His clunky attempt at an American accent was unmistakable.

'What have you done to your hair?'

Still maintaining a Texan twang, he replied, 'Walt sure is sleazeball; he kinda likes to slick on pomade for the little ladies.'

'Actually, he's almost bald, but never mind.' She ushered him into the internet cafe, towards the gents, and passed him the bag.

'He's a couple of sizes bigger than you, but you'll just have to manage. And hurry, the appointment's in fifteen minutes' time.'

Unable to risk being seen with 'Walt', Flora hugged him and said good luck before propelling him out onto the street. He looked slightly less confident than she would have hoped, but there was no time for a pep talk. She watched him weave through the crowds, and then she joined Dave behind the counter with her fingers crossed. Come on, Marty, don't mess it up. Had there ever been a time in her life where so much depended on one short meeting?

Without their passports they would have no option but to try their luck at the British Consulate. If only she'd known about them before she became embroiled with Lopez. Now all the dirty details would have to come out – the huge debt accrued by living in luxury; her work as a glorified pimp, luring lonely pensioners to fandango with prostitutes. Would they be sympathetic? And Marcola Lopez looked like Mr Magoo compared to Enrique and his gang, whoever they were. And there was her indiscretion in Mexico. The one-night stand with Jago. And the fact she'd freely handed over her credit card and both their passports. She already knew it wasn't fraud, just stupidity. Oh, the shame.

Dave passed her a mug of milky tea. 'Here, have a cuppa. And don't look so worried, I'm sure Marty the 'Merican will do you proud.'

'Thanks, Dave.' Something stronger would have been nice. Why was he the only person in Rio who didn't love Brazilian coffee?

'When this is over and you're back in Blighty, you'll remember to visit my old nan, won't you?'

'Don't worry, Dave, Leamington Spa is top of the list, as soon as I get settled.'

'Any ideas what's next? I mean, you were supposed to travel around the world, so what'll you do for adventure back in Coventry?'

'I've a few ideas, but first I need to get there.' She checked the clock. 'He's been gone forty minutes. How long does it take?'

'Didn't you say he might be followed by Lopez's men? Maybe he's having to shake them off?' Dave went to the door and looked out. 'Panic over. He's at the other end of the street. I can spot him a mile off in that get-up.'

Flora peered over his shoulder. 'He's got his suitcase back!'

'See, I told you,' said Dave, 'and look, even under that moose of a moustache you can see he's smiling.'

Flora couldn't wait for Marty to drag his suitcase fully through the door, 'So? Have got the passports?'

'Of course, babes.'

'So how did you persuade him? I'm sure he didn't just hand them over.'

'No. But the threat of telling the owners of Sunshine Forever Cruises about the Lopez Corporation's dodgy dealings was enough.'

'But that would implicate me as well. How have you left it with him? Is he going to come looking for me?' She had only thought of getting Marty in to see Lopez, not about how they would both extract themselves.

'Don't worry; the threat of going to the authorities about his tourist scam, and using you as bonded slavery, will create far more trouble. It took some doing, but I said exactly what Horado told me to, after he'd calmed down and stopped waving a gun at me—'

'Gun? Blimey, I didn't think he'd—'

'Don't worry, he's just a greedy bully. He soon realised the easiest solution would be to help us leave as soon as possible. He'll probably find someone else to take your place at Cafe Rio.'

'True. But a gun, Marty? I hadn't thought about that.'

'Actually, I don't think he'd ever use it. He's just a dodgy businessman, not a hardened criminal.' He took an envelope out of his inside pocket. 'I've even got you a little something extra.' He handed her two passports, a small wedge of banknotes and a brief note:

Mrs Marshall,
Your holiday pay is enclosed.
You are welcome to resume your employment
at any time in the future.
Marcola Lopez
Lopez Enterprises Inc.

'Sorry there's not more,' Marty said, eyeing the cash. 'It's just a token gesture to prove your employment was legal.'

'No matter, you got our passports. Well done.' Flora hugged him briefly, then quickly looked inside each one to check their mug shots. 'It's us. We're really real again!'

'Yes, we are,' said Marty while looking in the security mirror to peel off his false moustache. 'I even have my own clothes, but this uniform's done wonders for my mojo. I was wondering, do you think I could I keep it?'

'Walt's uniform?' Flora pictured the man who had been blackmailing her and having a fortnightly freebee at Carnival. There would be no more hustling at Cafe Rio from now on. Walt's arrangement was over. 'I don't see why not.' She chuckled. 'He'll have some explaining to do when he returns to ship dressed in whatever the girls find in lost property.'

TWENTY-TWO

As soon as the girls heard the mission had been a success, Bonita organised a whip-round; even the perfume vendor, indebted to Mamãe Flora's ingenious sale-and-return system, dipped into his takings. When added to Flora's savings, there was more than enough for two flights to Manchester and the rest of the journey home. Meanwhile, Marty had taken his suitcase of clothes to *Brechó do Homem Internacional.*

'It seems pre-loved European designer wear is in vogue,' he said waggling a small wedge of notes.

'Didn't you want to keep something?' Flora would have bet her life savings, if she had any, on Marty wanting to swap the second-hand faded shirt and jeans for something expensive and well made. 'What about when you get home you—'

'No. I don't want any reminders of you know who. Him.' Marty added the money to Bonita's collection. 'We might have enough to bump your ticket up to business class, babes, what d'you think?'

'No, economy is fine,' Flora said. Her days of wasting money on luxury were over.

~∞∞∞~

After a final breakfast the following morning and a hug from each of the girls, Marty left with a tightly packed money belt to collect the plane tickets from a travel agent. Without a bank account, the only way to pay for them was cash. Flora would meet him at Carnival, after he'd been to check in online at Dave's and found a taxi to take them to the airport.

On the pretext of packing, she went up to her room and sat on the bed. The little wall-mounted fan valiantly battled with the rising heat of the day; a rhythmic whirring to the backbeat of crying babies, motorbikes and street dogs. Add an argument here and a cheery greeting there and the whole cacophony that became the favela's song. She would miss all those hot-headed, passionate Brazilians going about their day with gusto.

Unable to put it off any longer, she stuffed a few items in her flamingo beach bag and went down the narrow stairs for the last time. Theresa came through from the kitchen, wiping her hands on her apron – she had soaked black beans overnight; today, she would prepare *feijoada* for her girls. Flora had copied the recipe into her notebook, though she had no idea where she'd find cassava flour or pig's trotters in Coventry.

Without speaking, Theresa stood on tiptoes and gathered Flora into a warm, firm hug. She smelled of tortillas and geranium soap. Finally pulling away she dabbed her eyes with her apron and said, 'I have *saudade*.' The girls often spoke of *saudade*; they had all experienced loss and grief.

'I am sad in my heart too,' said Flora. She tried to smile with her lips pressed firmly together, battling a surge of emotion. In between the urge to cry uncontrollably, she managed to say, 'Thank you for everything, my lovely, kind friend.' She gave Theresa the little home-made recipe book which she had dictated to Bonita, wrapped in a vibrantly floral Hermès silk scarf she'd found in Cafe Rio's lost property box.

Theresa nodded and smiled. The language barrier had hardly been a problem in recent weeks; they somehow managed to understand each other enough for their friendship and mutual respect to flourish. She gave Flora a handmade lace handkerchief, even more delicate than the one she'd borrowed from Alberto. It had a beautifully embroidered 'F' in the corner.

'Living with you and the girls has been *maravilhoso*. Your *casa* has been *mio* home.' She hoped the hand gestures conveyed all she felt.

'Yes, *minha casa é sua casa*,' Theresa said and then, in carefully measured English she added, 'Please, you coming back.'

'I will. And if you're ever in Coventry, you must come and stay with me.'

She already knew if Theresa ever had that kind of money she'd buy a scooter with a nice wide footwell to carry the shopping on market days, but it felt good to share open-ended invitations with a dear friend. With a last hug and a few escaping tears, Flora walked out of Vila Eloa, knowing they'd never see each other again. Her stay had been life-changing and now she must put all she had learned to good use.

She walked through the favela towards the underground station, past a burned-out patrol car and the house on the corner where men hung around outside, their guns clearly visible. She passed tiny shacks, crowded with half-naked children and proud-looking women, old before their years. Their entire lives to be spent squeezed together from birth to death and never knowing solitude. This time tomorrow she'd be back in her three-bed semi. On her own.

Before leaving the underground she gave her *cartão pré-pago* to a downtrodden old man queuing at the ticket booth; there was plenty of credit left and she wouldn't be needing it. She walked her preferred route to Carnival, stopping at the market to buy one last bag of freshly made *pão de queijo* and to say *bom dia* to the women frying street food, the stallholders and acquaintances she'd come to know on her route to work. She would never hear a cheery British equivalent to '*Bom dia*, Mamãe Flora,' back in Coventry.

She walked up the marble steps to Carnival's front door, just as she had on her first day. How naive she'd been – with Theresa's apron in her bag and thinking she was about to serve

275

cups of tea in a posh cafe. After a brief goodbye to Alanza and Chana in reception, she went downstairs. The girls crowded around, keen to share one last joke and hug the woman who had improved their working lives. Gradually they drifted back to the locker-room to change out of their jeans into regulation swimwear and apply false eyelashes. The first cruise ship would soon be disembarking, although they had no idea how many *velhos tolos* to expect, now there was no one at Cafe Rio to charm them.

Flora took Bonita to one side. 'Here, this is from Lopez – my so-called holiday pay. I want you to have it. Spend it on Kalisto.' She would miss this feisty little Brazilian, maybe even more than Theresa. 'I have to say goodbye now. Marty will be waiting with a taxi outside.'

'I also say goodbye,' whispered Bonita. 'Don't tell anyone but I am leaving.'

'Where are you going? Another *terma*?'

'No. I quit. I am taking Kalisto to my cousin in *São Paulo*. A new life, away from all this shit.'

'That's wonderful. I—'

'This is for you.' She shoved something into Flora's hand.

A small white box tied with a pink ribbon; inside, resting on a pad of cotton wool was a necklace made of tiny paper flowers, delicate and painstakingly detailed.

'I made it,' Bonita said shyly. 'Is what I do as a kid, for selling to tourist.'

'It's beautiful, thank you.' Flora's voice cracked when she tried to say, 'I will treasure it always.'

Bonita cut the awkward silence with a brief hug. 'You should go now,' she said. There was a faint smile, nothing more, then she thrust her hands in her pockets and walked away. There was no point waiting to see if she'd turn and wave. She knew Bonita, tough to the end.

~∞~

The flight was fully booked. Economy class burst at the seams with suntanned tourists heading home, and instead of 'Madam, would you like a glass of champagne before take-off?' Flora had to wait in the aisle while two families jostled for space in an overhead locker. Further along, a bewildered grandmother was sitting in the wrong seat. Somewhere on the other side, a baby began screaming. And because they had last-minute tickets, their seats were at the very back of the plane, next to the loos.

'It's still luxury,' said Marty, never missing an opportunity to mention his ordeal in the Brazilian jungle. 'What I would have done just to hear the sound of a flushing loo. And don't get me started on—'

Flora tuned out.

Saying goodbye to her friends had been emotionally exhausting. She patted her pocket to check Theresa's handkerchief was still there.

'—I should write to Dolce & Gabbana. Their swimwear isn't designed for real-life situations. The chafing was pure agony—'

She rummaged under her seat for her handbag and looked for Bonita's little gift.

'—I'm glad I didn't have a mirror. I mean, the state of my hair for starters. It's still not right even with that jojoba and aloe moisture mask.'

While muttering half to herself, 'You're not the only one who's suffered in life,' she opened the box. The tiny flowers must have been cut with nail scissors. She hadn't spotted it before but in the middle of each flower was a letter; altogether they spelled a word. BELIEVE. Flora knew it was meant for Bonita as much as her. They had such different lives, but both needed to believe in themselves and in the future.

Four months previously, alone and bewildered in a filthy, chaotic Brazilian ghetto, all Flora had been able to think of was how to get home, but finally landing at Manchester Airport, standing in an orderly queue at passport control, she felt strangely flat. A few hours later at Coventry Station, she parted from Marty with a heartfelt hug. They would meet again in a couple of days, once they had acclimatised. Finally alone, she wearily climbed the steps to the top deck of the number sixty-four on its way out to the suburbs.

The bus turned on to Beechwood Road, stopping with a hiss now and then to let passengers on and off. Everything seemed smaller, greyer than she remembered. She and John had travelled the same bus route home on their wedding day, past the turning to his allotment, towards her dream of domestic bliss. She would have been about Bonita's age, without any of her life experience or hardships – just a silly girl full of romantic notions.

From the bus stop, she walked down Grove Road towards the grey pebbledash of number ninety-three. Even after eight months, nothing much had changed. An oversized '41', daubed in dribbling white paint on a wheelie bin. The only bungalow in the street, its boot-shaped planter guarded by a platoon of weather-weary gnomes. An awkward branch, overhanging the pavement, now fully in leaf at next-door-but-two; the curtains twitching over the road at ninety-four. Len and his horrible missus. Flora gave them an ambiguous wave – somewhere between a 'V' sign and vaguely regal. May as well give them something to talk about.

The gate whined open then swung shut with a familiar clang. It had served her well as an early warning system when John was alive – thirty seconds to flick the telly off and jump to it before he was in the house. She'd squirt oil on the hinges tomorrow. Weeds had sprouted through cracks in the concrete path and clumps of dandelions flourished along the front of the house. She lifted a corner of the doormat and retrieved the key. There had been moments abroad when she'd heard John's voice: 'Have you no sense? What about burglars. Squatters?' Flora was half hoping someone *had* broken in – a bit of graffiti on the walls would cheer the place up. She turned the key in the lock and drew a deep breath. It didn't feel good to be home after all.

Stepping over the avalanche of free newspapers and junk mail seemed better than attempting to pick it up. She'd need a cup of tea first. In the kitchen with its still-broken cooker and careworn lino, she ran the tap for a while to let the germs out before filling the kettle. The caddy yielded a few musty tea bags, well past their best – she should have popped into the corner shop. Somewhere in her handbag were a couple of thimble-sized UHTs she'd snaffled from the in-flight meal. She'd make do till morning.

She took her cup into the front room and plugged in the telly. For some reason, she expected the Rovers Return to have had a makeover or at least a new landlord. A lot can happen in a few months. She flicked through washing powder adverts and celebrity game shows. Had she ever enjoyed watching this stuff? She would never want to sound like John, but 'inane chitter-chatter' came to mind.

Upstairs, she was pleased to remember there was new bedding in the airing cupboard. For her entire married life she had endured woollen blankets, topped with a mossy-coloured candlewick bedspread that made the room even more cave-like. Just the suggestion of a duvet had sent John into a mini-sermon on sleep quality versus expense. As soon as her inheritance had come through, she had taken great pleasure in choosing a luxury duck-down duvet, 'comfi-sleep' pillows and two sets of mix-and-match bedding in Honey Bunch Gold and Miami Spice.

She hadn't slept for almost twenty-four hours. Marty had only waited for the in-flight meal before pulling down his eye mask. She had escaped the flushing loos with 'The World of Love Songs' piped through complimentary headphones. Somewhere over the Atlantic, saturated by schmaltzy crooners, she'd switched to watching *Sleepless in Seattle*. By the time Tom Hanks and Meg Ryan got round to giving each other the longest meaningful look in history, another meal was served, then the crew prepared for landing. Now she was tired. She'd put the water heater on for a nice hot bath and an early night – tomorrow would be the beginning of a new beginning.

TWENTY-THREE

At first, Flora thought Bonita's bedroom fan had broken – and nor could she hear the sounds of late-night workers putt-putting past on mopeds, arguing drunks, yowling tomcats; sounds that always accompanied the little breeze machine. Struggling into a semi-upright position, it took a moment to realise the eerie orange glow was not the favela on fire or Theresa's long-awaited apparition of Christ the Redeemer – just a streetlight shining through gaps in the curtains. She glanced at the bedside clock and slowly exhaled. Half-past two in the morning. Grove Road. Home.

Had she ever had a decent night's sleep in this house? Soon after John and his nasal whistling snores had ceased to be, the wide-awake hours had been filled with loneliness and fear of the future. Funny then, how she had run away and ended up in Rio only to become even more alone, and penniless. What a life lesson. She reorganised the pillows and heaved herself upright to soak up the gloomy orange of the room and sighed. No more Brazilian nights, no snoring husband, just a peaceful moment, putting her thoughts into order. She had an idea brewing. Ever since coming home had been a genuine possibility, she had been planning what she would do once back in Coventry. First things first, she would sort out the financial mess; the bank was surely at fault, but it would take time. While that particular wheel was in motion, there were other bigger and much more exciting things to do.

Thoughts of The Plan propelled her out of bed into a frenzy of activity. She urgently needed cash and a small goldmine happened to be right there in the bedroom. It took a couple of hours, but she knew she wouldn't be able to go back to sleep without making a good start on what was to be the foundation of her new venture.

~ぐぉぬ゜～

The second time Flora awoke, neighbours were slamming their front doors and starting their cars to join the early-morning rush hour. Remembering her jet lag-induced activity, she glanced at the row of handbags moored along the skirting board, like colourful fishing boats on a shore of beige carpet. What a shameful sight; thousands of pounds squandered on buffed leather and bling with nowhere to go. All those boutique shopping trips, just because she was lonely and wanted to spend time with Marty. The price of one bag alone would feed Theresa and the girls for a month.

Nocturnal scribblings revealed the make, colour and size of each offender. After checking inside each one, she had struck gold in a cream Louis Vuitton clutch: two twenty-pound notes and a pair of byzantine-knot earrings, evidence of an outing to see *The Mikado* with Marty at The Guild. She had written 'used once' next to it on the list. A brand-new Chloé tote had yielded a rose quartz and diamond feature necklace, still boxed. She admired the pink hearts and pretty twinkly surround. Worth a fortune.

By nine o'clock, after double-checking her work and adding a stray Mulberry to the list, she pocketed the notebook and prepared to leave the house. In the hall, with her jacket already on, she flipped through the free newspapers for a local estate agent. She liked the sound of '*Everyday property for everyday people*' and phoned Ben Sykes and Co for their 'free market appraisal'. Satisfied the ball was in motion, she hurried out for breakfast and a proper cup of tea.

Thankfully, Gig-a-Bites was an internet cafe that actually sold food and drinks – Dave's set-up in Rio could learn a thing or two from this. Flora paid for a bottomless mug of tea, a surfer's breakfast butty and two hours' computer time. With pen poised, she scrolled through the pages of second-hand designer stores. Pre-loved labels were big business. There were specialist dealers too, none in Coventry but one in Birmingham and three in London. She jotted down the phone numbers and moved on to compare the secondhand prices.

Finally tracking down a particularly rare Judith Leiber Swarovski Minaudiere evening bag, she ticked the last item off the list. Four hours of intense research told her she could expect anything between five and eight thousand pounds for her collection, depending on condition and outer packaging. Not bad for a morning's work, but a headache was brewing. Too much interweb – she'd make a detour to the bus stop via the municipal gardens.

She shook out her arms and rolled her shoulders, not caring when a passing dog walker looked askance – clearly he hadn't heard of repetitive strain syndrome. Sitting on a bench near a little refreshment stall she clenched and unclenched her fingers while admiring the symmetry of bedding plants where there had once been a shrubbery of rhododendrons. She and John had sat in the same spot having a cup of tea and a Chorley cake on their wedding day. After the registry office and before opening time. Later, they had walked to the White Hart pub and were served by a waitress with acne and dirty cuffs. John had been at his best then. 'Chicken in a basket for my good lady wife.' She had giggled and squirmed in her seat at 'good lady wife'.

The waitress was impervious. 'Sauce?'

'Oh, yes, undoubtedly. Flora love, you like a bit of sauce, don't you?'

'I should say so,' she had said, giving the waitress an exaggerated wink. Still nothing.

It was one of the very few times they had shared a joke, and the last time they had eaten out. They chatted on the bus all the way to Grove Road, she in her white cheesecloth dress, still holding a bouquet of marguerites that were beginning to wilt.

'You have to carry me over the threshold,' she had insisted.

Was that the last time she had asserted herself too?

Enough of the past. She needed to get on with The Plan, *rapidamente*. All being well, Ben Sykes would sell the house without too much trouble. Meanwhile she needed to declutter and raise some quick cash. She rummaged in her handbag for the byzantine-knot earrings. There was a pawn shop near the bus stop – she could sell them properly when she had more time. She'd pop in the Spar for a few basics on the way, a microwave dinner for her and a box of French Fancies to help oil the estate agent's wheels. There was no time for proper shopping; she wanted to get home and phone the handbag dealers before closing time.

~~~

Flora spent the following morning preparing for Ben Sykes' free market appraisal. After wiping eight months' worth of dust off the furniture, she looked at each room with a critical eye and worked on a strategy of damage limitation. She moved two piles of books to the spot in front of John's chair where a succession of brown lace-ups had flattened the wool into bald submission. In the bathroom a discarded towel, seemingly flung off after a rub down, took care of hideous lino off-cuts.

Taking tips from the local paper's Property Guru, she then picked the dandelions sprouting along the front of the house and set them in the kitchen window, arranged in a milk jug for rustic charm. It still looked like a dungeon of doom in there, so she put the light on to jolly it up. Without the means to brew freshly ground coffee, she made a mug of instant and poured it into a cereal bowl to increase wafting efficiency, and walked it around the entire ground floor. Just as she was about to add some milk and drink the cooling evidence, someone rang the doorbell. She hid the bowl in the oven and after a quick *'sell, sell, sell'* mantra to herself in the hall mirror, she opened the door with a winning smile.

Ben Sykes and his thin red tie reminded her of the only other salesman she could remember calling in at number ninety-three. *'Save money on heating with double glazing at special show home prices'* had tempted John. At the time, Flora had hovered in the background, unsure what to say or do until John discovered how much a show-home price was and asked him to leave. But now she was 'Mamãe Flora' and a saleswoman with an outstanding record. No doubt she could show this salesman a thing or two. She led the agent around the house, making sure she stood in front of the worst of the worst, talking all the while about his lovely red tie being the perfect choice for such a beautiful sunny day. It took her a while to realise he was also waxing lyrical – about original features and the unspoiled nature of the house.

'What I'm saying, Flora – can I call you Flora? For the right price, your house will be snapped up.' He was smiling. 'Could I ask, do you have somewhere to move to?'

As it happened, he had some lovely little one-bedroomed flats on a new development. With no onward chain, it would be a trouble-free next step, especially as the developers were offering part exchange: no need to wait for a buyer if she didn't want to. They were on the same page. Flora made a cup of tea and arranged pink and yellow cakes on a plate. She'd keep the chocolate ones for a celebration later.

'Here we are, Ben, a nice cup of tea.' She placed the tray on the coffee table and plumped down on the sofa next to him, then held up the plate. 'Fancy a French Fancy?'

With the sale of the house and the purchase of a New Dawn Apartment, Ben estimated she would have about sixty thousand pounds left over. A nice little retirement fund for when the time was right. He would take care of the paperwork – all she had to do was say the word. She decided there was no harm in looking and accepted a lift in his silver Mondeo.

On the way, Flora listened to Ben's sales patter. New Dawn Apartments was an ideal next move for downsizers, 'such as yourself'. When he added, 'Very popular with single, mature ladies' she inwardly flinched; did he mean old spinsters? Marty had always extolled the virtues of her age. Fabulous and freewheeling. No matter. Ladies of a certain age, somewhere between forty-something and senior Saga, would be perfect in terms of The Plan.

'Here we are,' he said over the jangle of keys. 'Your very own front door, leading conveniently and directly into a state-of-the-art kitchenette.' Flora gingerly stepped onto the vinyl floor tiles. She ran her hand over the gleaming oven and hob and admired the mixer-tap with a degree of window shopper's knowledge. Nice chrome finish. Everything fitted so neatly together, even the fridge was disguised as a cupboard.

'Ergonomically designed,' said Ben, leading her through the archway to the dining-cum-living area with an architect-designed dado rail and far-reaching views over Coventry city centre. She could even see the treetops in the municipal gardens. The wet room was a stroke of genius; much easier to keep clean. By the time they came to the bedroom with a mirror-fronted wardrobe, vanity shelf and integral shoe caddy, she had already decided to take it. She'd keep that to herself and would allow Ben to complete his spiel, then ask for a few days to think about it. She'd check out a couple of similar developments and use the information to negotiate a better price.

Meanwhile, she would carry on with The Plan. Although she had no desire to travel anywhere for quite some time, she popped in to the National Express office and bought a Coventry to London day-return ticket. It was a small sacrifice she was prepared to make for the sake of raising some funds.

～∞∞～

Two days later, and several designer handbags lighter, Flora returned from London. Three hours of sitting with an over-stuffed money belt strapped around a celebratory cream tea had left her feeling queasy. She walked away from the bus stop in a self-styled nonchalant stroll while inconspicuously adjusting the seven thousand pounds stowed beneath her smocked top. It was important to celebrate the successes, and a High Tea Royale at Buckingham Gates Bakehouse had been the perfect prize, but maybe next time she'd wait till the mission was fully accomplished.

As she reached the home stretch, a 'For Sale' board outside number ninety-three stopped her in her tracks. Of course she wanted to move – she had a great future all mapped out, and selling the house was part of the process – but the sign also signalled something else. A failure in the community. Goodbye to a childless widow who barely knew her neighbours. The conversation she'd overheard on the bus still rang in her ears: 'We could do with a nice young family in that house. She should move away…'

Never mind the past. She was going to begin again, with a lovely new flat, neighbours she would befriend and, above all, The Plan. She walked past the last few houses with her chin up, fighting the urge to flash her money belt, muffin top and all, to whoever lurked behind the curtains. They had no idea who she was or what she'd been through and probably never would.

After stashing the bundles of notes beneath the spare room mattress, she made a cup of tea and carried it through to the front room. John's chair and a stack of new library books beckoned. She scanned the titles: *From Zero to Marketing Hero*, *The Magic of Business Unveiled*, *Accounting for Beginners*. She picked up *The Entrepreneur's Ultimate Guide* and flicked through the first few pages. It was going to be a long night.

TWENTY-FOUR

Flora muttered her mantra of the week – '*Plan the work and work the plan*' – and opened the wardrobe door. A second trip to London with a treasure trove of costume jewellery had added almost four thousand pounds to the kitty. Now there was just a tower of designer shoes, many still in their boxes, and assorted crimes of fashion to deal with. She would call a taxi and take everything to Encore Princess.

She roll-folded a Diamonique-studded bolero and shoved it into a bin liner, along with a ridiculously romantic pink tulle ballgown and a black leather catsuit that she suspected had made her look like Michelin Man's dream date. All evidence of giddy shopping sprees with Marty when her fear of loneliness had blinded her judgement.

There was no room for the old Flora in her new high-rise lifestyle apartment; everything must go. The rest of the household contents would be collected by the local women's refuge. She felt a pang of guilt about subjecting survivors of domestic violence to John's mother's taste in furniture. Perhaps they could sell everything and buy something more uplifting. Maybe have a party.

By the end of the week all that remained was a cardboard box containing the last few items she couldn't quite part with. She sifted through them again. Relics of the past. The velveteen baby-grow, folded into a small, soft rectangle, still stirred up a surge of sadness. A sparkly boob tube twinkled with dreams of dancing in an exotic life abroad. She knew now how that would have ended. She picked up John's last pocket diary. It had hardly served its original purpose – there were just a few odd notes scribbled here and there. *Pay electricity bill* circled in red. *Dentist 11.15 am* and *Flora – Doctor, AGAIN!* She smiled to herself – she had only to mention 'women's problems' and John had been happy to let her leave the house without him. Those furtive escapes to Gail's Cafe had been a lifeline.

Her wedding dress was next. White cheesecloth maxi. MacFadden's End of Summer Sale, 1970. She'd bought it with her final week's wages from Fine Fare, believing she'd wear it for picnics and romantic walks by the sea. Later she'd dye it purple; perfect for dinner parties. She'd been in such a fluster dressing on her wedding day with Dad shouting outside the bedroom door, that she'd forgotten to take the price tag off. Only worn once and looked almost as good as new. She held up her white go-go boots. She had loved zipping up the white patent leather and becoming three inches taller. Empowering. Not that she'd known the meaning of the word back then. Last worn on her first Christmas Day as Mrs Marshall when she'd tried to make a special effort. Yet still she'd kept the dress and the boots, ever hopeful, ever deluded.

She carried the box out to the small back yard and made a small fire with old newspapers and a broken kitchen chair. Should she say a few words? According to *A Guide to Happy Ever After*, letting go of the past was cathartic, not to be underestimated. She crouched down and set fire to a twenty-first birthday card, then grabbed *Flora's Housework Rota and Recipes*, the title on the front of the old school exercise book was written with a flourish in John's hand. She ripped out the pages, scrunching up jam roly-poly with faggots and peas. Here and there, she read snippets of pedantic instruction – '*rinse milk bottles*', '*once a month – dust skirting boards*', then dangled her wedding dress over the fire and watched thoughtfully as the fabric yellowed and charred in the heat. The acrid smoke drifted skyward and away.

Finally, when the flames had abated, she gently lowered the baby-grow onto the charred remains. A tiny velveteen foot caught alight. Half-blinded by the sting of smoke and sharp tears, she let it go and whispered, 'Goodbye'.

With the house stripped down to its miserable carcass, she spent the next few hours cleaning, squirting the past with citrus-scented detergent and wiping it away. By mid-afternoon there was nothing to do except call a taxi. She opened the front door to wait, remembering the day she first arrived, when she'd ordered John to carry her over the threshold; how he'd awkwardly shuffled backwards with her into the house, putting her down rather quickly on the mat inside. 'Welcome to your marital home,' he had said. That was before she'd realised he had only ever wanted a housekeeper.

She closed the front door, pressed her hand against the peeling green paint and thanked the house for the shelter it had provided. According to the book, she should have put her hands together and said 'namaste' afterwards, but the taxi driver was beeping his horn. Any residual spiritual karma completely evaporated when she saw Len and his wife over the road, openly gawping. She gave them one last ambiguous wave and got into the taxi. At the end of the road, she was already rummaging in her bag for her new mobile phone; there was no reason to look back.

She dialled the only contact in her 'friends and family' package deal and said, 'I'm on my way.'

'Perfect timing. I've popped a bottle of fizz in the fridge.'

'Oh Marty, that's probably half your wages gone. There's no need.'

'It's only prosecco, babes. But yes, it probably is half my wages,' he laughed.

'I can't believe the theatre won't put you back in the box office – you were so good at it. Are you still on cleaning?'

'Yes, but at least now I'm free to wander behind the

scenes. When no one's about, I have a little play. I had a go with Queen Nefertiti yesterday.'

'Shouldn't you look for something else? You know, maybe think of moving away from the theatre altogether?'

'I am looking – if something comes up, I'll be on it like sequins on a showgirl.'

She smiled to herself. He was prepared to leave the theatre. The Plan was taking shape.

'Now, before you get here, I have to warn you,' said Marty. 'I've rearranged the furniture again. I think it looks more spacious now.'

The new furniture had been a headache. Thinking ahead to the time when she might have guests to stay, she'd ordered a two-seater sofa-bed in cool grey and a Parker Knoll recliner in Misty Dawn plush. She'd imagined they'd look sophisticated yet welcoming on a cornflower-blue carpet, but according to Marty, they resembled a mother and baby elephant squeezed into a paddling pool. She hadn't thought about the dimensions-versus-space ratio, and the storage footstool-cum-coffee table had to be relegated to the bedroom. No matter. It was home and it was hers.

~~~

It had been difficult to find all the ingredients; compromises had to be made. After a couple of false starts and a few modifications, Flora had created a delicious spread worthy of launching herself and The Plan on her new neighbours. Her first-ever party would have a unique and memorable theme thanks to Mrs Beeton and an afternoon searching the internet.

Marty's brainwave of using little flags, Olympic Games-style, meant each edible treat proudly displayed its nationality. Bruschetta, empanadas, samosas and *coxinha* were placed on the two-seater dining table. Falafels, crispy won tons and chimichurri bites had to make do with the kitchen worktop next to a crowd of glasses, paper plates and an assortment of *tostadas*.

There was just enough time for hair and make-up before the doorbell chimed Greensleeves and someone called Sarah arrived, brandishing a potted orange gerbera. By seven-thirty, the windowsill was lined with pot plants, bottles of wine and a jar of homemade marmalade. Flora had already counted twenty-five guests, which was more than she'd catered for, when a silver-haired lady arrived with her son. She hadn't accounted for gatecrashers, but she let it go.

'Marty!' She had to almost shout over the chattering guests and her *One World* party CD. She gave up trying to speak and performed a pouring drinks mime instead. It had been his idea to serve fruity margaritas. After the whole Mexico debacle she'd never wanted to see another glass of the stuff, but he had already borrowed a beautifully embroidered *charro* suit from *The Day of the Dead* chorus line; she'd only be drinking mineral water in any case – the first rule of networking was to stay professional. Circulate. According to *Successful Entrepreneur in Five Days*, working the room was key. However, it didn't say what to do if prospective clients approached without warning.

'I don't know what this is, but it's delicious,' said a lady in her early sixties.

'Oh, it's a *coxhina*.' Theresa's recipe. 'I learned to make them in Brazil.'

'How exotic,' she said, popping the whole thing into her mouth. 'Isn't that in the Latin part of America? The furthest I've been is Fuerteventura. I don't suppose I'll go abroad again now.'

'Why ever not?'

'Roger's hanky-panky. It took us years to get to know all our neighbours out there.'

'The locals?'

'Yes. There was Debs and Mike from Essex, Pete and Sally from Walthamstow. We used to have such a laugh. Now he's with Tina the Tart, who used to be with Nigel from Northampton. The whole thing's gone south now.'

'So, your Roger and er, the Tina woman had an affair?'

'Couldn't keep it in his trousers. Been going on for years, apparently.' Her hand hovered over the buffet. 'I can't stop eating these little thingamabobs. I'm Eve, by the way. It'll be so nice to have another refugee here.'

'Do you mean a singleton? I wouldn't put myself in the refugee category. I can honestly say I couldn't be happier.'

'Really? I've been on my tod for four years. I miss all our friends, even that Tina. I'm too old to start—'

'Excuse me,' someone said behind her. 'Flora? Sorry for interrupting, I heard you've just got back from a world cruise and had a transformation?'

'Well, it wasn't quite like that—'

'My hubby Gary had a brave fight against cancer, but you know, in the end, well. The thing is, here I am seven years later. I thought the life insurance would be the answer to everything, but money—'

'Can't buy you happiness,' they all chimed.

'So, what's your secret?'

'Well.' Flora paused. They were getting ahead of her. 'Actually, if you don't mind, I'd like to save my answer. In fact, if you'll excuse me, I just need to make a little announcement.'

She stood on a chair and tapped her glass with her cubic zirconia dress ring. 'Excuse me! Excuse me, everyone.' She waited while Marty had wriggled his way through the crowd to turn the music down. She was glad of the few extra moments; preparation and poise were half the battle. The rest was down to the practice sessions she'd had in front of the bedroom mirror that morning.

'Thank you all for coming, I'm so glad you could make it. I invited you for three reasons. Firstly, and most important, to have the chance to meet my lovely new neighbours. Thank you for being so welcoming. Secondly, I wanted to introduce you to my friend, Marty. Where are you, Marty?'

'I'm here,' he said, holding up a jug of strawberry margarita.

'Since my husband passed away, Marty has been my rock, my absolute best friend. I owe him everything. Thank you, Marty.' There was a polite ripple of applause.

'And finally, I'd like to raise a glass to all the single ladies here today. Becoming suddenly single completely turned my life around. If anyone would like to find more about my secret to happiness, please come here for coffee and cake on Thursday morning at ten-thirty, when I would love to tell you all about it.'

After her announcement, the conversation in the room increased to an excited buzz. She had already done a quick headcount – at least half the guests were single ladies; she would have to buy more cups and saucers, *rapidamente*!

She caught Marty's questioning expression and wove through the chattering crowd towards him. 'Sorry I haven't told you about The Plan, but until now I wasn't sure it—'

'What plan, babes?'

'Well, I was waiting to see if there was a need for it, and there is. Obviously, it'll depend on people's budgets, but it'll be an investment in the rest of their lives, a road to happiness they don't yet know exists. To love life, they must love themselves first.'

'What? You sound like one of those evangelicals on American TV.'

'Sorry. I'll explain everything later, but just so you know, I've enough money put aside to pay you a basic salary. We can work out a bonus scheme later. I'd love it if you'd join me?'

～◦))))◦～

So much had happened in the months since leaving Rio. After moving to New Dawn Apartments, Flora had hardly had a moment to herself; everyone wanted to know her secret to happiness. Based on the initial feedback from a survey she and Marty carried out at a busy shopping centre, she developed a menu of options. Each client could have a tailor-made programme to fit their budget. It was clear: people from all walks of life could do with a boost now and then.

It wasn't long before the business was taking over her apartment. A new computer sat squarely on the dining table, blocking the far-reaching views of Coventry's municipal gardens. An extension cable trailed across the floor to the printer perched on the only spare chair. With no room for another filing cabinet, paperwork was dotted around on the blue carpet, like islands in the Aegean Sea.

The day Flora received the keys to her new office couldn't have come soon enough. The lack of space at home was one thing, but not being able to meet and greet clients in a nice environment had become an issue. When the right place came on the rental market, Flora was ready to pounce.

After a busy morning overseeing a furniture delivery and the installation of a networked computer system, she quickly ate a brie and cranberry baguette while watching the new sign go up above the front door. *The Bloom Agency*. Pink lettering on a dark-blue background. With a cosy armchair and display of fresh flowers in the window, the little office situated down a quiet side street was both tasteful and welcoming.

Back at the apartment, she had left Marty in charge of boxing up paperwork and office supplies. Later they would have a celebratory treat of a Chinese meal and a trip to The Guild to see *Oklahoma!*, a musical romance about a simple country girl with two love interests. Despite the incident with Smokey Brooks, she still couldn't resist a cowboy.

～≫))»～

Nursing a slight hangover from the after-show pink fizz cocktails Marty had insisted on, Flora was at The Bloom Agency for the first day of business by eight o'clock. She propped the door open to let out the whiff of fresh paint and new carpet. Mingled with the heady scent of white lilies in the window display, it was making her feel queasy.

The first clients were due at nine-thirty. Marty would take care of them while she had back-to-back appointments from eleven until four o'clock. As part of The Bloom Agency's launch, she had advertised free consultations with a complimentary coffee. She checked her supplies in the kitchenette. Milk, sugar and plenty of cups and saucers. She'd bought a job lot of Royal Worcester fine bone china, white with gold chantilly trim. She opened an airtight tin, inhaled the delicious waft of chocolate and caramel, then piled two dozen homemade *brigadeiros* onto the matching cake stand. A fiesta of colourful mini cupcake cases filled with Theresa's delicious recipe would always be a talking point.

By the time Marty arrived, clutching a packet of paracetamol, it was almost opening time. 'Sorry, babes, I would have been sooner but I've a banging head. After you left in the taxi I went on to Tropix. Met this gorgeous guy.'

Flora smiled. These days Marty rarely talked about his ordeal in the Brazilian jungle and never mentioned Enrique. Hopefully he was on the road to finding love again. She would catch up on his news later, but first there was a business to run. She gave him the itinerary for the following week's *British and Best* so he could book the transport and accommodation while she went to the bank. Although her old bank had repaid the unlawfully transferred funds, they were yet to get to the bottom of who was behind the Dominguez Corporation. No matter, Flora wanted to put the past behind her and had opened a New Enterprise Account at a more progressive bank with a female bank manager. Paying in cheques and sorting out petty cash was something she liked to do herself. By the time she returned to the office, Marty was talking to a group of ladies, with a swatch of colour-analysis fabric slung over his shoulder.

'As your personal stylist, I can't wait to take you on a fabulous day out. Included in the price is lunch at Bobo's and a lovely glass of bubbles.'

As the ladies put their coats on and headed towards the door, Flora pulled Marty to one side. 'Don't forget, they're on a budget, so no Prada for these three.'

'No worries, babes, we're doing high street basics, mix and match accessories, lunch, shoes, nails and back at four o'clock.'

'That's spot on.' She glanced at her watch. 'I'll have a quick coffee, then I'm meeting a pensioner who's always lived with her mother, never been abroad. Can you imagine?'

'Oh, sounds like she's overdue for *Gorgeous and Gold*.'

'That's what I was thinking.'

'Sign her up, babes,' said Marty, turning to his three waiting ladies. 'So, my lovelies, all set for your *Colour Awareness Safari*?'

Flora poured herself a coffee. Brazilian was still the best in her opinion, especially with a couple of caramel *brigadeiros* on the side. She carried her cup and saucer to the desk, sank into her new executive swivel chair and checked her emails. Five more enquiries and two more confirmations – she'd have to find an office assistant if she was going to grow the business *and* do more of the fun stuff. Marty was perfect for *Body Confidence*, but she had the edge when it came to *Expanding Horizons*. Rio had been a steep learning curve, but everything was now being put to good use. Her ability to talk to people, make friends and live on the edge had made her see life through a different lens. Possibilities were everywhere and she had a gift for finding them.

She flicked through a pile of post. She always opened the bills first and checked them against her purchase account; all income and expenses were noted down so she knew exactly where she was, money-wise. The office move had been carried out on a strict budget, and thanks to her negotiating skills she had managed to complete the whole thing with a little left over. She opened the rest of the post in random order. The last envelope was a 'thank you' card with a picture of a woman shrieking 'Wheee!' as she freewheeled a bicycle downhill, feet off the pedals. *'Take the brakes off and have fun'* said the caption.

> *Dear Flora,*
> *Thanks for a super time, it was so much fun!*
> *I know I said I'd never travel on my own,*
> *but I've just booked the Dublin Ferry next*
> *month and I'm just going to see what happens.*
> *Because of you and The Bloom Agency,*
> *I'm blooming again too!*
> *Love and best wishes,*
> *Millie M.*

Flora had recently escorted Millie and two other single ladies on *Balkans on a Budget*. Millie's husband had left her for a younger woman after they'd moved to Coventry for his work. She had no friends in the area and had completely lost her confidence. It was so rewarding to know The Bloom Agency was helping. She had tailored the business especially for suddenly-single ladies of a certain age, but clients seemed to come from all sorts of situations. Some were married but had become golf widows, others were happily single but wanted a bit of a boost or an adventure.

The Balkans tour had been a great success. Even though it was the first time Flora had been to Croatia, she'd still managed to wangle an invitation to a wedding by befriending the groom's mother. After starting with drinks and music at the groom's family home, the entire wedding party had then crossed the village in a joyful parade to collect the bride-to-be. Following the ceremony, there had been rakija-fuelled dancing to the *tamburaši* that only really got going after midnight.

In Montenegro, when they stopped for *bajadera* to enjoy with their coffee, Flora had struck up a conversation with the baker, and soon they were in the kitchen learning how to make it. While the sweet, nutty, chocolate layers were cooling, the baker's daughter had taken them on a walking tour of the town. Later they'd joined the extended family for *buzara*, a traditional seafood dish, served with freshly baked bread to mop up a delicious wine sauce.

During the trip Millie had gained enough bravado to go to a market on her own, and had come back with a selection of fruit for breakfast. Yes, mused Flora, she would invite her for a coffee and find out about her trip to Dublin. She propped the card up and quickly keyed Millie into the Christmas card database. It was a good job the addresses could be printed on labels, she was gathering friends so quickly these days it was hard to keep up.

Looking around the neat new office, with its high-tech computer system and the small forest of 'thank you' cards on top of the filing cabinet, it was hard to believe how much had happened since John's accident. Thirty-five years of marriage hadn't amounted to very much, but in the year and a half since then she'd come further than she imagined possible. All the way from Grove Road to Coventry's city centre, via the Americas.

Flora opened the bottom drawer of her desk and gently eased out an ornate gold picture frame. At last there was a moment of calm to hang the finishing touch behind her desk. She had spent quite some time at the designer's studio, deciding on a setting to accommodate Bonita's necklace of delicate paper flowers spelling out B.E.L.I.E.V.E, and a montage of Marty's photographs. There were flamingos in

Bolivia, Mexican dahlias, a spectacular snowscape with the Kulusuk Mountains in the background, and her favourite snap of Theresa in her flowery pinny, haggling over tomatoes in the market. In the middle of the montage was a section of John's original list, complete with notes in his school-teacher handwriting, suggesting a detour here, an overnight stay there.

On tiptoes, Flora reached up and hung the frame on the wall behind her desk and then took a step back to admire her handiwork. No longer a promise on paper. The lottery-winning fantasy had finally come to life in a most unexpected way.

'You're missing all the fun, John,' she murmured as she sat back down to finish her cup of coffee.

ACKNOWLEDGEMENTS

If I hadn't been stuck in bed with an elevated foot, Flora may never have found her fabulous. Thank you, Clare McVey, for arriving with a stack of books and the encouragement to start writing. Later, I'm grateful to Shelley Weiner and the many inspiring people I met at Faber Academy, who taught me what should happen in between the beginning, middle and end.

Without editors, beta readers and proofreaders I would only have words. Special thanks to brilliant Anna Davidson who has been a fountain of all knowledge throughout. Huge appreciation to a posse of beta readers: Chandy Rodgers, Jules Lampshire, Shivanthi Sathanandan and Elizabeth Price, your enthusiasm for the book has been wonderful. Anna Bierhaus, thanks for a great developmental edit; a big thumbs up to Anita Sargeant for her collaborative edit; and thank you, Jessie Raymond for the final proofread.

Without fellow writing pals, I would be lost. Anna, David G, David H, Di, Jules, Lizzie, Lucy, Shivanthi and Tamara, you've been a cornucopia of inspiration and joy! And Di, thank you also for getting my website started.

For the language translations, *gracias*, *obrigada* and *danke* to Isabel Ward, Natascha Azevedo, José Oliveira Nunes and Juliette Reilly.

Fondest love and thanks to my Kiwi family – Patrick in spirit, Oriel, Ben and Megan, Claire and Nick and all the Golden Cherubs for your encouragement and a place to write. Also in New Zealand, I'm grateful to Gerry and Brett, Ming and Sue for their friendship and wifi.

As most of this book was written while travelling, I have many sofas, kitchen tables and cups of tea to be grateful for. Thank you for your welcome and generosity, Jane H, Ineke and Guy, Jude and Hugh, Jenny and Duncan, Gai and Tony, Steve and Ayns, Sarah C, Rosie and Chris, Sue B, Sandy and Ian, Julia and Martin, Claire and Keith. For hosting me in London in the early days, many thanks to Lottie G.

For ensuring I had a screen break and daily exercise, I'm grateful to a stampede of furry friends who have contributed to my happiness and wellbeing throughout: Jimi, Devon, Buster, Millie and Chase, Bertie, Ellie and Misty, Florence and Frieda, Cuda and Nylah, Percy, Pip, Phin and Big Edward, Nonu and Kiana, Maz, Grace and the talented Mr Quazi.

~◦◦◦~

If you enjoyed *How Flora Finds Her Fabulous* please leave a review as this helps writers to be recognised and helps other readers choose a book they will enjoy.

If you want to be one of the first to read Stella Stonestreet's next book or to receive the latest news, bonus content, book promotions and updates, go to the official website and subscribe.

www.stellabookchat.com

If you'd like to connect on social media:
Instagram: StellaBookChat
Twitter: @stellabookchat
Facebook: stellabookchat

READING GROUP
QUESTIONS

1. Do the historical aspects of the book, especially music, fashion and food provoke memories for you?

2. How unlikely is it that Flora and John became a couple? What motivated them individually to get married?

3. Is John's behaviour due to his upbringing or part of his inherent personality?

4. Is Flora's marriage a product of the times? How have things changed since 1970, especially for women?

5. When Marty befriends Flora does he have a motive? Later, in Rio, is he as innocent as he claims?

6. Are Flora's dreams of romance her downfall or her saviour?

7. How are the themes of loneliness handled in the book? Discuss the how John, Marty and Flora deal with this individually.

8. How would you have dealt with the obstacles Flora faced in Rio?

9. How does Stella Stonestreet use food to magnify situations and relationships?

10. Do you believe it is possible for anyone to **Find Her Fabulous**, especially later in life?

PREQUEL IN THE
FINDING FABULOUS SERIES

Enjoy the first chapter now!

FLORA

Flora had him in her sights. The only possible beau-to-be in the penny arcade, his flower-power shirt drawing her like a bee to nectar. She had watched him arrive at Seashells Guesthouse, then clocked him in the queue at the fish and chip shop and now, on the pier. His lovely shoulder-length mop of blonde hair flopped over his face as he leaned forward, concentrating on a game of Shindig Pinball.

'I'm Flora, what's your name?'

'Colin.'

'Are you here with your family?'

'Yeah, worse luck.'

'Me too. We're here for the week.'

'Bummer,' he muttered, nudging the machine, still not looking up.

'Yes, it's a bummer,' she said, enjoying the use of the word bummer, despite the fact she'd been crossing the dates off in her diary and had underlined 'Hooray! Holiday Starts Today!' in red pen. 1968 was going to be the year when everything changed for the better. She had been planning her first holiday romance for weeks and according to Cupid's Secret, the newest and most reliable-looking fortune-telling machine on the pier, love, luck and marriage were on the cards.

'Is this the first time you've been to Western-Super-Mare?' she asked.

'Yeah.'

He wasn't a talker; she would just have to increase her allure.

'I'm going to be a model. One day soon I'll be on the front cover of Nova.'

With that, he let go of the machine and appraised her. Flora struck a well-rehearsed pose with something between a knowing smile and a pout.

'Farmer's Weekly, more likely.' He smirked and launched another pinball.

'Hey! Don't be like that,' she ventured, but Colin didn't seem to hear and as soon as his game was over, he walked off without a word.

Flora re-examined the little printed card from Cupid's Secret; it said good things were going to happen, but maybe not immediately and definitely not with Colin. No matter, she was used to rejection and besides she still had six more days to find her dream date. She looked around the arcade and settled on a group of boys crowded around the mechanical grabber, trying to win a ten-shilling note, wrapped around a packet of cigarettes. She pictured herself sashaying over, taking the controls and dragging the prize to victory; they'd be so impressed, they'd probably fight over who would be the first to take her dancing. A collective groan told her they had failed and as the group broke up, someone shouted, 'Let's do the Dodgems!'. Should she win the prize and take it over to them at the Dodgems or just go straight there and get in a car next to the dishiest driver? She was still lost in the daydream of living happily ever after in a little country cottage with one of the Dodgem boys when, just like a knight in shining armour, the only man who truly loved her was making his way towards her.

'Ah, there you are, Pickle, how about an ice cream and a bit of fresh air?'

Walking along the promenade on her father's arm was as close as she'd been to any man, but all that was about to change. Sweet sixteen and never been kissed – how she hated that phrase. But now she'd left school, the world was waiting and she had the assurance of love, luck and marriage in her pocket.

~~~

It soon became apparent why the place was known as Western-Super-Mud: the rest of the holiday had been a washout, horizontal rain lashed across the dismal expanse of grey sand while redundant donkeys sheltered under the pier and seagulls went inland. Even the arcade lost its appeal and to top it off, the only boy Flora had a decent conversation with was ten-year-old Neville at the guesthouse – a bespectacled little nose-picker who challenged her to a tiddlywinks tournament.

Back home in Coventry, the Summer drizzled on. With nothing more to do than stay indoors and entertain herself, Flora avoided being asked to help with the housework by spending most of the time in her bedroom. She enjoyed re-reading back issues of Jackie magazine; *Twenty Ways to Make New Friends* had some useful tips and *Give Your Looks a Fling!* had been most inspiring. If only she had somewhere to go, she could try out Mary Quant's '*lovely pair of shiners* 'in the real world, instead of just at home. She applied black mascara, allowing each layer to dry until she had a satisfactory build-up, then carefully drew a line of whitener inside her lower lashes. The best part was swiping on the eyeshadow and hey presto! Twiggy's doe-eyed look. She found a jar of Vaseline in the bathroom cabinet and applied it to her lips for guaranteed kissability. Her campaign to be ready for anything was right on target.

She had refused her mother's offer to run up a new outfit from her collection of Simplicity patterns. The days of looking like a child of the fifties in frocks with over-zealous smocking or ill-fitting slacks were gone. That also applied to the mortifying phase of mother and daughter outfits, made in the same fabric. Mum's with elaborate frills and buttons, Flora's the plain dumbed-down version. Those dresses were a visual summary of their relationship. Mother first, daughter an afterthought. Or in truth, a mistake. She'd known that from a young age; she was the reason her parents had to marry and although they seemed to have made the best of it, Flora was all too aware she was an unwelcome guest at a party for two. Well, not for much longer. If everything went to plan, she'd soon meet her Prince Charming and Mum could 'get her life back', whatever that was supposed to be.

At sixteen, she had her own ideas on fashion and asked her father for a ten-shilling clothing allowance. The hot pants she'd ordered from Freeman's catalogue were a good fit, but the top was a disappointment; if only she had the bazookas. She would have to stop sleeping on her front and do at least twenty press-ups a day if she were ever to be selected by Pan's People. With the bazooka-growing still in progress, she had better work on her high kick and twirl. She copied the moves off Top of the Pops and gave them her own names: the scissor spin and the wiggle jump. They were surely guaranteed to impress at her interview, so long as she remembered to smile and somehow managed to increase her cup size. Meanwhile, she had a job at Fine Fare, starting Monday.

Although disappointed to not have been accepted at secretarial college, she would be earning her own money and was looking forward to more freedom. After four miserable years at St Margaret's High School for Girls she had only had a handful of so-called friends; other odd-balls forced together by circumstances rather than choice. She hoped a job would also mean meeting a couple of nice girls she could go dancing with at The Regent on a Friday night. If she was ever to get a boyfriend, she would have to go there; everyone knew the last dance of the evening was the perfect beginning to a dreamy romance.

With just a few days to go before life-changing friendships were formed, she had better rearrange her bedroom; whenever anyone came to visit, she wouldn't want to give the wrong impression. Teddy bears would have to stay in the wardrobe, although still sitting comfortably on the top shelf and probably her ballerina jewellery box had better disappear as well. An assortment of Tufty Club posters definitely had to come down but there was no way she would be moving her crushes. Ever since *Dr Zhivago*, she had been mad about Omar Sharif. Slightly stern, brooding and handsome – what more could anyone want in a man? If he wasn't too old for Julie Christie, then she was in with a chance and if he were ever to propose, she'd say yes in a jiffy. Next to the love of her life was a newspaper clipping of BBC newsreader, Robert Dougall, looking authoritative in his sober suit and tie, passing on the shocker of the day in a calm, collected manner.

JOHN

John's teenage years had been set up for disappointment while he was still in short trousers. At Elgar Primary School, where bomb damage still pock-marked the playground, he was considered a good enough goalie. Even with his crippled leg, the lack of agility hardly mattered in the small space between dustbins; and the fact he couldn't swap places to run with the scoring champions made him a popular choice. In the classroom, his ability to respond with witty one-liners increased his popularity and as one of the brightest in the school, his ever-so-slightly arrogant undertone was overlooked by teachers keen to chalk up another success on the educational leader board.

When John became the only boy to pass his Eleven Plus with flying colours, he celebrated by sharing a Gentleman Smoker's Selection Box with a few of his classmates. While pretend-puffing their way through sickly sweet cigarettes and chewy liquorice pipes, they all agreed the cleverest boy in school was destined to become the next Prime Minister. Another Churchill they cheered and slapped him on the back while sucking on chocolate cigars. Little did John realise, that was his finest hour and by the end of the Summer holidays, the happiest days of his life would already be over.

Upon entering grammar school, where every boy was his academic equal, John discovered the cruel reality of competitive sport. With his leg in a brace, his awkward gait became the brunt of jokes and bullying. Then a few weeks later, the addition of prescription glasses provoked someone to call him The Limping Spectacle and before long everyone joined in — even some of the teachers. The fervent teenage fantasy of being attractive enough to get a girlfriend quickly disintegrated to zero and was confirmed by the arrival of acne. To be bullied or ignored by the boys was one thing, but knowing girls giggled and whispered about him was far worse...

Cliff Richard smiled down from above her bed in his petrol blue velvet suit and fabulously romantic white ruffle. He had earned his place for being such a dish in *Summer Holiday* and for almost winning the Eurovision Song Contest with '*Congratulations*'. She had listened to him continuously on the Dansette until her parents agreed she could keep the player in her room if it meant they didn't have to hear it ever again. Neither of them seemed to like music which sometimes made her wonder if she was adopted.

With roller-skates and a collection of dolls in various stages of undress shoved in a box under her bed, Flora was ready to tackle her bookcase. Barbara Cartland's fragrant reads, arranged alphabetically from *Cupid Rides Pillion* to *The Unpredictable Bride* filled most of the space, while Catherine Cookson's *Fanny McBride* and *The Blind Miller* jostled for space at the end. After an inner debate on how she wanted her new friends to perceive her, Flora decided Lady Chatterley and Enid Blyton should hide in the wardrobe, on top of a stack of Bunty Annuals.

The top shelf of the bookcase was now free to display her impressive collection of nail polish passed down from her mother, who claimed she had to spend the family allowance on her appearance because having Flora's had ruined her looks. In a circuitous route of just injustice, the resulting overflow of beauty products found its way to the perpetrator. Flora clustered pearly pinks and ravishing reds together in a knowing beautician's display with the most popular colours at the front and the moody purples at the back. She doubted any of her soon-to-be Fine Fare friends would have half the selection and she already knew which colours she would be prepared to give away.

COMING SOON!
SEQUEL IN THE
FINDING FABULOUS SERIES

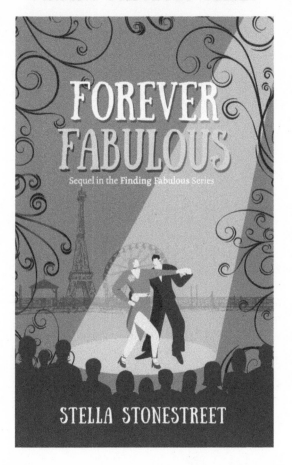